My Name is Eleanor

Val Scully

Courage is not the towering oak that sees storms come and go;
it is the fragile blossom that opens in the snow.

Alice Mackenzie Swaim

Val Scully is the maiden name of Val Boyle.
She was born in Salford in 1956 and has lived in Newcastle-upon-Tyne for thirty years. This is her second novel.

Also available:
Under the Spreading Chestnut Tree

For more information, please visit
www.valscully.co.uk

Cover image

Original photograph of Gibside Chapel by Catherine Martin
NationalTrust/CatherineMartin. Edited by Tom Carr.
Detail from the portrait of Maria Theresa, Archduchesse of
Habsburg by Rosalba Carriera (1730) is in the Gemäldegalerie
Alte Meister in Dresden. The photographic reproduction is in
the public domain. (Wikimedia Commons)
Composite image by Emily Davison
www.EmilyHannah.com

Printed by
Martins the Printers
Sea View Works
Spittal
Berwick-upon-Tweed
Northumberland
TD15 1RS

My Name Is Eleanor
ISBN: 978-1-326-48892-5
Copyright 2016 Val Scully
All Rights Reserved

A note from the author

Mary Eleanor Bowes lived from 1749-1800. Her life is well documented, both in her own words and in the words of others, but none of us can really know 'the truth' about anyone else's life. All the places, names, dates and public events in this novel are real; I have wrapped the fiction around the facts, describing things that might have happened in private, imagining how it might have felt to be Eleanor.

For those readers who want to know more, appendices are provided:

Who's Who

Chapter Notes

Gibside Timeline

Truth and Fiction

Bibliography

There is more information and illustration on my website

www.valscully.co.uk

Chapter 1

I dreamt of Gibside again last night, a lovely dream of a time when all was well and the world was full of hope. It was just after dawn on a summer's morning and I was down by the river in my nightgown.

If they could have seen me from the house, which they couldn't, I'd have looked like a ghost, but I had never been more conscious of my flesh and blood. It had rained in the night and a dewy mistiness floating above the grass hid my footsteps across the water-meadow. As I walked, I spoke the names of the sleeping flowers like a magical incantation: meadow foxtail, sweet vernal-grass, Cardamine pratensis, fritillaria meleagris... My feet in their soft leather slippers tingled with cold, and the fingertips of night-time lingered in the air. My naked face breathed through every pore. I had loosened my hair from its night-time braids and it sprung out about my shoulders and down my back in unruly coils, refusing to be bound.

I blush to tell you how my breasts felt, but you, my imaginary reader, are my friend from whom I conceal nothing, so I confess to you the simple joy of freedom from constraint. (For you should know my breasts are large and much admired, in fact I have often wondered whether I should have had quite so many suitors had not nature been so generous in that regard!) But with amplitude comes discomfort, and the fashions of the day dictated that they would be lifted and constrained beyond the design of nature. I was yet only seventeen, so the sense of imprisonment was fresh and raw: I have never lost the taste for freedom in all its manifestations.

And so, picture this wanton maiden wandering across the water-meadow towards the riverbank, where two fine oaks frame a view of the water. She could be anyone: a spirit of the place, the water and the trees; Persephone newly released into the world after half a year in darkness; some village lass early abroad to meet her lover. Had you met me on that morning, you would never have taken me for the mistress of the place, let alone the richest heiress in all of England.

When I was eleven years old, my father died. This is a fact that cannot be changed, cannot be told any other way. All his wealth and power and status, all my love and the love of his family and friends, his tenants and his workers could not save him. My world changed in that instant: I was flung out of Paradise.

And yet, as long as I was at Gibside, I would always have my Eden. I was safe there. His spirit was everywhere around me.

If I was Persephone, then my Demeter lived a curious reversal, for my widowed mother inhabited the dark. Since the day he died, she had become a woman of darkness, dressed entirely in black, inhabiting a darkened room where she prayed to dark paintings and was visited by obsequious clergymen with whispering voices, downcast eyes and outstretched palms.

I would not be drawn into that darkened room, but would insist that she should come to me. 'Come out, Mother, come for a walk, a ride, a trip. Come and admire the roses, smell the honeysuckle, see my garden. Greet our visitors, talk to the housekeeper, taste this delicious peach. Live, Mother, live!'

On this morning I remember so clearly, it had been six long years, and I had become used to taking my liberties where I could. The suitors had circled, the princess had chosen, the negotiations had begun: the net was tightening. The more I felt it close around me, the more I craved freedom.

Reaching the shelter of the oaks, I turned and leant against a rough trunk and gazed back up the hill to where Lady Liberty glittered atop her column, and how I envied her. A sudden swelling of frustration and anger burst out of me, and I thumped the trunk in temper, denting my hand, my face contorted in grief. I slid to the ground, careless of the moist soil on my pristine nightgown, and huddled at the base of the tree, staring across the river with unseeing eyes.

Gradually aware that I was being watched, I perceived a heron, priestly and disapproving, regarding me with haughty disdain from the opposite bank like one of Mother's more dignified churchmen. I snatched up a pebble and flung it across the river, where it plopped ineffectually in the water. The heron heaved itself into the air with languorous disdain and drifted ghostly downstream.

'What's he done to you?' A voice, sudden and deep, from below me!

2

Startled, I scrambled to my feet and peered over the retaining wall to see who had spoken, though in the same moment, my body recognised his voice.

His dark head was bent over his fishing rod, attaching a worm. His long wavy hair hid his face from me, and I watched in silence as he cast the line out into the river. Bare feet, wet sandy soil between his toes. Broad shoulders, grey cotton collarless shirt open at the neck. There would be dark hairs at his throat. I slowly craned to see before he should look up, ready at any moment to avert my eyes. But he did not look up.

Calmer now, I shifted to the edge of the retaining wall and lowered my legs over the edge, managing my nightgown with what decorum I could muster. Still not speaking, I was conscious of him casting a sideways glance at my feet dangling an arm's length from his shoulder. A few years ago, he might have risked gripping my ankle and pulling me in, but I was a grown woman now and he would not dare. Alas.

I thought of the last time he'd touched me and wondered whether he remembered. It would have been soon after my father died: I'd have been about twelve and he'd have been sixteen. It was when he and his father came to my garden on Green Close to build the cold-frames and I had helped to hold the planks steady. His hand had closed over mine, by accident I think, and he could not have known the effect it had on my insides, young as I was.

If we had not been friends as children, if he had not built a swing for me and tried it out first, if he hadn't carried me piggy-back in a Mayday race, if he hadn't helped me onto my first pony and ridden a donkey alongside, laughing as he jolted along the Avenue, his feet scraping the ground on either side of the comical beast. Or shown me Orion from the walled garden one Bonfire Night. Or sucked a bee-sting from my finger.

If it wasn't for these memories, I would have abruptly arisen and vanished, affronted by his intrusion on my rare moment of solitude, and not afraid of showing my irritation. I might have commanded him to move away from this spot. Any other estate worker might have moved away without speaking or looking at me, but not him. There was something fearless about him and there always had been. Once I had spoken haughtily to a groom, not knowing he was in the next stall, and he had cast me a sideways glance, amused. I remembered how I had blushed to think that he saw through me.

I had never been alone with a man before, not even old Mr Avison, my piano teacher, and I felt a curious tingle up my spine that made me shiver with the daring of it.

I stayed quiet and watched the float bobbing on the water. The river was low: it had been a dry summer, and pebbles were clearly visible in the shallow water near the edge. Small dark fish poked between them and as I watched, one nosed the big toe on his left foot. If he felt it, he gave no sign.

The quiet deepened, my breathing deepened and slowed and the moments lengthened until I fell into a kind of dream-state, watching the water flow endlessly. When a blackbird struck up its cascade of song across the river, it seemed to come from far away and barely disturbed my reverie.

It was only when his hand closed round the toes of my right foot that I came back to awareness, and even then it was like waking from a dreamless sleep.

'Your toes are cold.' He peeled off my damp slippers and held my feet. The warmth of his hand against my skin brought an aching, and then he let go and I watched, dazed, as he bent to jam his rod between two rocks and turn in one swift movement to enfold the toes of both my feet in both his hands. Although my thighs tensed in the shock of being touched, I held still, looking down and feeling a blush rise from my neck to my cheeks. I tucked my head down further, not wanting to break the moment but completely at a loss: for the first time in my life, I simply did not know what to do.

The world of propriety suddenly felt as distant as the sea, always there, always around this island of my lonely soul, pressing on my shores, invisible to the eye but there nonetheless. Instead, the deep heat of desire spread from my belly upwards to meet the blush that suffused my face and neck and downwards to the source of the heat that radiated through my body. I realized he had shifted so that the soles of my feet were pressed against his chest, and his hands covered the rest. The heat he was generating seemed beyond human to me, and I was lost to my senses.

I kept my head down, thankful that the cascade of my unruly curls hid my face and neck while I struggled to take control of my body. I could not have trusted my voice, even if I had known what

4

to say. All tension had been displaced to my fingers, which gripped the edge of the wall as though I should fall into his arms, which I have to admit I did briefly consider. How liberating to simply do what my body wanted to do, though for propriety's sake I would have to pretend to have fainted. But I would not have deceived him and I knew it.

In the end, it was he who broke the spell, abruptly letting go and stepping away, though my traitor toes reached out yearningly as he left them.

'There, that's better. You shouldn't be out here so lightly dressed, you being a delicate girlie an' all.'

It was the perfect thing to say: he had always teased me about my hardiness.

I laughed and tossed back my hair, grateful for the cool morning air on my overheated skin. Determined not to look at those dancing eyes, I turned my head away and spoke to the tree-trunk. 'You know fine well that I've the constitution of an ox. Besides, I can do what I like.'

'Ah yes, so you can. I forgot.' He sounded sad and I could not help but glance sideways to see his expression. He was standing very still, looking up at me, his head to one side. When our eyes met, his as clear and forget-me-not blue as ever, a stab of something very like pain in my chest made me flinch. I looked away. When I looked back, he was still watching me. Long moments passed until he spoke again.

'So you're to be married?'

I lifted my eyes to the treetops on the opposite bank, and I know I paused too long before I answered.

'Yes, yes I am. Apparently.'

'Now now,' his tone was teasing again. 'We all know you had the choice of the matter.'

With all the haughty disdain I could muster, I looked down at him. 'You know nothing whatsoever about it.'

There was a silence, in which even the birds stopped singing. For a moment, I actually felt afraid that I had hurt his feelings. This was such a new experience for me that I was lost in examining it when he said, 'Then tell me,' in such a low, warm voice that my eyes pricked with tears.

All the unspoken feelings of the past months crowded to the front of my mind, jostling to be heard: the endless parade of suitors and their raptor-eyed mothers; the effortless disdain of the aristocracy, unable to keep their covetous eyes from the paintings and sculptures; the way they all surreptitiously looked me over like a brood mare they were considering buying; my mother's refusal to be involved, even when it came to considering the proposal I favoured, from the handsome Earl of Strathmore. The negotiations had gone on for months, and the longer it took, the more doubtful I was feeling about my choice.

'I...' There were so many possibilities of what to say that in the end, I could say nothing.

He stepped closer to me and lightly touched my ankle, 'Go on, tell me.'

In the end, I summoned the last vestiges of my self-control and decided that this had gone far enough.

I straightened up, took a deep breath, mustered my dignity and asked him to avert his eyes whilst I got to my feet.

In answer, he put both his hands on the wall beside me and, apparently without any effort, lifted himself and twisted: suddenly he was sitting beside me, whilst I looked on in amazement.

'Are you going to tell me about it?'

I didn't turn my head so that I would not have to look into those eyes again, so tempted was I by the offer of intimacy.

'No, Gabriel, I am not.'

With one fluid movement, he was on his feet beside me and extending a hand to help me up. I did consider struggling to my feet without his assistance, but decided to accept one last illicit touch.

When I was standing before him, he seemed so tall that I could not look up at him without my stature seeming like a rebuke, a reminder that I was, after all, just a girl in a night-gown.

He, on the other hand, seemed more reticent than he had been when below me. He took a step back and bowed his head before he spoke. And the words that he said have stayed with me always: 'This is difficult for me and I've a feeling it is for you too. We have known each other a long time. Would that I were your equal, but I am not. I am, I like to think, your friend. I am part of this place and you are too. If ever you should go away, know that I will always be here. If ever you should need me, for whatever reason, know that I will come to you.'

With that, he reached out his hand. Unsure what he wanted or how to respond, I extended mine and felt heat close around it. He lifted it to his lips, kissed it lightly on the fingertips, and he was gone.

It is a dream I return to, again and again. I can summon it at will, I find. That early-morning encounter is to me a kind of touchstone. We all have these moments, do we not? Memories which, the moment they are formed, go straight to the heart of us and make us what we are. It seemed to me then, and it seems to me now, almost thirty years later, that everything about it was pure. And I use the word deliberately, regardless of how you might judge me in the circumstances.

The clarity of the memory infuses me with strength whenever I revisit it. In my darkest moments, when the core of me shrank for want of light, like a forgotten bulb lying in the darkness, away from the soil and moisture and warmth that would give it succour, when I felt I wanted to die, that memory was deep and immovable and gave me strength.

Chapter 2

My father was a fine man, the finest I have known. Tall, handsome and commanding, with clear grey eyes and a laugh that rattled your ribs. In one of my earliest memories, we are standing on the summit of a gentle wooded hill on the estate, surrounded by activity. Working men, wooden scaffolding, huge blocks of stone higher than my head. The air is full of stone dust and noise — hammers, chisels, loud voices. I am bewildered and I hold my father's hand more tightly, press my face against his knee, my other hand clutching its sorry clump of bluebells clamped against my ear.

Suddenly his voice booms out — I feel it vibrate in the bones of his leg — and all sound stops. The air is still. I raise my head. The men have ceased their toil and all faces are turned towards us. The one nearest to me is on his knees, his chisel poised in the air; his face, not a yard from me, is dark underneath but with a thin layer of dust like icing sugar. His eyes are as blue as my flowers. He looks at me and winks then takes his cap from his head and wipes his brow with the back of his hand as he rises to his feet. He is tall, like Father, and as I squint up at both their faces cast into darkness against the bright sky, the outline of the column looms between them.

We can see the column from the house: I have been watching it grow from my bedroom window, but this is the first time I've been here. These men are building it, and now they cluster round us, not too near, and my father speaks to them. Their legs are like a forest. There is a lot of talking. My father says a short sentence, then another man, old and a bit fat, with a wide leather belt, says some longer ones. There is much pointing. Then the man with the blue eyes joins in and there is some laughter. My father laughs loudly, boomingly, and lets go of my hand. I'm not frightened now, so when a boy appears next to me and asks to see my flowers, I show him. He bends down to look, and I see his eyes are exactly the same as the tall man's, but the white bits are as white as white can be. And the lashes are thick and dark and curled, like a girl's. And when he smiles at me, his teeth are white too. I think it is the most beautiful face I have ever seen on a real person. Father has many paintings, and this boy looks like an angel.

I don't remember any more about that day, but I have never forgotten that first time I saw him.

There were so many people on the estate and in the house that I was never lonely. Inside, I was mostly with the maids and governesses and nannies, but I liked it best outside when I was nearly always with Father. We walked about the estate, up hill and down dale and sometimes he led me riding on my pony because when I was little, I couldn't walk fast enough for him, and there was a lot of ground to cover and people to see. I liked it best when we went along the riverbank to where the mills and forges and ironworks clanged and belched smoke, and you could sometimes see a flash of blue dart along the Derwent. The kingfishers and herons were used to the noise, and so was I.

When we walked through the woods, we always had to be careful and stay on the path. Once, when I was small and knew no better, I ran away from Father and found a tunnel in the hillside where I hid, breathless with giggles in the damp darkness. I listened to him shouting in the distance and I hugged myself for mischief. But then his voice changed from angry to scared and I started to cry. He found me in the tunnel, sobbing in the darkness and he pulled me out into the sunlight and hurt my arm and bent down and shouted into my face and then I was really scared and cried louder, then he cried and hugged me and we both calmed down.

After that, he marched me back to the house and sat me down and drew a big bowl shape and told me that this was the valley. And just under the valley he scribbled a thick black bowl-shape and he told me that was the coal. And then he drew little lines from the valley to the coal and told me that was where I had been, in the entrance of the tunnel. And that the tunnels were dangerous places, that they were called adits and that sometimes people got lost in them and never came out, and that sometimes there were explosions that boomed out of the tunnel like the fires of hell, and that all the miners that I saw walking about, with their pigtails and their funny clothes and their black faces, went down there and worked really really hard in the pitch black and risked being crushed or blown up so that we could have a fire and the forges could make iron. And

10

that when I was older I would learn all about the mines and the coal and how it got from Gibside to London, about the wagonways and that big arch that Father had built to make it faster getting the coal to the Tyne, and he would take me to Derwenthaugh and we would watch it being loaded into flat-bottomed boats called keels and we'd see the keelmen row the boats away towards the sea. And that we had to look after all these men and their families. That was our job.

There was another kind of men: the ones who arrived in carriages or on horseback and always came in through the front door. They mostly had big booming voices like Father. When I heard carriages I always went to see who it was, because it was exciting to see new people. I would be at my studies, engrossed in reading or writing or drawing, and I would hear the wheels crunching the gravel long before my governess. (She said I had ears like a bat.) And I would jump up and run out of the room, ignoring her calls, ribbons flying out behind me, along the gallery and down the stairs like the wind. I would sometimes be at the door even before Frederick the footman!

When I was tall and strong enough, I could pull down the handle myself, and it was funny to see the big grand person on the doorstep look to see who had opened the door, and there would be nobody at head height, just me laughing on the threshold.

Some of the men were not pleased to see me though, I could tell. They would smile with their mouths but not with their eyes, then step past me into the hall, handing their hat and gloves to Frederick and marching into the reception room or even, if they were really important, straight into Father's study.

Sometimes, out of mischief, I would follow these visitors: the more they didn't like me, the more mischievous I felt. I'd sit on a chair in the same room and smile at them sweetly. If they didn't smile back, I'd say, 'Would you like to hear a poem?' If they didn't answer, I'd recite it in Latin.

There was one in particular. I had seen him before when I was smaller and couldn't resist the governess taking me away by the hand. I had heard him say hateful words to Father as he watched me being led away up the stairs, scowling at him through the bannisters. 'Pity you have to make do with a girl yet, Bowes. You'll be getting on with the job of making a proper heir, I'll wager.' He was trying to sound posh but I could hear his accent underneath. Father hated people who pretended and I did too.

The next time he came to Gibside, I was bigger and a lot more pert. He marched straight in, looking neither right nor left, let alone down at me, and closed the door of the reception room behind him. I waited outside for a moment, choosing a poem out of my head. I heard a quiet voice from the stairs behind me, and when I looked round it was father's lovely valet, George Walker, watching me from the stairs. He spoke softly, his eyes crinkling: 'What are you up to, little miss mischief?'

I raised a finger to my lips and gestured at the door, then mimed a big fat belly and wobbly jowls. Walker smiled and winked and went on his way.

I turned back to the door, opened it wide and waited a bit longer. I heard his deep voice come out of the room: 'Bowes?'

Then I went in, head held high, a bright smile on my face. 'No, it's me.'

He made a harrumphing noise and sat down in a big leather chair with his back to me, so I walked round the front of him and climbed onto the window seat. My feet didn't quite reach the floor, so I slowly arranged my skirts, crossed my ankles neatly and folded my hands in my lap before I looked up at him.

Silence. Finally, I spoke: 'Fine view, isn't it?'

He cocked a bushy eyebrow at me then said, 'Where's your father?'

'Do you like the column? It's higher than any other in the whole of England! The statue on top is Liberty, and she's covered in gold leaf.'

He looked at me more fiercely then and said in a sneering voice, 'Run along little girl. I'm here on important business.'

I smiled sweetly. 'I never doubted it. Would you like to hear a poem while you're waiting?'

'Pah!' he turned his head away from me like a petulant child and crossed his arms and legs.

Latin it was then. I'd start with an innocent one, the one about the death of a girl's pet sparrow. Just to irritate him a bit more, I hopped off the window-seat and struck a coy pose directly in front of him, my hands clasped in prayer, eyes rolling heavenward. 'Lugete, O Veneres Cupidinesque!' Mourn, ye Graces and Loves and all you whom the Graces love! My lady's sparrow is dead!' Here I flung my hands towards the floor and mimed gently picking up the tiny body, lifting my tear-stained eyes towards him. As I sobbed the words about how beloved the pet was, I held out my hands towards his appalled face as if begging him to kiss its lifeless body: 'Deliciae meae puellae, quem plus ila oculis suis amabat!' He was pressing himself into the back of the chair, his face a mask of revulsion, and I nearly burst out laughing at the effect my performance was having. To disguise the threat of giggles, I turned and did a bit of hopping about like a little bird as I chirruped the bit about how it used to play 'modo huc modo illuc' and then abruptly straightened up and dropped my voice to a sepulchral low for the line about how the poor sparrow was now walking a dark and lonely road whence there was no return. When it came to cursing the shades of Orcus, I flung out my arm towards him and issued the words towards his horrified face in a loud accusatory tone, as though I was banishing his malevolent spirit from the house: 'Male sit, malae tenebrae Orci!'

I ended, like poor bereaved Lesbia, with downcast eyes, and when I raised them, pretending to be blinking back tears as I gazed at him for approval, he was pressed back in his chair, as far away from me as he could get, looking at me with outright loathing, and not a flicker of understanding did I see in his piggy little eyes.

So then I had a flash of inspiration: there was another Catullus poem mocking a pompous buffoon for his airs and graces and affected speech. Just the ticket. Whilst I rehearsed the poem in my head, I fluttered my hand prettily in front of my face, as if trying to gather my emotions after the sad lament for the long-dead sparrow.

When I was ready, aware of the mouth hanging open in his appalled face like a split in an overripe plum, I climbed up to stand on the window-seat and struck an orator's pose. I smile to think how comical I must have looked, like a delicate little doll pretending to be Mark Anthony. I cleared my throat theatrically and then I began: 'Chommoda dicebat, si quando commoda vellet.' A sly glance from under my lashes told me that he didn't understand this one either, so when I got to the line about how marvelously posh he thought he sounded, I rolled my eyes at him and wobbled my voice as though I was speaking words of great tragedy: 'et tum mirifice sperabat se esse locutum!' As I built up to the bit about how everyone's ears are grateful when he leaves, I kept my eyes firmly fixed on the chandelier to stop me losing control. I could see out of my peripheral vision that he had got up and started pacing about the room like a caged bear, muttering imprecations, and finally bursting out with: 'Really, this is not to be endured! Where the devil is Bowes?'

I had just got to the finale when he flung the door open and bellowed, 'Bowes!' then backed into the room holding out both hands, practically pulling my father into the room.

'What on earth's the matter, William? Oh, hello Mary!' His face lit up most agreeably and he came over to give me a kiss and help me down from the window seat. Smiling down at me, his eyes twinkling, he said, 'Have you been entertaining Sir William with one of your renditions? Which item from your repertoire did you choose, my dear?'

When I told him, he laughed aloud, a great bark of a laugh, and turned to his guest's puce face. 'Come along, Will, I'll explain as we walk. Mary has a rich and varied repertoire of classical poetry, and she selected a special piece for your delight and delectation.'

Captain William FitzThomas waited years for his revenge, and by then his disdain for me had curdled with his resentment and jealousy of my father: he was to be a formidable enemy.

Chapter 3

Life in London was always a contrast to life at Gibside: as a child, I hated being there, but by the time of my engagement, the *bon ton* had quite turned my head.

I had spent long dull winter months imprisoned in the nursery at our Grosvenor Square house whilst parliament was in session, longing for Father to come home and tell me why we had to endure this for the good of the people of County Durham, who I thought should represent themselves in this choking city and let us go home.

My pretty slippers barely touched the dirty pavements: I would be lifted from the carriage like a mutinous parcel and passed along to the steps between a channel of footmen and housemaids. The gleaming marble hall so alien after the creaking dark wood floors of Gibside; the echoing ceilings, the shutters, the brass, the hard bed, the slippery stairs: everything conspired to chill and repel me, to confine and bore me.

Once, seeing my stricken face at the window when he arrived home early one April evening, Papa came bounding up the stairs before he had even taken off his coat, and bursting through the door of my nursery, swept me into his arms and twirled me around, to my great glee and the dismay of my mother, who happened to be in the room. 'George! For goodness' sake, put the child down. You will make her vomit!'

Just for sheer devilment, though I did in truth feel a bit dizzy, I shouted, 'No! More! More!' My Papa always loved it when I showed how tough I was, and I loved it when he did what I wanted regardless of Mother's protestations. In the end, clever compromiser that he always was, he whirled me twice more round and then wound me down towards the ground and tumbled with me into a laughing heap on the carpet, where we lay side by side until we got our breath back.

Never so much as cracking her long face into a smile, Mother regarded us from above, then said, 'Really George, you over-excite the child and it is nearly her bed-time.'

'Nooo! Papa please! I haven't been out of the house this livelong day! It's spring! I want to be outside!' and with the drama only the young can muster, I grabbed his labels and spoke earnestly into his face: 'I NEED to be outside!'

Lying across his chest, the great boom of his laughter punched me in the ribs. 'Then what my little princess needs, she shall have. Come, we shall go and take a turn about in Chelsea Gardens.' Pleased and excited, I clambered to my feet and made to pull him up.

Still holding my hand, he spoke to Mother: 'Coming, Mary?'

'No, no, you two go without me.'

'Oh, come come, my dear, just an hour or so's stroll.' He murmured something in her ear, and her plain face broke into a smile at last. Whatever it was had mollified her, and when the maid passed her my cape, she fastened it around my neck, saying, 'Certain it is that there is no kind of affection so purely angelic as of a father to a daughter.' She bent down and cupped my face between her hands. 'Joseph Addison said that, Mary Eleanor, and there never was a truer word.'

Mother had never been a sociable creature, so while Father was going about his business in the daytime, I would be at my studies and she would be engrossed in her endless correspondence. She occasionally entertained visitors, and I might be summoned to the morning room to make my appearance and be petted over, but mostly I was happy to be in lessons. I was rarely introduced to a girl of my own age, and when I was, I invariably found myself tongue-tied, for I quickly became conscious of how little I knew of what was considered polite conversation for young ladies of my class. I would try to talk about whatever I was currently interested in, but would be met by an open mouth and a vacant gaze so I would try to turn the talk to ribbons or embroidery silks, but I must have been a patronizing little moppet and the women soon stopped bringing their daughters.

Boys were an entirely different matter. I was always keen to find out what they had been studying at school and compare notes. It took me a long time to realize that it was I who was lucky: the girls I met were far from stupid, simply deprived of an education. Father always promised me that we would do a Grand Tour of

16

Europe when I was eighteen, exactly as if I was a boy. But of course, it was not to be.

The first time we went to London after Papa died, things were entirely different. Mother had stayed in mourning at Gibside for two whole years, and I was left to my own devices. When I look back, I marvel at the self-containment of the little girl I was then, for I was only eleven years old when he died and I cried until I felt myself utterly drained of all feeling, so prostrate with grief and loss, bewilderment and impotence that there were fears for my sanity, and when I stopped eating altogether, for my life.

But then one day in his study, where I sat and sobbed with my head on my arms at his desk, I heard a sigh, close enough for the hairs at the side of my neck to prickle. I looked up, expecting to find one of the footmen sent to find me, but there was no-one there. The room was dark in the pallid autumn morning, grey light seeping in the air, but I saw that a framed text on the wall was strangely illuminated. With an intuition that seemed entirely natural, I accepted what I had heard and what I was seeing, for the illumination grew brighter as I watched. I wiped my eyes on my skirt, took a deep breath and crossed the room to stand before the picture. It was a favourite of my father's, a quotation that he said had been the guiding principle behind his design of the estate: 'True happiness is of a retired nature and an enemy to pomp and noise. It loves shade and solitude, and naturally haunts groves and fountains, fields and meadows. Joseph Addison.' I had never noticed before that it was the same person who had spoken of the special bond between a father and his daughter.

My father was sending a message to me, and I felt a swelling of warmth in my chest. We had always been happy wandering the groves, he and I, and now I must do it alone: I would learn to love solitude. I blinked slowly and read it again, memorising it, then I smiled for the first time in weeks. I took myself outside that very moment: I remember vividly how I swung open the heavy oak door and stood on the threshold, breathing deeply, deliberately filling my lungs with the woodsmoke air and looking across to where the late autumn sun floated behind a veil. A sheep called from Cut Thorn Farm on the hillside and I mimicked it exactly, as I had often done to make my father laugh. In my heart, he laughed again.

He was with me now, and he always would be. We walked to the woods together.

One bright February day I was busy in my garden – there was so much to do – the crocuses were out and there was so much winter detritus to be cleared. It was a wonderful feeling to be out and active amongst all the promise of spring, and when a shadow fell across a clump of snowdrops, I was irritated to be interrupted, so I didn't look up.

'Miss Mary, your mother would like to see you in her study.'

I carried on forking gently round the snowdrops. 'I have told you to call me Eleanor. Could you step out of my light please?'

The maid didn't move. We always had a rather free-and-easy way with our house-servants: it was something London was to teach me to be ashamed of.

'I said,' and now I dropped my voice from its habitual treble, hoping to convey some authority. I was, after all, practically the mistress of the place. 'I asked you to move. Kindly do so.'

To my immense frustration, the maid bobbed down beside me and spoke confidentially into my ear. 'We need to make you presentable before Mrs Bowes sees you, and she insists we call you Mary. Would you come to your dressing room please, miss? Martha has hot water ready and a morning dress.' Cajoling now: 'Come, it will not take long.'

An hour later, writhing with discomfort inside a tightly-laced bodice, I knocked on my mother's door. Her voice, when it bade me enter, had its habitual quaver, which increased my irritation. The room was dark, as I expected, the heavy drapes partially closed against the spring sunshine, though I could sense that a window was open. In the distance, there was a clang of metal against metal and the raised voices of the workmen engaged in constructing the chapel which was to be my father's mausoleum. A wave of fresh grief swept over me and washed away my temper, leaving me bereft.

'Come here my dear.' When I stood before her, she reached out her hands and I placed mine inside them, palms up. Martha had scrubbed them but despaired of getting the nails clean, so I hoped Mother wouldn't turn them over. Instead she bent her head and placed a kiss on my palm. It had become so rare for her to show me any affection that I was quite taken aback.

'Such fine, delicate hands,' she mused, 'and so very small.' She looked up at me and appeared to study me for a few moments without speaking. Her face was pinched and pale like a plant too long denied the light.

Abruptly, she dropped my hands and turned back to her desk. 'We are going to London.'

I couldn't help myself: 'No, please Mama, it's spring! There's so much to do in the garden.'

'Forget your garden, Mary, we have more important matters to attend to.'

'But there's nothing more important to me, Mama! Not in the spring! Please, can we leave it until autumn? I have such plans, and London will be so smelly and boring.'

Sudden inspiration struck: 'You go! Leave me here! I shall be perfectly well looked-after here. We can correspond, and then when you come back, you will see what a fine garden I have made for you!' Although I lacked conviction: Mother had never shown the remotest interest in the natural world.

She didn't answer and I could feel my temper rising. I would not let her misery inflict itself upon me.

'Really, Mother, what would draw us to London, now there's no need to go? We belong here.'

She looked at me sharply then. 'I don't, Mary, not any more. If I ever did.'

'I don't know what you mean?' I couldn't imagine that she might feel any differently from the way I did about Gibside.

'I know you love it here and you barely know anywhere else. I have loved it here too. There are many reasons why we are leaving.' Looking at me, her expression softened, and she drew me to the window-seat to sit me down by her side. I twisted round, however, and opened the window further so that I could lean out and breathe in the sweet air. Across the green, the voices of the stonemasons rang with laughter.

'I loved your father, Mary, and I think he loved me, in his way.'

I always bridled at any implied criticism of my father, but I held back a sharp retort and merely said, 'Of course, Mama.'

She was silent for some moments and I surreptitiously watched her face in profile, its pointed features so dissimilar to my own. I saw her gather breath, and then she said, 'Of course, he loved his first wife more, the sainted Eleanor of revered memory.' She gestured across the room at the portrait. I had never heard my mother speak with bitterness in her tone. It was a new feeling for me, as though she was confiding in me as a friend. I was so used to the portraits of Eleanor that I barely gave her a thought, but now it dawned on me that she had died when she was not much older than me. Why, her life had barely begun!

'Six portraits, Mary. Six. All about the house, the favourite in his study. One even over our marital bed. I ask you: was it fair of your father to expect me to see them with equanimity?' She shook her head and reached for my hand without looking at me, dabbing her eyes with her other hand. 'I'm sorry, child. I should not burden you with my grief.'

She was quiet for a moment, and then she turned to me and spoke with the tone of a governess imparting a serious lesson, which indeed it was, had I but known it then. I know it now.

'Your father and I had a good marriage, Mary. We worked well together; we had mutual liking and respect. These are vital for a contented marriage. We were fortunate in that regard.' She stood up, brushing off her black gown as though the past was dust.

Not knowing what was expected of me, I looked out of the window, stayed quiet and waited.

When the silence had gone on too long, I turned away from the daylight to look at her. My eyes took a few moments to perceive her, deep in the room, darkness within darkness. She was staring at me, a sombre expression on her shaded face, as though somewhat fearful of speaking, but then lightly shook her head and seemed to dismiss the thought.

'We are going to London for my own satisfaction, because it is time, and because the estates demand it: I have neglected certain aspects for too long. There are lawyers I must see. I must make decisions about properties. Streatlam will take care of itself: your father didn't much care for the place but we have good staff. We will call in at Ledstone on our journey: I may sell the place and simply rent whenever we travel between London and Gibside. We will stay at Grosvenor Square for now, then I will travel to St Paul's Walden, leaving you with your Aunt Jane. My father is not well. I may stay there for the time being.'

She brightened: 'Meanwhile, Mary Eleanor Bowes, you shall be introduced to London society. I think you will find much to interest you.' In a simulation of coquettish delight that I found horrifying to behold, she wafted an imaginary fan in front of her face and made cow-eyes over the top of it. I did not smile: she dropped the pretence abruptly and returned to her habitual dour expression.

'We leave tomorrow.' I was dismissed.

She was right: three years older than I had been on my last visit, I did find much to interest me in London society. In fact, as I said, it quite turned my head.

From the moment we arrived, I sensed that I was being regarded in quite a different manner. Servants were more solicitous of my well-being. I was introduced to a fresh-faced new governess, Mrs Parish, and given to understand that academic lessons would be taking up a good deal less of my time. Instead, I was to be dressed in finery and shown about the place. When news of our arrival spread (and all such news spreads like ground elder) callers proliferated. Some afternoons the silver tray in the hallway was piled high with their cards. Fashionable women brought their sons and daughters to meet us, to take tea, share gossip, and invite us to theatres and assemblies. Excited and flattered, I barely knew what to make of all this attention. At first (poor deluded fool) I put it down to my sparkling conversation, and redoubled my efforts to entertain and impress, whilst my mother looked on, astonished and amused. I blush to think of how I must have seemed.

It was George Walker who made me see things clearly. George held a special place in my heart and I in his: he had been Papa's valet and friend and now liked to see himself as my father-substitute. He was much given to telling me what my father would have said, and sometimes I found it touching. Other times, I found it painful and presumptuous, little madam that I was.

One morning, having seen the latest visitors to the door, he returned to the reception room, where mother was reclining against the arm of the sofa, declaring herself quite exhausted by my chatter. Too exhilarated to have any patience with her, I snapped, 'Well go to bed then!' and caught George's disapproving glance as he closed the curtains against the midday sun.

With a solicitous bow, he extended his arm to my mother, and casting me a reproving look, escorted her to the door. I had stood up and was pacing the room, fizzing with energy and plotting how I could get to the theatre to see a play I'd just been hearing about from an entertaining gentleman caller. Mother heartily disapproved of the theatre, believing it to be a den of iniquity, but I must get there somehow!

When George reappeared without knocking, my first response was a haughty look, but he knew me too well and smiled, ignoring it completely. He stayed still, by the closed door, and watched me, an amused expression on his kindly face.

'What? What is it George?'

'You're plotting how you can get to Drury Lane, aren't you?'

There was no use pretending. 'Yes I am. Mother will never take me.' I brightened. 'But you? We could go together, you and I. I would go incognito in a black velvet cloak! She need not know.'

'Now now, you know I would not do that. Your mother fears the theatres with good reason.'

'Pah! Tosh and poppycock!' My father's favourite expression.

'You would be allowed to go with an escort, and it seems to me you could have the pick of your recent visitors. The gentleman who was here just now would no doubt be happy to take you.'

'Him? It would not be seemly, surely, for me to be seen with so old a man. He is not a relative, merely a new acquaintance: she would never accept it.'

'She would have to accept it if you were to consider his suit.'

'His suit?'

'Yes, his suit. Why did you think he was here?'

'Why, so that he and his mother could meet us, of course!'

'And why would they want to do that?'

'Well,' I faltered, 'why, to be neighbourly I suppose. We are a novelty, being from the north...' but I was far from convinced, even as I said it, and a horrible suspicion grew. 'No! You cannot mean that, George. The young man who was here yesterday with his mother, yes, I can accept that she was looking at me in a rather speculative way, but I thought that was merely because she was impressed with my knowledge of Renaissance architecture.'

'Really? You really think that was what she was thinking as she watched you talking with her son?'

22

'Her eligible young son. That's what you're saying, isn't it? Oh for goodness' sake, we had a lot in common. We enjoyed each other's company, but he was just a boy and I am just a girl.' I caught his bemused expression. 'Yes, yes, when it suits me. But marriage? It's not in anybody's mind, George!'

'I'm sorry, but you are entirely deluded, little miss.'

I stood up straight, struggling with my temper. George knew he could get away with a lot if I was in the right mood. In fact, when I looked at his eyes like a pair of twinkling sapphires, I sometimes found myself yearning for a fatherly hug. But at that moment, I could for two pins have ordered him from the room and banished him from my house.

My voice low, I said, 'Don't call me that, Walker, not any more. You may leave now.'

'Forgive me, Miss Eleanor, but I will say my piece though you don't want to hear it. For nobody else will say it. You may not be aware of this, but you are rumoured to be the richest heiress in all of England.'

I was genuinely flabbergasted. 'I am?'

He nodded gravely. 'And that makes you vulnerable. I just want you to know that. You have grown up surrounded by honest people.' He laughed and his smile was wry: 'With your father around, they would not dare to be any other way. But he is gone now, and your mother has ... other things on her mind. So I feel it my duty to speak.'

Suddenly deflated, I sat down in a hard chair.

George softened his tone and patted my hair. 'I will just say this one thing and hope that you will always remember it: People are not always what they seem.'

Oh George, if only I had listened.

Chapter 4

My mother soon tired of the society matriarchs and they of her. She made so little attempt at conversation: she seemed to me to draw all the energy from the room like a draught from a chimney. Except mine, of course, but then I was used to her. I soon noticed that her widow's weeds were regarded with distaste by our fashionable lady callers and once plucked up the courage to broach the subject, in the hope that she would rouse herself out of her lassitude. I didn't handle it very well.

'Mama, Father has been dead for three years now.'

She turned her head slowly, her eyes already brimming. 'You think I don't know that?'

'Of course, it was clumsy of me, I'm sorry. I simply meant to ask whether you intended wearing mourning for much longer. People …'

'Yes, do not think I am unaware of their revulsion: they see widowhood as a plague they must not catch.'

I thought it a cynical remark, and couldn't see how there could be any truth in it. Whenever the women mentioned their husbands, it seemed they only wanted to complain about their drinking and gambling. In my naiveté, I assumed that if that was how they felt, surely they would be relieved to be widowed. My mother's response was always a reproachful look which clearly implied that the women were lucky to have husbands at all.

After a couple of weeks of these strained gatherings, where undercurrents swirled confusingly, the parade of visitors dwindled and then ceased.

Mother departed for St Paul's Walden and I was left in the charge of my father's sister, Aunt Jane, who being plagued by gout, was not the most cheerful company. Mother had told me that Jane had once been a celebrated beauty. Looking at her now, with her small wrinkled face on an outstretched neck, I was reminded of a drawing of a tortoise I had seen in a natural history book. It was difficult to see the remnants of any beauty, try though I might, and there was certainly no trace of resemblance to my handsome father.

Aunt Jane had never married, but was quite animated by the prospect of finding a husband for me, despite my protestations that I was only fourteen. I had no intention of choosing a husband for a while yet, if ever: I saw no need for one. I was thoroughly enjoying myself making the acquaintance of a wide array of young men - and women, of course, but I always enjoyed male company more than female. The banter was so much better, the range of reference so much wider, the topics of conversation so much more fascinating, though I tried to bear in mind that it was not the fault of the girls.

Aunt Jane, for all her failings, was a sociable creature, and within a fortnight of Mother's departure my life became a glittering round of assemblies, dancing, card games, going for walks and rides in parks. I quickly lost my taste for solitude and lost myself in the dizzying whirligig of London society.

Many of the young men I was meeting were from other countries which I one day hoped to visit: I was particularly enamoured of a light-hearted young Venetian with whom I could practise my colloquial Italian. Most of the Englishmen had been on the Grand Tour and could regale me with stories of museums packed with Renaissance treasures, oratorios in elaborate rococo churches, descriptions of indigenous flora and fauna. I felt myself quite parochial and was hungry to know more of the world, plying these young men with question after question. My curiosity was always genuine and I knew I was never more pretty than when animated by some fascinating topic of conversation. I had often been told that they enjoyed talking to me for that very reason. I soon learnt that most of them loved the sound of their own voice and given such encouragement, could talk for hours. I drank it all in and paid no heed to how my rapt attention appeared to others: I see that now.

One day, Aunt Jane was listlessly looking through the cards on the silver salver when she picked up a letter, scrutinized its seal, and then airily wafted it, affecting to be uninterested. 'You have a letter from Mrs Montagu.'

I knew of the Montagu family of Denton Hall, and my father had spoken of Elizabeth Montagu with great respect, referring to her as a woman I should seek to emulate. I was keen to meet her and waited impatiently to be passed the letter.

26

'You are no doubt invited to one of her Blue Stocking Assemblies. You are just her sort.'

'Pardon, Aunt Jane?'

'I have never been privileged to receive an invitation myself, but then I am a woman of simple tastes and little education beyond the feminine skills in which you yourself are so notably lacking.' She looked at me disapprovingly over the top of her pince-nez.

I made a great effort to keep my smile, though these oft-repeated criticisms were beginning to seriously irritate me. Mrs Parish had been quick to tell me that she had been instructed to rectify the deficiencies my mother perceived in my education: I listened with incredulity as she explained to me, in all seriousness, that my posture, my etiquette, my polite chit-chat all needed urgent attention, as did such other demanding pastimes as sewing, knitting and drawing. I was speechless with indignation and disdain. Luckily for the future of our relationship, Mrs Parish did share some of my interests in the natural world, and had a brother who worked at the Natural History Museum, so I endured her tedious 'lessons' and waited to be introduced to the members of the Royal Society whom she boasted of numbering amongst her acquaintance.

'Have no fear, you will not be required to wear blue stockings. It is merely a nickname for the type of party given by Mrs Montagu and her ilk. They are - how shall I put it - rather unconventional. Quite respectable, I can assure you, but somewhat mocked.'

'By those who have no hope of an invitation?' I kept my eyes wide and innocent, but when she turned her head slowly to look at me again, I had the distinct impression she had not missed my meaning.

She reached for the bell-pull to summon tea before she continued whilst I sat suppressing my irritation, my interest piqued.

'Of course, Elizabeth Montagu might simply want to meet you because of the Newcastle connection. She and her husband were friends of your father's, you know, and he very much admired her. She has always been a sparky individual, a lively and very clever woman.' Here she cast me a meaningful look: 'And we all know your father admired learning in a woman. Myself, I believe it to have been a mistake to educate you to quite such a degree. I am of the same mind as Lady Mary Wortley: in order to attract a husband, a

27

young lady must hide knowledge with as much solicitude as she would hide crookedness or lameness.'

I stared at her. 'You cannot mean that, Aunt Jane.'

'Oh, believe me, Eleanor, I do. And you would be particularly well-advised to remember it.'

Now I could not hide my disdain and abruptly got up to snatch the letter from her hand. 'This is addressed to me, I think.' My temper fluttering in my chest, I considered flouncing out of the room but luckily thought better of it as the door suddenly opened and two maids entered with tea-trays. The rigmarole of china and sugar-lumps distracted my aunt, who I had already decided had the attention-span of a goldfish, and by the time we were furnished with our side-tables, she seemed to have forgotten all about my outburst.

'The family has a similar background to our own, with a fortune made in the Great Northern Coalfield. Since she lost her only son, she has busied herself with the cultural life of the city. Her salons are famous but somewhat ... unconventional. Whereas fashionable people favour card-games and dancing at their gatherings, blue-stocking assemblies are always presided over by the ladies and the topics of conversation are, shall we say, scholarly. You will find no enjoyable distractions such as gambling or dancing, oh no no no, far too low-brow for the likes of Mrs M! I think you will find yourself quite at home, my dear, but have no hopes of finding a husband there.'

'I know you have trouble comprehending this, Aunt Jane, but finding a husband is not uppermost in my mind. In fact,' I took a breath, 'I may never marry.'

'Not marry? Don't be foolish, Eleanor. You have a duty to marry.'

'A duty? To whom?'

'Why, to us all! To your family and to all the people whose livelihoods depend upon our continued success! You are merely a cog in the great wheel of destiny. Do not be deluded that you have any significance beyond that.'

I was speechless. It was as though a great pit had opened at my feet and I stared into the void. Falteringly, I spoke: 'You cannot mean that, aunt. Surely you want me to be happy.'

'Mary Eleanor Bowes, your head may be crammed with learning but you have little comprehension of the ways of the world. You will marry. You will marry an aristocrat, I'll wager. There are many aristocratic families willing to bestow their titles on a girl like you from what they would term,' and here her voice took on a bitter sneer that I found chilling, 'the mercantile class. They will lower themselves to do that in exchange for your wealth, which they will then use to repair their crumbling castles and country-seats. And, if this is not too indelicate, to improve their blood-line.'

'Like a race-horse?'

'Exactly like a race-horse. You will not like to think it, but many of these young men who cluster round you like bees to the honey-pot are not so intoxicated by repartee, your clear grey eyes, your chestnut curls and your, ahem, generous embonpoint. You are, in their eyes, a brood mare.'

I stared at her, horrified, buffeted by such a tumult of emotions that I struggle to describe them for you. I had had little regard for Aunt Jane before, though I had always been dutiful and obedient, but this speech hardened my heart against her. It was not that there was any great surprise in what she had said: it was the green-eyed glee with which she had delivered it.

'However,' she examined the card again, 'I notice that you are invited for a breakfast rather than an evening gathering. That is unusual, and implies it will be an intimate event.' She looked up with a cold smile. 'I think you are going to be interviewed, Eleanor.'

And she was right.

George Walker had warned me that Hill Street was in an area notorious for footpads, but I was unprepared for quite how dirty and crowded it was. It was a novel idea to me that not all people of our class had pavements in front of their houses. As we approached, the press of carriages and horses on all sides became claustrophobic, the air full of shouted imprecations that burnt my ears, and the carriage rocked alarmingly as we turned into the street.

When I stepped down from the carriage, my foot slipped unpleasantly on a thin layer of slime: a strip a yard wide had been swept, and on either side of it a bank of unspeakable mud and manure grazed my skirts: I lifted them higher. I had only to take a few steps before I attained the threshold, and thankfully the door was already open and a liveried footman took my cloak and showed me into the morning room.

'Mary Eleanor Bowes, ma'am.'

There were two ladies in the room, and the older one arose from a wing-back chair and came towards me with a warm smile.

'Welcome, my dear, I have so looked forward to meeting you properly.' She bent her head to look into my face, then nodded and patted my hand. 'You have your father's eyes.' She smiled, drew me towards the sofa and sat down beside me. I had time to perceive that the other young lady was a few years older than me, though less than twenty, I would judge. Her dress was modest and I wished I had worn the gown I'd chosen, but Aunt Jane had been eager to impress and so I was attired in a tight corset and huge pleated skirt which felt uncomfortable and looked, I believed, somewhat ludicrous on my tiny frame.

'Mary Eleanor, this is Hannah More from Bristol. Hannah has just published a notable play, which is how I came to hear of her. Hannah, Mary Eleanor is from County Durham, and her father was a friend of mine.'

Instantly impressed and somewhat overawed by meeting a published playwright, I was keen to find a way to impress Hannah with my own literary aspirations, but suppressed the urge and simply smiled in imitation of the gracious serenity I had observed in others. But the excitement was too much for me and I couldn't stop myself from speaking: 'How do you do, Hannah. Please call me Eleanor. What is the name of your play? Is it to be performed?'

'It isn't quite published yet, although at the printer's as we speak. It is called The Search After Happiness.'

'I would love to write my own play! Do please tell me about it.'

Hannah opened her mouth to reply, but Mrs Montagu held up a hand. 'All in good time, my dears. You will indulge me, I hope, if I explain why I have invited you both here today and how my house differs from the prevailing customs of pleasant conversation.'

Hannah and I made a slight bow of acquiescence and Mrs Montagu continued: 'We three are educated women.' I blushed to be included so warmly. 'Our parents were enlightened and they conferred on us the privilege of an education more usually bestowed on our brothers.' She studied my face gravely. 'Now that you are of an age to enter into society, you will find that the presiding arbiters of taste and decency would rather we stayed in our parlours embroidering a cushion and confined our minds to tittle-tattle.

'London society is, as you are no doubt already aware, dominated by largely male pursuits. We are meant to be merely decorative and light as air. The English aristocracy is quite obsessed by drink, gambling, horses, and the ... market.'

'The market?'

'The market in land and in marriage.' Here, she looked meaningfully at me. 'I hear the Prince of Mecklenburg is desperately in love with you?'

Meeting her gaze, and relieved to see the mischief dancing there, I laughed outright. 'Yes, he and many others. It's amazing how attractive a vast fortune makes a girl! At some assemblies, I have to step over the bodies of notable aristocrats prostrating themselves at my feet!'

She patted my hand kindly. 'You enjoy yourself, Eleanor. It is not often a single woman has such power.'

'Oh I do! I'm enjoying all the attention, but I won't let it go to my head.'

'You must have had a very quiet time since your father died, my dear. How have you been occupying yourself up at Gibside?'

'Oh, I never have a moment of leisure! The gardens take up much of my time. They are my great pleasure, you know. I still have a full timetable of lessons, for my father was most anxious that I should continue my studies after he ...' Suddenly, I could not speak for a great well of grief that rose in my chest.

She squeezed my hand again and waited until I had gathered my senses and steadied my voice. 'I know, my dear, I know. Your father had great foresight. He waited so long for a child, and it was greatly to his credit that he invested as much in you as he would have done in a son. He was very proud, you know.'

I blinked back tears. 'I know. I strove always to make him proud. I still do.' I paused. 'I have never told anyone this before, but I still speak to him and ask his advice.'

Her expression was enigmatic. 'That is quite understandable and I think very healthy. It must be a comfort to you. I perhaps should not say this, but your mother is not the most...'

Mrs Montagu's friendship with my father made me somehow feel I could confide in her. 'No, Mother is not the most ... communicative person. We are not close.'

'And so in whom do you confide, if I may ask?'

'Oh, I am never alone. We have very loyal servants, and of course there is my old nanny at Gibside, and my new governess, Mrs Parish, who shares my love of Botany. And there's Aunt Jane...' though my tone must have indicated a good deal about my feelings in that regard.

She studied my face for a long moment before patting my hand again. 'Well, I hope that you and I will get to know each other, and you and Hannah will meet other educated and enlightened young ladies at my salons, although in fact there are none quite so as young as you, Eleanor. I make it my business to introduce people and ideas. We have some fascinating speakers, and cultural, enlightened conversation is de rigeur chez moi.' She laughed, the playful, tinkling laugh of a much younger woman. 'I trust you two are not devoted to the card games which preoccupy so much of London society?'

'I do enjoy card games, but I much prefer conversation. I've been a little disappointed that some evenings have been so dominated by gambling that no-one talks about anything else! That's partly why I love dancing, because then at least people are looking at each other and talking. But yes, I like cards.'

'As do many of my friends and acquaintances, but we agree that card tables stifle the exchange of ideas. And there are many ideas abroad, particularly in Scotland, and of course in France. My friends and I refuse to accept that we should be excluded from the life of the mind simply because of our gender. We enjoy the company of writers, artists, historians and thinkers, and to that end, we invite others of like mind to assemble and enjoy conversation.'

All of a sudden, there was a great roaring in the street outside, raised voices and the thunder of scores of running feet.

Mrs Montagu's smile was sad but reassuring. She waited until the mob had passed and then she said, 'Do not fear, my dears, this is a monthly event. You will have heard of the public hangings at Tyburn? I'm afraid that half the drunken and yelling spectators pass by here on their way to fresh scenes of debauchery and riot. Our society is in sore need of reform.'

'But how can these people be reformed?'

'Education. Public debate. A responsible press. And all of this can only happen if the people at the top of society improve their minds instead of deadening them with drink and gambling. Enlightenment ideals of culture, conversation and friendship are in the air. Those of us who are engaged in promoting the improvement of society's morals believe in the union between the scholarly and the sociable, the masculine and the feminine. We aim for what David Hume perceives as essential for the creation of a reformed republic of letters.'

I looked to see whether Hannah wanted to speak, but she was only smiling vaguely, so I said, 'I understand now why you and my father were such great friends.'

Mrs Montagu smiled in a way that showed she knew what I meant, but she encouraged me to elaborate by saying, 'Go on, my dear.'

'He explained to me about the Whig concept of society's inevitable progression towards greater liberty and enlightenment, and how we should put our faith in the power of reason and education to reshape society for the better.' I suddenly felt shy, but Mrs Montagu's smile had grown wider, and so I carried on. 'He believed England's constitution to be a social contract based on the Magna Carta. He was a great believer in liberty, but told me that individuals consent to surrender some of their freedoms in exchange for the protection of their remaining rights.'

'Quite so. Perhaps you have heard of Lord Mansfield's recent ruling, in which he invoked habeas corpus to argue successfully for the release of a slave called James Somerset?'

'No, Mrs Montagu, I had not, but I am glad to hear it. Slavery is abhorrent.'

'Indeed it is, Eleanor. As John Locke said, "All mankind being equal and independent, no-one ought to harm another in his life, health, liberty or possessions." Would that it were so. I am an optimist, Eleanor, as was your father. We can improve society.'

I cannot tell you how I felt at that moment: it was as though that one short exchange had given me a passport to a new life, and as she got up to ring a bell chord, I sat back and breathed out. If I had been invited to an interview, I was fairly sure I had passed. I hadn't realized until that moment quite how much I had wanted to be accepted into Mrs Montagu's circle, young as I was. It felt like having a grown-up conversation of the kind I would have had with my father.

'When I had my first gatherings, we would hold them at breakfast-time, so I thought I would have a special breakfast to introduce you both to some of the younger ladies of my acquaintance. Follow me.'

We were shown into a room with exquisite Japanese hand-painted wallpaper in which a long table was laid out with the finest linen. Glittering china cups, plates and saucers held delicate delights such as biscuits, and toasts with delicious bowls of cream, butter and chocolate. I gasped, 'I've never seen such a beautiful, artistic room!'

Elizabeth laughed, 'Ah yes, I must confess I am aware that it is pretty enough to make me a thousand enemies!'

It was a delightful morning and wonderful to meet girls and young women who shared my interests and wanted to discuss science and the arts, philosophy and the tenets of a civilised life. My father was with me that morning: I had found a group to which I felt I belonged and for which he had prepared me well.

As we left, Mrs Montagu bade farewell to each one of us. To me she said, 'I look forward to seeing you again very soon, Eleanor. Now that I know of your interest in Botany, I shall ensure that you are on the guest list the next time we have speakers from the Royal Society. You will, of course, meet Benjamin Stillingfleet on our forthcoming trip to the theatre. He and I are good friends. Dr Johnson will be there too. And I have noted that you would like to meet Joshua Reynolds and Horace Walpole, though beware of the latter: he has a wicked tongue and you had best keep on the right side of him.'

As I stepped into the sedan chair, I looked forward with great excitement to the next time I should visit Mrs Montagu's house, with the promise of more such lively conversation and perhaps even seeing some of the famous scholars she knew.

When I later learned that Mrs Montagu had described me as 'a fine girl, lively, sensible, civil and good-natured, ' I hugged the words to my heart: I had at last found a woman I could look up to.

Chapter 5

I had heard of 'the beautiful Lord Strathmore' long before I saw him, but wasn't prepared for the impact he had on me. Now, with the benefit of hindsight, and having brought up daughters of my own, I can see that I was ripe for what happened: it was, for me a *coup de foudre*.

I was finding London life increasingly oppressive: the crowded streets, the constant noise, the choking air, the black rain, the grimy fog. The novelty of constant socializing was wearing off, and the press of insistent young bucks was becoming wearisome: they were all so eager to catch my eye, to sit beside me at card games, to fill my dance-card with commitment, that I felt constantly pressed on all sides by unwelcome attention.

Looking back on that time, I can see that I was making enemies even then. I really had no interest in marriage and found it tiresome when some strutting cockerel of a boy would make assumptions simply because we had enjoyed a little banter during a quadrille. He would then scurry over to his doting mater, sitting with the other dowagers like a row of climbing plants past their prime. I would see her look over at me, the gleam of avarice in her eye, then turn to her companion and speak excitedly, her gloved hand raised to the side of her face. All three would regard me speculatively for the rest of the evening, and I would later hear that the family had approached my mother with a proposal of marriage.

When these young men had the effrontery to speak to me personally on the topic, I would waft the subject away with a flick of a feather. 'No, no no, I am having far too much fun to think of marriage. Why should I marry? I am only sixteen and have no need.'

'But might I approach your mother for permission?'

'I care not what you do: I am off to dance.'

I meant what I said, I always have done, but they invariably took such remarks as coquettish banter. Once or twice, I caught a glimpse of the venom that could ensue from such misunderstandings, but had not the wisdom to protect myself.

'You are a tease.'

'I? A tease? How so? I am simply enjoying myself. I have no favourites!'

'But you have sat beside me at supper three times now.'

'Good Lord, you are ridiculous! That shows nothing, merely that I was enjoying hearing about your travels in Greece!'

I genuinely found it bewildering. Why did these people persist in misinterpreting my words and actions? Was a young woman really not free to enjoy the company of a young man without conclusions being drawn? In the absence of lessons, I derived all my stimulation from these conversations. I sucked all the interest from a beau like nectar, and when it seemed there was no more to learn, I moved on to the next flower.

Soon, the press of attention made me actively crave peace and solitude, and I was becoming homesick. I wanted woods and hills and moors, big clear skies, birdsong. I wanted my garden, the fast-flowing clear waters of the Derwent, the cool moist air of the old oak forest. I wanted to see the red kites wheeling over Gibside. I wanted Liberty. I wanted people I knew and who knew me. But the longer my mother stayed away, the more I despaired of ever getting home.

One evening as I left Almack's and climbed wearily into my carriage, the coachman chatted amiably to me as he often did. 'Too much dancing, Miss Eleanor? Let's get you home to your bed and a good book.'

'Oh, Francis, I wish I could go to my real home. I miss Gibside.'

'Aye, me an' all, Miss Eleanor. In fact I was just having a good chat with a fellow from Durham and we were both craving some clean air. It's funny, isn't it? Half the muck in London air comes from Newcastle mines. Makes you think, doesn't it? He was saying his lordship doesn't want to stay long down here in the smoke. He's just back from Italy and finds London …what was the word…abominable.'

'Oh? Who is his master?'

'Lord Strathmore.'

A face swam into my mind's eye, but I was so tired it barely registered. 'John Lyon, yes, I think he visited when I was a little girl.'

My first glimpse of him was at Almack's. I was standing as usual in a noisy circle of other debutantes and dandies, trying to muster enough interest to follow the increasingly combative conversation between two young men, both of whom wished to sit next to me at supper.

Unbelievably, it seemed to be escalating. When I caught a mention of a duel, I lost all patience: 'Oh, for goodness' sake. You are both ridiculous. I shall sit with someone else entirely!' and I moved purposefully away from them, thankful for once of the enormous skirts which prevented either of them from detaining me by slipping a possessive arm around my waist, a common technique which I found irritating beyond belief.

As I moved in amongst the other girls, I happened to look up and noticed a group of men on the balcony above us. Two gentlemen with their backs to the balustrade were speaking to a third whose face I could not see, but who was distinctly taller than his companions. When one briefly stepped aside, I had a clear view of a handsome face with regular, rather austere features. It was his stillness that struck me, and I thought of a Greek statue and the serenity of Michelangelo's David. The other gentlemen were quite animated, but the one in the middle was looking straight over their heads as though he couldn't even hear what they were saying.

The press of young ladies around me broke the spell as the tide turned to move towards the supper table, and I went with them, slipping one last look over my shoulder, but he was hidden from view.

I didn't see him again that evening, but the image of that godlike face stayed with me, serene and unruffled by the hubbub around him. As I lay down that night, it was the last thing I saw in my mind's eye, and my dreams were unusually heated.

The next morning over breakfast, with what I hoped was airy nonchalance, I raised the subject with Aunt Jane.

'The Strathmores? Yes, we do know them but your mother has no fondness for the dowager duchess, and besides, they are Scots.'

'How so?'

Somewhat impatiently, Aunt Jane pushed away one of my puppies with her foot. 'Dratted thing! Really, Eleanor, they shouldn't be in the breakfast room. George, take the puppies to Eleanor's room.'

'Not my room, thank-you George. Aphrodite is nursing new kittens and I don't want them to be alone with the puppies whilst they're so small. If you wouldn't mind taking them to the garden please. Perhaps one of the parlour maids could stay with them while they run off some energy? Thank-you.'

'I can't imagine what your Italian was thinking of, sending puppies all the way from Paris.'

'He's not my Italian, Aunt Jane. And I was rather touched. It was a sweet present. They are adorable.'

She carried on grumbling into her cup.

'Gout bad this morning, Aunt?'

She gave me a look of pure malice. 'One day, young lady, you'll understand what it is to be old.'

We carried on eating in simmering silence, our mutual resentments having no outlet. I turned my mind back to the face I'd seen and cast about for someone else I could find information from but could think of no-one else from the north apart from Mrs Montagu, and she was out of town.

Finally I tried a different tactic, hoping to get Aunt Jane to embark on one of her garrulous, gossipy monologues, from which I could extract the information I wanted. 'So do tell me more about our neighbouring families in County Durham, Aunt. Forgive me, as a child I barely took any notice, only registered vague impressions. I'm looking forward to the end of the London season and when we go back to Gibside, I'd like to start getting acquainted with our neighbours as an adult.'

She flashed me a look. 'You're not an adult yet, young lady.'

'I beg to differ, Aunt. In the eyes of society, I am clearly eligible for marriage, which I consider something of a marker.'

'Off your high horse, Miss Priss. Remember who you're talking to.'

'Why, Aunt Jane, how could I forget?'

She regarded me coldly for a long moment. 'You're getting rather above yourself, Mary Eleanor. All this attention is going to your head. Your mother writes that she has now had to fend off a dozen proposals of marriage. We both think it's high time a husband was chosen for you who will demand your obedience.'

'Obedience?' Once again, she had dismayed me with her view of marriage, which I then regarded as rather antiquated. How I would live to regret my naiveté.

'Yes, obedience. Once you are married, you will learn your place in the world.'

'And you would know about that, would you?'

'How dare you? If you continue in this vein, Missy, you will find your allowance cut.'

'I think you will find that in the terms of my father's will, my allowance is not within your gift.'

'We shall see about that, Mary Eleanor. I shall write to the other trustees this very morning, recommending that for your own benefit, your wings should be clipped.'

I doubted very much that she could do that, but reflected that there was nothing to be gained from continuing in this vein. It had all gone horribly wrong and I didn't know how to get the conversation back on track. Luckily, at that moment, George came back into the room and Aunt Jane rose slowly to her feet. 'George, clear the table. I have quite lost my appetite.'

I protested: 'But I haven't finished.'

'Oh yes you have, madam,' and she flounced from the room in a rustle of fabric.

George gently closed the door behind her and looked over at me with a sympathetic expression. 'Oh dear, Miss Eleanor, have we trodden on a corn this morning?'

I broke out into laughter, the tension instantly dissipating into hysterical giggles. 'Shh! Shh! She'll hear!'

'I think not, miss. Sadly, your Aunt is losing her hearing.'

'Oh dear, as well as her eyesight, soon to be sans everything. It's quite sad, really.'

'Sorry miss?'

'Shakespeare on old age: Sans teeth, sans eyes, sans taste, sans everything.'

'I don't understand, miss. Do tell.' George was a country boy who had grown up on a farm at Pontop Pike. He was a clever man, quick-witted and with a prodigious memory, but he had never been to school, which was a source of deep regret, and he had often sat in on my lessons. He loved Shakespeare and only had to hear a speech a couple of times before he had it by heart.

I smiled a smile of real affection. George was my rock, I decided.

'Really? Do you want to hear the whole speech?'

'If you wouldn't mind, miss. I love to hear a bit of Shakespeare.'

'It's from As You Like It. Just a moment.' I could remember the beginning and the end but wasn't sure the rest would follow. 'I'll do my best. I shall stand. Imagine you are in a box at Drury Lane and I am David Garrick.'

'That's quite a stretch, miss, but I'll try.' He lifted the chair I had just vacated and positioned it where he could see me properly. 'I am in the royal box.'

Excited, I felt the thrill of adrenaline that had powered my command performances in front of my father and his friends. 'Then I shall appear from behind this curtain.'

I stepped back into the alcove and obligingly, George pulled the cord which closed the plush folds of red velvet.

From behind the curtain, I cleared my throat: 'Ahem. Ahahahem.'

I heard George clapping and giving an approximation of a hubbub dying down, then, 'Shhh, shhh.'

I left a few moments' silence and then opened the curtains and held them at arm's length whilst I acknowledged the cheers and clapping from my audience. Smiling graciously, I waited for the anticipation to subside, and then I began:

All the world's a stage,
And all the men and women merely players:
They have their exits and their entrances;
And one man in his time plays many parts,
His acts being seven ages. At first the infant,
Mewling and puking in the nurse's arms.
And then the whining school-boy, with his satchel
And shining morning face, creeping like snail
Unwillingly to school. And then the lover,
Sighing like furnace, with a woeful ballad
Made to his mistress' eyebrow. Then a soldier,
Full of strange oaths and bearded like the pard,
Jealous in honour, sudden and quick in quarrel,

40

Seeking the bubble reputation
Even in the cannon's mouth. And then the justice,
In fair round belly with good capon lined,
With eyes severe and beard of formal cut,
Full of wise saws and modern instances;
And so he plays his part. The sixth age shifts
Into the lean and slipper'd pantaloon,
With spectacles on nose and pouch on side,
His youthful hose, well saved, a world too wide
For his shrunk shank; and his big manly voice,
Turning again toward childish treble, pipes
And whistles in his sound. Last scene of all,
That ends this strange eventful history,
Is second childishness and mere oblivion,
Sans teeth, sans eyes, sans taste, sans everything.

The whole performance was accompanied by a pantomime of actions, by which I told myself I was aiding George's understanding, but in reality I was indulging my enjoyment of dramatic expression. In contrast to my mother, I loved the theatre from the very first show I had seen at the Haymarket, a rowdy and bawdy revival of a Restoration comedy. She'd have loathed it. In my months in London, I'd seen performances of every kind, from low comedy to high drama, and found the whole experience riveting, not least because of the unruly antics of the audience below.

I nursed a secret ambition to see a play of my own devising performed at Drury Lane one day, preferably starring David Garrick or Sarah Siddons, the actress who had audaciously and successfully played Hamlet. I had it all planned: I would attend the first performance incognito, sitting under a black velvet cloak at the back of an obscure box and watching from the darkness as my words unfurled and caused the audience to stop their chatter, cease their trading and eating and whoring, until a rapt silence fell upon them all, so dazzled would they be by the verbal dexterity, the poetic flights of fancy, the spellbinding lovers, the Amazonian heroes, the devilish plotting. And as the curtain fell into the rapt silence with a swoosh, David Garrick himself would step forward, announce my presence, indicate my position with a grandiloquent sweep of his arm, and I would stand, move forward and drop the cloak from my head to bask in the waves and waves of cheers and applause as they rose to the heavens.

Remember, I was only a child.

It was at the theatre that I next saw Lord Strathmore. It was, somewhat ironically, The Country Girl: a comedy, altered from Wycherley. All unaware, I was actually looking at the box opposite when I saw his imposing form emerge from the darkness, and I felt an unaccustomed flutter in my chest. He took his seat at the front, between two other men, acknowledged no-one and sat immobile throughout the performance. I was anxious to catch his eye, and after the interval, when I had hoped to see him in the lobby, I took my seat rather more slowly than usual, making a great show of waving to friends in the stalls and even an imaginary one in the box above his. When my peripheral vision indicated that I had caught his attention, I casually let my eyes wander before settling on his face. I saw his gaze register mine and waited for some reaction. Surely he knew who I was? But his eyes had already moved on and there had been nothing to indicate that he knew me: the final acts of the play passed in a miasma of distraction.

So I was startled when we were leaving to be approached directly. I was chatting to my companion, Louisa, when I heard a deep voice at my back say, 'Miss Bowes?'

In my face and neck, I was conscious of an immediate sensation of heat. I had enough self-control to feign deafness, and when I finally turned round, affected merely to be following the gaze of my companion, whose face had taken on the look of a stunned calf.

I had not expected such great height, and was somewhat disarmed to be confronted by a row of shiny buttons. I blush to think of the view he must have had of me, for my dress was rather daring, in accordance with the fashion of the day, and my generous breasts billowed forth in a froth of lace.

I like to think there was distance in my voice, but I fear not, for I was quite possessed by palpitations, the like of which I had never experienced before.

'Have we been introduced?'

'A very long time ago. You were just a little girl.'

'I'm sorry, I have no memory of it. Do excuse me.' In truth, his voice, with its soft Scots burr, brought a sudden vision to me of an impossibly handsome young man high above me on a chestnut bay, but I know not whether it was a memory or a fantasy which had evolved from a heated dream.

'John Lyon, Lord Strathmore. I hunted with your father in County Durham once or twice.'

'Oh, I'm afraid I have no memory of that. When would it have been?'

'It was twelve years ago. I had just succeeded my father, the eighth earl, so I would have been sixteen.'

'My age now.'

'Indeed.' He inclined his head and it seemed that the conversation would have been at an end if I had not taken it upon myself to extend it, rather to my shame.

Feeling an unaccustomed nervousness, I ventured: 'Did you enjoy the play?'

His face darkened, 'No, to tell the truth I did not. Not to my taste. I have no fondness for the theatre.'

Instead of taking that as a warning, as I should have, it piqued my interest. 'No? Whyever not? I find the theatre most enjoyable. Have you seen any other plays you enjoyed more? I have: I saw...' As I burbled on, my tongue having taken on a life of its own, I caught a surprised glance from my companion, and a few moments later, I felt her tug my skirt.

Irritated, I turned to her, 'What is it, Louisa?' Her eyes burned into mine trying to convey a meaning that was not lost on me. My fevered brain considered ignoring her and carrying on, but luckily a quiet little voice of common sense whispered, 'Steady, Eleanor. Have a caution.' Though my brow darkened, and at that moment I hated her, luckily her intervention had the desired effect. When I turned back to Lord Strathmore, I thought I caught a certain look of mild amusement and then his expression settled into its usual complacency.

I inclined my head with all the dignity I could muster and said, 'Well, it has been pleasant to meet you but our carriage awaits.'

Without speaking or smiling, he nodded once and turned away.

When we were safely in the carriage, Louisa was beside herself with amusement. 'I have never seen you so flustered, Eleanor! I swear, the blush on your neck is quite red!'

Embarrassed to have had my performance witnessed, I considered answering coldly, but in truth I was still feeling that fluttering sensation. I stayed silent, replaying the conversation, mortified by the simpering fool I had become in his presence.

Meanwhile, Louisa chattered on, which thankfully gave me reprieve to gather my senses. 'So that is the beautiful Lord Strathmore! He certainly is very handsome, like a Greek statue. But rather forbidding, don't you think? And actually rather old. I can't believe he made you so nervous, Eleanor! I do not need to ask whether you like him, but I cannot see it myself. He's rather *dourrrr*. I can't imagine he'd be much fun.' She affected a Scottish accent and a sepulchral monotone: 'Ay hev no forrn-dness forrr the the-ay-tarr.' Ha ha! Pompous ass! Do you really not remember him? Ah, I see that you do! And yet you would have been no more than four years old! Is he from Scotland or County Durham? He's old enough to be your father. Don't think about him, Eleanor, he's not for you. Much better to concentrate on Lord Mountstuart. We're all so jealous you know. He's quite the catch. You will accept his proposal, won't you? My mama was speaking to your Aunt Jane, and she says your family is hoping you'll accept him. Lady Bute is already telling the town that the match is made.'

'Enough!' My tone startled both of us. I took a breath. 'Louisa, please don't make assumptions. The match has not yet begun.'

Chapter 6

The night before our wedding, I sat alone in my room watching the dying embers of the fire and my eyes were full of tears. I had waved away the maid who had come to replenish the coals and declined the help of the one who had come to brush my hair. My mother's light knock had grazed the door, but when I failed to answer I heard her footsteps retreat along the landing. She knew by then, perhaps as well as I did, that I was making a mistake, but pride prevented me from talking to her.

She had been against the match from the start and had been unusually vociferous in her opposition: 'Oh Mary, no. He's a Scot! They'll drag you off to Glamis!'

The Lyons had a large extended family: an only child herself, my mother had a horror of what she called The Clan. Instead of listening to her, I decided that she and I were very different so I would do the very opposite of what she wanted. The more she objected, the more I dug my heels in. You know how it goes.

I wish I could say it was the biggest mistake of my life, but as you will learn, it was far from being that.

It seemed to me as I gazed into the grey cinders with their barely-perceptible dying light, that the fire was a perfect metaphor. Not for the feelings of the beautiful Lord Strathmore, which I doubted had ever generated any heat, but for mine. That girl, the one whose blush burned for an hour after their first encounter, the one whose dreams took on a heat and urgency that left her embarrassed upon waking, the one whose every thought was to capture this remote and disdainful man, to entrance him with her wit, to entertain him with her stories, to impress him with her knowledge, and shamefully, to bewitch him with her body – she seemed to me now a poor deluded dancing puppet.

I thought of that morning encounter with Gabriel the summer before last. I had revisited it so many times in the intervening months that I had polished it into a gemstone, a shining vision of two innocents in Eden, a love that could never be, and the dream of it had taken its place at my core.

On that shining morning, I had seen with utter clarity that my engagement was a mistake, but I was too proud to stop the process I had started.

Here I sat, almost two years later, having endured the seemingly endless rigmarole of family politics and legal negotiations with barely-disguised impatience; here I was, on the eve of my eighteenth birthday, my wedding day, the society wedding of the year, and what did I feel? I felt nothing but regret.

Regret that, for all my much-vaunted intelligence, I had misread the situation so completely. That sixteen year-old girl, used to attention and power, had found herself coolly regarded from a great height. And I could see now that it had quite deranged her senses.

Where she saw dignity, I now saw coldness. Where she saw mystery, I now recognised emptiness. Where she saw experience, I knew there to be cynicism.

And yet, and yet... He was undoubtedly a good man, a well-regarded man, a man my father had admired, a much-travelled man, a well-educated man, a friend of Thomas Gray, whose poetry we both loved. At the thought of Papa, a trembling began in my heart and I lost myself to grief once more.

I found myself on my bed, my coverlet wet with tears. My body drained and exhausted, I resolved to sleep, and crept from my bed in the cold of the room to rinse my face in the tepid water on the night-stand.

Dust motes floated in the pale moonlight as I parted the curtain to look out on the London night. The same silver disc would be looking down on Gibside, illuminating the mullioned windows of my bedroom, casting faint shadows under the leafless trees, bathing the walled garden in ghostly light. It would be looking in at the windows of the workers' houses while they were sleeping. The river would be running on, as it always did, glittering in the darkness, parting round rocks and the legs of night-hunting herons; the Octagon Pond would be lying still under a sheen of silver, reflecting Liberty inverted in the mirror of its surface.

I slept fitfully, my dreams a juddering kaleidoscope, and awoke exhausted in the pale grey light of a February dawn. Molly had already lit the fire in my room and through the wraith of my breath, I watched the young flames leap and crackle. Nobody would bother me until I rang the bell, so I lay there gathering my senses and made a determined effort to be optimistic.

It was 24th February 1767. I was eighteen years old. My childhood was behind me. My father was gone and would never come back. The responsibility for all that he had built and for all the people who had helped him build it had devolved onto me.

Today I would be married and tonight I would not sleep alone.

I tried to imagine how Lord Strathmore – John - would look without his fine clothes and was surprised to find that it brought forth tenderness in me. We might have nothing in common, he might have a complete absence of humour and a haughty disapproval of so many things, but he would still be a very handsome, dignified and gentlemanly husband. I tried to imagine how it would be when we were alone, and found it difficult to picture quite how events would proceed. He was, I knew, very experienced in these matters and although I was afraid, I felt I could trust him to be gentle, and for the first time in a long while, experienced a frisson of something like excitement.

Ready to face the world, I pulled the bell-chord by my bed. Immediately, the door burst open and my two ladies-maids came giggling into the room, their eyes wide with trepidation. I knew I had been moody lately, snapping at nothing, and my heart softened to see their excitement: this was a big day for them too. The wedding gown - and oh it was so beautiful! – waited in my dressing room in isolated splendour, glowing like a full moon studded with diamonds.

I greeted them with my biggest smile and flung back the covers, ready to submit myself to their ministrations.

Their faces lit and they hastened towards me. 'Your bath's ready miss. We've been waiting outside. We thought you'd be awake early. Happy birthday!'

Together, they handed me a small package wrapped in tissue.

'We've embroidered a pair of handkerchiefs for you.'

As I unwrapped the fine linen and cooed over the sweet gift, I wondered whether any of John's friends would be giving him presents with his new initials and doubted it very much. The clause in my father's will which made it mandatory that my husband should take the Bowes name had been the cause of much discontent in the Strathmore household, and part of the reason that the negotiations had taken so long. But in the end, as Mother had pointed out so cynically, the lure of my inheritance, 'All the collieries, lead mines, ironworks, farms, houses, fine art, jewels, stocks and racehorses,' had broken down the walls of their resistance.

At the thought of John's family, soon to be mine, my spirits began fading fast, but I only had to look into the bright eyes of these girls, who were so devoted to me, whose joy at my engagement had been so innocently complete, who genuinely wanted me to be happy, who were actually excited about travelling to Scotland with me, and I could put those thoughts from my mind.

As I was bathed and dried and primped and preened and painted and adorned in all my pomp, I found myself caught up in the joy of it all. Never had a bride had such a beautiful dress, with so many precious stones! Why, it belonged in the Tower of London with the Crown Jewels! The stomacher was indeed a wonder to behold, studded as it was by diamonds, which my mother had reverentially told me were worth £10,000. Diamonds glinted at my ears, at my throat, in my bosom, their lights flashing and refracting in the silver threads of the fabric.

By the time I saw myself in the mirror, I was entirely transformed. The girls themselves stood back in awe when they were finally done.

When at last I stood ready in the great marble hallway, surrounded by a ring of cooing serving-women, the men of the household lined the walls, their faces a mixture of awe, impassivity and indulgent smiles. The coachmen and stable-lads were at the front of the house, readying the procession of coaches which had been brought down from Gibside for the occasion, and I saw that the scarlet-jacketed figure with his back to us at the half-open door was George Walker. I thought at first he hadn't yet seen me, but when he turned, his eyes were downcast and his lower face was working. He was crying, and the sight hurt my heart. I knew that he too was thinking that my father should be here by my side. I had to look away: I could not bear it.

My mother and aunts had already left: Papa would be in their minds too. How would I get though this day without breaking down? Only by being what my father had wanted me to be, what I would have become if he had been with me. I would not be a frightened and lonely girl. I summoned the Mary Eleanor that he had made me: a strong woman with a heart of oak and a will of iron.

I took a deep breath and stood up straight. The servants moved back and opened my way to the door.

It was a bright cold day, the sun low over the rooftops opposite, gilding George's profile and the strands of silver in his hair. He and another red-jacketed footman stood on the top step, their heads bowed. On the pavement below stood two others in green livery; they were both looking up expectantly, their backs to the glittering emerald lacquer of the open landau.

I moved forward, the hoops of my skirts swaying heavily, and stood for a moment on the top step beside George. I reached for his cold hand and held the fingertips lightly in my own.

At last, he looked into my eyes and for a few moments we took strength from each other.

On an impulse I said, 'Ride with me.'

His rheumy blue eyes widened, and I saw the flicker of disbelief, then doubt, then he stood up straight, turned towards the coach, extended his elbow for my hand, and escorted me down the steps.

As he handed me into the coach and waited whilst the maids arranged my skirts, I know he doubted again, but when I was ready and the girls had stepped down to the pavement, I nodded to him, and he mounted the landau to sit opposite, his face alight.

All along the route people clapped and cheered as the procession went by. I saw eyes widen when they saw such gleaming splendour, such a blaze of colour in the monochrome winter streets. As the sunshine bounced the lights around, I heard people declaring themselves dazzled.

Many of those we passed will have thought that George was my father, and he acted the part with dignity and pride.

When we emerged into Hanover Square the crowds went wild. On the opposite side, at the entrance to George's Street, a line of constables tipped their hats and the scribblers and cartoonists from Fleet Street were already busy with their pens. As we pulled up in front of the grand portico of St George's Church, the six great Corinthian columns gleamed in the cold sunlight. I looked up and thought of my father's chapel at Gibside, so far from being finished.

I resolved there and then that I would make it a priority when John and I had our first business meeting.

You may think that is a strange thing for a bride to be thinking as she steps down from her wedding coach, but it was just the start of a chain of distractions with which I occupied my mind throughout the ceremony. When I walked down the aisle alone to the Entry of the Queen of Sheba, I thought of Handel worshipping in this very church and, instead of meeting the eager gazes of the guests, I focused on watching for his dedicated pew.

When I looked up to the galleries, it was to wonder how they could be built to take the weight of so many people with so little evidence of support.

While the priest intoned the vows, I was admiring the wood-carved altarpiece and wondering whether it was by Grinling Gibbons: I had seen his exquisite work in St Paul's. The muted colours of the stained glass I knew to be Flemish: perhaps we could have stained glass in my father's mausoleum.

In this way, I kept my mind occupied with anything but the reality of his absence and the presence beside me of a lofty aristocrat who had just received my promise of obedience in all things.

Only when the voice of a boy soprano arose and I recognised the opening chords of Bach's 'Sheep May Safely Graze' did I almost lose my composure.

It could not have been a more moving choice of solo, though my husband could not have known it: he had clearly chosen it because it is also known as the Birthday Cantata. Tears sprang to my eyes and I was back in the music room at Gibside, Mr Avison at the harpsichord, my childish soprano straining to the unfamiliar German. My father opens the door: he has been listening outside. He stands still, a rapt and indulgent smile on his face as I wobble my way to the end.

When I finish, he claps and then he holds my hands and tells me: 'If I were to choose a cantata for Gibside, my darling, it would be this one: 'Sheep may safely graze where a good shepherd watches over them. When ruled by a good king, his subjects sleep in peace.'

The tears that swam in my eyes elicited a kindly pat from my new husband.

We emerged into the cold sunshine man and wife. Behind the lines of constables, the street was crowded with a sea of roaring, waving people. I waved back, then lifted my posy of ivy and white roses and waved that too until I felt John slip a hand round my elbow and gently bring down my arm.

He bent to whisper, 'Decorum, Eleanor.'

I carried on waving my free arm in defiance.

When he handed me into the landau, his grip on my hand was unnecessarily tight, and when I was seated and he released it I jutted my chin and carried on waving. He took his place opposite me with an icy stare until he was sure I had registered his disapproval. For the remainder of our journey through London, he never looked at me once, preferring to stare impassively over my head, his mouth clamped in a tight line, while I turned from side to side smiling and laughing and acknowledging the cheers and waves of the people.

When at last the crowds faded away as we were passing through Barnet, he spoke at last, leaning forward so that the coachmen would not hear.

'I asked you to desist, Mary Eleanor.'

He always called me Mary Eleanor when he was annoyed with me. It rankled.

'But really, people are so kind. What harm can it do to wave back?'

Instead of answering my question, he simply gave me a cold glance and said, 'Obey.'

I looked at him for long moments after that, considering my response. Luckily, I resisted teasing him, though I resolved to do so once we were alone together.

The custom being that the bride's parents host the wedding breakfast, we had to turn off the Great North Road to St Paul's Walden instead of carrying on north to Gibside. I suddenly found myself overwhelmed with emotion, and I began to cry quite openly, making no attempt to hide my tears. He did at least show some tenderness then, reaching across to pat my hand. I blinked my gratitude and dabbed at my eyes with one of the embroidered handkerchiefs. I would let my husband believe they were tears of happiness, though when he found me inconsolable, I think even he must have begun to doubt it.

The feasting and festivities passed in a blur, from which my mother's fixed smile occasionally emerged like a retribution. I played my part, there at the centre of the feast, glowing in my rigid cluster of gems and smiling, smiling, smiling. People loomed into my vision, offered congratulations and then faded into the crowd, and most conversation seemed to go on over the top of my head.

At last, at last, the ladies had retired and my mother signaled for the maids to take me to the bedchamber. I was so tired that I could barely stand. My eyes were dry and each blink was longer than the last. I had drunk and eaten little and the weight of the dress bore me down when I rose to my feet unsteadily. I saw my mother's eyes soften, and she lifted her chin, signaling me to do the same. One last effort. I made my unsteady way out of the room, acknowledging the nods and gruff greetings of the gentlemen at the table, already embarked on the port and cheese.

I climbed the stairs slowly, a maid on each arm, whispering encouragements. When we passed the door of the room I had been used to occupying, I registered that Mother had allocated the master bedroom for our honeymoon, and the thought of it made my soul shrink, but I was so tired that I yearned to be released from this gown and allowed to lie down on a bed, any bed.

When the maids had finally gone, I floated at last in perfect comfort on a feather mattress and sighed deeply with pleasure, not least because for the first time that day, I was alone, left in precious peace, my body free of the constraints and discomfort of splendour.

The room was warm, the silence deep, my comfort complete, and I was soon dozing. I don't know how long I had slept when I became aware of men's voices in the corridor outside. Two voices, John's deep bass and the higher, clipped notes of his brother Thomas.

A fluttering began in my chest. Suddenly my solitude was a source of fear, and I wanted female company. I wanted giggles and shared confidences, the innocent pleasures of the dressing room.

The room was dark, the fire's glow barely discernible, and I was chilled. I recollected that I'd been so warm after my bath that I'd flung away the blankets and spread myself out like a starfish in my lace nightgown. I turned onto my side and pulled the coverlets up to my neck, curling up and breathing into my chest to warm myself. I

52

would pretend to be asleep. Perhaps he would not want to consummate the marriage immediately. Perhaps he had partaken of too much port wine and would be relieved if he found me sleeping.

Warmer now, and safe in the nest of my own breath, I relaxed and thought I would begin to doze again, but curiosity kept me alert to the voices still murmuring outside the door, and soon my curiosity turned to resentment. What could he mean by keeping me waiting so long? What could they possibly have to talk about? On our wedding night?

And still it went on. I had just decided that this was unacceptable and I was going to call out, when I heard a hand upon the doorknob and counted myself lucky that I had not relinquished all dignity through such a display of impatience.

There was more murmuring of a different, more staccato tenor, a bark of laughter from Thomas and then, at last, the door opened and a shaft of light fell across the bed. I did not stir.

Now real trepidation grasped my belly and I lay rigid with fear. As he moved about the room, presumably divesting himself of his garments, I steadied my breathing through a sheer effort of will. I knew the mechanics of the act in principle, simply through observation on the farm, but I found it hard to reconcile that with human intercourse. Without wishing to be indelicate, I had no idea about scale, and that's what frightened me most. I knew there would be pain – that was as much as my mother had told me to expect. No matter how much willpower I tried to summon, I was afraid to my very core.

When he finally lifted the blankets and slipped into bed beside me, I was unprepared for the heft and heat of his presence, and felt for the first time the pleasure of the warmth of another body, so different in volume and nature from the snuggling cats and the stone hot-water bottles I was used to. He lay still for a few moments, perhaps listening to my breathing, and then a warm hand slid round my waist and pulled my hips backwards until they came to rest against the hard muscles of his belly. At the same moment, his knees pushed gently into the backs of my calves – he was so much taller than me that the action pushed my legs straight.

Then he gave a deep sigh, seemingly of contentment, and I relaxed into his embrace, thinking nothing more was required of me; but soon I became aware of something pressing against me and I knew the day was not yet over. Please, just let him speak to me first. If he did, I felt everything would be all right.

When he spoke, his face was close in against the back of my neck, and his gentle whisper sent a tingle down my arm. 'Are you afraid, little Eleanor?' To which there could be only one answer.

Part of me wanted to stay still, let him do as he wished without my involvement, but a greater part of me wanted this to be a shared endeavour, and so I squirmed round to face him, finding as I did so that he had lifted my legs over his hips and now held me close, all of me enveloped in his arms.

I spoke in a whisper that sounded more nervous than I now felt: 'Yes, I am.'

'I will not hurt you.'

'How can you not? I do not understand…the mechanics…of scale.'

He laughed softly and kindly, and I smelt the sweetness of the port on his breath. 'You are a bright child, Eleanor, but you will not need your brains for this act, I assure you. Just trust to your body.'

'Please don't call me a child.'

He appeared to consider this, and the longer it took him to process his thoughts, the more indignant I felt, but I could not risk disturbing the moment by letting him know he had irritated me.

Finally he said, 'I'm sorry. It was thoughtless of me. I shall not do so again.'

He was quiet then, and a sadness seemed to have come over him. I watched his face, fascinated by its closeness. I saw that dark hairs lay beneath the skin of his chin and the sides of his cheeks, some of them long enough to feel when I reached out a tentative finger to stroke them. His brows were thick and dark and described decisive symmetrical arches. I was used to seeing them knitted in perplexity or lowered in disapproval, but now I saw that they were joined by a finer line of brow above the bridge of his nose. I softly traced the twin ridges that ran vertically between his brows, which I had seen so pronounced when he looked at me in recent months. They were softer now, and when I looked into his dark eyes, I saw that he was looking beyond me and into the past.

I knew, in fact all of London society knew, about his Grand Tour romance with Constanza Scotti, Countess Sanvitale of Parma, though we had never spoken of it. We had never spoken of anything close to our hearts, which was the core of my misgivings about this marriage. But we had gone through with it now and if we were to make it work, I strongly felt we must make it a marriage of equals, hearts and minds. Oh how naive I was.

And so I said, 'Are you thinking of Constanza?'

Startled, he blinked and looked at me directly, defensive, affronted, resentful. I saw all of these feelings flicker across his face. I saw him consider how to answer and finally settle on rueful acceptance. 'Yes, I am thinking of Constanza.'

I really thought this would be our breakthrough: he would show me his heart and I would show him mine. We would learn to understand each other, and then we would learn to love each other.

Full of hope, I said, 'Did you love her?'

Abruptly, he turned over and brushed me off like a tick.

When we finally consummated our marriage some days later, no words were spoken. He was gentle with me, true to his promise, and physically he could not have been more considerate, but my heart yearned for comfort, for emotional contact, for anything that made me feel less like a vessel for his seed.

He evidently found pleasure in my body: his caresses were sweet and he was appreciative of my flesh, there was no question of that, but if ever I tried to speak or even turn his face to mine, he would lay a finger across my lips or bury his face in the pillow beside my head while he went about his business.

I soon learnt to take my pleasure where I could. The smell of him and the feel of him was such that I sometimes felt a melting sensation in my belly, but there was never a moment when my mind could abandon itself: instead, it hovered above the bed, looking down in cool consideration of the proceedings.

There was much to occupy us in the daytimes, or more accurately, there was much to occupy him, whilst I spent the time reading or walking. The gardens at Waldenbury were formal and manicured, so I found little to interest me there. He and his brother spent many hours with my mother and various officials and lawyers, presumably taking stock of accounts and making plans.

Once, when I happened to come upon John and his brother in the garden, I risked a teasing, 'What do you two find to talk about all hours of the day and night?'

I remember how they both turned slowly to look down on me from a great height in astonishment, as though one of the statues had suddenly spoken. They both had the same capacity for keeping their faces entirely devoid of expression. Finally, John spoke, whist Thomas looked on, one brow arched in disdain and amusement: 'I beg your pardon?'

Unable to bear Thomas's condescending stare, I stared straight back and said tersely, 'I would like to speak to my husband alone, please.'

With a barely perceptible incline of his head, he turned and strolled away at an insulting snail's pace, ostentatiously looking around him with what I took to be a proprietorial air.

In a low voice, I hissed, 'I was simply asking what you are discussing. I imagine that at least some of it will have some bearing on me?'

'On you? What relevance would it have to you?'

'Oh really, John. You are being obtuse. We are staying in my mother's house, shortly to depart for Gibside, which may I remind you is my home. You will have much to learn about the estates, and surely there are subjects under discussion which involve me and my properties...'

The disdain and bewilderment had turned to puzzlement and then hostility.

'My dear, I think you need to adjust your perceptions of your place in the natural world order. You are no longer entitled to refer to anywhere or anything as yours. Now go about your business.' And with that, he turned from me and hastened after Thomas.

On the journey to Gibside, we were all subdued, partly due to the effects of some of mother's vintage port wine, which had caused stomach ailments in John and Thomas as well as several of our guests. With frequent comfort stops, the coaches made slow progress in the freezing March weather.

Despite all of this, the further north we travelled, the more my spirits lifted, and when we turned onto the Roman Road out of Whickham, I was in a positive frenzy of excitement, barely able to keep still. John was dozing beside me, his head against the cushioned headrest and a blanket over his knees. Thomas was watching me from the dark of the corner opposite.

As we turned into the gates, I finally succeeded in wrestling the window open and an icy blast entered the carriage. John sprang to instant wakefulness. 'Eleanor, what on earth are you doing?'

'We're just entering Hollinside! We're there! Smell that sweet air! Oh, I can't wait to get outside! There's so much I want to do this season. I thought perhaps a hot-house. I have been corresponding with the gardener about the possibility...'

'Yes yes. That's all very well, but I hope you are going to comport yourself properly.' I was regretting my impulsiveness in opening the window: John was always grumpy upon waking.

True to form, he went on as he sat up and smoothed down his hair. 'You are no longer a child. Have a care, my dear. Take your cue from me. When we arrive, I shall assemble the servants and make it quite clear that Gibside is under new ownership.' He shared a complicit smile with Thomas and I was left to look out of the window and swallow the mutinous lump in my throat.

When they began to show interest in the grounds as we passed, I was somewhat mollified. John spoke first, 'Ah, this makes me feel quite at home! It's like descending into a Scottish glen!'

'Yes, father planned it as such: at the start of the descent, the pine and birch are interspersed with some standard oaks, as you see. This is Snipe's Dene, planned as the natural outer zone. Further on, the driveway is bordered by clipped yew at twenty-foot intervals, and then alternating limes and yews for light and dark. When you reach the laurels, the garden begins. The oak was Father's favourite.' I looked shyly at John, and risking rejection, I said, 'I cannot wait to show you the ancient oak woodland. It is where we loved to walk.'

Still looking out of the window, he did at least smile.

Taking this as encouragement, I knocked and spoke to the driver. 'Pull up at the Crow's Foot please.'

When we rocked to a stop, I indicated out of the window and sat back so that Thomas could see, although he made no move to look.

'You see straight ahead of us is the Octagon Pond.' I was gratified to see the cloudless sky reflected in the serenity of its surface. John obligingly looked out of the window, but Thomas remained where he was, watching me with an inscrutable face which I knew masked hostility.

I decided to ignore him and concentrate on charming John with my father's vision: 'To our left, the Banqueting House, which commands beautiful views. We might choose to entertain guests there after eating in the main house: it is most pleasant to take a walk there through the pleasure gardens after a meal, to listen to music and partake of sweets and cheeses. The views over the valley are delightful.'

John's smile was warm and gratifying. Encouraged, I directed him to look out of the right side of the coach: 'And there is Liberty atop her column, but perhaps you have seen her before?'

'Only from a distance. She was not completed when last I hunted with your father, but as you know, she is visible from outside the estate: I have glimpsed her in passing along the Derwent Valley. It is a curious thing, is it not, the way she seems from some angles to be low in the valley, and from other points she towers.'

'Quite so: her placing is deliberate. Father could have positioned her at the highest point of the estate, but he had a vision of inclusion, of liberty for all, and so she is at the heart of Gibside. And of course, the people of the locality are welcomed onto the estate.'

There was something I hesitated to ask in front of Thomas, for I feared the answer, but decided that now was the time. 'You do intend to continue that tradition of having the estate open to the people, don't you, John?'

His smile was genuinely warm, and I felt my heart swell: 'Yes, of course. I hold your father in the greatest esteem and I respect the reputation he built. Your mother has made it quite clear to me how he earned the affection and respect of his flock. We shall have a public feast to celebrate our marriage.'

My face must have lit, for John smiled at me in the most open and natural way I had yet seen. He knocked for the coachman to continue and I slid a sly smile of quiet triumph towards Thomas, glowering in his corner.

What a joy it was to finally descend from the coach to be greeted by the wide and warm smiles of a row of familiar faces. Had I been alone, I had no doubt that I would have been closely surrounded and plied with questions and chatter, but the servants were evidently on their best behaviour and I saw from their faces that when John descended from the coach into the warm spring sunshine, they were instantly impressed by his looks, his serene confidence and regal manner.

When we attended Whickham Parish Church that Sunday with a retinue of family and friends, we were received by a cheering throng, many of whom I recognised. I actually felt quite giddy with happiness at being home among my people, as though their warmth and evident affection could make up for the habitual cool condescension of my husband. I raised my hand to wave to the Stephensons, but when I brought it down, John took a firm hold of it. Then the faces of the Pallisers appeared in the crowd, so I waved my left hand in defiance.

Surveying their upturned faces following our progress towards the church like a field of sunflowers following the sun, I felt a shift in my soul, feeling for the first time my new status: this was what mattered, these people whose work laid the foundations of our fortune and who depended on us for their wellbeing. Suddenly, the dread word 'duty' which had so often been leveled at me as a reminder and a reprimand became something to aspire to, something to focus on and I made a promise to myself that I would never forget that.

Those first few months at Gibside were among the happiest in my marriage: John was much preoccupied with business and integrating himself into the coterie of influential gentlemen in Newcastle, and I was very much left to my own devices, which suited me just fine as I could devote myself to my garden at the time when it needed me most. It was a beautiful spring and Gibside was very heaven.

Robert Thompson, the head gardener, was visibly elated to have me home, and could not wait to show me what he had been working on. Dear, sweet man. The promise of a hot-house and the challenge of exotic specimens to nurture seemed at first to initimidate him, but a few well-chosen words of flattery and encouragement from me and he was suggesting sites for the proposed building.

Soon, too soon, June arrived and preparations began for our journey north to Glamis, which had taken a positively gothic connotation for me. I could barely think of myself as Countess of Strathmore, let alone imagine myself in such a place. In my mind, the castle was synonymous with Macbeth, dark deeds, regicide, witchcraft. When once in an unguarded moment I confided my fears to John, he laughed but then failed completely to provide any reassurance when he told me that the mother of the seventh earl had indeed been burnt at the stake as a witch, while the earl himself had been imprisoned under threat of execution by James V.

None of this reassured me, and I began to deeply resent being uprooted from Gibside, but despite my pleadings, John was adamant: 'Of course you must accompany us: your place is by my side. There there, Eleanor, it is not so bad as it seems, though I must confess I have not much fondness for the place. Thomas and I have begun purchasing materials for its refurbishment, and by the time we get there, most of the furniture and furnishings from Edinburgh will have arrived, and you will be able to help supervise the decorations. Well, inasmuch as my mother will allow.'

I gave him a penetrating look, which did not go unnoticed, and he looked away somewhat sheepishly. The furnishings to which he referred had been ordered from Edinburgh during our engagement, much of it chosen by his mother the Dowager Duchess, a dour and formidable woman whom I had disliked instantly. The relish with which she and her sons had set about spending my money before they actually got their hands on it still galled, and I knew my own mother would never get over it. 'See? What did I tell you? Rapacious Scots! Don't say I didn't warn you Mary. Well, you've made your bed and you shall have to lie on it.'

Chapter 7

And lie in it I did.

The birth of my first baby, Maria, was dreadful, like some medieval torment in Dante's Inferno. I felt I was being rent asunder: I am a small person and Maria was a large baby: I need say no more. Such was the damage to my parts that I thought I would never recover, that I would never again be able to walk unaided or without pain, let alone entertain the thought of doing the whole thing again.

She was born in April, my favourite time of year, and yet a deep depression settled on me as though I was viewing the world through a dark haze. I cried and cried, lost to myself. Nothing could lift my spirits, least of all the sight of the squalling red-faced infant who had caused it all. Do not mistake me: she was well cared-for, just not by me. As is the custom, wet-nurses and nannies enveloped the precious little bundle in swaddling clothes and love.

I cared not a jot for anything. My husband's joy in the child was unalloyed, and his glowing enraptured eyes as he gazed into her little red face did at least bring me a quiet pleasure. I thought more kindly of him for the fact that he never once expressed any disappointment that I had brought forth a girl. If he had, I fear I should have flown at him like a wild-cat.

I lay in my room for long dark days, animated by nothing, my body a miasma of pain and my mind a dark forest where devils lurked. The doctor who attended to me spent some time outside the door speaking in a low voice to my mother, whose anxiety was growing with every passing day. Though I could observe her distress and feel nothing, I don't know what I would have done without her quiet presence. It was as though I was floating alone on a dark sea, and she was the faint light that showed me the direction of the shore.

For the first time, I understood that she and I had something in common: we were both women, both wives and now both mothers, though I only apprehended this as a fact, I did not feel it in my heart. I felt nothing, nothing at all.

In those dark days, she mostly sat in silence, but sometimes she talked to me and I heard her voice as if from a distance. She spoke of her childhood, of her love of God, of her hopes of finding a husband who would help her find a way to make the world a better place. She told me of meeting my father in London, of how his formidable reputation as a 'Coal Czar' preceded him and how she had seen in him a gentleness and a loneliness she had not expected. She knew, she said, that he would never get over losing his first wife, but she had hoped that love would grow between them. And it had.

She told me of the five years of disappointment she had experienced each time her monthlies came around and of her deep joy when she had finally become pregnant.

'Your father was beside himself, Mary. He once said to me that for years he thought he would never be a father, but instead put all his creative energies into Gibside. He came to see it as his legacy to the world. But when you came along, he thought his heart would burst for happiness. I have known no man who has loved his daughter more that George Bowes loved you, my dear. In fact, I sometimes think...'

'What, mother?'

'I sometimes think he spoiled you.'

I was dismissive, not at first understanding what she meant. 'Pah! Of course he spoilt me. How could he not?'

'No, I don't mean materially...'

I imagine my voice took on a lecturing tone: I've heard it in my own daughters' voices, and I expect you have too: 'But you know, mother, you don't understand. It wasn't thoughtless indulgence. By giving me such a great and wide education, he gave me perspective, aesthetic appreciation...' I blush to tell you what I said to her, but I know I included the phrase 'things you wouldn't understand.'

She gave me a long level look, her lips pursed. 'Don't patronize me, Mary Eleanor. I may not have had the benefits of your intellectual training, but I am far from stupid.'

I might have had the grace to be suitably chastised, but then again, I might not. I could barely rouse myself to engage in any kind of thought, let alone self-examination, so deep was my lassitude.

'Listen to me Mary.' Suddenly, she grasped my hand and spoke with urgency in her voice, which I heard as if from a long way away.

'Mother, I need to sleep. Please would you close the curtains on your way out?'

'No. I want to say my piece and I may not get another chance. Are you listening to me? Look at me please.'

I turned back to her, my face deliberately obscured in the cloud of my curls. She reached to brush the hair away from my face and her dry hands were far from tender.

'Listen to me. I have wanted to say my piece for some while now. You and Lord Strathmore. Your job is to make him happy. You must modify yourself, make yourself agreeable to him. You cannot go on defying him and being petulant when you don't get your own way. Don't give me that look – I've heard more than you think. I have heard you deliberately provoke him.'

I went to turn my head away, but she grasped my chin and turned me back to face her. 'You have to know your place. You must obey him in all things. You must speak to him with respect. It is your duty. It is what he has been brought up to expect in a wife. If you do not change, he will take his pleasures elsewhere. Men such as he are used to being petted and adored...'

'Pah!' I made to turn away again, but she restrained me by the shoulders. I was indignant: 'Mother! What are you doing? Let go!'

Her face came close to mine and she held my face between her hands. 'Your father spoilt you, Mary Eleanor Bowes. You have grown up thinking that the undivided attention of men is your right, that you somehow deserve it. That is wrong Mary: you are doomed to disappointment. You are a married woman now and a mother. You must put aside all else.'

I was so astonished by being forcibly held still and made to listen that I could not comprehend what she was saying. Instead I was distracted by the animation in her features, their piercing focus on me, the urgency with which she spoke.

I took her wrists in both my hands and prised my head free. I spoke coldly: 'You may go.'

She blinked and I saw her struggling to decide whether to do as I said.

'Just let me say one more thing and then I will leave you. Happiness is in your own hands. Do not look to John to give you fulfillment. He cannot fill the space that your father left in your heart and mind, and you must not hate him for that. Accept it, Mary. You will never again be the sun and the moon to a man.'

She stood up and looked away. When she turned back to me she said, 'I will put this in a way that you will understand. You were raised in a hothouse and now you must live in the walled garden. I leave you with that thought.'

I am ashamed to tell you that as she left, I turned my head back into my pillow and cursed her for a bitter old woman.

Her words have come back to me over the years, many times, and of course now I understand the truth of them. We do not know what we have until it is gone.

Unbelievably, no sooner had I recovered and begun taking tentative steps in the summer sunshine than John wished to lie with me again. I put him off for as long as I could, but finally, one night when he had been carousing until the small hours with his friends, he forced himself upon me. He was all teasing charm, but his smile and his words gave the lie to his actions. He would have what was his by right. It appears I have no rights.

Soon I was pregnant with my first son, whose birth the following April was greeted with such effusive celebrations by the Strathmore clan that I never felt he belonged to me at all. I had an easier time of it, giving birth to John Bowes-Lyon, and was even able to nurse him a little, though it was painful and rather unsuccessful. At least I tried.

I have a clear memory of looking down at his scrunched little red face and balled-up fists and lifting my head to see my mother watching with an indulgent smile. Behind her, two wet-nurses whispered together, waiting for me to fail.

'I know what you are thinking, my dear. It is quite different, is it not?'

Obtuse as ever, I pretended not to know what she meant. In fact, I was not dwelling on the fact of the baby's gender, I was willing them all to go away and let me be alone with my son.

'You are thinking how astonishing it is that such a tiny creature will one day grow to stand before you as the 10th Earl of Strathmore and Kinghorne.'

'I am not thinking that Mother. I am thinking how much more of this can I endure before I remove his mouth from my breast.'

'Then think on it now.' She turned to dismiss the wet-nurses, who went away shaking their heads and muttering. She sat down on my bed and stroked the baby's soft head, an intrusion from which I recoiled.

'Mother, please give me some time alone with my son.'

'I'm afraid I cannot do that, Mary.'

Startled, I looked up: 'Whyever not?'

She did not answer at first and I could see she feared my response.

'We are all under strict instructions not to leave you alone with him.'

I was slack-jawed with astonishment.

'I cannot really blame him, you were … not yourself after Maria's birth and the doctor warned us that it might happen to you again.'

I closed my mouth into a tight line and went back to my suffering.

The silence between us vibrated and we both watched the baby's efforts to feed. If my mother hadn't been there, I would have taken him from the breast half an hour ago, it was so painful, and the more unsuccessful his efforts were, the more he redoubled his efforts.

Eventually, she said, 'So, a son.'

Terse, I wanted her gone. 'Yes. As you see.'

She took a deep breath and I knew she was struggling to stay patient with me. 'I was blessed with only one child, and you were hard-won.'

'But worth it though, eh Mother?' I smiled and saw her face relax.

'Of course. But I felt sad for you being a girl.'

'Sad for me? Why?'

'Because I knew it would be difficult for you to have the life you wanted. It just is. For women. Even rich women.'

It was hardly a new thought, and I lost interest, gently inserting my little finger into the baby's mouth and feeling the power of his suction as I guided the little limpet away from the nipple. He started to grizzle and hiccup, so I lifted him to my shoulder and began stroking and patting his back.

I hoped she had said her piece, but there was more.

'For mothers of boys, there is greater hope, however. Of achieving some power over your life. You must nurture this boy, Mary Eleanor. Make yourself special to him.'

'For heaven's sake, I am his mother! How much more special can I be?'

'Keep him by you. Make him adore you. Don't lose him. He is your passport to influence once you have lost all else.'

'Mother, I'm tired and I don't understand you. Lost all else? What can you mean?'

'You own nothing – marriage has taken it all from you. You have no independent existence, no more than one of your husband's horses. The only power you have is if your husband loves and respects you and enjoys your company. When you lose that, or if you never try, he will look for it elsewhere. He may go wherever he likes, take whatever pleasure he wants from wherever he wants it. You have no protection in law or in convention. Think on it.'

I was growing tired of this constant lecturing, but at least by then I had learned to pretend that I was listening, so I simply said, 'Yes, Mother.' It seemed to satisfy her: she nodded, complacent in the belief that she had imparted her wisdom successfully. Standing up, she held out her hands for the baby, waiting for me to concede defeat. All I felt was a burning sense of powerlessness and impending tears, so I handed him over.

It is a fault with me that quotations from literature, once they pop into my mind, frequently pop out of my mouth. Being married to the Thane of Glamis (and his family) words from Macbeth often came to me, and it was something of a joke between us, though often his smiles were terse. Once, at dinner, and still possibly delirious with the fever that ensued from infections in the aftermath of a birth, he had airily announced that he had changed his mind about an outing he had promised me. Before I could stop myself, I had said the first thing that came into my mind:

'I have given suck, and know
How tender 'tis to love the babe that milks me.
I would, while it was smiling in my face,
Have plucked my nipple from his boneless gums
And dashed the brains out, had I so sworn as you
Have done to this.'

66

It was meant to be a joke, but I can see now that it was more than a little ill-advised, especially in front of his mother. Abruptly, silence crashed around my ears and everyone froze. I must have been delirious or a little drunk, because I laughed when it struck me that they looked as though they were playing Grandma's Footsteps: a servant stopped in the act of pouring John a glass of wine; the Dowager Duchess held her napkin to her mouth as though to prevent herself from vomiting up my father's good claret. John, his eyes like saucers, stared at me as though I had grown two heads.

We never spoke of it again, but the incident often came into my mind when I caught wet-nurses exchanging frightened looks. I never got used to seeing my children in the arms of others or ringed all about by protective nannies who looked at me with hostile eyes. I was not to be trusted with babes in arms: whenever I held them, anxious women hovered at my shoulder.

Those first years of my marriage, it seemed that I was constantly either pregnant or recovering from a birth, and by the time I was twenty-four years old, I had been delivered of five children, two girls and three boys, all fine healthy children. My second daughter, Anna, was born a year after John, and the following year George was born on that dreadful November morning when the Tyne Bridge was swept away.

It had rained heavily for days, and the coach bringing the doctor had become stuck in the mud in Snipe's Dene. When he finally arrived on foot, drenched and chilled, a fretful midwife came with wide eyes to tell me that he was shaking and not fit to attend the birth until he had dried off and his teeth ceased chattering. By the time he came to see me, I was delivered of my child, who came more quickly and easily that his three siblings, and was lying contentedly snuffling at my breast.

My husband was at that time in London: it would be a few days before he would hear that he had another son, 'an heir and a spare,' as he would subsequently never tire of saying. My mother was at home in Hertfordshire, and the Lyon hangers-on were up at Glamis, so I felt quite relaxed and self-contained in my own home with my people about me.

When the doctor finally knocked, it was early afternoon and the wind and rain were still lashing at the windows. He was a well-built man with a florid complexion, but his hands shook when he took the baby from me, and he started to pace about the room instead of examining the child. Alarmed by his demeanour, I said, 'You seem troubled and distracted. Give him back to me, please, and take a seat. What ails you?'

He came to a stop by the dark and rain-lashed window, the baby held out before him like an offering. 'Terrible news from Newcastle. You need not concern yourself, your ladyship.'

Exasperated by his very presence, which I felt unnecessary, having been perfectly well taken care of by the midwives, I confess I was more abrupt than I should have been with the poor fellow: 'Give me back my baby. Now.' Startled, he moved towards the bed. 'Of course I must concern myself! Out with it, man! What has happened?'

He sat down heavily and placed the baby on the coverlet where I could not reach him without sitting up. This I did, though my gasp of discomfort went unnoticed. Once I was lying back, safely cradling little George, I tried again.

'Tell me, please, what has happened. Is there a flood?'

He turned tragic eyes to me and it all came out: 'Yes, a dreadful flood. A torrent has swept away the bridge.'

'The bridge? But people live on the bridge! Are they lost? When did it happen?'

'Two o'clock this morning. High tide. They say it swept through almost fifteen feet higher than even a spring tide. The bridge collapsed. The bridge-dwellers were in bed.'

'But I know those people! I have bought shoes there, from Mr...'

'Mr Weatherley. I too, I have bought shoes from Mr Weatherley. A good man, skilled, kind.'

It was all coming back to me now, the narrow street across the bridge, a closely-packed hive of voices and things to buy, banter and laughter, washing strung between the windows up above, the smell of leather and the strong wafts of tobacco. Walking past the cheesemonger's holding my breath, for I never could abide the smell of cheese. The hat shop. A face and then a name came to me: 'Mr Haswell the milliner, his wife and daughters? Are they lost?'

'Yes, and their servants, it seems so: I heard there was a family stranded on one of the remaining pillars in the centre of the river, but the current was too fierce to rescue them.'

'Oh dreadful, dreadful! I cannot bear to think of it!' I cried, overwhelmed by the enormity of the tragedy and pity for those poor people, out there in the lashing wind and rain, at the mercy of the vast indifference of nature to their plight.

The following day, we heard more of the disaster: the water had not only swept through the river channel but also up the Close and the Sandhill: ships and cargo were dashed upon the Quayside and when the tide withdrew in the afternoon, three sloops and a brig were left stranded. We listened to the catalogue of devastation, of lives lost and lives ruined, until we could bear no more. No-one knew how many had died, but everyone knew someone affected, if not in the centre of Newcastle, then among the keelmen at Dunston, Swalwell and Blaydon, or as far up-river as Newburn and Wylam.

How random fate is, how unpredictable life is. Astonishingly, that family who had huddled together with their servants on a small area of stone pillar no more than six feet wide, the family whose fate had haunted my dreams in the storm-lashed night, that family had survived. Who could have predicted that? There is always hope, as long as there is life. Fortune had sent them a saviour in the form of an ordinary working man who found within himself the courage and the ingenuity to thwart fate: a brickmaker called George Woodward had heard of their plight and had rushed to the scene to construct a system of ropes and pulleys and, in the teeth of a gale and against all the odds, had saved their lives. It was the shoemaker and his family.

And the following day brought news of one more miracle: a ship at sea had picked up a wooden cradle and in it a baby, alive and well. When I heard this, I held my own babies tightly and wept as though my heart would break.

Chapter 8

In those nine years of my marriage to John, time had a curious quality. It felt as though I existed in a bubble, my body and mind no longer my own but dominated by pregnancy and birth, whist all around me there was action and drama and interest, none of it involving me. I can remember only feeling discontented and weepy, constantly thwarted and discouraged, my body an alien thing of swellings and pain and fluids, my babies taken from me, my freedom to walk, to ride, to go where I wished, all gone.

In reality, now I look back, there was much more to my life than I felt at the time. I cannot feel angry with the girl that I was: the loss of liberty that marriage and childbirth entailed had been a shock to her and she had, I think, a kind of mental incapacity as a result of all those difficult births. She could not see the life she had for what it was. When I look back at those years, they seem gilded to me now, and yet at the time, young Lady Strathmore found it difficult to be happy. Perhaps it is ever thus: we do not know what we have until it's gone.

In reality, as long as I was at Gibside I was fairly free to follow my interests and inclinations as far as pregnancy, childbirth and its physical and mental effects would allow. It was a different matter in London, where John supervised my activities far more closely, and I cannot bear to think of how entombed I felt at Glamis, but Gibside was home, and at home I had a kind of freedom.

It heartened me greatly that John enjoyed being there so much: he had his study and his gaming room, his friends and his hunting. Meanwhile, I supervised the work on the east wing of the house, adding a new dairy, bake-house and laundry. We made much-needed improvements to the servants' quarters, and everywhere I went, apart from the nursery, I was greeted with warmth and affection. Out of John's sight, I could be as I always had been with the staff, and they with me.

Where I was happiest, and the same has been true throughout my life, is outside. It gave me so much happiness to spend time with the estate workers: they were a kind of family to me, and many of them had known me all my life. My father had always instilled in me that respect had to be earned. He respected their skills, their hard work and their loyalty, and they respected his management, his fairness and the success he brought to the estate. Although I cannot say I always behaved as I should have done, for I was indeed a spoilt little moppet, as a young married woman I did feel privileged to have inherited some of the respect they had for my father. I was conscious of not having earned it, and anxious to make my contribution to the development of the estate.

John's brother Thomas was the source of a good deal of my unhappiness, for he held the purse-strings. He was a gloomy, pinched-faced man with the aura of a ghost. I swear the room became colder when he entered. He had taken a room in the west wing of the house, and I avoided that staircase after the time I saw him emerge silently from the shadows, where he must have been watching me playing with a kitten on the landing. Startled, I froze and he stood immobile, staring with an unreadable expression, before gliding down the staircase without making a sound. At dinner, he would often talk over me: to him, I was little more than a constant irritant and I was dimly aware that he regarded me as some kind of threat.

I often clashed with him on matters to do with the management of the estate, and our disagreements were widely known, because he refused to keep me apprised of his decisions, so I usually found out from estate workers or, even worse, casual labourers. Many's the time I gave him the sharp edge of my tongue and took my complaints to John. I soon found out that was useless: in his eyes, Thomas could do no wrong. I cannot imagine that any two brothers were ever closer or more inter-dependent.

The worst row by far was when I found out that work had ceased on the chapel.

It was on what would have been my father's birthday, 21st August. I always marked the day by laying flowers on the altar of the beautiful church in Whickham where he lay in the vault, waiting to be taken home. Every year since his death I had whispered a promise that next year he would be back at Gibside in the crypt of his own chapel, and every year I had meant it. Surely he would be home by Christmas?

It was a beautiful morning and I was walking along the Grand Avenue, breathing deeply of the sweet warm air and savouring the feeling of the sun on my face. I think it was the first time I had thought of my father's absence with a sense of peace, for there could be little left to do in the chapel, although I knew the decorations were taking a good deal of time.

I had ordered a carriage for eleven o'clock, and this year, in addition to my own flowers, I would take a posy from his first grandson. How happy he would have been to hold little John and Maria.

As I approached the chapel, I felt a rising sense of frustration that yet again an anniversary would pass without my father coming home. How could it still not be ready? He would never have stood for it himself, especially having spent so long over the plans. I remember he was much preoccupied with the stone, fearing that his quarries would not provide blocks of sufficient length for the pillars: he need not have worried: the pillars looked splendid.

When the foundations were dug, Father still had a few months to live: though he rarely left his bed, he always asked how the building work was going. At eleven, I doubt I understood the real reason for his interest: I knew it as a chapel, and in my hearing it was never referred to as a mausoleum.

I stopped and looked, comprehending perhaps for the first time the impact of this building as a focal point for the estate, the harmonious beauty of its symmetrical design. My father had conceived its location and appearance and the architect had designed it to his specifications, but men and materials from this place had made it. The stone from Wheatley's Quarry, the wood grown out of this very earth, the metal and the bricks from our own factories, the iron band securing the dome made at the Crowley works, which my grandfather had supported years ago by supplying timber for the furnaces. I thought of all the care and craft that had gone into the chapel's construction and decoration, all the lives and skills and materials had worked together to produce a lasting memorial of such grace and beauty. The grey-blue of the Devonshire slate roof was the colour of his eyes, and the colour of my own, which swam with tears. Why was he not here, in his own mausoleum? When I started

73

to walk again, I had resolved to ensure he was brought here before Christmas.

I thought of the child I was when he died, and how a year later I had visited the newly-completed vault: it had now been waiting for him for eight long years.

He passed away in the September, and the by the end of the following summer, the crypt was complete. Joseph Palliser, the master carpenter, came to me one day where I was sitting disconsolate on a bench he had made for my garden. He sat down beside me in the sun, chatting of this and that, asking after my plants and admiring the row of climbers on the trellis he had made. In lieu of answers, all I could do was sniff: as he well knew, I had been crying again.

He lapsed into silence, watching the robin that pecked about my feet waiting for the seeds I always carried in the pocket of my pinafore.

And then he said, 'I've finished the doors.'

Only half-listening, I threw the robin a pinch of seed and then said, 'Doors?'

'There's a lot going on, as you know, what with repairing the balustrade for the Bath House, the work on the bank, painting the statues and whatnot, but the doors had to take precedence.' He put his arm around my shoulder and gave me a swift hug. 'We want him home, don't we, Miss Eleanor?'

At that, I sat up straight. No-one ever spoke to me about Papa, and if I said his name, people looked at me with startled eyes as if they expected me to melt into a puddle of tears. My mother had shut herself in her room and the women of the household had an unnerving way of hugging me to their aprons and sobbing. All the doe-eyed avoidance of the subject of my father's absence just made me feel more lonely and excluded than I could ever have imagined. Now here was Joseph Palliser talking to me directly about him.

I looked up, squinting into his weather-beaten face. 'Yes, Mr Palliser, we want him home.'

The thought of having him here, even under a stone slab, gave me a strange kind of hope. I looked around my garden at the graves of the two cats and a dog that I had loved and lost. I thought of the comfort of knowing where they were, near me, safe in a neat grave that I could tend lovingly any time I liked, and I wanted the same for my Papa.

I stood up and faced him. 'Can I see?'

He thought for a moment, and looked over at Martha, sitting sewing in the sun. She lifted a hand to shade her eyes, then I saw her nod at him and go back to her sewing.

He stood up. 'I can't see any harm in it. Come with me.'

As we walked, he said, 'I would not suggest such a thing to my own daughter, Miss Bowes, but I know you are a spirited young lady and will not be afraid.'

'No, Mr Palliser, I am most certainly not afraid to see where my father will lie. It gives me comfort to know he will soon come home.'

In fact, I was fascinated, though I remember my heart trembled as I descended the steps. The air was dusty with cut stone and sawdust and, coming in from the bright sunshine, the light was dim. I knew from Mr Paine's plans that the vault was circular with a central column, but I was unprepared for the beauty of the design. Where I had expected a simple Ionic column like the ones planned for the portico, I saw a glorious fountain of pale golden stone flaring upwards, opening into the smooth arch of the low ceiling and curving down the walls.

I let go of Joseph's rough hand and walked forward to put my own small one against the cool stone.

'Why Joseph, this is glorious! Such skillful work!'

My back to the column, I looked around in the gauzy gloom. As my eyes accustomed themselves, the shadowy greys and blacks of the encircling wall resolved themselves into stone blocks and dark arched niches, each the size of the end of a coffin. I took a deep, dusty breath and held it.

Bless him, Joseph waited in silence until I breathed out, and then he spoke in a normal voice. There would be no whispering here: George Bowes never could bear a whisperer.

'There are eleven, Miss Mary. You can choose, if you like.'

'Choose?'

'Where you would wish your father to lie.'

'Oh, yes, of course.' I went forward to touch the rim of the niche in the centre, facing the steps. I took a breath and slowly stretched my arm deep into the blackness, pressing my ribs against the edge until they hurt. My ear against the arch, I could hear my heartbeat as though listening to a seashell. I trailed my fingers down the wall, forcing myself to register the skill of the stonemason, for it was very smoothly carved, with faint ridges like wavemarks on a beach. Slowly withdrawing, my fingertips left darker stripes in the pale gold stone-dust and I lifted them to my face in wonder.

Such an epiphany had come to me that it changed me forever.

I looked round to where Joseph stood in the entrance, half of him illuminated in the bright sunshine from the world outside.

I spoke softly, in awe. 'One day, I will be here too, won't I Mr Palliser?'

His face was in shadow but I saw his lips part in surprise and then tightly press together as he came across and put a fatherly hand on my shoulder to gently guide me out. 'Now now, Mary Eleanor Bowes, we'll have no more of that. Not for a very very long time yet, and who knows what you will have achieved by then? You will be a world-famous botanist, they tell me.'

Though dazed and disorientated, the child that I was responded: the combination of the sudden sunshine and the dizzying possibilities of life hit me at once, and I burst into chatter. 'Yes, and an adventurer and a writer. I'm going to write plays and grow amazing plants from hot countries far away. I shall go there myself to collect them.'

'You'll need a glasshouse.'

'Yes, you can build it for me, and I will have a desk in there and write my poems and plays whilst I tend my plants. And I shall be perfectly happy.'

Only eight years ago, but it felt like a lifetime, and although the glasshouse was under construction, I had made little progress with my other ambitions, I thought ruefully as I climbed the steps into the cool of the loggia.

The doors were closed and there was no sound from within. I stood for a moment with my hands on the stone balustrade and looked towards Lady Liberty, high atop her column half a mile away, gleaming gold in the morning sun.

'Morning, Lady Eleanor.' A man's voice from below me. 'You look quite a picture up there, like a painting in a frame.' It sounded like Joseph Palliser, of all people, but I knew it was more likely to be his son Cuthbert, who was doing more of Joseph's work lately.

'Morning Cuthbert. How are you and all the little Pallisers?'

'All well, thank-you miss, and my father asked me to pass on his greetings if I should see you.'

'Do you know where we are up to with the chapel, Cuthbert? It is surely almost finished?'

'Well, you would think so. I must say, I was surprised when the work was stopped and they sent away the plasterers.'

'Sent them away? When?'

'In the spring, Miss. You were taken abed with little master John. Congratulations, by the way. I don't believe I've seen you out and about since then.'

'Who sent them away?'

'Well, the estate manager, but the decision came from the house.'

By the time I found Thomas, I was utterly irate, having fuelled my indignation by going over all the instances of his rudeness and high-handedness which I had allowed to pass without protest, and some I hadn't. I burst into his office without knocking, and there he was, bent over some account books like a solicitor's clerk.

His head jerked up: 'What is the meaning of this?'

'I am here to ask you that very question!'

'How dare you burst into my room in this way? I suggest you leave immediately. Go elsewhere and calm yourself. If you have something to say to me, come back when you have mastered your temper.'

My voice, when it came, was low and threatening. I had learnt quickly that Thomas reacted to female proximity with a shudder which he never bothered to disguise and sometimes even accentuated deliberately to provoke me.

'How dare you. How dare you talk to me like that in my own home. No, don't speak, you will listen to what I have to say and you will give me an answer. Sit down.' Clearly somewhat frightened by being confronted so unexpectedly, he had risen to his feet and at one point seemed ready to make a bolt for the door.

'There are many things you have done with which I take issue, Thomas. We have a mutual antipathy, but it seems I must accept your constant presence in my home and in my marriage. No. Don't speak. I have heard your opinions on a woman's role and I will not listen to them again. Be silent. I have come straight from the chapel, which is near completion. Why has work ceased?'

'Because I ordered it to cease.'

Anger threatened to choke me, for he had lounged back in his chair and was regarding me with outright disdain.

'For what reason?'

'Because it is not a priority.'

'It is a priority for me.'

In answer, I received only a look, a look of the most patronizing, eyebrow-arching condescension that it was all I could do not to fly at his face with my nails.

Palpitations fluttered in my chest, my blood pumped in my neck, and suddenly I was looking down dark tunnels. I must have staggered, for in a moment he was beside me and helping me to a chair.

His voice sounded a distance away, though I was conscious of his presence at the side of the chair where he had placed me. 'Really, Mary Eleanor, you must not excite yourself so.'

His feet swam into focus as my vision returned, and he walked back to his desk. I could not trust myself to speak.

'The chapel has been a considerable drain on the estate's finances. You may not be aware that it has run vastly over-budget. Even your mother concedes as much. It will be finished one day, but no more will be spent on it for the time being.'

Feeling hot and dizzy, I rested my elbow on the arm of the chair and propped my head upon my hand, regarding him with what I hoped was still an angry gaze. I focused my attention on not falling to the floor, for I was quite sure he would leave me there if I did.

He turned back to his ledgers.

The winters were fierce in those years. 1773 was a particularly hard one for the north-east: the river was frozen solid for over four miles below the new bridge, so coal ships were unable to leave the Tyne and the region was deprived of London's money. My father would have anticipated that there would be hardship and acted accordingly, but we were oblivious until the agent came to see John to talk about the trouble he was having extracting rents from our tenants. Greatly to his credit, John did not hesitate in coming to an arrangement which ensured that our people would not suffer unnecessarily.

Over dinner that night, he spoke of a neighbouring landowner who was not being so understanding.

'You'll know Hannah Newton, I expect?'

'Newton? Yes, I met her once or twice at the Assembly Rooms. Her father is a mine-owner.'

'Was. He died and it seems young Hannah has made a sorry match.'

'How so?'

'The fellow's a scoundrel, by all accounts. Gambling all the Newton money away and threatening the tenants with eviction if they cannot pay their rents.'

I made a sound of disapproval and took a sip of wine. 'Coal Pike Hill, isn't it? Don't the Stephensons have a brother who works there?'

'Yes, name of Rowland, he's acting as agent, though he's not getting paid, such are this chap's debts. He's even trying to sell off their ancient oak woodlands, would you believe? Keeps advertising them in the Chronicle but Hannah's uncle is threatening to sue anyone who bids.'

He put down his fork and sat back, replete. 'The Stephensons are good workers: I've told our man to tell Rowland to come to see me if he wants to come back to Gibside. We'll find a job for him.'

It was one of the times when I looked at John with real affection. It warmed my heart when he showed care of our estate's families.

'And Hannah, how is she?'

'Not good apparently. This fellow treats her badly, by all accounts, and her health's suffering. They spend a deal of time at Bath: she to take the waters and he to gamble and fornicate, or so I have heard.'

'Does she have children?'

'No, poor girl has had several stillbirths. There's a rumour this fellow had the bells rung at the cathedral, pretending there'd been a live birth, so desperate is he to hold onto her estate.'

I hope I had the grace to feel sorry for Hannah. I often think that if only I had shown more curiosity, if only I had asked this scoundrel's name, my own life would have turned out very differently.

And then there was Gabriel. What can I tell you of what he meant to me at that time? Living as I did under watchful, often disapproving eyes, knowing as I did that my husband did not love me in the way that I wanted to be loved, I began to depend on thoughts of Gabriel's devotion, expressed so long ago. Perhaps it was wrong: I know many will say that it was, that if I did not betray my husband with my body, I certainly did with my heart and my imagination. To them I say, Judge not lest ye be judged. I am many things; I have made many mistakes; I have many regrets, yet I think it is true to say I never sat in judgment on anyone.

What I do know is that though I saw him rarely, and then only in company, the idea of him made my life more bearable. I liked to think of him as my knight, in fact it was this that gave me the idea for my first play, though I chose to set it long ago and far away, the better to give distance to my thoughts. I called it The Siege of Jerusalem.

In the writing of it, I was able to give a tragic, romantic dignity to my own situation:

'A virgin princess matches not for love
Her ev'ry thought devoted to the state.'

Often, alone in my bed whilst John was carousing in Newcastle, I imagined a simpler life in which I would never be left alone in echoing halls or feel lonely in a room full of people. Instead, I would live close to the land, and earn my crust shoulder to shoulder with other working people. No-one would look at me with envious eyes, for I would have nothing but the love of a good man. And at the end of a day of honest manual labour, we would tumble into bed exhausted and sleep wrapped in each other's arms:

'In real happiness no pomp is seen,
But gloomy grandeurs ere attend a queen,
While the poor peasant in his humble cot
Lives to the world, forgetting and forgot;
With meek content he spends his guiltless days,

Peace in his paths and pleasure in his ways.
No kingdom can a sacrifice command –
He reigns sole master of his heart and hand.
He's free to choose the partner of his bed
And love alone directs him where to wed.'

I often considered arranging myself prettily at my writing somewhere outdoors where I knew Gabriel would come across me, though I chose to overlook how difficult that would be, as he was mostly at that time working in the fields on Cut Thorn Farm. However, in my fantasy, he would sit down beside me and ask me what I was writing - something John never did. Blushingly, haltingly, I would read my words aloud and slowly the truth would dawn on him:

'Would we had been some neighbouring shepherd's babes
Together bred in equal humble state:
We then had frequent met at rural sports,
In sweeter converse oft beguil'd the day
'Til love insensibly had crept into our hearts
And our glad parents had with rustic joy
Join'd willing hands, and heard our nuptial vows.'

In my wildest fantasies, he would, upon hearing these words, fall to his knees and beg me to run away with him. I think when I conceived this idea, it was inspired by the elopement of Bessie Surtees, who had recently climbed out of the first floor window of her father's house on Sandhill to be with the man she loved. It seemed to me then the most passionate, romantic thing I had ever heard.

Much as I enjoyed writing my play, I would never have had the courage to show it to my friends in London if it had not been for the encouragement of the governess, Mrs Parish, who knowing nothing of its role in sublimating the secret yearnings of my heart, read the play at face value and found it marvelous.

And as for my botany ambitions, I had got so far as building my glasshouse, which I called the Green House and others the

Orangery, for I had ordered seven large tubs and the orange trees were thriving. There I grew some camellias and delargonium grandiflorum, but was looking forward to experimenting with new species.

These were exciting times in the botanic world, with explorers bringing home specimens and seeds of exotic new plants. Through Mrs Parish, I had made contact with other serious natural historians: her brother, Joseph Planta, worked at the British Museum, and her sister, Eliza, taught the children of George III, whose enthusiasm for botanical discoveries had led to the expansion of the Royal Gardens at Kew. I had not yet met the great Sir Joseph Banks, but it was a real thrill for me to be introduced to Dr Solander, who had also voyaged to Terra Australis Incognita on Captain Cook's Endeavour. It was on one of the rare occasions that John had agreed to accompany me to Chelsea Physic Garden. He was so disdainful of my interest in botany that I had to resort to feminine wiles to entice him to accompany me.

'Shall we go for a walk this afternoon?'

'That would be most agreeable,' he said, not looking up from his newspaper. 'Where had you in mind?'

'I thought perhaps Chelsea. It is rather a cold day, but the climate by the river is so much warmer. It might be pleasant to walk in the gardens there.'

He arched an eyebrow and looked at me over the top of his paper. 'The climate?'

'Yes.'

'Gardens by the river? I take it you mean Chelsea Physic Garden?' His indulgent tone made the muscles of my neck tense: he spoke to me exactly as though he was considering indulging one of the children.

I had learnt by then to master my natural impulse to rage, though not quite. I imagine I jutted my chin and averted my eyes, which will have been fierce with indignation as I struggling to maintain a coquettish lightness, girlishly discovered in my innocent strategy.

'Yes.'

'I wonder whether there is any particular reason that my little poppet would like to go there this particular afternoon?'

'Why, yes there is. William Curtis is to give a lecture.'

'A lecture.'

'Yes.'

'And why would we want to attend a lecture when we are out for a walk? Surely one has to remain motionless in order to attend to whatever is being said. Perhaps even be seated. Inside, even.' He ruffled his paper and resumed his reading position, with the perfectly elegant posture of a man constantly aware of the image he presented. 'No no, I think not. I think we'll have a far more pleasant stroll in Kensington.'

I hesitated, torn between continuing to act in a girlishly persuasive manner and leaping up out of my chair to tell him what I thought of his patronizing condescension. I decided to go for the middle line and speak in a reasonable, adult tone.

'Then perhaps you won't mind if I go to Chelsea with Mrs Parish and the children? Her brother will be there, and perhaps the botanists from the Endeavour.' I had a flash of inspiration. 'Possibly Captain Cook himself.'

At this he looked up. Captain Cook was a man's man, none of this namby-pamby mincing about with flowers.

And so we went, and as luck would have it, so did Captain Cook.

After the lecture, Mrs Parish's brother, Joseph Planta, was at the front talking to a tall gentleman. I saw him look over at me and then speak to his companion. The two of them came towards me, and I confess my hand was shaking when Dr Solander took it in his own. I admired him greatly, had been to several of his lectures, read all his papers and was conscious that Linnaeus himself had shaken this very hand. Perhaps you do not share my enthusiasm for botany, but imagine being introduced to someone whose heroic adventures have been the subject of your fascinated interest for years.

'Lady Strathmore, delighted to meet you.'

'The honour is all mine, Dr Solander. I am a great admirer of your work. Is it true you returned from the Pacific with over ten thousand plant specimens?'

'Indeed it is, including over two thousand new species of flora and fauna. It is a great pity that you were unable to attend our presentation at the Royal Academy.'

'Yes. I am not alone in considering it an outrage that women are excluded. But I have read all about it and seen some of the beautiful paintings and sketches you made.'

'I believe you bought some of the seeds. How are they faring?'

'Yes, I sent them to Gibside and some to my mother's hothouses at St Paul's Walden.'

'You have hothouses at Gibside?'

'Yes, a heated Orangery, just completed in time for the seed sale. I would love to have a greenhouse in London, but Grosvenor Square is unsuitable and ... circumstances do not permit me to purchase a property in this area.'

Dr Solander followed my eyes to where my husband and Captain Cook stood smoking cigars and guffawing loudly.

He smiled kindly and spoke softly, 'Perhaps one day.'

Grateful for the hope his response gave me, I smiled. 'Yes, perhaps one day.'

Chapter 9

Be careful what you wish for.

The beautiful Lord Strathmore's decline was dreadful to behold.

When I first lay with my head upon his chest when I was eighteen years old, among the new sensations of lying in a man's arms was amusement at the strange whistling noises that emanated from his chest. It was just something I quickly got used to, something that came with the intimacy of sharing a bed. I had no way of knowing that such a fine, strong, well-built man could have a fatal weakness: in his lungs lurked an ailment which was to kill him in the prime of his life.

By the time we had completed our family, his health was declining, though he denied it for as long as he could: that whistling and rattling was much worse and no longer a source of amusement. The moist air of Gibside in which I thrived was anathema to my husband: his breathing became more congested and his cough more pronounced. He often used to stand facing the fire, his hands on the mantel, taking the hot dry air into his lungs and trying to hold it there. Cold air always made him cough persistently, and climbing the glen on the walk that he had once loved began to cause him to struggle for breath. I had no concept of the seriousness of his condition: he did not tell me that there had long been blood in his handkerchiefs. When I think about it now, I see that the washerwomen must have known before I did that their master was not long for this world.

He was twelve years older than me, but I began to feel that I was married to a much older man: by the time he began to decline, he was only in his mid-thirties. In his final two years, he spent much of his time taking the waters in Bath. By then I was used to his absences, for gambling and horse-racing often took him away from us: he had always spent time at the Streatlam to see to the stud; he was a regular at the gentlemen's clubs in Newcastle and Durham; in addition there were his frequent trips to Glamis and London.

It was by then quite usual for myself and the little ones to be uprooted from Gibside and transported to London, though none of us wanted to go. Like my father, I was determined to bring up my children to be hardy, energetic and independent, and at Gibside they had an outdoor childhood very much like my own. Once we were transplanted to London, we all felt confined, so you can imagine how I reacted when Thomas, who had become his brother's fierce protector, suddenly announced that he was taking John to Bath and we were to remain at Grosvenor Square. It happened several times in John's final years, though I had not the faintest idea that his ailment was so serious. I used to think they were simply making the spa an excuse so that they could go off unencumbered by wife and family, to live the bachelor life of drinking and gambling.

At first I was deeply resentful of John's absence, for the children's sake as well as my own, but it wasn't long before I started to enjoy the freedom from that constant sense of being an irrelevance and an irritant. When I was left in London, I began to host a tentative salon to which I invited people of my acquaintance, people whom John did not encourage or had forbidden me to socialize with. Bluestocking friends and acquaintances, people I had known in my girlhood, a few notable academics. Horace Walpole came once, briefly, and I felt the honour acutely: The Castle of Otranto was a favourite of mine.

The servants loved it all. Though of course it didn't stop them grumbling, it was happy grumbling: they were kept busy and enjoyed being able to compare notes with their peers at other society houses. These gatherings gave me a guilty and defiant consolation, but it also stimulated my dormant brain, and the children enjoyed meeting new people. The London house was a busy and mostly a happy one, but in the midst of it all I often felt lonely.

As that last Christmas approached, I began to realize that I missed John in a new way, and became full of regret, wishing things could have been different between us. I had hopes that he would join us for the festivities, and resolved to try to be more amiable with him, even if Thomas was there. I still had no idea that he would be leaving us for ever. But he never came home that Christmas, nor ever again.

It was January 1776 and the streets were calf-deep in dirty sludge and melted snow, churned up with mud and filth brought on carriage wheels and expelled from horses. John was still in Bath: he and his new physician were preparing to set sail for Lisbon to take a cure in the warm dry air of Portugal. The children and I had spent a strangely solemn Christmas with my mother and she had pressed me to leave them there when I returned to town. I could still see their beseeching faces, but I knew she would begin to spoil them as soon as my carriage had passed the gates. I'd received a cold letter from Thomas, who was comfortably ensconced at Gibside, the thought of which was a worm squirming in my mind.

It was one of those winter nights when we pine for light, our energies depleted. The sky had been a dirty grey all day and I felt the want of daylight as a want of sustenance. Sometimes we can find pleasure in hibernation: I had had an early bath, and anticipated a peaceful night with my book. But somehow I could not give up on the day; I was restless and melancholy. I had received a letter from Thomas on some financial matter, and his words still rankled: he had refused me a simple request for no good reason other than to exercise his power.

I thought of him now and the grip of resentment fastened on my heart. What right had he? He would perhaps have been for a walk in the bracing northern air, or taken one of the horses for a canter over the hills. Perhaps he had walked in the ancient oak woods and felt the wisdom of ages in their presence. The charcoal burners would have greeted him or he might have come across one of the bonfires that the estate workers sometimes lit on a winter's afternoon to warm themselves and share a glass of ale. He would choose a book from my library and settle into my father's chair to read by the light of the fire. My hearth. My wood. My home. I yearned to be at Gibside with every fibre of my being.

We all, no matter how privileged, have moments of self-pity. I pressed my head against the icy window and my ever-present homesickness, always there like distant sad music, welled up and threatened to drown me. I saw a figure emerge from a carriage, muffled up against the cold, and as he turned, I saw that it was my old friend George Gray: he looked up and smiled that great warm smile. I heard his knock from the floor below, his friendly chat with the footman. John was always so cold and distant with the servants, a fact that never ceased to pain me.

My eyes were still swimming with tears and I suppose I didn't want anyone to see me at my most vulnerable, so for a moment I felt I should refuse him entry. But I was so very lonely. When he came in, he saw my distress straight away, and without a word he took my hand and led me to the chaise longue, where he put his arm around my shoulders and pressed my head to his chest. The floodgates opened.

I cried and cried. I don't remember any words being spoken, only the overwhelming warmth of his presence and his acceptance of my distress. He asked no questions, just let me cry, and occasionally kissed my brow fondly. I think he even said, 'There there.' I had not abandoned my control for a very long time, but suddenly I was a rag doll. All will and wit and energy and purpose left me.

When the crying subsided and my handkerchief was drenched with tears, I passively accepted his, and I remember the unfamiliar sensation of Indian silk. When he opened the door to my bedroom, I was momentarily disturbed, but when he brought forth a fresh towel which he had immersed in cool water from the night-stand, I pressed it against my face gratefully. Still no words were spoken. When he stood and held out both his hands, I placed my own inside them and allowed him to lead me to the bedroom. When he slipped my dressing-gown from my shoulders and lifted the blankets, I lay down without a word.

When a few minutes later, he lay down beside me and I felt the heat of him against my side, I turned and nestled into his arms, questioning nothing, seeking only companionship and, yes, love.

I have no belief in God: the Bible was taught to me in the same way as the Iliad. My father believed that we should direct ourselves to the goodness that is in everyone. If I ever felt the need for a religion, I would be drawn to the Quakers: for them, as I understand it, God is simply the light within us all.

In the morning, I felt sad that I had broken my vows, but comforted myself that John had broken his promises to me first. When I was pregnant with my first baby, I overheard him and his friends talking about a recent visit to a brothel and from what he said, it was clear that his promise about forsaking all others meant nothing to him.

I was sure our servants would be loyal and discreet. George had left before midnight at my request, though it had been tempting to let him stay. The night-watchmen would certainly have seen him leave, and there would be gossip, but in the bedchamber, the closet and at breakfast, the faces and bearings of the servants were as natural and relaxed as normal. Only George Walker gave any indication that he was aware, and even then I might have been being over-sensitive. When he brought the previous evening's post to the breakfast table, there was none of his usual cheery banter and he did not meet my eye. Ordinarily, I would have asked him whether he was quite well: I was afraid to do so. I think we both knew what the matter was.

When I returned to my room mid-morning, I saw that the sheets had been changed. Although some members of staff could sometimes be overfamiliar, no-one gave any indication that anything was amiss and no knowing glances were exchanged: I chose to believe I could count on their discretion.

Of course, in the eyes of the world, that night I went from respectable married woman to transgressor. Whereas a man is almost expected to have mistresses, any woman who has relations out of wedlock risks everything. I had no fear of society's disapproval: I did not yet know what it was. I was to learn.

Though there was no farewell communication from John, I knew he was due to set sail for Lisbon in mid-January and would be gone for at least three months. Although I saw no harm in taking comfort from George, I did initially keep him at arm's length, but he was so attentive and solicitous that I soon began to accept his visits. I had hoped that he would not press me for more physical intimacy, but when he did, I lacked the will or the desire to deny him. Though I missed the peace of mind that came with being a virtuous wife, I saw no other reason to reject him. The words I had written in the Siege of Jerusalem seemed remarkably prescient to me now:

> 'Oh virtue! I would yet resume thy paths
> And tread thy peaceful ways; but thou art fled,
> And with content art lost to me forever.'

George was warm and steady, a man I felt I could trust, and his steadfast devotion gave me great comfort. Soon, our relationship was no longer a secret, and here I see I was unwise. Perhaps I thought to provoke John into showing some emotion, even if it was jealousy, shame or anger. If he had lived, my indiscretion would have simply been meat for the gossips. It would have filled a few column inches for a couple of weeks, John would have returned home, there might have been a scandal, certainly not a duel: Lord Strathmore would never have demeaned himself to publicly defend my honour. George would have slunk away, the press would have written admiringly of the patrician bearing of the aristocratic earl and the chastened little wife, brought to heel. Perhaps she'd have been given a beating: she deserved it, as long as the stick was no thicker that his thumb. Can you believe that a husband's right to suitably chastise his wife is enshrined in law, thanks to Judge Buller? I find it absolutely reprehensible and it is my fervent hope that one day the law will protect women from this most heinous ruling.

But no, Lord Strathmore did not return.

By the beginning of April, he had been gone for over ten weeks, and still I had heard nothing from him. I was not worrying unduly, but I had begun to feel real concern. Sometimes I feared that he had returned to Italy to seek out Constanza, and other times I considered writing to Thomas to see whether he had heard anything, but my pride prevented me. For the children's sake, I pretended that I had heard from Papa and he was sunning himself in Lisbon, his health improving every day.

It was 6th April when the news came, just a week before John's seventh birthday. The poor little chap had just started at a boarding school in Neasden. Needless to tell you, I had no say in the matter: his father and uncle had chosen the school where the formal education of the future earl was to begin. It was clear they intended to mould him into a suitably stoical and emotionless heir to the Lyon family: his future lay in Scotland, as I was told on many occasions, and I was to consider my role in his life to be secondary to his destiny. I had learnt by now to hold my tongue when John and Thomas presented me with their faits accomplis: they spoke with the air of unarguable authority that centuries of power and

90

entitlement confers on families who have squatted on the same piece of land since the Norman Invasion.

I would see John on his birthday by hook or by crook, and had written to the school requesting that he be allowed home for the weekend. I was not yet aware that the school had forwarded the letter to Thomas at Gibside as they had been instructed to do, and that my request would be refused.

He had been begging for a dog of his own, not a yappy little thing like the family dogs, but a proper dog, a hunting dog, a retriever or a Labrador. Perhaps unwisely, I had bought him a black Labrador puppy, and I was pretending for all the children's sake that it had been sent from Portugal by their doting Papa.

That morning, I was breakfasting with little Maria, and her brother's puppy was sitting on her lap, drinking milk from her bowl. Her own birthday was only two weeks away, and she had just announced with confidence that Papa was certain to send a puppy for her too, maybe even bring it himself.

When the door opened, she looked up, excited, and her face fell when George Walker came into the room bearing the silver salver on which he was in the habit of bringing the post. He stopped just inside the door, and something about his demeanour arrested my attention. There was only one letter on the tray, and the envelope was large and blue with a number of stamps in different-coloured inks. I raised my eyes from the letter to George's face and I went cold. As if from a distance, I heard Maria scold the puppy for trying to climb onto the table. I stayed still, staring at the letter and I felt the colour drain from my face. At some signal from George, the maids ushered Maria and the puppy from the room. He sat down at the table.

'It is from Portugal.'

I could not speak.

'The handwriting is unfamiliar, and it bears the mark of Lord Strathmore's surgeon. Would you like me to open it?'

Faintly, I assented.

He opened the envelope and took out a large sheet, which he unfolded. Inside was a smaller envelope. He read the sheet quickly and in silence, and then he put it down to take my hand in both of his own. His voice, when it came, was gruff. 'Lady Strathmore, I regret to inform you that your husband died on the 7th March.'

I was watching him as he said those words and I took in their meaning only slowly. My mind felt sluggish and drugged.

Stupidly, I said, 'In Lisbon?'

'No, they were almost there. He died aboard ship off the coast of Portugal. The physician was with him when he passed. He knew he was dying, and he wrote you a letter. Here it is.'

He handed me the smaller envelope: on it were the words: 'Lady Strathmore – for her eyes only.' It was John's writing.

I swallowed and my eyes burned but no tears came. I straightened my back.

'Thank-you, Walker.'

I thought idly how strange it was that we should address each other so formally at this moment: we were two old friends set upon a public stage. 'Thank-you. You may leave me now. I shall be quite fine. Please ask that I am not disturbed.'

Bless him, George did not hesitate. He gave my hand one final squeeze, and then he left, closing the door softly behind him. I have no doubt that he stood sentinel the whole time I was reading, for he was there when I opened the door some time later and stepped into the world as a widow.

The contents of John's letter I have kept to myself until now, but I want you to know the gist of it, dear reader, for it will give you an understanding of my tale. Far from making me cry, it made me angry, and that no doubt helped me through what was to come.

I have it here. I hope you are not expecting a tear-stained love-letter, for you will be sorely disappointed when I tell you that it opened thus: "As this is not intended for your perusal till I am dead, I hope you will pay a little more attention to it than you ever did to any thing I said to you while alive."

Are you surprised? I must admit, I was not, only sad that John had gone to his grave in bitterness. Having noted the tone, I braced myself to read on. In what followed, he took the opportunity to lecture me in all my faults: my willfulness, my sharp tongue, my contrary nature, my literary aspirations, my over-familiarity with the servants, my excessive generosity and my trusting nature. He bade me lay aside my "prejudices" against his family, to give up what he called my indulgences, by which he meant botany and writing for pleasure. There was not one word of fondness, no message for the children, no sense of peace. His tone throughout was bitter and his purpose to lecture me and try to extend control beyond the grave. Indeed, the missive ended with a barely-disguised resentment that my fortune would revert to me, and he ended with no softness, only self-justification: I must trust no-one, for "A dead man can have no interest to mislead, a living man may." Those words certainly came back to haunt me, as you will hear.

I hope by now you know me well enough to understand my reaction to this letter: contrary to its desired effect, it hardened my heart and liberated me from many of the feelings I might otherwise have suffered. My main concern was breaking the news to the children, though in truth it is no exaggeration to say that the little ones barely knew who he was: he had been absent for almost the whole of baby Thomas's two years on this earth.

I will be open and honest with you at the risk of your disapproval: when I stepped into widowhood, I felt liberated, and I make no apology for saying it.

Chapter 10

In the immediate aftermath of the Earl's death there was much to do, and I dealt with all of it with dignity and perspicacity. I tell you that with no little pride, for it was as though my adulthood, so long denied, came to me in an instant. The transition from infantilized wife to mistress of my own life brought forth the strength and independence I had begun to fear I would never be allowed to exercise.

It would take at least two days for the news to reach Thomas at Gibside, and his first concern would be to take it north to Glamis. My priority was the children, especially John, whose transition from six-year-old schoolboy to tenth Earl of Strathmore and Kinghorne threatened to take him from me. I acted quickly, and after dealing with the immediate business of contacting lawyers and ordering mourning clothes for the whole family and household, I sent for a carriage and went directly to Neasden to bring him home, brushing aside the protests of the hatchet-faced head-teacher and using my new imperious voice: 'Send for my son, Mr Raikes, and on no account must he know of his father's death until I tell him myself.'

In the carriage, John turned his serious pale face to me and said, 'Am I really going home for my birthday, Mama? It is a week away.'

All at once, tears sprang to my eyes. John sat immobile, his back straight, his grey eyes wide.

I do not know what I had hoped, perhaps that my first-born son would come to me for a cuddle, that we would comfort each other. But as he watched me with interest I thought I detected in his expressionless face something of his uncle Thomas's disdain. All at once, I wanted my son's respect more than anything. In truth, we barely knew each other, and he had so often heard me spoken to in a condescending tone that of course he would adopt it himself. He sought to emulate his father and uncle in all things. If I could gain his respect, I felt sure that warmth would follow.

I mastered my voice and stopped my tears. 'John, I have some very sad news for you.'

He blinked once and then spoke as though I had mentioned an interesting scientific fact: 'It's Papa, isn't it?'

'Yes, it is.'

'He's dead, isn't he?'

'Yes, John, I'm afraid he is. He died in his bed on board ship before they reached Lisbon.'

Still in a dispassionate tone, he asked, 'Would it have been painful? Dying, I mean?'

'No, no, I'm sure he just went to sleep.'

'I'm sure he did not, mother. I rather think it would be painful, to cough blood.'

Startled, I said, 'You knew he coughed blood?'

'Yes, he told me. He and Uncle Thomas, before Christmas. We had a meeting.'

I almost smiled, to think of those two overbearing aristocrats sitting formally at a table and speaking to a six-year-old boy as if he were already a man.

But I must not smile. 'Oh? I was not aware that you had had a meeting, John. What else did they tell you?'

'That Papa was likely to die, and that when he did, I would become Earl Strathmore and Kinghorne. I am the tenth, you know.'

'Yes, John, I know.'

'We are descended from Sir John Lyon, the first Thane of Glamis, in the fourteenth century. Our ancestors came with William the Conqueror, who came from Normandy. I would like to go to Normandy one day.'

'And so you shall. I shall take you.'

'Oh no, Mama, I'm sorry. Uncle Thomas is going to take me.'

'Oh, is he?'

I must have looked crestfallen, and I turned my head to the window. I was conscious of him watching me thoughtfully, and then he said in a gentle voice, sounding for the first time like a child: 'But I shall ask Uncle Thomas whether you can come too.'

I kept my head averted so that he did not see the flash in my eyes. When I turned back to him, my voice was meek and compliant. 'That would be very kind. Thank-you, John.'

I had intended to keep the puppy secret to provide a distraction once the news was broken to all the children, but when we got back to Grosvenor Square, he could be heard barking down in the kitchens. We were standing in the hall, being divested of our cloaks, and I saw John cock his head to one side to listen. He looked up at me, and read my face in an instant. Then he was gone. George Walker told me later that he was so enraptured by the puppy that he insisted on sitting on the floor with it while they ate their lunch.

I broke the news to the other children over tea and biscuits in the nursery, and I was again surprised by their equanimity, though the girls did come over from the window-seat to sit on either side of me and lean in silently. I put my arms around their shoulders and squeezed them to me. Maria reached up to whisper and I felt her sweet hot breath on my cheek.

'I knew, Mama, when that letter came this morning. I told Anna. We cried. But don't worry, we are fine now.'

I kissed her softly on the temple. But she hadn't finished yet, and she reached up to whisper again: 'Mama? If Papa had sent a puppy for my birthday too, would it be already here?'

In answer, I gave her one of our secret smiles and kissed her cheek.

George was sitting on a rug with his adored nanny. I can see him now, just four years old, his cheeks chubby and rosy, his clear grey eyes so like my father's, his normally smiley face solemn. Thomas, just starting to walk, was pulling himself to his feet and staring intently at a plate of biscuits on the rug. There was only one chocolate one left. George realized just in time, and his hand shot out like a lizard's tongue, grabbed the biscuit and shoved it into his mouth whole. It bulged out of his cheeks and it was so comical watching him trying to regain an appropriately solemn expression that we all burst out laughing, except of course Thomas, who set up a wail that could have shattered glass.

The lawyers came the following day and confirmed that all was as I had hoped: my father's properties – Gibside, Streatlam, the mines, farms and other lands reverted to me: it was enshrined in law. The warm glow those words engendered spread from my chest and up my neck until my face felt heated and I had to ask for a glass of water. The lawyers and their clerks were most solicitous: Lady Strathmore was clearly overwhelmed. Should they leave until I felt well enough to carry on?

'No, no, gentlemen, thank-you. I shall be fine. Pray continue. Could you just confirm my understanding of what you have said so far? I will keep the allowance which was granted to me in the marriage settlement, and now, in addition, the incomes from the mines and other properties will come directly to me?'

'Yes, my Lady, this should give you an income of approximately £18,000 per year.' He kept his face impassive, but we both knew that there were few incomes in the country that were quite so considerable.

'And what of the capital?'

'You should know, Lady Strathmore, that the capital is considerably depleted but of course still substantial. Would you like me to outline the major items of expenditure or did Lord Strathmore keep you apprised?'

'Perhaps we should leave that for now. I believe the capital is held in trust until my son comes of age?'

'Yes, until the tenth earl reaches his majority, the capital will be held in trust, the trustees being your Ladyship, his uncle Thomas Lyon and two other gentlemen from Scotland.'

It was as I suspected: I had had no hopes of recovering my father's fortune, but given my annual income, I had no need of it, and although I knew my relationship with Thomas Lyon was not about to get any better, I knew him to be honest and to have the best interests of the children at heart.

Poor Thomas: I like to think that although I loathed him, I did spare a thought for his distress. It must have been a dreadful time for him. He had lost his adored brother, whose life had been so closely intertwined with his own. And on top of that, he would have to beat an ignominious retreat from Gibside before I returned to take possession. Although I could find it in my heart to let him leave in his own good time, I was determined to send very clear signals that I would no longer be an adjunct to the Lyon family. I was an independent widow and had no need of his permission to do anything, ever again.

In the first flush of excitement, I confess I did have possessive thoughts about the children, but soon realized that any rebelliousness on my part was doomed to failure and would only cause pain and awkwardness for them. They were fond of their

Scottish aunts and even their uncle. If I set myself up in opposition, I would gain nothing and the children would suffer.

As I sat alone at dinner that night, surveying the silver salvers and the porcelain decorated with the Strathmore heraldry, it suddenly came to me how I would send my signal. The porcelain was packed the very next day: it was soon on its way north with several of the Scottish members of staff whose hearts lay at Glamis. I gave them no opportunity to protest, for I knew that although they would profess their loyalty to me, I would never be able to trust them.

I wrote a message and asked George Walker to read it to them, "her Ladyship being incapacitated by grief." In it, I thanked them for their service to the late earl, and expressed the understanding that "now he is gone, you will want to return to Scotland. Certain household items belonging to the Strathmore family will accompany you on your journey."

I often wonder what Thomas thought when the procession arrived, but by then he had far greater worries, for he had discovered the extent of his brother's debts. Soon after John's remains were interred at Glamis, I heard through my lawyers that all renovation work had been halted. On the same day, with a deep sense of satisfaction, I signed an order for work to re-start on my father's chapel, and I wept for relief: it seemed such an obvious and significant signal to send to Gibside ahead of my arrival that I could barely wait.

I was at Gibside in July when I read about the American Declaration of Independence having been signed on the 4th, and you can imagine with what a frisson I read the words: "Life, Liberty and the Pursuit of Happiness."

I find it hard to convey to you what happiness I experienced that year, what a dizzying round of emotions I experienced. I mourned, of course I did, and I even felt pity for the Lyon family, forced to hold an auction to raise funds to pay John's debts. I felt, but did not show my anger when Thomas brought his lawyers to seize items from Gibside and Streatlam which had been bought by John and could therefore be claimed as his assets. Indignant messages came flying from the Streatlam stud and from tenant farmers: racehorses and livestock were being taken away to be sold. When I heard that the Lyon contingent were coming for certain pieces of furniture and the contents of John's wine-cellar, I simply left strict instructions with my agent, Thomas Colpitts, and departed for London. My lawyers would be present: I would not risk a scene.

In London, I was keen to establish myself as a serious botanist, and my academic salons quickly became known. Botany being such a popular pursuit, and ladies being excluded from the Royal Society, I was excited to provide a meeting-place for those who shared my interest. The eminent scientists whom I had previously had to admire from a distance soon became my friends.

At one such meeting, I was approached by Dr Solander himself.

I took my leave of the person I had been speaking to and turned to him.

'Lady Strathmore.'

'Eleanor, please.'

'Then you should call me Daniel. This was an exciting lecture, wasn't it? The Cape is ripe for exploration. Virgin territory for the botanist.'

I glanced at him, understanding his hint immediately. The idea had already occurred to me and I had been quietly watching for an opportunity to make my commitment clear to the Royal Academy.

'Yes, I thought the same. Do you know of any forthcoming expeditions?'

'There are plenty of ships trading with the Cape, any one of which would be happy to carry natural historians.'

'And are there any botanists of your acquaintance who would relish such an expedition?' I spoke with heavy irony, fully expecting him to jump at the suggestion, but he surprised me by stroking his beard thoughtfully.

'None that immediately spring to mind.'

'Wouldn't you consider going yourself? For the right terms?'

'Oh no, thank-you! My adventuring days are done, and now my energies are fully utilized at the British Museum. I love my work there. We are creating a collection that will be the envy of other European nations: a lasting legacy.'

'Oh, then perhaps you could make discreet enquiries on my behalf?'

'I will. I am sure there are many young naturalists who would jump at the chance. In fact one comes to mind already.'

'His name?'

'Forgive me, I would rather make some enquiries about his character before I recommend him to you.'

'Please tell me who it is? Perhaps I know him.'

'Perhaps you do. He's from Melrose, which I understand is not far from your late husband's Glamis Castle.'

'Really? A trained horticulturalist?'

'Yes, and a gifted artist. A delightful, earnest young man, just back from serving in India. His name is William Paterson.'

'Oh, do bring him to meet me.'

'As I said, I will make discreet enquiries. There might be another candidate.'

'No, I feel it in my water. This William Paterson is the man for me.'

And indeed he was. Poor William. For him, I was a blessing that turned into a curse. Young Paterson became a casualty of what happened to me, but I remember him now as he was then: such a bright-eyed, serious chap, his pale Scottish skin burnished by the Indian sun, hair like thistle-down. He barely seemed old enough to have travelled the world and made a name for himself already, and in the years that followed, I always felt a motherly concern for his resilience. But I am getting ahead of myself.

Dr Solander had moved the conversation on: 'I remember you once said you would like to purchase a property in the vicinity of Chelsea?'

'Yes, I would love to have my own greenhouses here, where so many exciting developments are happening.'

'You might be interested to hear of a house which may well be ideal.'

Stanley House was not far from Chelsea Physic Garden, and as I was shown around its grounds for the first time, I breathed in the moist warm air from the river. I had asked for the head gardener to accompany us, and the more we saw, the more my enthusiasm threatened to burst though the veneer of *haute monde* which I was trying to maintain. The gardener's face broke into a warm and relieved smile when I finally gave in to my impulse to gush with excitement.

'This is marvelous! The microclimate here is ideal. I intend to grow non-native plants, perhaps even an olive tree like the one at Chelsea. In this area, I envisage creating a variegated terrain: we'll need some flint and fused bricks. Perhaps it will be possible to buy some of the Icelandic lava that Joseph Banks brought to England. Oh, I have such plans!'

Such plans...

Chapter 11

I place before you a man, tall and commanding, with broad shoulders and a piercing gaze. A Roman emperor in profile. A man whose erect bearing, stillness and confidence causes everyone to look and to listen, to believe his words, to care for his approval. All heads turn when he walks into a room: men as well as women find he draws their gaze, despite their best efforts to resist.

Imagine, if you will, such a man dressed in military finery: scarlet coat, white breeches and a cold determination like frost on a horse's flank. Now place him in a room amongst fops and simperers, conversationalists and wits. Hangers-on.

The furniture is plush, the wall-hangings opulent, the carpets deep. In the shadows, footmen and maidservants watch and keep their counsel. The room is a cacophony of voices: bass and baritone notes of heat and power, tenors expressive and various, and above them, the staccato sopranos shrill, their laughter ascending scales, their fans fluttering: an aviary of light and feathered females in a cage they cannot see.

Centre stage, the sun around which all planets rotate, is a young woman, small of stature, ample of bosom, innocent of nature. Look, she is aglow with happiness! Her eyes are bright with laughter, her cheeks flushed with rude health. She is from the north, you know: they breed them outdoors, even the gentry. See those ruddy cheeks, those strong teeth: milk-fed, fine breeding stock. She has five children already, does she not, our merry widow? And such a fortune!

Ah yes, the fortune. She is under no illusions, this young woman. She knows her power, and the taste of it is fresh and thrilling on her pink lips. I summon it now, all these years later, when so much has happened in the intervening years, and the zest for freedom is as intoxicating to me now as it was then. For she is me, of course, in that brief golden time when I was master of my own ship. I was to be wrenched from the helm and thrown overboard, did I but know it, and it all began with the coming of that fine Irish soldier.

Chapter 12

Such happiness I tasted in that golden year: I was blossoming and busy, my children were happy and healthy, my estates were in safe hands, and I was free to follow my interests, spend time with whomsoever I choose. This, at last, was liberty.

It was all an illusion. In reality, a net was closing on me, though I had no awareness, none whatsoever.

Do you ever think that men abhor a free woman? It is beyond their comprehension. How can it be so? She must be captured and tamed: she must learn her place. Or perhaps that is unkind, for we all know good men: men who do not fear us, who do not resent their need for us. Good men, strong men, kind men, honest men. Men like Gabriel, my lodestar.

Captain Andrew Robinson Stoney. Not a captain, as he asserted, but a half-pay lieutenant. He was dressed as a soldier and he took me prisoner by stealth. It was all planned, and now that I look back, after all these years, I find that I can even summon a degree of horrified admiration for the means by which he achieved his purpose.

He came to London with the express intention of snaring himself an heiress far richer than the first, and he knew whom he wanted.

He began by observing me, long before I had noticed him. I was to learn later that his first sighting had been at the theatre: of all things, it was the premiere of The Bankrupt by Samuel Foote at the Haymarket. The reason he knew that I would be there was that he had befriended one of my coach-drivers. He always had a way of charming, of presenting himself to people in the way most calculated to draw them into conversation and gain their confidence. I have watched him do it, many times. James had been in the military and so his trust was easily won. Idle chatter, this and that, plans revealed. Bingo!

He boasted to me later, when he had me in his power, of how cleverly he did it. He began by learning my territory, the theatres I favoured, the assembly rooms I frequented, where I sat, which card game I preferred, the routes I took between them. And he watched and followed, blending into the background.

Then, by not drawing attention to himself - though how that must have pained him! – he was able to observe who had my trust, who made me laugh, who whispered in my ear. Once he had identified my coterie, he isolated them, one by one, like a lion hunting antelope, snaking along the ground, blending into the scenery, and all the while, watching, watching...

The first time I noticed him was in the foyer of the Drury Lane Theatre after a performance. He had his back to me: I saw only a tall, broad-shouldered figure in a red military jacket who was partially obscuring Mrs Parish's sister, Eliza Planta: she was smiling and laughing up at him, unaccustomed animation in her dark eyes.

From my closest friends he learnt my that I loved poetry, gardens, the north, that I longed to travel to Italy, that the Strathmores treated me badly, that my husband had shared none of my interests, that I had a beau named George Gray but that my friends felt that he was not right for me, having a preference as I did for taller, more imposing men. He learnt that I favoured cats over dogs, that my bedroom at Grosvenor Square was decorated in shades of green to remind me of Gibside, that I grew my own vegetables in London and loved to be muddy, and fatally, that my favourite poet was John Donne.

This last pains me. I had once confided in Eliza Planta that of all the poets I knew, John Donne was the one who would have had no problem at all in seducing me. I love his mischief, his boldness, his open love of women, his teasing, his cleverness, his mixture of the sacred and profane. What other poet could make of a flea-bite something erotic? I fell in love with John Donne at fifteen, tired of polite conversation from potential suitors dressed in lace and velvet, their honey words attempting to disguise their real intentions. When I read The Flea, I recognised a powerful seduction technique – boldness expressed through humour. Indulge me: I will tell it to you, for it makes me laugh still:

> Mark but this flea, and mark in this
> How little that which thou deny'st me is;
> Me it suck'd first, and now sucks thee,

And in this flea our two bloods mingled be;
Confess it: this cannot be said
A sin, or shame, or loss of maidenhead,
Yet this enjoys before it woo,
And pamper'd swells with one blood made of two,
And this, alas, is more than we would do.

How could a girl resist?

And so, armed with this knowledge and ready to emerge from the long grass, the lion waited for his moment. And when he finally approached me, the first words he spoke were Donne's.

It was in the interval of a performance. I was, as usual, surrounded by friends and fluttering fans, for it was a warm night in late summer. George Gray was by my side, which made it all the more remarkable when I noticed that I was being stared at. At first, I thought I was imagining it, and that the tall, striking fellow with the military bearing who was standing so still in the corner of the room must be looking at someone else. I was soon engaged in conversation and thought no more about it, but when the tide parted again, there he was, in the same position, still looking intently at me. I turned away immediately and spoke to George, something inconsequential, I know not what, but I was unnerved and wanted to make it clear to my observer that I was accompanied.

Unfortunately, when the time came to mount the stairs to our box, we had to pass close by this audacious and somewhat chilling presence. George had linked my right arm as he always did, and so it was impossible for me to avoid passing close by as we waited to mount the staircase. I know now that it was all planned and he had chosen his position with care. I deliberately raised my fan to the side of my face so that it blocked his view, but astonishingly, he leaned down and whispered these words through the lace of the fan:

"Twice or thrice had I loved thee,
Before I knew thy face or name;
So in a voice, so in a shapeless flame
Angels affect us oft, and worshipp'd be."

I experienced a frisson of such potency that for a moment I was quite unable to mount the next step, and George looked at me, concerned for my well-being when I failed to respond to his movement.

'Are you quite well, my dear?'

'Yes, yes, just a moment of dizziness.'

All through the first half of the play, my mind was quite elsewhere. When the lights came up, the throngs of heads in the seats opposite and below us were universally turned to the side to speak to companions, or downward to adjust dress as people got to their feet, but one face in all that sea was turned upwards, regarding me still and I was drawn as though to magnetic north.

When our eyes met, he inclined his head slightly and then disappeared into the crowd. I looked for him after the performance and as the crowds poured onto the street to find their waiting carriages, but there was no sign, and of course that had the effect of leaving me wanting more, as he knew it would.

The next time I saw him, it was at a meeting of a botanical society to which I belonged. I had certainly never seen him there before, but saw nothing sinister in his presence as he was with Captain Magra, who brought him over to be formally introduced. Always rather obsequious, Captain Magra bowed low before saying, 'Countess Strathmore, may I present Captain Andrew Robinson Stoney.' Fortunately, the talk was about to begin, and after acknowledging the introduction with a nod, I took my seat in the front row, which was reserved for wealthy patrons, and had no trouble in concentrating on the speaker's voice, for it was a riveting account of a plant-seeking expedition to the Galapagos. I was at this time involved in the preparations for Paterson's departure for South Africa, and knew he was in the audience: neither of us was to know that our nemesis was present.

At that time, there was much to occupy me – the purchase of Stanley House had been completed and the plans for hothouses and greenhouses took up much of my time. I had always had irregular monthlies, but by early August I could no longer ignore the fact that I had not bled since the end of June. I hope you don't find it indelicate of me to say this, but how I wish it were possible for a man and woman to make love without the possibility of pregnancy. There are so many unpleasant procedures attached to the prevention of unwanted babies, and none of them is foolproof. Like many women, I had to resort to asking someone I trusted completely to procure me a potion to bring on my bleeding; Eliza had by then become my closest friend, so it was to her that I turned.

I was to live to regret ever confiding in her, but I had no choice. I had no wish nor any need to marry again, but our society is so cruel to children born out of wedlock that if I had allowed the pregnancy to continue, I would have been obliged to marry George for the child's sake. I could not bring myself to drink that foul black tar again. There would have to be a pre-nuptial contract, but George with his gentle warmth might make a good ally against the Strathmores, and my position in the eyes of society would be stronger as a married woman than as that unaccountable thing, a wealthy, independent young widow.

As summer faded beautifully into autumn, my life continued busy and serene. Stoney had become a frequent participant in my salons and was often to be seen at the theatre and in the parks I frequented, but I was always accompanied and he did not approach me again. I purposefully avoided him: I was, however, often aware of his eyes on me. How I felt about that, I cannot say.

Yes I can: I am being completely honest with you. Every woman enjoys being admired. There was no harm in it, or so I thought.

In late September, Eliza came to me in tears. She was pregnant, and would not tell me the name of the father. She would only tell me that he was in love with another woman and had refused to marry her. I was, I confess, surprised at Eliza, who I had always thought had aspirations: she and her siblings were born in Italy, and though I knew nothing of their status, they were all well-educated and charming people. I offered to give the father, whoever he was, a position in my household if he would "make an honest woman of her" (how I loathe that expression!) but she told me that there was no hope: he had his heart set on another.

'Well, if you are determined to go ahead with the pregnancy, and you wish to be married, I have an idea. I know of a clergyman who is looking for a wife. His name is Reverend Stephens. He approached me quite recently. He said that he had long admired my father when he was an MP, and if ever I should require a family chaplain to look after the spiritual welfare of the children, it would be an honour to serve me. He seemed a very personable gentleman, and if you would like to meet him, I shall arrange it.'

And so it came to pass that Eliza became Mrs Stephens and the two of them moved into Grosvenor Square. I had let a pair of vipers into my nest.

One morning in October, the post brought a letter with a Durham postmark written in an unfamiliar hand. At first I assumed it was from Gibside or Streatlam, and was confounded when I began to read that it was apparently from a woman spurned by Andrew Robinson Stoney. Without any further preamble, she told me that Captain Stoney was besotted with me and begged me to reject him so that she might regain his heart. But more astonishingly, and much more worryingly, she spoke of my lover, George Gray.

I struggled at first to understand what she was saying, but it soon became apparent that she was advising me how much happier I would be with George because he was the Strathmores' man. Her exact words were: 'Cultivate Mr Gray's affections, because your late lord's friends and relations will accept him as your husband, but not Captain Stoney.' But as far as I knew, George had no connection whatsoever with the Strathmores.

I stared at the words for a long time, my mind racing. Was it possible? George, to whom I had confessed all my true feelings about the Lyon family? Until him, I had always been faithful to John, always, though his heart was never mine, though I felt neglected, exploited and unloved, as powerless as one of the children. I had had plenty of opportunity, heaven knows, for my husband had often been away, and during his illness he had withdrawn from me more and more, rejecting my concerns, spending all his time in Bath and never wanting me with him.

Meanwhile, the more absent he had become, the more present George had been. He had inveigled himself into my arms by his honey words. Had he even then been in the employ of the Strathmores? Perhaps recruited to keep watch over me? Was it that they knew that poor John was doomed and that if they were to maintain their power over me, they would need a proxy, for they knew full well by then that I would never accept any member of their

110

family to live with me in London, whilst Thomas squatted at Gibside like a malignant toad?

Was it really possible that George was their agent? Our relationship was warm, affectionate, easy-going. He shared my interests and was demonstrative and biddable. I really had no need of commitment and unless I was unfortunate enough to become pregnant again, I would not consider marrying. By the time the letter came from this unknown woman, I had in truth become reconciled to the idea that I might one day find it necessary to marry George for the sake of an unplanned child.

(I did not yet know it, but the seed was already sown: whatever happens in a woman's womb is a secret known only to nature, but the spark that was to become baby Mary had already occurred.)

This letter had rocked my complacency completely: if George was indeed in the pockets of the Strathmores, I would be consigning myself back into a prison of their designing. They would have me back where they wanted me and my hopes of evicting them from my life would be lost forever.

When George next called on me, he noticed immediately that I had cooled towards him, but he always was afraid of conflict, so as soon as he detected my mood, he made to go.

Irritated further, I snapped at him: 'Where are you going?'

'I … why, I was on my way to my club for lunch and I thought to call in to see you, but it is clearly not a good time.'

'No, George, it is not a good time. I'm not sure it ever will be again.'

His gentle face was stricken: 'Dearest, is something amiss?'

'Why, should it be?'

His mouth opened but then he stopped himself and said sadly, 'I'll take my leave.'

Such a defeated attitude had opposing effects on me: half irritated and half apologetic, for I could not believe it of him, I said nothing but stared at him intently, challenging him to meet my gaze.

This he did, and I detected no sign of guilt in his warm brown eyes. I have learnt that when one of the children wishes to deny a wrongdoing, they will habitually look down and to the left: it is something many mothers recognise. So I decided to come out with it: 'George, do you know any Scots?'

111

'The language, dear?'

'No, George. People from Scotland.'

'Why no,' he put his hand to his chin in some comically unconscious approximation of a thinker, 'no, I don't believe I do. Why do you ask?'

'You don't, for example, know anyone from Glamis?'

His eyes widened, and his bafflement was clearly so complete and so open that I believed him, though perhaps not entirely.

By November, I knew I was pregnant, and so the die was cast. In early December, accompanied by trusty George Walker, I took a hackney cab to my lawyers' offices in Holborn. I did not want them coming to the house as I wanted no tittle-tattle, and I could not entirely trust my coachmen, but travelling with devoted Walker felt almost as though my father was with me.

There was still a possibility I would not need to marry George, but it was best to be pragmatic: a married woman has no existence in law, and I had absolutely no intention of handing my inheritance and income over to anyone ever again. The baby might not come to full term, but if it did, I would ensure that we were married by then and on a long tour abroad, so that her date of birth would be obscured. I would have no child of mine bearing the stigma of illegitimacy, much as I abhor society's attitude to babies conceived out of wedlock.

Together, the lawyers and I drafted a pre-nuptial to protect my assets and incomes from any future husband. George Walker swore on oath to keep it secret, though I trusted him so completely I felt there was no need. Wisely, the lawyers overruled my objection and George laid his hand on a Bible.

On the way home, we passed Fleet Street, where many of the newspapers are printed, and saw the usual hubbub in front of the windows: people pointing and laughing and sharing the latest salacious gossip. George and I shook our heads over the modern preoccupation with the private lives of prominent figures, and then, without a trace of irony, went on to share some gossip of our own. We were laughing when we arrived back at Grosvenor Square and didn't at first detect the averted faces of the footmen or the subdued atmosphere as we were greeted in the hall. It was Mrs Parish who handed me the newspaper, and her face was grave.

It was a copy of that day's Morning Post, folded to the letters page. I looked up at her face, and she indicated with a movement of her head that I should go into the morning room to read it in private.

The letter was signed 'A Conscience-Stinger' and my first thought was to despise the writer for his or her cowardice. I almost knew what I would read before I looked, and yes, there it all was: I was immoral, I kept an immoral house, I insulted the memory of my esteemed husband, I had taken a lover whilst he was fighting for his life, my children were suffering by association with me. I was destined for the place where all sinners were punished for all eternity.

Suffering a tumult of emotion, my feelings came in quick succession: the mention of my children concerned me most, for they would surely hear of this, especially little John in a boys' school. My personal embarrassment and indignation, together with the acceptance that I would have to marry George Gray was swiftly followed by the conviction that this letter emanated from the Strathmore camp. In the face of such a message of venom, my heart quailed. But I was my father's daughter and I would not show the world I was afraid.

I emerged from the morning room with a straight back and a direct gaze. Mrs Parish and her sister Eliza, standing with their heads together in the hallway, jumped when I appeared and looked at me with fearful and excited eyes.

I summoned a complacency I did not really feel and smiled and waved the paper carelessly, 'Don't worry ladies, a flash in the pan. This is merely tomorrow's firelighter.'

Of course, the correspondence did not end with that one letter: London loves a scandal, and the furore emboldened the anonymous accuser to go further in his accusations. In one, I was scheming Lady Macbeth, then faithless Gertrude, caring nothing for the memory of her husband or for the torment of her son.

At last, almost a week after the scurrilous articles had started to appear, someone wrote a letter in my defence; they signed themselves 'Monitus' - a warning voice - the implication being that this was only a first salvo in what would become a real fight.

My fiancé was there when I read it, and I looked up at him in surprise and delight.

'Why George! Thank-you! It is rather flowery, but I do appreciate this. Now perhaps they will move on to some other scandal.'

He looked up from his book, preoccupied with its content as he always was. George's powers of concentration amazed and irritated me in equal measure. His face told me what I think I already knew in my heart

'Mmm? Sorry, my dear, what was it you said?'

I took a deep breath. 'A letter in my defence is published in today's Morning Post. Did you write it?'

'Why no, dear. But I'm glad to hear it.' And he went back to his book.

At the next lecture of the Botanic Society, I attended alone and took my usual place in the front row. I was mortified when an attendant was sent over to ask me to move as the place was apparently reserved for a particular gentleman. Feeling quite dumbfounded but unwilling to make a scene, I rose obediently and looked towards the seats he had indicated as an alternative, where several wives were already sitting. If they had not all had their eyes on me, I think I would have refused to move, but the gaze of groups of women has always intimidated me, and my courage failed: dignity was all I wished to retain.

To my horror, as I took my place, the women on either side of me rose as one and relocated to seats further away. My blush burned all the way through the lecture and I barely heard a word of it.

When the lecture ended, I was about to hastily make my departure when the imposing figure of Captain Stoney appeared before me, made a slight bow and extended his arm. I took it gratefully and left the room in silence.

As he handed me into my carriage, he broke the silence: 'I have read the scurrilous correspondence in the Morning Post and am considering calling out the editor in a duel.'

'No, really, it will die away.'

'It is not to be endured, Eleanor. I must defend your honour.'

'No, really. And it is surely not your place...'

His eyes twinkled with what I now know to be the scent of victory. 'And whose place is it, if not mine? I do not see your lapdog leaping to defend you.'

114

I looked away, mortified: I had had the same thoughts myself. George seemed remarkably unaffected by the scandal. In fact I thought once I had detected a smile and my suspicion of his allegiances was renewed.

More urgently now, he clasped my hand with a firm grip and leaned into the carriage: the smell of leather and cigar smoke made his maleness suddenly overwhelming, and I backed away involuntarily.

'You must know that I love you. I will always love you. I know you cannot be mine, but I will defend your honour to the last drop of my blood.'

I did not know how to respond: I hardly knew what I felt, so shaken was my self-confidence. This man, striking though he was, barely knew me. I would not be intimidated into gratitude for his apparent devotion. I could trust no-one. How I longed, in that moment, for the ground to swallow me up. For safety and anonymity. For home. To my horror, the threat of tears burned my eyes.

No. Not tears. Not now, with him looming into my carriage.

Thankfully, I managed to muster some humour with which to fend him off, and I said: 'You may be my parfait gentile knight. You must write me courtly sonnets. I shall be your Dark Lady.'

He studied me, a serious (and I now perceive, calculating) look upon his face. 'No, Eleanor. That is not my style. You will be hearing from me.'

As the carriage pulled away, I studied my own reactions: something in me was deeply stirred by this masterful manner, though I cautioned myself against it.

When a few days later I departed alone for Hertfordshire to see my mother, it was with great relief and as we passed through the outer reaches of London and into the countryside, I began to relax and consider my situation from a distance.

The baby was due in August, and thanks to the fashions of the day, I could disguise my pregnancy for at least four more months. We could marry in February and leave for an extended honeymoon, a Grand Tour of Europe, during which our child would be born. I began to get excited. At last I would be able to visit all the places I had yearned to see. My Italian is excellent: the idea of giving birth in Rome or Florence held no fears, in fact just the opposite: I saw myself basking in the golden light of a courtyard of a rented palazzo with yellow stucco walls and frescos by Michaelangelo. Little George and Thomas would blossom in the unaccustomed warmth, and I would breastfeed my baby in the shade of a pergola, bathed in the scent of jasmine and bougainvillea. This time, I would do everything right. I would not have a wet-nurse, I would bond with this child. No disapproving nannies to come between us, just a person of my choosing who would help me but always know that I was the mother and she must defer to me. And when we came home, the child's siblings would adore her and we would all live at Gibside; the boys would go to school in Newcastle and live at home and I would perhaps find a school that could provide the education I wanted for my girls. The thought of this scenario, with all my children and my people about me, warmed those winter days.

My recent conversation with Lady Elizabeth Montague had helped enormously. I had wanted reassurance that, with the pre-nuptial contract and sweet biddable George Gray by my side, I could live the life I wanted. We had talked of marriage, of how freedom could be achieved within it: her own marriage was a perfect example, but also that of my hero, Margaret Cavendish, the Duchess of Newcastle. I too would explore philosophy and ideas as well as the natural sciences: I would write more of my plays and poems as well as learned essays. I would be entirely fulfilled and I would make my family proud. Yes, even the Lyon family.

Given the confidence that she imparted to me, I found the maturity to swallow my pride, put my defiance behind me and embark upon a different course with the Strathmores. I had to accept that because of my children, my life would forever be entwined with the Thanes of Glamis. It was their birthright, and my first-born son and daughter were particularly close to the Lyon family. If we could achieve a more amicable relationship, I felt that I could mend fences.

By the time I arrived at St Paul's Walden, I had achieved a vision of a wonderful future and I remember the pleasure with which my mother remarked upon the transformation in me.

But of course it was not to be.

Chapter 13

I returned to London in early January, and George came to dinner that evening. He was most effusive in his greetings, and in his arms I felt safe. I had decided to put aside my mistrust as well as my all-too-short period of restless freedom.

When we settled down to supper alone, I began to put my plan into action.

'I have been thinking.'

'Thinking about what, dearest?'

'Everything really, but most especially about my relationship with John's family.'

I watched for his reaction, but he went on eating then looked up with what seemed to me genuine curiosity: 'And what were your conclusions?'

'I feel I should move on now, try to forge a new relationship. It is almost a year since John's death. It will soon be springtime and everything will be renewed. I think, for the children's sake, I should seek to reconcile the Bowes and the Lyons.'

'That seems to me an eminently fine idea. How will you go about it?'

'Well, there are things to forgive on both sides, but I feel it would be wise to simply put them behind us.'

'Water under the bridge, that kind of thing.'

'Yes, quite. I thought I would write a letter suggesting exactly that.'

'And what would you wish to see happen?'

'Well, I need to think it all through and I would appreciate your suggestions.' I had, in reality, decided exactly what I wanted: I had already drafted the letter, but I had learnt enough by that stage about how men like to be flattered, so I innocently solicited his help and tenderly let him believe he had thought of it all.

'Gladly, my darling. Whatever you would like me to do, I will do it.' Frustratingly, he went back to his food with a ruminative air, and I felt irritation stir in my jaw. Taking a deep breath, I exhaled silently whilst I decided how to proceed.

'I thought perhaps I would have a birthday party. And invite them.' This was so clearly an appalling idea that I awaited his response with interest.

Mildly, he carried on chewing, and after what seemed an age, swallowed and picked up his wine glass. 'Well, I think it a capital idea that you should have a birthday party, but as for inviting the Strathmores, I'm not so sure.'

When it became clear that he wasn't going to elaborate, I was driven to ask why, though he and I both knew the answer.

'Well, I find it hard to imagine Thomas in particular at any kind of celebratory gathering. I fear his presence would cast a kind of dampener on proceedings, don't you?'

As I smiled, I felt real warmth towards George and his mild-mannered steadiness.

Encouraged, he dared to go on: 'And as for his mother…it would be rather like having a kind of black gargoyle at the table… or a giant crow… or a witch!' Chuckling to himself, he took another swig of wine.

I felt quietly satisfied by his complicity – this was the first time he had ever actually spoken a word of criticism of the Strathmores, having previously been content to pat my hand while I raged about them.

'Yes, perhaps you're right. A letter then. So what shall I say?'

'Well, of course what you really want is independence and freedom from interference.'

This startled me in its directness: I had intended cloaking my deepest desires in concern for the welfare of the children.

'Yes, yes I do.' I gathered my thoughts: 'Of course, if we as a family were to base ourselves entirely at Gibside, we could provide a wonderful childhood for them. And we would be so much closer to Glamis, so the children could see their father's family often.'

'Yes indeed.'

'And you, George? What of you? How would you feel about living in the north-east?'

'For myself, I must confess I'm not sure. I fear the climate, of course, used as I am to the heat of the tropics! But really, my dear, it is whatever you want. Whatever makes you happy.'

118

He sat back, replete, and dabbed at his mouth with the corner of a napkin. 'Do you think you could live amicably with Thomas back in the house, running the estate and all that?'

This was a vision so repellent to me that I had trouble hiding my real feelings. I struggled to keep my voice level: 'I doubt Thomas would want that any more than I.'

'So how would you get him to leave?'

'I thought perhaps by signing over Streatlam to him.'

'Relinquishing all claim?'

'Yes. Like my father, I have no feeling for Streatlam. It suits Thomas, being isolated and grand.'

He looked up at me, a twinkle in his eye. 'Aha, I was rather intrigued as to whether all your animosity could truly have evaporated with the old year.'

'But what do you think, George, do you think that I would have a chance, that we would...of making a life at Gibside?'

'Truly, I don't know, Eleanor. Wouldn't you miss London?'

'No, I have had my fill I think. I might come down here once a year or so, but Newcastle has fine attractions of its own, and a strong intellectual life. I would like to become a leading light. The boys could go to the Royal Grammar School, and if I cannot find a suitable school for the girls, why I will buy one!'

I settled back, a satisfied smile on my face and in my mind. The wheels were in motion.

They came to a sudden halt only three days later.

It was Monday evening, 13th January and I had spent the evening with John and Maria: we had been making a play based on Ulysses. The cats were curled up on a rug by the fire and the children were fast asleep. I was suddenly sleepy, and had just decided to go to bed with my book when there was a knocking on the door.

When the footman came into the room, he was accompanied by a gentleman I had never seen before. Without waiting to be announced, he said, 'Forgive this intrusion, Lady Strathmore, but this is a matter of some urgency.'

My thoughts flew to my mother and younger children, whom I had thought safe at St Paul's Walden. A fire? I leapt to my feet, grasping his hands: 'Tell me! Is it my children?'

'No, no, madam, please keep calm. There is no threat to you or your family. No, I come from the bedside of a gentleman who is dying from wounds inflicted in a duel...' he looked round to where the footman still stood in the doorway, uncertain whether to leave. 'It was apparently fought in your honour. I am a surgeon, Lady Strathmore. My name is Jesse Foot. An hour ago, I was called to the Adelphi Tavern to attend to a person who had been involved in a duel.'

A sense of dread rose up in me. 'His name?'

'Stoney. Andrew Robinson Stoney. A soldier, by all accounts. He is mortally wounded in the chest. My colleague is with him. He is asking for you.'

I sat back down, dumb-founded. I had no idea whatsoever how I should react. I had not asked for this. But the poor man. To be so incensed by my mistreatment that he would give his life in my defence. There was no alternative. I must go to him.

I summoned the carriage and Eliza from her bed and we hastened to the Adelphi, whose dark corridors were lined with stricken faces illuminated by tapers.

When we were shown into the room, the candles flickered in the draught from the door. An elderly gentleman whom I recognised as Sir Caesar Hawkins, surgeon to King George, stood up from the side of the bed and came forward, his face grave.

He took my hand and looking sorrowfully into my eyes, he said, 'Lady Strathmore, my condolences.' Then he moved aside so that I could approach the bed.

Captain Stoney lay there in full dress uniform, his shiny boots hanging over the edge, so tall was he, like a shattered column or a toppled statue of a Roman general. Grasping Eliza's hand, I moved closer. The white face upon the pillow seemed drained of blood and his eyes were closed. His bloodied shirt lay open, and the dark hairs upon his chest were matted and smeared red. A sword lay beside him on the bed.

The surgeon shook his head, his eyes downcast and the two of them stood back and conferred in low voices. Dr Foot came forward and gently touched Stoney's shoulder, bending to speak to him: 'Captain Stoney, Lady Strathmore is here.'

His eyelids flickered and he stirred. The movement seemed to pain him, for he groaned and clutched his side, at which I let out an involuntary gasp. The thought that such a man should die for me was an agony: it constricted my chest and made it hard for me to breathe. Beside me, Eliza grasped my hand and whimpered, 'Oh mistress!'

I watched as his eyelids slowly opened, focusing first on the ceiling as though dragging back his soul from seeping out into the cold winter air. He blinked slowly, seeming to gather his scattered senses and emitted a low groan which was echoed by the creak of a floorboard.

My emotions were in complete turmoil: compassion for his suffering, shame that, however innocent, I had been the cause of it; horror at the blood and the violence that had caused it; fear at the consequences and beneath it all, a sense of the sands shifting under my feet. Suddenly I was staring at the bed down a dark tunnel and the sea was hissing in my ears. I toppled and nearly fell.

When I came to, Eliza was still holding me and the other doctor was pressing a cold compress to my forehead. The first thing I saw as I swam up out of the darkness was the face upon the pillow, eyes closed, mouth slightly open revealing the edges of white teeth.

I struggled to regain my composure. I had no idea what to say. The doctor spoke softly against my ear. 'Perhaps just hold his hand, Lady Strathmore. It will not be long.'

I looked at the large hand lying near me on the coverlet, the wonder of its construction, the strength implicit in the muscles, the life ebbing from the veins and I thought of Michaelangelo's David. The mystery of life and death came upon me then, and I lay my own hand on it to offer some comfort. Slowly, I felt it stir, and then it twisted and held mine loosely, dwarfed across the palm.

I looked back at his face and saw the glimmer of light under the closed lashes, then his eyes opened and he looked at me directly for a long moment.

Some movement of his mouth made me reach for the water glass and press it to his lips. The doctor gently lifted his head to allow him to drink and then softly laid his head back on the pillow. His eyes were closed again, but then I realized he was trying to speak. I inclined my head toward his and caught the words:

> "Before I sigh my last gasp, let me breathe,
> Great Love, some legacies…"

John Donne.   Now the tears came and I pressed my handkerchief to my mouth to stop myself from sobbing aloud.

He was struggling to speak again.

'I'm sorry, I cannot hear what you are saying.'

'My sword.'

'It is here. Do you want to hold it?' Some memory of Roman soldiers and honour made me say it. I thought he must want to die with the sword in his hand.

'No, please... please keep it. And always remember me.'

It felt the least I could do. 'I will. I will keep it with me always and I shall always remember you.' The emotion of the moment threatened to overwhelm me again and I went to grasp his hand more strongly. I was startled to find he had found the strength to reciprocate and my hand was in a firm grip.

'Eleanor.' He had never said my name before, and it felt too raw, too intimate.

'Yes, I am here.'

'I love you Eleanor. I did this for love of you.'

'I know. It was honourably done, but I so wish you had not.' And now I crumbled into open crying and my shoulders shook. 'I don't know what to say. I wish there was something I could do! I turned a beseeching tear-stained face to the two doctors who looked on, their expressions grave. 'Is there really no hope?' They shook their heads wordlessly, eyes downcast.

His voice came again, weaker now: 'There is something.'

'What? What can I do?' I spoke between my tears. And then I spoke the fatal word: 'Anything.'

The moment swelled: everyone seemed to be holding their breath; only my sobs broke the silence.

'Marry me.'

I was startled beyond words. 'Marry you? How can I marry you?'

'It is all I ask. And then I can die happy.'

The effort of speaking so much seemed to have exhausted him, and he lapsed into silence. For a brief moment, I thought that he was gone, and I watched the doctor take his pulse, my own breath held.

At length, the doctor spoke without looking up. 'He is sleeping. His pulse is very weak. We can only wait.'

122

The two doctors retired to the doorway, conferring again in low voices, and I turned with troubled eyes to Eliza. 'Oh, Eliza, I cannot bear this. We must go. I can do nothing here.' But she was watching me with steady eyes.

'It is a small thing he asks, Eleanor.'

I hissed at her, feeling like a small creature backed into a corner. 'A small thing? How can you say that? I cannot marry him!'

'He will die soon. If you deny him this, it will haunt you forever.'

'I cannot! How can I?' I was becoming slightly hysterical and I know my voice rose for the two doctors looked up.

Jesse Foot came to stand behind me and spoke softly. 'Lady Strathmore, if you are considering agreeing to this man's dying wish, we can arrange it discreetly.'

I looked into Eliza's eyes and she reached out to hold both my hands. 'Let him, Eleanor. It is the right thing to do.'

And so my fate was sealed. Eliza and I travelled home in silence, both staring ahead. I wish that I could say my mind was in turmoil, but I was strangely calm. Everything else seemed to have faded into the background and this one thing became the still centre of my mind. I have never knowingly taken drugs but I imagine that the numbness I felt was similar to the mind-altering sensations of laudanum.

Two days later, I went through the ceremony in a curious daze.

I have the strangest, vaguest recollections: standing at the altar with Eliza, watching the two doctors and two other men carry the stretcher and lay it on the ground beside me, the respectful silence, the droning voice of the priest, the warmth of Eliza's presence at my side, the passivity with which I watched my hand extended to the priest to receive a ring which I knew to be my own. When I recognised it and wondered how it came to be here, it was as though my brain would not engage with the mystery.

When he spoke his vows, the priest had to kneel beside him the hear them, so weak was the voice of the dying man.

It was a performance worthy of David Garrick.

Chapter 14

Eliza and I travelled back to Grosvenor Square in silence. I remember I had the sensation of watching the world go by as though through darkened glass. I thought idly of George Gray, who seemed to have completely evaporated. There was nothing of him in the house, and if it hadn't been for the child growing in my belly, it would have felt as though he had never existed.

The house was strangely silent and even George Walker, normally so warm and welcoming, avoided my eyes as he opened the door. Eliza went straight to her room and I was left alone in my sitting-room to stare out of the window and try to summon my thoughts.

When Walker brought tea, I begged him to sit and talk to me. 'Please tell me what everyone is saying, George. I feel so strange.'

It was a relief to see real concern in his crinkly eyes, but he was noncommittal. 'Strange times indeed, madam.'

'I feel quite bewildered by events. Hopefully things will return to normal now. I find it hard to believe that Captain Stoney has survived so long.'

'I agree. I felt certain he would expire that night.'

'You saw him? How?'

'I followed you. I was worried.'

I squeezed his hand, overcome. Neither of us spoke.

And then he surprised me again. 'Mr Gray saw him too. Shook his hand. Thanked him for defending your honour.'

'You astonish me, George. I have not seen Mr Gray since that night. What more was said?'

'I have no idea. I left them alone.'

I felt greatly reassured by this, and as I studied this new revelation, it felt like seeing a small light in a dark forest. I felt my strength begin to return. I could trust my two Georges. Of Eliza I was not so sure.

'So now, we can only wait.'

'Yes. Wait and hope.' He was saying the unsayable and I was grateful to him for that too. Stoney would die in the night, I felt sure. There had barely been a murmur from the stretcher and all the men present had stood as though attending a funeral. I would go to bed now so as to bring the release of the morning a little bit closer. But first there was something I must do.

'George, I trust you with my life.'

'Well, I should hope so, little lady. You know I like to think of you as the child I never had.'

I smiled but my face was serious. 'I have something very important that I must ask you to do for me. A document I would like you to look after for me. You know the one. The original is safely lodged at the Inns of Court, but I have need of a safe place for my copy. I need to keep it with me but not in an obvious place. Not in my desk. Where will you keep it, George?'

'In my trunk, Miss Eleanor. If you need it hidden, I can stitch it into the lining.'

'Yes, hidden. It needs to be hidden. And only you and I must know where it is. I cannot know what the future holds, but that document is my security. I have tried to protect myself and my...' I had not yet told anyone that I was expecting George Gray's child, and stopped myself now. 'When Stoney dies, as he surely must, I may or may not marry Mr Gray. The events of these last few days have been...But if I do marry again, that document is very important indeed. Remember that George, and promise me you will keep it safe, no matter what.'

And thank heavens he was true to his word.

When I awoke the following morning, I was instantly aware of a commotion in the street outside. Two fine carriages deposited two statuesque generals on the footpath, and they embraced warmly, their great booming voices rattling the window-panes. I watched in bewilderment as their attendants escorted them up the steps of my house and then their laughter was shaking the chandeliers in the hall.

There was some raucous conversation with whoever had let them in and then their voices came from beneath my bedroom floor: they had apparently been shown into the morning room.

A hesitant knock came on my door, and a maid with the face of a frightened rabbit told me that Generals Armstrong and Robinson were here to see me.

'Who are they?'

'They're great-uncles of Mr Stoney, ma'am.'

My blood chilled. Their demeanour made it quite clear that they were not bringing news of his demise; in fact, on the contrary, they seemed to be in a celebratory mood.

'Kindly tell them I am unwell and ask them to leave. Then come back and tell me what they say.'

She bobbed a curtsy and disappeared.

I lay still, my mind racing, and a cold chill was creeping through my bones.

The maid reappeared. 'Ma'am,' she said, her eyes wide. 'They say they are here to offer their congratulations.'

My face set. 'Why have they not left?'

'Ma'am, they say they are here for the wedding breakfast.'

'The wedding breakfast?' Now I was quite flummoxed.

'Yes, ma'am. We are preparing the table now. Things have been arriving since dawn.'

'Things? What things?'

'Food and wine. From Fortnum and Mason.'

It was with a sense of complete helplessness that I watched in horror from my bedroom window as four more men arrived and then the carriage bearing my new husband, who was carried over the threshold sitting upright on a chair and followed by the two doctors who seemed to have been in continuous attendance since the duel. I cannot describe my feelings: it's a cliché to say that something is like a bad dream, but that is exactly how it felt.

When I finally descended the staircase, dressed in a luminous cream gown, I could hear carousing from the dining room and when I entered, the fug of cigar smoke and the overwhelming smell of men en masse made me recoil. I stood in the doorway, my heart quivering in my chest. I had been determined to brave it out, queenly and serene, to take charge, to welcome my guests with what graciousness I could muster, but my spirit quailed. It was such an invasion, such a shock, that I could barely make my body obey me.

Conversation died away and all except my new husband rose to their feet in a scraping of chairs. A moment's reprieve, a heavy silence. This calmed me. I deliberately stayed motionless: no-one here could pretend that this was a conventional occasion.

Finally, when I was sure they had all registered the fact that the mistress of the house had entered the room, I acknowledged their courtesy with a gracious nod. There was creaking of leather and more grating of chairs as they sat down. I was aware that whilst some still watched me, others were smirking at each other.

Finally, Stoney spoke, and in a strong voice such as I had never heard from him: 'Gentlemen, may I present my wife, Mary Eleanor, the Countess of Strathmore!'

Stung, I replied with my chin up: 'Your health appears to be much improved this morning, Mr Bowes.'

While the others erupted into puzzled guffaws, Stoney's eyes hardened in a way that gave me a sudden chill.

Catching his look, one of the generals guffawed, 'What nonsense is this, Andrew?'

'Pish! Some tomfoolery of her father's. I've to tack on her name to my own. It matters not a jot. Cheers!' but though he lifted his glass in a jocular manner, his eyes still glittered on me.

Chastened, I took my place at the opposite end of the table, mentally reprimanding myself for having provoked him in public, but to be honest, I was so astonished by this turn of events that my mind was in turmoil. How was I to behave when in truth I felt like melting into a pool of tears?

I could not eat, nor could I drink. I sat at the opposite end of the table feeling entirely invaded, powerless, cancelled out. Servants replenished plates and poured more and more wine, none of them even daring to look at me. No-one spoke to me, no toast was proposed: all the talk was of horses and betting. The soft Irish burr which I had found so endearing was gone: in the company of his uncles, Stoney's accent was as impenetrably Irish as can be.

It soon became clear that my presence was entirely incidental to the proceedings: more champagne was called for, and when George Walker respectfully replied that there was none in the house, I felt again the chill of those glittering eyes upon me.

George was sent to buy more, and as he left the room, I looked to him for some glance of commiseration or reassurance, but there was none. As he closed the door slowly, it came to me with a creeping chill that Stoney was now the master here, not I.

When the opportunity arose, I took my leave of them and retired to my room, and it felt like a surrender. In the ensuing hours, while they caroused and laughed and sang, I sobbed alone in my room: I had given away my freedom once again.

I had no-one to blame but myself. I tried very hard to feel some optimism. If he loved me as he said he did, and had risked his life for my honour as he appeared to have done, I had married a man of passion and integrity. He shared my love of poetry, in particular John Donne; he was interested in botany; he was handsome in a rather intimidating way; he was certainly charming and sociable. Perhaps I should not have spoken to him as I had when I entered the room, for the mood had changed markedly: on reflection, if these were all good men, my tone must have sounded waspish. He had clearly confounded his doctors: it was cruel of me to show my dismay in front of his friends and his distinguished uncles. I decided I would apologise when we were alone.

By the time night fell, I had reconciled myself to the fact that I was married.

I fell asleep to the sounds of laughter and music from downstairs and when I awoke in the night, it was to the creak of floorboards outside my room. I heard George Walker's voice quite clearly: 'This way, sirs. Lady Strathmore is asleep. The master bedroom has been prepared for you.' There was the sound of several pairs of heavy feet, an outburst of smothered laughter, and the sound of a heavy body brushing along the wall.

I must have dozed, for the next thing I knew, a weak light was seeping through a gap in the curtains. No fire had been lit, and someone was tapping at my bedroom door. 'Madam?'

'Yes, Ann, come in. I am awake. What is it?'

'Mr Bowes is dressing, madam. He would like to come in shortly.'

'Come in? Into my room?'

'Yes ma'am.' Ann could not meet my eyes. What must the servants think of me? This whole scenario must be beyond their comprehension. I hoped I could rely on George Walker to explain it all sympathetically.

I sat up and spoke with more confidence than I felt. 'I would prefer to be dressed first. Kindly arrange for Mr Bowes to be attended to and I will ring when I am ready to receive him. In my sitting room.' I looked at her meaningfully. 'Ann. You understand me?'

I had some news for Mr Bowes which I doubted very much he would receive with equanimity.

He was helped into the room by his valet, whose name I later learnt was Thomas: he saw his master to the chair opposite me, then bowed respectfully and retired. Not once did he meet my eyes.

We regarded each other in silence for a few moments. My mind was in turmoil but I kept my face still.

Finally he spoke, 'So...'

I poured the tea. 'So. Here we are. And how are you feeling this morning?'

He looked at me sharply, perhaps to judge the tone of my question. 'I am in some pain this morning. I slept too heavily on my injury.'

'Perils of the demon drink, perhaps?'

'Yes, quite.'

'Thank-you for not waking me.'

'Your man Walker was most insistent. He needs to learn his place, I think.'

'Walker has known me since I was a little girl. He is very protective of me.'

'Well, he need trouble himself no further. You have a new protector now.'

I did not know how to reply, so I didn't. I knew I must be very careful. I sipped my tea and awaited developments. Now that he was here in front of me, the idea of Andrew as a husband was not so frightening. Though he was clearly in some discomfort from the wound in his side, his posture was erect, his shoulders broad, his face striking in some way I found hard to define. The eyes were slightly hooded, and when I saw him in profile as he turned to replace his cup, there was something of the hawk or the eagle in the hook of his nose.

Finally, after regarding me in silence for a few moments whilst I sipped my tea with all the complacency I could muster, he spoke. 'I have written to your mother. I have it here. Would you like to read it?'

All inner watchfulness and outer compliance, I said, 'Yes, please. I would.'

130

He took from the inner pocket of his morning coat a folded sheet, and I was relieved to see that he had not availed himself of the Strathmore-crested writing paper which I suddenly remembered was still in the desk in John's study, adjoining the master bedroom.

What he had written gave me deep reassurance, for it was an apology to my mother for the unconventional nature of our nuptials. He wrote: 'I wish to atone for that breach of duty, and to ask your pardon under the promise of dedicating the remainder of my life to the honour and interest of your daughter and her family. My grateful heart will make me her faithful companion, and with unremitting attention I will consult her peace of mind, and the advantage of the children.'

It was such a relief to read those words that I decided to lose no time in breaking the first item of news.

As I considered how to word it, I felt there was still a chance that upon hearing it, he would request an annulment of the marriage. Of course I had no such right.

I took a deep breath. 'I have something you must know. I am with child. George Gray's child.'

Thunderstruck, he did not speak for some minutes, and I watched the reactions move across his face like clouds across the moors.

Finally, his jaw muscles clenched once and he brushed it aside: 'No matter. He is unaware, I take it. We shall pass it off as our own. You will not hear from George Gray again.'

'That hardly seems fair.'

'Fair to whom? Think of the child, Eleanor. It will be entirely confused otherwise and known to be a bastard.' I flinched at that word. 'No, I shall pay off George Gray. He has already proved himself ... amenable.'

'What do you mean?'

'Nothing. You need not trouble yourself. Business between men. Speaking of which, I have sent a message to the estate manager at Gibside. He is on his way to London.'

'You have?' I was entirely astonished. 'You have been very busy for a dying man.'

He smiled the smile of a crocodile and my blood froze in my veins.

'As you see, I am much recovered. I have astonished my doctors.'

'Indeed. I have to tell you that you have astonished me, too.'

His look was long and steady, head on one side as though considering how to answer. We studied each other in silence for long moments. I was tempted to break the silence, but for once I simply did not know what to say or how to be. I felt at a distinct disadvantage: he had clearly been learning about me whilst I had been barely aware of him, beyond his status as an admirer.

Far from being a handsome man, my new husband had an undeniable magnetism and a quality of stillness. I have always admired a man who can hold a silence, and this one was prolonged.

Finally, he spoke: 'What are you thinking, my dear?'

'I ...I hardly know what to say or how to behave. The circumstances are extraordinary.'

'I know. This is not how you expected events to proceed. I understand.'

'No indeed. I feel I barely know you.'

He brightened: 'Ah, but I know you, Mary Eleanor Bowes. I have made a study of you.' There was a cocksure pride in his tone that gave me some concern, but I must confess to a frisson of something I had not expected. It was a long time since I had been in the presence of a powerful man whose focus was entirely on me. He reached out and took my hands in his, in the manner of a promise: 'I am here now. You are no longer alone and a prey to the designs of others.'

'A prey?'

This he ignored. 'I shall protect you and keep you safe.'

Oh the irony of those words!

Chapter 15

I quickly became aware of what his protection entailed.

After a pleasant breakfast in the warmth of the morning room, during which he entertained me with anecdotes about his uncles and his upbringing in Ireland, Stoney took his leave of me and was helped from the table by Thomas.

I got up to look out of the window feeling quite calm. I had simply no idea what the future held: it was as though I had been holding the reins of my own carriage, riding along quite happily, fully able to steer my own course, and someone had jumped aboard and taken the reins from me without a word. Nothing whatsoever had been said about the practicalities of this marriage, and as far as I knew, Stoney had made no approach to any lawyer or agent other than his letter to Thomas Colpitts. He could hardly have been aware of the terms of the marriage since he had apparently been barely conscious when he signed the hurriedly-prepared marriage contract.

It was a grey icy day and I resigned myself to waiting passively to see what it would bring. I didn't feel like moving from the cosy morning-room where the fire always burned so well, and I took comfort in adding more Newcastle coals to it myself. I rang the bell and asked for my post: Walker usually brought it to me on the silver salver, but there had been no sign of him this morning.

The footman returned empty-handed and his tone when he said it was entirely neutral: 'Mr Bowes has your post, madam.'

'Mr Bowes? Why would he have my post? This is surely some mistake. Kindly go and get it for me.' I know my voice was high: I was so surprised that I had no time to hide the fearful indignation I felt upon hearing this news. I still had not found the courage to tell Stoney something vital to the future conduct of our affairs and I feared there might be a letter from my solicitor.

'Mr Bowes requested that all post should be brought to him.' He looked at me intently, his eyes dark and serious. ' He was most emphatic.'

I stood up, brushing crumbs from my skirt and avoiding his eyes. 'Thank-you, James. You may go.'

I found him in John's study, a dark and wooded room on the first floor adjoining the master bedroom. As I paused before the closed door, I considered knocking, decided not to, took hold of the handle, but then fear gripped me, and I knocked lightly, hating myself for doing so. This was, after all, my house.

But it wasn't.

He was sitting at the desk with his broad back to me and he did not turn before he spoke: 'What is it?'

'James tells me that you have my post. There is surely some mistake.'

'No mistake.'

'May I have it please?'

'No, you may not.'

'Whyever not?'

'Because I am the master of the house.' He said it on an amused, languid note, as though the reason was patently obvious, slowly turning as he did so. 'You need no longer concern yourself with business matters, and any social correspondence is of course relevant to me. You are a married woman now.'

I considered how to answer. His face was cast in darkness, and I spoke against the light, straining to hide the irritation I felt. 'Thank-you for your concern, but until we have had a formal discussion, it seems somewhat presumptuous of you to have taken command of my private correspondence in such a fashion.'

There was another long silence, but I was becoming used to this and refused to be intimidated. I walked over to stand before his chair. Such was the disparity in our heights that, in this position, we were eye to eye. I could still not see his expression, and I was desperate to get my letters. Apart from my fears about the legal document, there could be something from George Gray.

His stillness unnerved me, but I steeled myself to smile sweetly as I moved towards the desk, saying as I did so, 'I am free this afternoon. Perhaps we could have a marital business meeting then.' I reached out for the pile of letters, some of which I saw had already been opened, and my fingers had just closed round them when I felt the skin on the back of my hand gathered into a fierce pinch. Startled and in instant pain, I instinctively grabbed for his wrist with my other hand and when he tightened his hold, dug my nails in, but his free hand folded over mine and I felt the fingers crunched into a tight ball until I feared they would break. I let out a yelp and looked into his face, my eyes wide with fear and pain. He was smiling.

This was so unexpected, treatment so alien to me that I felt real physical fear for the first time in my life. Something inside me was instantly cowed and my innards trembled. When tears sprang to my eyes, he released the crushed hand but not the flesh of the other.

'I fear you have a lot to learn, Mary Eleanor. I do not like to hurt you,' his eyes told a different story, 'but sometimes I have found it is the only way.' At last, he let go, and sorrowfully regarded the deep purple bruise that was already developing on the back of my hand. To my complete astonishment, he then lifted it to his lips and planted a kiss.

Smiling at me with what seemed like real warmth, he released my hand and said, 'Now you may go.'

Ann noticed it when she was dressing me for dinner. I told her I had dropped a candlestick on my hand.

When I came downstairs, George Walker was standing in the hall in quiet conversation with James, and they stopped talking as soon as they saw me, but neither of them looked away. They watched me descend the staircase, their faces unguarded and gentle. No word passed between us, but James gave a slight nod and then left. I looked around at the closed doors, and then spoke softly to George in a voice that was calmer than I felt. 'Keep the deed safe, George. I do not know whether I shall be able to lead my life with Mr Stoney.'

He had clearly been waiting for some indication from me that all was not well: he smiled a tight-lipped smile and taking both my hands, held them up enclosed in his own as if in prayer. When I flinched, the warmth on his face turned to concern. When he saw the bruise, his look hardened to anger and he made to speak. I lifted a finger to his lips and shook my head.

It's strange. Now, with the benefit of hindsight, I know that that first pinch was a sign of what was to come. Then, I had half a mind to think I had deserved it. I cannot tell you how much I wish I could speak to the young woman that I was and tell her that any man who could do what he had done on so little provocation, and smile while he was doing it, was capable of doing much worse. Bewildered as I was in those days, all I could think was that I had embarrassed Mr Stoney in front of his friends, and then revealed to him that I was carrying a baby conceived out of wedlock. I told myself that it was no wonder he had been angry with me.

The first time he slapped me, I stood holding a gloved hand to my cheek and found myself strangely jubilant. Here, at last, was honesty. Here was how he really regarded me. It had been building up for days. First there had been the sharp reprimands in public: 'Sit there! Leave the room! Speak English!' this last when I was conversing with an Italian friend at dinner.

Then it progressed to sudden flashes of temper which manifested themselves physically. Returning from a shopping trip one morning, only a fortnight into our marriage, he was waiting in the hall on my return, his face a thundercloud. When the door was closed, he strode forward and snatched the bonnet from my head, stamping it onto the hall tiles before my astonished gaze. I was so stunned I hardly knew how to react, and turned to James, who was standing up very straight, his back pressed against the wall by the door, his face impassive, staring at the opposite wall. All the servants had become silent and watchful in those first weeks: two maids had already been sacked, though the nature of their offence was never revealed to me.

Stoney took my arm with false gentleness and as he escorted me up the stairs, he said in a low, controlled voice: 'I believe I have made it made quite clear to every member of this household that Lady Strathmore is never to be allowed to go out alone. I am her husband. This is my household. You are my servants. I command it. James, I trust you will reiterate this information to your colleagues. Their future employment depends upon it.'

One night he was late for dinner, having been absent all day. He was not in the habit of telling me his plans and I had quickly learnt not to ask. I sat alone at the end of the table and felt my sense of injustice and powerlessness rise in my chest. I rang the bell to request that they begin serving. To my great surprise, it was Ann who responded.

136

'Why, Ann, this is not your place. Where are George and James?'

Ann did not look at me when she replied, 'Ma'am, Mr Bowes has instructed that only female servants should respond to your bell.'

I was never good at hiding my feelings, and saw no need to pretend a loyalty to my husband that I did not feel, so I said, 'What on earth can he be thinking?'

Ann closed the door behind her and spoke hurriedly. 'Forgive me ma'am, but I think he does not want you to be alone with any man. Thomas got into terrible trouble when he fetched Mr Bowes' cane from your dressing-room.'

'But I told him it was in there!'

'Yes, ma'am, but there was no-one else in your suite, and the men have been expressly forbidden to be alone with you.'

I actually laughed, I was so astonished.

Ann misinterpreted my response, and she gave me a hesitant smile. 'Perhaps it is his devotion that makes Mr Bowes so?'

My face and tone must have shown her my true feelings: 'Yes, Ann, perhaps it is.'

It was a strangely silent meal. George Walker and James were both present at one time or another, supervising the maids as they flitted in and out bearing dishes and glasses, but neither of them spoke. They were both excellent and trusted footmen, elegant, controlled, discreet and efficient: James, though thirty years younger, was learning from George all the skills that had made him so valued by my family. Normally, if I had been alone, we would have chatted between the courses like the old friends that we were. I missed it, of course I did, but I could not entice them into any action that would put their jobs at risk. It was a great comfort to me, therefore, when George, unnoticed by the maid, lightly squeezed my shoulder as he poured me a glass of dessert wine.

I had just put down my coffee when there was a thud against the door; it opened and Stoney staggered into the room. I must confess that my first thought was hope: I hoped that he was injured, weakened somehow and that some balance would begin to be redressed in our relationship. But when his eyes came to rest on me, it was clear he had been drinking heavily.

'Ah, here we are, Lady Muck. Been dining alone have we? Dear dear.'

Not wishing to antagonize him, I kept my voice low and neutral: 'You sent no message so I assumed you were eating elsewhere.'

'As indeed I have.' He burped loudly, as if to illustrate the fact, and pulled up a chair beside me.

Smiling a smile I did not feel, I tried to lighten the mood: 'And was it a pleasant repast?'

'Oh yes indeed. And pleasant company too.' He winked lasciviously and I felt a nauseous stirring in my chest. What fresh hell was this? Still I feared questioning him in this state, so kept the placatory smile on my face. 'I'm glad to hear it. I have had a pleasant day too: I have been to Kew Gardens where I...'

'You have been where?' His voice was icy cold. 'I do not recollect you asking for permission to leave the house.'

I could not help myself. I laughed, such was my indignation and fear.

Instantly, his expression changed. 'Laugh, do you?' and he took my face in both his hands and pressed hard until I felt my skull must crack. I held his wrists and tried to pull but had no more effect than a feather.

'Please. You're hurting me.'

Abruptly, he let go and reached for a wine glass then turned his head and bellowed at the closed door. 'Thomas! Bring wine!'

The door opened a crack and his valet's sandy head appeared. He said, 'Yes sir', but his eyes were on me.

'Be quick about it.'

Thomas vanished.

'So, my dear, let us once again establish the facts of the matter. I am your master. I am master of this house. I decide whether you may or may not go out. And I decide with whom. Do you understand?'

Now was not the time to challenge him, so I said yes. But fatefully, thinking I was clever, I added, 'I understand,' expecting the distinction to go unnoticed. It didn't.

Accepting the wine bottle from Thomas, he poured himself a glass, lifted it to me in an ironic toast, and took a drink, his eyes never leaving my face.

Without turning round, he said, 'Thomas, you may go.' I did not dare to lift my gaze to watch Thomas leave the room, but I was aware he had left the door open and I was grateful.

Watching me still, Stoney took another drink of his wine then sat the glass on the table and picked up my hands, gently separating them, for they were clenched together on my lap in a fearful locked embrace.

He studied them for a few moments, then with tender fingers, he stroked the faded bruise, looking up at me with smiling eyes. I thought for one hopeful moment that he would apologise for hurting me.

When he said firmly, 'Close the door, Thomas,' my heart dropped like a stone.

He shuffled closer towards me and spread his knees so that mine were wedged between them through the thickness of my skirts and petticoats.

'Poor baby. I have hurt you. I am sorry. You know that. But you must learn, and it seems to me that you find it difficult.'

I did not speak, fearful that whatever I said would change his mood in an instant.

Letting go of one of my hands, he helped himself to another glass of wine and then took it up again and turned it, pretending to study my palm.

'An interesting specimen, don't you think? See here,' he suddenly lifted his own palm in front of my face and I flinched involuntarily. 'Oh my sweet, be not afraid of me.' He reached out and cupped my cheek then kissed the tip of my nose.

'Look here. See my lifeline? It is strong and long and deep. Now look at your lifeline.' He lifted my bruised hand and indicated the palm. 'So faint and so short.' He studied it for a while, sorrowfully, and then smiled a rueful smile. 'Your hands are so small, my sweet.' He planted a kiss on the palm. 'You are delicate. We must take care of you.' He raised his face to mine, a gentle and mischievous look upon his face. 'Come. Come to bed and let me take care of you.'

I think by this point we had been married for three weeks or so, and still he had not explored that aspect of his marital rights. I had put it down to the fact that I was pregnant, and with another man's child. I chose to believe it a sweetness in him at first and was touched by his sensitivity. But soon after we returned to London from my mother's house and it became clear that he intended to continue the life of a single man, I thought myself dignified in my acceptance. If he was availing himself of the services of courtesans, I could only hope that he would be discreet. By the fourth week of our marriage, however, it had become clear that when he was in drink he enjoyed making heavy hints, as though boasting of his prowess.

When we left the room, he was still holding my hand as we ascended the stairs. I hoped very much that drink would disable him as it so often had my first husband, for I was full of fear and every muscle in my body clenched. And indeed it was so: by the time I was undressed and bathed, loud snores were rattling the handle of the closed door between our rooms.

Ann was putting away my clothes, and she turned when she heard the first of his snores. I smiled in a way that I hoped indicated female complicity, but her face was serious when she said, 'Would you like me to lock the door, madam?'

I affected to be startled. 'Lock the door? Why on earth would I do that?'

She held my gaze and jutted her chin. 'Forgive me for saying this madam, but...'

I wrapped my robe more tightly around me and considered how to answer. It would be a betrayal to show a servant that I was afraid of my husband, but the thought of having Ann as an ally was sorely tempting.

I compromised by turning my back to her and pretending to fiddle with something on my dressing table. The snores continued unabated as the silence, which was in itself a confession, stretched between us.

To my horror, Ann appeared at my side and whispered hastily in my ear. 'Madam, I have to say this. I am afraid for you. Thomas was telling me...'

I whirled on her, to my great shame. 'How dare you, Ann? This is servants' tittle-tattle. Do not bring it to me. You presume too much.'

Her face was pinched, white and fearful: I remember it to this day. Plucky girl, she persisted, animated not by the heat of gossip, but by genuine fear. 'Madam, please. Listen to me, though in truth I know not what to say. I had not planned this. Thomas says...'

'Ann. You are dismissed.'

Such was her heightened sense of self-preservation, that she took me to mean that she was dismissed from the house, and tears sprang to her eyes. 'No madam, please!'

Poor girl, I softened to see her distraught face. 'Silly goose, I only mean from my bedchamber.' I touched her cheek gently. 'Do not fret, Ann. I am fine. Mr Stoney and I only have to get used to each other, is all. You go to your Thomas. He is your Thomas, is he not?'

She blushed instantly. 'Yes, ma'am. We have become very close.' She looked up at me, a beseeching expression on her face. 'I must tell you though...'

I turned from her, angry now. 'Leave me, Ann. Good night.'

Tenacious little thing, she spoke in a low voice from behind my back. 'Please do not tell Captain Stoney, but Thomas is looking for a new master. He has reasons, Lady Strathmore. I would like to tell you the reasons, in private. I understand that you do not wish to talk any further tonight, and I am sorry if you feel I have presumed too much. I am your devoted servant, madam.'

When I did not move or speak, she softly said, 'Good night' and I let her leave the room without acknowledging anything she had said.

It was one of those pivotal conversations and I often think of it. If I had handled it differently: if I had told George Walker the extent of my fears and enlisted the support of Thomas and Ann. If we had formed an alliance, perhaps I would have felt stronger. Sometimes we turn away help when it is offered in the belief that to accept it would be to admit our weakness. It was, I now see, a terrible mistake, for in refusing their help, in denying that there was a problem, I isolated myself.

After Stoney beat me with the hilt of his sword, Ann and Thomas were so appalled that they came to me together. And I turned them away.

It seems incredible to me now, but that night, when my back and side hurt so much that I had to spend the night in the chair, I blamed myself for what had happened. I had never found the courage to tell Stoney about the pre-nuptial contract: when he found out from my lawyers that he had no access to my assets or future income, he had returned to the house in a rage of such ferocity that I counted myself lucky to be only badly bruised.

Ann and Thomas left Grosvenor Square that very night and I never saw them again.

Chapter 16

That dark winter held tight for so long that there were times I thought it would never yield its grip. The weak grey sun remained shrouded in a heavy bank of cloud the colour of dirty snow. I spent my time alone, and quickly came to value solitude: I could no longer trust anyone. Ann was swiftly replaced by a slovenly girl with dirty nails and a brazen stare who wore her waist-length hair loose. The other female servants had developed the look and demeanour of startled deer and could barely stay in the room long enough for any kind of interaction with me.

Young John was safely back at school, and the other children remained with my mother in Hertfordshire, where the air was clear, the mornings were crisp and there was a plentiful supply of wood. I thought of them constantly and wrote to them every other day, inventing stories of parties we had held, plays we had attended, lectures I had heard. Seeking inspiration, I painted a picture of a wonderful automaton I had seen the previous summer in the Mechanical Museum of James Cox, a silver swan in a moving stream whose neck arches and bends for it to catch a fish from the shimmering silver stream. It was a thing of such marvelous beauty that my spirits lifted to remember it and to recreate it for my children.

I often felt that my imaginary life was sustaining me and would wake, blinking, into the wan grey light of another London day where air hung heavy with soot from the coal mined in Newcastle.

It had been customary for me to write my correspondence at the escritoire in the morning room. I would ring the bell and ask for coffee or lunch, and if any letters were ready to be posted, whoever came would take them away. But nothing was so simple any more.

In the second week of our marriage, my writing paper and pens had disappeared from my desk, and when I rang the bell to enquire as to their whereabouts, it was Stoney who opened the door. His face was alight with a veneer of charm. 'What is it, dearest?'

I confess I was so startled by his appearance that I sat dumb, hardly knowing how to frame my question.

'Oh, I see you are at your little desk. I had your papers moved into my study, I do hope you don't mind. I thought it would be cosy and convenient.'

'I...I don't understand. Cosy and convenient for whom?'

He came across and took my hand, indicating that he expected me to rise.

I did as he wished, and he kissed my hand tenderly.

'Why, for us, my dear. As you know, I have a good deal of correspondence to deal with in the management of our affairs. I'll occasionally need your signature, and I expect you will want to write to the children, and I thought it would be cosy if you do your little letters in my study. And of course convenient as I will be reading and signing them all.'

After that, if I was alone and rang my bell, no-one came. I cannot tell you what a strange and isolating thing that was for me. As I think I have made clear, I had been brought up to be fully aware of my position of privilege and to appreciate and respect the people whose work kept me in comfort. My father had always impressed upon me that our fortune was based on three things: the mineral wealth of our lands, the hard graft of our people and the perspicacity of our family. I was fortunate and I knew it, though I confess that I sometimes lost sight of it – it's human nature to take things for granted. I think we all do it, losing sight of how easily they can be taken away from us.

The sudden loss of power bewildered me entirely, and I simply did not know how to deal with it. My confidence was knocked from me in one blow, as though I had been winded by a fall from a horse. If I had no influence on the world around me, what was I? Suddenly, I felt bereft, alone to the depths of my soul. Until I thought of the baby within me and I felt my core of strength re-shape itself.

The one person I felt I could speak to was George Walker, and I watched and listened for him for many days before I found the courage to speak. I did not want to draw attention to his special place in my life, for fear of what would ensue.

One morning when I had breakfasted alone, I took the opportunity to ask James when he came to supervise the clearing of the table. I had by then become uncharacteristically silent, and so I startled him when I spoke: 'Is George ill? I haven't seen him for a few days.'

James ducked his head and stood still, as though contemplating his answer. When he looked up, he cocked his head to one side, listening. The little maid whose name I did not know stood still, her head bowed like a child who thinks she cannot be seen.

Bewildered and somewhat frightened, I said, 'James?'

Gently closing the door, James spoke urgently: 'Lady Strathmore, George has been confined to below-stairs duties.'

I was horrified. If I lost George, if Stoney knew how much he meant to me, if he ever found out that George held a copy of the pre-nuptial deed...

'For how long? What has he done?'

James was just about to answer when we both heard the front door open. He left the room without saying another word.

I yearned for Gibside with every fibre of my being, so the morning when Stoney looked up from his newspaper and announced we were going north, my heart leapt. I kept my face still, lest he should see how much the news had delighted me. My heart had begun to race and the child within me quickened: we sensed safety. No matter how illogical, I felt that nothing could hurt us there. The belief buoyed me and made me brave. I pretended languid interest: 'In February? It will be an arduous journey. Why not wait another month until spring?'

He stood up, his features animated in a way I had not yet seen. 'Because, oh light of my life, I am on my way to parliament!'

Now I was entirely bewildered. 'To parliament?'

'There is the small matter of an election to deal with, but yes, the master of Gibside shall once again be MP, not for Durham but for Newcastle!' Pausing only to peck me on the cheek, he left the room at speed, there being no longer any trace of a limp, then he was bellowing good-naturedly in the hall: 'Walker! Ready the household. We leave for Gibside today!'

Below, I heard voices raised in surprise and consternation.

He had thrown the morning paper onto the table, and I hastened to read it. I struggled at first to find anything that would have prompted this, but as my thinking brain caught up with my eyes, I knew that what I would see would be an announcement of the death of Sir Walter Blackett or Matthew Ridley. It was the former. I sat down, felled for a moment by a wave of grief, not just for Sir Walter and his family, but for my father, who had been his friend.

Sir Walter, the pride of the north-east; Newcastle's Mayor throughout my childhood, and a man with such a caring nature that he was known as The Father of the Poor. I'd known him since I was a baby, though my first real memory of him was at the benefit concert in aid of the new infirmary for the poor. Until then, I had thought Mr Avison just a music teacher, and Uncle Walter just a jolly friend of my father's, but that night I saw my father on the stage with the two of them, and everyone clapping, and I realized they were all special men. Sir Walter especially was universally loved and respected, his great florid face like a child's painting of the sun. His bellowing laughter and the warmth he spread wherever he went.

I remembered him coming to sit beside me at the funeral after carrying my father's coffin into church. The other bearers, Lord Ravensworth, Sir Thomas Clavering and Edward Montague, all bowed their heads, but Sir Walter was not one for ceremony. He looked around him, and his eyes fell on me in the front pew beside my mother. He said later that my face had looked like a spring flower exposed to the winter winds. When the others formed a stately line and processed down the steps to join their families behind us, Sir Walter dispensed with the formalities and came directly to sit down beside me, take my hand in his, and smile reassuringly into my upturned face. He smelled like Papa and I leant against him, grateful for the human warmth: my mother, lost in her own grief, had no comfort for me. He put his great heavy arm around my shoulders and held me tight throughout the service.

Remembering this, I remembered all that was lost and I cried. And once I started, I found I could not stop.

That grief cleansed me somehow. There was a catharsis in it, and I was released from the trembling fear that had held me in its thrall these past few weeks. Perversely, although the twin giants of my childhood were now both dead, I felt as if their spirits had risen up in me. I was not helpless and powerless. I was my father's daughter. The feeble frightened rabbit was dealt a kindly blow. It was as if by summoning up Sir Walter and my father, I had called their spirits to me to arm myself.

146

I was that spring flower exposed to winter winds, but I would withstand their icy blasts. We were going to Gibside: I would start to thrive when transplanted. There, I would be surrounded by people who knew me, had known me all my life, families who, like mine and like the sturdy oaks, had grown out of the soil of that fertile valley.

Stoney's power over me was bound to be diminished: there I would be amongst my people.

The journey was long and arduous, but it passed quickly because Stoney was in such high spirits, talking aloud about his plans and plying me for information about the wealthy families.

'Old Blackett, fat old Tory. I hate his sort. Handed it all on a plate, like you.'

There was so much I could have said, should have said, but we were alone in the carriage and I feared to provoke him, so I simply stated, 'He was a friend of my father.'

'Think I don't know that? Don't worry, missy, you'll be providing me with plenty of ammo.'

A voice in my heard told me to be brave, so I took a breath and said, 'He did a great deal for Newcastle. Granted, a Tory, but a kind and generous one. He was a great benefactor, and served his city for almost half a century. They called him 'The Father of the Poor,' you know.'

'Yes yes, I know Newcastle far better than you think I do, lady.'

This was still a mystery to me. He had mentioned arriving with his regiment, a whirlwind romance and a short marriage. He had told me that his wife had died, but would not be drawn on any detail.

I tried again. 'Of course. Do tell me about your time there.' But he ignored my question. 'Trevelyan will no doubt think he'll inherit a seat in Parliament along with Wallington Hall. We'll see about that.'

'Will you look to challenge him for the Whig candidacy?'

'No, I'd be onto a loser there. I know how those toffs operate.'

'What will you stand for?'

'Not sure yet, but I've an idea brewing. I think I'll make myself into the right man for the Radicals.'

'How so?'

'Bowes and Freedom! I like the sound of that. I have men already on the ground: we've been waiting for this moment.'

'On the ground?'

'In the Toon, moving amongst, taking the temperature, staking the enemy.'

'The enemy?'

There was a flash of irritation then, and I saw his eyes come to rest on me in a way that I found disconcerting. I kept my face still and held his gaze until he looked out of the window and spoke again: 'You, my dear, will be most valuable to me in this enterprise.' He reached across and slipped a hand into the side of my bonnet, his hot palm cupping my cheek. I kept still, mistrusting what appeared to be an expression of affection. I felt him trace the outline of my ear, and it was all I could do not to recoil: the muscles of my neck and shoulder tensed. True enough, he took hold of the lobe and gently stroked it while he looked at it thoughtfully before moving his eyes to mine and tightening his grip. 'You'll behave as befits the wife of a prospective candidate and you will do everything in your power to ensure my success. That is the case, is it not?'

'Yes, of course.' In truth, I hoped he did succeed and would spend all of his time in London and leave me at home to bring up my baby in peace. It was with a sense of resignation that I felt him twist the earlobe until I knew it must tear. I kept still and bit my lip to keep myself from crying out in pain. When the carriage jolted, he withdrew his hand and went back to gazing out of the window and carrying on the conversation as if nothing had happened.

'The tactic is to be anti-establishment, inherited privilege, that sort of thing. My fellows are self-made, as am I. A chap should get on though merit, as I have done.' I watched him raise his chin, clearly congratulating himself. This was a new idea to me, and it seemed an insight that I would store away and consider at a later date. For now I must stay on the alert. Know thine enemy.

'Who are your agents?'

'The Scott brothers. You won't know them, moving in elevated circles as you do.'

'Newcastle born?'

'Yes, damned clever fellows. My sort.'

'William Scott?'

This startled him and he regarded me with a watchful expression, suddenly wary, and I relished the frisson of power it gave me. There would be many more moments like this once I was home.

Eventually, he spat out the question: 'Know of him, do you?'

'I've heard of him. Clever young lawyer. Rising star.'

'Yes, and he has two brothers, equally sharp. Good men to have on my side. Our side.' Suddenly expansive, he burst out, 'Let us break the closet-combination of the magistrates and gentry, whose glory is to treat their inferiors as slaves! How does that sound?' Clearly not really needing an answer from me, he went on as if to himself: 'Yes, I'll be a natural on the hustings!'

We passed through Whickham at speed, and when we turned off the Roman road and pulled up between the gate-houses, my soul breathed out. Softly-falling snow enveloped the turrets and I stretched out my hand to watch the flakes melt on my palm. The wheels of the carriage were hushed by the thick cushion as we wound our way down the Scottish glen towards the stables. I pointed nothing out and he did not ask. When the Palladian frontage came into view, I saw his eyes sharpen, and he said, 'I had heard the house was old and draughty. This looks new. But small.'

I kept quiet for as long as I dared, only answering when he turned to look at me: 'That is the stables.'

When the house came into view, emerging from the snow in glimpses that quickened my pulse, my fluttering heart started to settle and a sense of peace spread warmth throughout my body, so much so that I felt a blush rise from my neck to my cheeks. As we approached, the wheels crunching on newly-settled snow, we watched the mullioned windows pass and glimpsed the fire-lit rooms within.

When we came to a standstill, Stoney flung open the door and stood on the threshold, looking up into the falling snow with a beatific smile. I knew it was a pose for the benefit of the servants watching from the windows and the footmen who came forward to help us dismount.

'Greetings, my fine fellows! Ah the sweet northern air! How good it is to be home in Newcastle!' I smiled to myself at his gaffe, for he could not know how it would rile these men to hear their beautiful part of Durham thus relocated to the north of the Tyne.

He jumped down, startling the footmen, who took a step backwards in unison. Standing with his hands at his waist, feet spread, he laughed at their discomfiture, then putting a hand on each of their shoulders, spun them round and gave them a playful shove, 'I shall help her ladyship. Wait indoors.'

Turning to me, he inclined his head and extended his hand, all the while watching me with a glittering eye. 'My dear.'

For one mad moment, I entertained the thought of dashing past him into the house and locking the door, but I took his arm with a demure smile and entered my childhood home with my dignity intact.

Everyone was there in the hall, and my eyes brimmed at the warmth of the greeting. It only needed me to smile and the assembled faces lit up as one: I was borne away in a phalanx of women, leaving Stoney to supervise the arrival of the other coaches and issue his orders.

The fire was already lit in my bedroom, and I stood before it warming my hands whilst Martha and the maids fussed about me, exclaiming over my fine kid gloves and asking excited questions about London fashions. When we heard men's voices in the adjoining room, everyone hushed, startled, watchful, but it was only a pair of manservants bringing up my trunk.

When they had gone, the girls opened the adjoining door and went through to explore the contents of my boxes, and I was left alone with Martha.

'And so, mistress, are you quite well?' She was looking at me closely and I kept my eyes on the fire. 'Quite well, thank-you. As you see.'

'I am glad to hear it, madam. We have worried.'

'Worried? Why would you worry about me? On the contrary, I have worried about you. It seems so long since I have been home.'

'It is, madam. It is almost six months. You were in mourning.'

'Yes, so I was.' My last visit in the wake of John's death had been brief and formal. It seemed so long ago, and so much had happened in the interim that even if I had wanted to tell, I would not have known where to begin.

'And now you're married.' Her voice was flat.

'Yes, as you see.' I did not like where this was going, and felt that our usual intimacy was a dangerous thing. I needed time and tactics before I could start to think of how to conduct myself at Gibside, and a lot would depend on the face Stoney presented. He had clearly already begun to conduct a propaganda campaign designed to get him elected. Although these servants had no vote, they and their kind had the ears of the men who did.

'And how was the wedding?'

I gave her a long look. 'I think you will have heard the circumstances of my wedding, Martha.'

She spoke quickly, as though she had only been waiting for the opportunity to say it: 'Yes, and when we heard his name...'

'His name? It was familiar to you?'

Suddenly abashed, she busied herself with brushing snowflakes from my coat. 'Yes madam. His name is...somewhat familiar.'

Women communicate in such subtle ways, don't you think? We both studied each other for long moments, our thoughts flickering in our eyes. I could trust Martha in a way that I could never have trusted little Ann back in London. And after all, I had asked no disloyal question. I knew her well enough to be aware that I only needed to give her my assent, and she would talk. She knew me well enough to know that if she talked, what she said would never be used against her.

I must not put her at risk. She was an honest soul, as were they all: all our staff had been with us for generations. I kept my tone light. 'A friend of a friend, perhaps?'

'George Stephenson. His cousin works at Coal Pike Hill.' It was all she said, but the tone in which she said it was enough to convey its dark significance.

Coal Pike Hill. I think I knew even before she said it, but now, unwilling to face the truth, I edged my way towards it. Perhaps Stoney had seduced the girl when he arrived in Newcastle as a young soldier. The scarlet jackets had enlivened many a gathering at the Assembly Rooms, though I had usually been escorted by my father so had made no personal acquaintance with any soldiers.

'Coal Pike Hill? I'm not familiar with the Newtons.'

'But Mr Stoney is.'

'Mr Bowes,' I felt I had to correct her to give some semblance of loyalty. 'He hasn't mentioned it.'

By then, I had composed my face into an expression which indicated I was resigned to hearing a bit of tittle-tattle that had no bearing on my life; in my heart, though, I was preparing for the blow.

'Mr Stoney was married to Hannah Newton.' By that single simple statement, our complicity was ensured. She now knew that I had been unaware, and I knew that there was more. She dropped her voice and spoke urgently, clasping both my hands to force me to confront the import of what she had to say: 'Hannah was sorely mistreated by Mr Stoney. He was seen to beat her.'

'Sadly, Martha, the law allows a man to chastise his wife. Though the stick must be no thicker than his thumb. Hadn't you heard?' I laughed ruefully, a bitter laugh that sounded hollow even to me. My back still bore the bruised imprint of the flat of Stoney's sword.

Martha was goggle-eyed, diverted for a moment from her course. 'Truly, mistress? A judge has said this in court?'

'Truly, Martha. A marvel, is it not? Perhaps one day there will be a female judge and we shall have our revenge.' I laughed again and turned from her to compose myself.

'There is more, mistress.'

'But you see, Martha, I don't want to hear it. The marriages of others are another country with its own language, and no-one can truly know what goes on there. Fear not. You have told me something I did not know, and I am grateful to you. You have implied that there is more I should know, but I will stop you there. Mr Stoney…'

'Bowes.'

I accepted the correction with a smile. 'You are a bold woman, Martha, and I am glad you are my friend. And oh!' with a sudden burst of exuberance, I flung open the casement to breathe in the sweet Gibside air and the soft flakes of pure white snow. 'I am so very very glad to be home!'

For the two weeks prior to the election, Stoney was charm itself, and he made it his business to keep me close by his side whilst he presented to the Newcastle voters a prospective candidate to represent their interests in parliament. I trusted him not one inch, for I had been witness to the hollow shaping of his policies and the venom of his personal opprobrium. I watched him at the hustings and distributing leaflets in the Bigg Market. He was a marvelous actor, though of course I knew that already. In his efforts to present himself as a man of the people, he was careful not to alienate powerful men who he thought would one day prove of use to him. His anti-establishment stance was a controversial one: the prominent families of Newcastle were largely philanthropic, and his tactic of haranguing them for their privilege and exploitation of the workers was a risky one.

My actions in appearing to support him met with universal disapproval. Edward Montagu, the husband of my erstwhile friend Elizabeth, was aghast to see me there and I soon received a letter from his wife, full of rebuke disguised as earnest advice. She urged me to remember the treatment meted out to Georgiana, Duchess of Devonshire for her campaign in support of Fox. Much as I wished I could distance myself from Stoney's campaign, I bridled at the implication that politics should be left to the men. Why should it? In fact, I was proud to align myself with Georgiana and took a kind of perverse pride in being accused of canvassing 'in a most masculine manner.' Some leaflets went even further, the most notorious of which, The Stoniad, described me as a whore.

Through it all, my feelings were ambivalent. Anything that would take him away from Gibside gave me hope. I felt within reach of a future where I could stay at home with my children and make my life there whilst my husband lived largely in London. It was a vision that sustained me through the indignities of that campaign.

In fact, I will be honest with you, my unknown friend. I sometimes entertained myself with a secret fantasy which I shared with no-one. In the darkest and loneliest nights, whilst my husband was out 'campaigning' in the drinking dens and brothels of Newcastle, I nurtured a dream.

It will be no surprise to you that it focused upon Gabriel, and I no longer blush to think of him. Let me try to explain to you what he meant to me at that time. Throughout my marriage to Lord Strathmore, Gabriel's place in my mind grew. I deliberately pushed him away from my waking thoughts, but in my dreams he came to me often. We were always as we had been that morning, the only time we had been alone as adults, but freed from the constraints of propriety, the outcome was very different. In my favourite dream, he took me by the hand and helped me to my feet, then slipped an arm across my back and held my waist as we walked slowly along the riverside path away from the house, across the meadow and into the oak wood. Nothing was said for we understood each other completely.

Once we were under the canopy of trees, he turned me to him and held me close, my cheek against his chest and his face buried in my hair. He breathed deeply and kissed me gently on the forehead, then on each of my brows, the tip of the nose, then my cheek, pausing each time to linger and smell my flesh. And I, wanton dreamer that I am, felt my body moisten and melt. We made love on a bed of bluebells.

For the seven years of my marriage to John, I rarely saw the real Gabriel, and when I did, I could not meet his eyes. I felt that if I let him look into the window of my soul, he would know of my yearnings and imaginings.

I think now, with an understanding that distance lends, my fantasy of perfection made it harder for me to reconcile myself to the reality of my marriage to John. I am a romantic at heart and if that marriage was to work, I should have been more pragmatic. But to be fair, there was more that John could have done to reassure me that he was not dreaming of his Italian Contessa.

And now the nature of my second marriage made me nourish the hope that I could make my dream a reality, at least in some measure. And so, when I supported Stoney in his election campaign, I felt it a step towards emotional freedom. My hopes were unformed, but they sustained me.

I could barely wait to see Gabriel in the flesh: the very thought of it gave me a tremor in my chest. I was desperate for news of him, but Stoney monopolized the estate business and I could not ask without drawing attention to my interest. I thought I would be driven to ask Martha, perhaps in the guise of enquiring about the estate families, but she had already given me a potted history of births, marriages and deaths and his name had not been mentioned. She knew me so well that I was frightened of her sixth sense detecting anything.

I finally got my opportunity one bright cold morning. Stoney had not come home, which concerned me not one jot, as it was another of my secret hopes that he would be killed in a pub brawl. The campaign leaflets against him did not often come into my

154

possession, but from what I'd seen and heard at the hustings, he owed large amounts of money to several people, was a profligate gambler and, as I was already aware, a frequenter of brothels. None of this dismayed me, in fact it gave me strength to know there were people in Newcastle who could see past the posturing and the charm. On the other hand, he had a gang of devoted admirers who clearly saw his vices and yet sought to emulate him and ingratiate themselves. I learnt a great deal in the course of that campaign.

The other great benefit was that it distracted him from the business of controlling my activities when I wasn't with him. As far as I knew, none of the servants had been given any orders with regard to me, so as soon as I was dressed that first morning, I sent a boy to find the head gardener and ask him to meet me at the Orangery at 10 o'clock.

How sweet it was to open the front door and breathe deeply. The sun shone low over the chapel, pale orange in a clear blue sky as I walked across Green Close and into the Ice House Woods. The snowdrops shone, tiny white lights amongst the fallen leaves.

The stone arches of the Orangery gleamed pale gold, and there, sitting on the steps with his walnut face raised into the sunshine, was the head gardener. When he heard my skirts, he jumped to his feet and almost ran towards me, his hands outstretched. We had never stood on formality, he and I, though the manner of his greeting made me smile:

'Lady Strathmore! How wonderful to see you!'

'No need for that now, Robert. You know I never did agree with Lord Strathmore's insistence on formality.'

'No indeed, mistress,' and here he took off his flat cap and held it against his chest. 'God rest his soul.' Quickly replacing it, he took my hand and led me up the steps to open the door. A wall of heat bent out into the cold February air, and I waited whilst Robert opened some vents, chattering all the while about the boiler, a few problems with leaves scorching, signs of life in some rare seeds. 'So much to show you, mistress!'

The heat inside was stifling and moist when he came back to where I was standing, admiring the alien red of an exotic I had never seen in flower before.

'Why, these are wonderful! I have never seen their like! Are they the ones from the Endeavour?'

'Yes, I thought at first that they would fail, but I soaked them overnight and moved them into direct sunlight and they germinated the very next day!'

'I had quite forgotten how many packets of seeds I had acquired! Some, as you know, are at Stanley House in Chelsea, but I think the gardeners there are not having half the success you've achieved, Robert!' This was not strictly true, but it did not harm to encourage the man: he had laboured so long and with so much love and patience, nurturing plants and seeds the like of which he had never seen before. 'I am quite in awe of your skill! You must be very pleased.'

'I am, but it is good to hear you say it. I am so happy to show you what we have done, Miss Eleanor.' Spontaneously, he grasped my hands in his and his blue eyes shone.

It was so pleasant to see everything surviving and even thriving in the soon-to-be-spring sunshine, that the time flew, and I lost myself in absorption.

'It is so pleasant here, Robert, I feel moved to do some watercolours of this specimen. I think I would like a small desk to be moved into one of the garden rooms. Would you arrange that for me please?'

'Aye, no trouble at all. I'll send a pot-boy.' He went to the door and called over one of the little lads who were working in the shrubbery.

I felt so wonderful that I could take on the world, though I knew that Stoney could appear at any moment, grasp my elbow and steer me back to the house.

I decided to make the most of my opportunity and sit and have a talk with Thompson.

'You have achieved miracles here, Robert. I am so impressed and so grateful. But come, sit here with me and tell me all the gossip.'

Smiling shyly, he sat down on the low wall. 'I hardly know where to begin, miss, so much has happened and yet not really anything at all.'

'Well tell me about the farmers and estate workers? Any babies born in the last six months? Anyone courting?'

'Oh, you'd have to ask my wife about that. We only know the gardeners, really, with living in the walled garden. You know me,

I'm not much of a one for talking.' He shook his head, 'No, though there's a baby in the Minto house. I heard it when I was passing on my way to Whickham.'

'There we go, that's a start. What else?'

'The Palliser lads are doing all the carpentry now. I see Joseph bossing them about in the workshop. It must drive them mad. They know what they're about; learned it at their dad's knee, they did. They're canny workers like.'

I laughed, 'I don't suppose Cuthbert minds. He's a lovely easy-going chap, they both are.'

'Ah well, you say that, but when it came to that row between him and Gabe Thornton... We saw a side of him we'd never seen.' Here, at last, was some news.

'A row? What about?'

'Dorothy Stephenson.' He smiled. 'There was always going to be trouble over that one. She's a beaut and no mistake. All the lads were after her, but she was most often seen walking out with Cuthbert.'

'So what happened?' Lest he think it unseemly of me to be so keen to hear stories, I risked diverting him by adding. 'Oh, it's so good to be home! I've missed all this!' and lest he thought I meant the gossip, I hugged my knees and looked about me, then flung my arms wide, 'All of it!'

Somewhat bemused, he watched me with a smile but said no more.

'So go on, Cuthbert and Gabriel?'

'Well, Gabe had been working over at Darlington for a few months – you know he's got family there – and when he came back, he made a beeline for Dorothy. He's always held a candle for her, you know. They were proper little scamps as kids.' I didn't know, but I kept my face still, not that I needed to worry – Robert wasn't the most intuitive chap.

When he still didn't go on, I said, 'So... what happened?'

'There was a proper fight. Fisticuffs. The Pallisers and Stephensons are church-goers, but Gabriel's not, which is funny when you think of his name.' He broke off and started chuckling to himself, and I felt my temper stir. The suspense was killing me: church? Was Gabriel married to Dorothy?'

'Anyway, they came out of church together, Cuthbert and Dorothy, arm-in-arm like. And there's Gabriel, sat on the wall, cap in hand, waiting for her. And he jumps up and says, "What's going on?" and you know, he's a big lad, bigger than Cuthbert anyway, and everyone stops, and Dorothy drops Cuthbert's arm and says, "Nothing's going on, Gabe. We've been to church is all." And Cuthbert chimes in: "What's it to you, Thornton?" and grabs her arm again. And Gabe comes over and stands in front of them like this.' And here Robert creaked to his feet and stood in imitation of a strapping six-footer with something on his mind. 'And he says, "Let go her arm." And Cuthbert says no, and Gabe takes a step closer and says, "Let go her arm or I'll make you." And Dorothy's trying to get her arm away and going, "Lads, lads," but Cuthbert won't let go and she goes, "Cuthbert, let go, you're hurting me!" and then Gabe goes, "I'll fekkin hurt him!" and punches Cuthbert in the face and he drops down like a dead 'un, spark out.'

He sat back down on the wall, drained by the drama and clearly thinking the tale is over. But I had to know. 'So how did it end?'

'Well, he says, "Come on Dorothy, we're going for a walk," and she says, "There was no need for that! He's just my friend. Am I not allowed to have friends just cos I'm walking out with you? Look what you've done to him!" And she kneels down, going "Cuthbert, Cuthbert!" and eventually he stirs.

'And what did Gabe do?'

'Well he just stands there, wringing his cap in his hands and watching them, and then Cuthbert tries to get up and falls back down and Dorothy, you know how soft-hearted she is, she goes, "Oh Cuthbert!" and Gabe goes, "Dorothy, he's just play-acting." And he turns on his heel and goes. And d'you know what? He was right! As soon as Gabe's gone through the lych-gate, Cuthbert's eyes are wide open and he's lying there like King Arthur, stroking Dorothy's hair.'

'And what did she do?'

'Well, she jumps up and she goes, "You bloody men! I'm having nowt to do with either of you!" and she goes to her mam and dad who've been watching all this and rolling their eyes, and she stalks off with them, head held high.'

'And so now? Who's she walking out with?'

'I've no idea. All I've heard is that Gabe's gone back to Darlington.'

I took a moment to absorb this news, and then I changed the subject: 'Have you received any letters from William Paterson?'

'Yes, I got one just this week. I have it here.' He drew from his pocket a crumpled piece of yellowed paper covered in stamps: shaking the soil from it, he held it out to me. 'He writes that he's sent some seeds under separate cover. Tritonia Flava, native to the Cape of Good Hope. See here, his drawing of it: he says it has a yellow flower. He has sent some also to Kew. He says it has a roundish capsule with round wingless seeds.'

I read eagerly news of the gallant young Scotsman exploring South Africa on my behalf: 'Oh, how wonderful! I cannot wait to see if we can cultivate this exquisite specimen!'

One thousand, one hundred and sixty-three burghers of Newcastle voted for Sir John Trevelyan and only one thousand and sixty-eight for Andrew Robinson Stoney Bowes. He came home drunk and raging about the £12,000 the election had cost. I do not want to think about his treatment of me that night. The next day, we left Gibside, my face shrouded in a veil to hide my tears and my black eye. I felt as though I was being torn out by the roots.

Chapter 17

The journey back to London was a nightmare for me: I experienced it as an abduction, which in a way it was. I pleaded with Stoney to let me go back, and everywhere we stopped, I asked again, but not only were my feelings clearly of no consequence to him, but he actually seemed to take pleasure in the grief he caused me.

The first day of the journey he passed in raging at the establishment in general, Trevelyan in particular. 'Stitched up. The whole thing. The toffs closed ranks, bought votes.' (This last an irony of which he seemed entirely unaware.) 'I'll appeal at Westminster. I've got evidence. I'll show those bastards. I'll be back, and next time the gloves are off.' Whilst he satisfied himself with plotting revenge, I pressed myself into the corner of the coach, feigning sleep, for I feared drawing his ire. At the inn that first night, he drank himself into a stupor from which he failed to awake in time for breakfast.

As I breakfasted alone in my room, my spirits in my boots, I thought briefly of hiring a coach and heading back north to safety, for I felt in the core of myself a visceral fear of returning to the isolation of London, to a houseful of sullen servants whom I could not trust. Eliza, my so-called companion, was asleep in the next room, her pregnancy in advance of mine, and when I heard a man's voice through the oak paneling, I stopped eating to listen. Despite our estrangement, my first thought was for her safety, and I strained to hear the tone of the man's voice. She spoke, and then him: sleepy morning-murmurs. I was astonished: Eliza's husband was in London: who could this be? A moment later, I heard a distinctive bark of laughter and I knew.

I got up and went to the window, my eyes smarting with tears, not for his betrayal but for hers. We had once been close, and now that I knew they were intimate, I began to wonder how long it had been going on. I thought back to that evening at the theatre when Stoney was on the periphery of my group: I had seen them laughing together then. Could it be that they had been having a relationship even before my marriage? It was she who had accompanied me to his so-called deathbed, she who had whispered words encouraging me to do as he asked. I knew by then that he had plotted to obtain my hand, but had Eliza helped him?

Suddenly possessed of a renewed determination, I started to assemble my things in readiness for departure. My departure. North. At last, I had concrete evidence of his adultery. It must confer on me some power. My trunk packed, I sat on a chair and composed myself.

The door opened at last. 'Good morning, oh light of my life.'

I turned on him a gaze of impassive disdain and then said coldly, 'You have betrayed me.'

He looked disconcerted for a moment, and then sat down and reached for the coffee.

'And what of it?'

'With my friend.' Tears started to my eyes and he looked on, unmoved.

He took a long drink of coffee and then poured himself a second cup before he answered. 'You should never have counted her your friend. She is our employee.'

My temper rose at his insouciance and I struck the table emphatically as I spelled it out: 'She. Was. My. Friend. Are there not women enough for you in the brothels? Did you have to foul my own house with adultery?'

'Ha!' He took a swig of coffee and spoke as if to an invisible audience: 'Harken Miss Priss! Faithful unto death to the beautiful Lord Strathmore!' His laugher choked me and he grinned malevolently. 'Or perhaps not.' He gaze me a lascivious wink. 'I think the whole of the *bon ton* knows about your adulterous ways, milady. You are hardly in a position to lecture me! And as for that bastard you are carrying...'

But something had dawned on me now, and when he saw my face, he knew it.

'Are you the father of Eliza's baby?'

Somewhat abashed, he looked away, only for an instant, but it was enough.

'You are, aren't you? She was already in your thrall when you plotted to marry me. She helped you to entrap me. Didn't she?' Suddenly enraged, I rose to my feet and reached out to scratch his face, but he seized my wrists in a grip like a vice. I subsided in uncontrollable tears.

I was so lost in my grief and sense of hopelessness that at first I wasn't aware of him rising to stand beside me until I felt a heavy hand on my back. It was some moments before I registered that he was patting me awkwardly, and I lifted a mutinous, tear-stained face, forgetting in my anger to be afraid of him.

His hand resting on my shoulder, he said, 'There there. Don't upset yourself so much. Nothing is lost. We have a partnership, you and I.'

I was so astonished that I stared at him, mouth agape. 'A partnership?'

'Yes, a partnership. We are as bad as each other.'

'I think not.'

'We are a match for each other, I think.'

'Sir, you are sorely deluded.'

'You cannot see it at this moment, but we are well suited.'

'You jest, surely?'

He didn't reply at first, and appeared to be troubled, like a little boy who doesn't know what he's done wrong. Suddenly he thought of something to say in his own defence.

'I have not troubled you for sex.'

'No indeed, and for that I am grateful.'

'Quite so. So you cannot begrudge me taking my needs elsewhere.'

'Elsewhere? Under my roof! Here? In public!' Another thought dawned on me. 'At Gibside? Did you defile my father's house too?'

'Do not distress yourself with wild imaginings, Eleanor. Concern yourself with the here and now.'

'Yes!' My indignation was mounting again. 'Here and now I sit and hear my own husband in the next room with my friend, who carries his baby! My feelings are so in turmoil I barely know myself!'

'Look, what concerns you the most? Eliza? She was never your friend. You can never count an employee a friend, for the relationship is most unequal. Her welfare? We have her safely married off to your confidante and trustee, the Reverend Stephens, who seems to believe the baby is his own. The baby? The baby will not trouble us.'

'How can you say that? It is your own child!'

'My child? Pah! That means nothing to me. It is not the first bastard born to one of my mistresses, I can assure you.'

I stared at him, quite confounded. This man was the very devil. 'Not your first child? And where, pray, are the other fruits of your prolific loins?'

He smiled then, the slow smile of interest and respect. 'There you are! I have missed the spiky Mary Eleanor I fell in love with.'

'Love?' I was truly bewildered now and my bewilderment seemed to anger him.

'Yes, love. What did you think? That I married you for your money?'

He did not fool me for one moment: this man was an actor to his fingertips. 'Yes, Andrew, I think you married me for my money. As you did Hannah Newton.'

It did not give him even pause for thought. 'Hannah was nothing in comparison to you. She had not a fraction of your beauty or spirit.'

'Or money.'

He smiled a smile of confident complicity. 'Or money.'

He poured himself another coffee, smiling all the while. 'Speaking of money, I am going to need your help.'

'My help? How dare you ask for my help at a time like this? Do you have no conception of the import of what I have just learnt?'

The slap came before I was even conscious that he had raised his hand. As I sat holding my scalding face, frankly astonished by this turn of events, he sipped his coffee and regarded me over the rim of his cup.

'Remember your place, Eleanor. I was enjoying our discussion. It is good for us to …how shall I put this…clear the air. But you forget your place again, and I must punish you. If we are to have a peaceful marriage, a working partnership, you must obey me and afford me the respect due to a man in my position.' I saw his face darken as he remembered that his position did not include a place in the Houses of Parliament.

'The election campaign in which you were so involved leaves us with something of a problem.' I waited. 'It cost a large amount of money, as you are no doubt aware.' He put down his cup and

164

glanced at me out of the corner of his eye. But I caught it. He was afraid of me in some way I could not define or account for.

'Which accounts for our rapid departure from Newcastle.'

He affected a businesslike tone, as though he were performing in a court of law: 'As you are well aware, you have deceived me on two counts.'

My outburst was indignant and heavily ironic: 'I? Have deceived you?'

His eyes took on that menacing glint with which I had learnt to fear, but I was not afraid. I was angry.

'Yes, Eleanor. Though you clearly perceive yourself as a perfect paragon, you are deluding yourself. You are not only an unfaithful wife, an entitled and over-indulged exploiter of the working classes, but also a liar.'

'I … am a liar?'

'Indeed. Yes. Good to hear you confess it. That is the first step to making amends.'

I stood up and walked to the window, the better to protect myself. Down in the yard, the horses were being harnessed in readiness for our departure and the clopping of their hooves on the cobbles calmed my agitated heart. The scene was one of such timeless normality, working people going about their business, that I suddenly felt stronger. George Walker appeared in a doorway and I waved to him. That contact further emboldened me. I stayed where I was, in full view, and turned back to the darkness of the room.

'I think I can safely say that I have never told a lie in my life.'

'Oh come come, Miss Priss. All of us lie to a greater or lesser extent.'

'I sincerely can think of not one single instance when I have felt the need to lie.'

'Ah, that is because you have always had whatever you wanted without having to use stratagems to get it.'

I let that statement linger on the air and stood up straighter but did not reply.

He went on: 'And so I would be interested to hear you account for the fact that you married me under false pretences.'

There were so many ways in which I could have challenged that representation of the facts of our marriage that I barely knew how to respond. I blinked and blinked again. I was surely speaking to a

165

madman. A Geordie voice rang out from the yard and George joined him in laughter. Out there in the pure air were honest fellows: it made me stronger.

'And yet again, Andrew Robinson Stoney, you astonish me. How, pray tell, did I do that?' My mind was cool and I was genuinely interested to hear this unaccountable man explain himself.

He laughed, shaking his head as if unable to believe his ears. 'You people! You live in such a swarm of sycophants and servile arse-lickers that no-one challenges your view of the world, let alone your swaddled selves.'

He stood up and advanced towards me slowly, but I stood my ground. Taking me by the shoulders, he turned me round so that we were both looking down into the yard. I saw George's smile die on his face. Stoney raised his hand and I know I flinched, but he merely waved the fingers at him in a mocking salute before bending to nuzzle my ear, all the while watching George from the curls of my hair. 'Don't think I don't know. You and that lackey as soon as my back's turned. Well, if you know what's good for you, and for him, you'll be visiting your lawyer as soon as we get back to London.'

'My lawyer?' Now I knew where this was going.

'Yes, my sweet, you think it right that you should lure me into marriage and then reveal that you've put your money out of my reach? You think it right that you should hide the presence of the bun in your oven? You are a liar, Mary Eleanor Bowes.'

'I am no liar. But you…' Suddenly his hands were at my back and he was pushing me, slowly but insistently, towards the open window.

'Stop, please, my belly, my baby.'

His arms came round me and enclosed me in a bear-hug.

'Fear not, my lovely. I will not let you fall. You are too precious to me. As gold is precious. As silver is precious, so you are to me.'

I heard footsteps thundering up the stairs. George had vanished from the yard. If he came in, I feared for his welfare, let alone his position in my household. Suddenly, Stoney released me, a fraction of a second before the bang came on the door. He stared at me unperturbed. I could not risk it, and so I answered in as light a voice as I could muster: 'Yes? What is it?'

There was a pause before he spoke. I imagined us both, well aware of the true nature of the situation, play-acting in the presence of this madman. George's voice, when it came, was strained: 'The carriages are ready, madam. Shall we take your bags?'

I looked to Stoney to see how I should answer and he smiled with leering confidence, before bending to whisper in my ear. 'Say goodbye to the lackey, whore.'

George was dismissed on our return to London.

Chapter 18

'I'm considering having you committed to a lunatic asylum.'

I heard those words often during the first years of our marriage, and every single time, my blood froze in my veins. I endured so much, suffered greatly, lost my friends, my devoted staff, my health, my self-confidence. Of all my children, only baby Mary was left to me, for the Strathmores had taken possession of the others, and had them made Wards of Chancery. In my darkest hours, I thanked them for it.

But this was my greatest fear, and it is a threat that hangs over every woman. If even the wife of a king can be locked away, then no-one is immune to the threat of it.

That fateful time he said those chilling words, we were at Gibside, and as Stoney often noted, I showed more spirit when I was there, depleted though I was. It was a cold dark February morning, and he had followed the maid into my bedroom. He was dressed for the hunt but seemed distracted and restless, which was unusual for him. Somehow it was less frightening than the stillness and cold intensity with which he usually regarded me. The maid, whose name I did not know, put more coal on the fire and then busied herself wiping condensation from the mullioned windows, square by square. It wasn't something she usually did, and slight though she was, I felt protected by her continued, determined presence. I felt strong enough to challenge him, 'You jest, surely.'

'No, I do not jest. You are become tiresome. A thorn in my side. An embarrassment to me, to all of us, and to your children.'

That he should say such a thing in her hearing made me instantly afraid. Such was my deep visceral fear that my voice shook, though I did my best to control it.

'No doctor would commit me. I am known.'

'You are known for a whore.'

Injustice has always galvanized me. I feel it in the core of me and it cuts through any other emotion. I jumped up from the bed and approached him, anger blazing from my eyes. I summoned enough self-control not to raise my voice but to stand face to face with him where he lolled in my father's chair. 'You call me a whore. How dare you? You think I don't know of your unpaid accounts in the brothels of this town? You call me a whore and yet you bring your mistresses into my house?'

I saw a flicker of something like surprise, but when I spoke of the house, his eyes hardened and he rose to his full height before bending at the waist to thrust his face right into mine. He spoke with sardonic disdain and I smelt the sour whiskey on his breath: 'Your house? I think you will find you have no house. I think you will find that in the eyes of the law, you barely exist. You are no more than one of my possessions. Icelander is worth more to me than you are.'

He straightened up and turned his back on me. 'On the contrary, my dear, I have suffered you to live in *my house*, and frankly I am growing tired of it.'

I knew nothing then but raw anger. I gave no thought to the consequences but flew at him to scratch that smug sardonic face. He grasped me by both wrists and without any effort at all, lifted me from my feet.

'Ha! Fly at me would you, you madwoman? You have truly lost all sense of reason. I will send for the doctors now and have you tied into a straitjacket.'

All anger and all strength were gone from me in an instant. 'No! Please, no! I will do anything.'

He looked over to the window, where the maid was standing rooted to the spot. 'Jessie, go and fetch Dr Foot. He's in my study.' I did not see her go, but only heard the door open and close.

My head hung and I cried and cried, struggling for breath the longer he held my arms above my head. My shoulders burned and my lungs dragged every breath until it seemed to me my heart would stop. When he flung me on the bed, my ribs banged hard against my elbow and I lay winded, powerless, like a broken doll.

I was barely conscious that he had sat down on the edge of the bed, but lay there lost to myself for I know not how long. I heard a knock at the door. He went out into the corridor; there was a brief hushed conversation and when he returned, I was actually relieved that he was alone. Had the obsequious Dr Foot been sent to get another doctor, one I did not know and who did not know me, a

170

man who had heard of the strange behaviour and appearance of Lady Strathmore, a man who governed an asylum?

By an effort of will, I struggled to steady myself. My heart was pounding in my ears and my ribs ached with every breath I took.

When at last my breathing had steadied itself, I saw that he had lit a cigar and was staring out of the window, motionless. I rolled onto my side away from him and rubbed my aching shoulders, still sobbing quietly.

I have to tell you, my unknown friend, I thought then that I could not be more lonely, frightened and helpless. Sadly, it was not the case, as you will learn. While I lay there, I focused my thoughts on baby Mary, for whom I must survive. If anything happened to me, I knew Stoney would have no hesitation in getting rid of Mary somehow, for though he pretended in public to be a devoted father, in private he called her 'the bastard.'

For her, I decided I would do anything he asked. Anything. I would surrender my will to his, if that was what it was going to take.

He was still uncharacteristically quiet and contemplative, and I feared whatever monstrous thought was taking shape in his brain. I decided to mollify him in any way I could. I spoke softly: 'Andrew?'

He did not answer at first, but merely took another puff of his cigar. I waited, tense, for in his hands, a cigar was a weapon, and I still bore the scars. I recoiled further from his reach.

When the cigar finally burnt out, he ground out the stump on the rug and got to his feet. 'I think I shall not go hunting today.'

Was he regretful? Was he waiting for the doctors to come and take me away? The thought rose in me that he was the one who should be bound in a straitjacket but I pushed it away. If the black carriage did not come, there would be no more rebellion.

If it was on his way, I still had time. Subservience might disarm him. He might leave me alone.

'I have another idea of an agreeable way to spend a dark winter's day with my wife.' He turned from the window and strode over to the small desk in the corner of the room, opening the drawer and examining the inkwell in a way that made me bridle. That was my desk. He had no business... But no. I must not object.

Seemingly satisfied, he came over to my side of the bed and sat in the chair beside me.

'Sit up.'

I sat up, brushing my hair from my eyes.

Sorrowfully, he examined my face. 'Tut tut. See what a mess you have made of yourself. Things have come to a pretty pass, Mary Eleanor Bowes.' He sat back like a judge and folded his arms. ' Go and look at yourself in the mirror and tell me what you see.'

I thought quickly as I rose from the bed. What answer would best please him?

My image in the vanity mirror was a shadowy one, for which I was thankful. I knew I looked a sight: my face was thin, my cheeks sunken and the eyes stared out at me as though I would save that woman in the mirror.

'I see a fearful woman.'

'What more?'

'I see a wife.'

'What kind of wife?'

'A dutiful wife.'

'Ah, interesting. Dutiful and obedient?'

'Yes, dutiful and obedient.'

'As a wife should be.'

'As a wife should be.'

'So, dear dutiful and obedient wife, are you ready to turn over a new leaf?'

'Yes, I am.'

'Come here.' When I stood before him, he reached out a hand, drew me onto his lap and held me against him, so that my head lay against his chest where I could clearly hear his heartbeat, steady, slow, deep and booming. My own heart fluttered in my chest like a caged bird. When he spoke, I felt the reverberations of his voice throughout my head.

'You have been a willful and foolish woman, Mary Eleanor. Have you not?'

'I have. In many ways.' The irony of my words I would keep to myself. For now I must be watchful, careful. His arms held me in a heavy and lifeless grip, but that was as nothing in comparison to a straitjacket.

'Let us enumerate the ways in which you have been a fool. For you know, if you are truly to repent, you must acknowledge your sins.'

172

For the life of me, I could think of no sin to confess. Then I knew he meant Mary. 'I have lain with a man who was not my husband.'

'Indeed. You are a sinner in the eyes of God and a whore in the eyes of society. You are in fact a whore, are you not, Eleanor?'

My heart formed into a tiny fist and started to try to beat its way out of my chest. 'Eleanor?'

The warning was implicit in his tone. I must not waiver. I, who always asserted pride in speaking the truth, must adapt to survive.

'I am a whore.'

I felt the earthquake in him: he made himself more comfortable and relaxed his crushing hold on my shoulder. He even kissed my hair.

'Good girl. We are making progress. This is excellent, Eleanor. I am most pleased. Now, I think what we must do, together, is to cleanse you of your sins.'

I kept my voice small and in my own ears I sounded like a child. 'How can we do that?'

'We are going to write every thing down.'

'Everything?' In truth, I could not think what he meant, what more there was to say. He misunderstood, missing entirely the note of mystification in my voice.

'Yes, everything. You will find it cathartic I think.'

'Cathartic?' I felt him tense: he must not sense the challenge in my incredulity. I thought quickly, and even as I said the words, I feared that he would recognise my pretence. 'What does it mean?' I held my breath: he surely would not believe that I did not know the meaning of the word.

'It means that you will feel cleansed.' Warming to his theme, he got to his feet and set me carefully on mine. Surely he would see through me, but no, he was enthusiastically setting my chair at the desk and beckoning me over. 'We shall start immediately. Strike while the iron's hot, as it were.' He took off his riding jacket and set it over the back of the chair, so that when I sat down, the stiffened lapels dug into my back. He set a sheaf of creamy yellow paper before me and put a pen in my hand. Speaking almost to himself, he said, 'We will need more ink. I shall send for some tea to sustain us. You may make the title page: let's call it The Confessions of the Countess of Strathmore. Yes, capital!'

I stared at the page before me. I was clearly in the hands of a madman but the crisis had passed. Soon a servant would come with tea and I would have a glimpse of a gentle face. Out there in the world, people with kindness in their hearts were going about their business, and there were many of them. He was only one man. How was this even possible, that I was alone in the power of this creature? But I must not think of that now: I must only survive this, do as he wanted and soon I would be with my baby. At the thought of her, tears rose in my eyes. I almost lost control, and could not stop the evidence of my grief from dripping onto the paper. Behind me, I heard him speaking to someone at the door, and I hastily dried my eyes and slipping the dampened sheet to the bottom of the sheaf, I laid a fresh piece onto the surface, running my finger down the tooled leather. I was chilled and my arms ached, but I must write.

When the words were down, I stared at them as though someone else had written them. What had I to confess? I could think of nothing save my open heart, now sealed.

Suddenly, he was there, looking over my shoulder. 'Good good. Capital. I think we should add "Written by herself", don't you? To confirm authorship, as it were.'

I did as he suggested, and he took the sheet, smiling broadly.

'Tea will be brought shortly, and fresh supplies of ink. While we are waiting, perhaps you would like to order your thoughts.'

'How shall I begin?'

'I have a form of words in mind for the introduction, but first let us enumerate your sins, starting with … what was the name of that boy who broke your heart?'

This startled me: what possible connection could this dreadful exercise have with an innocent childhood flirtation? Surely I would be confessing the extent of my relationship with George Gray. I could not think of my childhood friend in the context of sin. At the thought of his sweet face and the fun we had had in those innocent days before the Fall, my eyes burned with tears. I struggled to make my voice inexpressive before I answered. 'James Graham.' I felt his name and all those memories contaminated in that instant.

'Ah yes, James Graham. You practised your wiles on him in your apprenticeship to whoredom, I imagine. We shall start with him perhaps. Ah! But I have another idea. You once told me of your aversion to your first son, unnatural woman that you are.'

174

I could not accept this. I had indeed told him of the grief I had felt in the first few months of baby John's life: I had never used the word aversion. How I wept every day and how all seemed dark and hopeless. This was surely no sin? Since then, I had learnt that I was not alone in this reaction to childbirth. Other women suffered similarly. Though I was ashamed to confess it, it had coloured my relationship with the child, so like his father, so watchful of me. Right from a baby, he had watched me with those deep blue eyes which seemed never to blink, which looked into my heart and found it wanting. Why even Martha had commented on his gaze: 'He looks so serious, this baby! He has an old soul indeed. You've seen it all before, haven't you, master John?'

'I ... I have repented of that, and I have tried as best I can to make it up to the child. It was my health at fault. I ... I cannot count it a sin.'

'It was a sin, Mary Eleanor. And it shall have pride of place at the start of your confessions, for you can blame no-one but yourself. Are you ready to begin? Write these words: I have been guilty of five crimes.'

'Five?'

He turned slowly, the side of his face illuminated in the fire like the very devil he was. I wrote those words, my hand shaking as it moved across the page.

'Now, that poor child. Write about the sin of unnatural motherhood.'

'I ... I do not know what to write.'

He came across and loomed over me and I could smell the sooty heat of the fire on him. "I have been guilty of five crimes. The first, my unnatural dislike of my eldest son." Write that. Write of his innocence and your regret.'

The words came easily, though they swam in front of my eyes.

'Good, good. Now, to your adultery. Write about that.'

As he watched the words spool out across the page, I heard him tut as I wrote. ' "Connection to Mr Gray?" Cowardly, Eleanor, a milksop word for a carnal deed. An act of sin. Sins of the flesh should be acknowledged for what they are. I can see I'm going to have to help you out here. You and Gray committed your first sin when?'

'In January.'

'In January. When poor Lord Strathmore, all unawares, was taking the waters in Bath, I imagine. Your poor sick husband, dying of consumption. Instead of being by his side, as you should have been, you were in London cavorting with a nabob.' This was such a distortion of the facts that I opened my mouth to speak, but the look in his eye silenced me.

'So, you and Gray enjoyed your...what was your word? Your "connection"... throughout the winter months, even while poor Lord Strathmore was risking his life aboard a ship to Portugal on the advice of his doctors. While he was tossed about the ocean, his wife...'

'Please Andrew. Enough. I have owned my shame. I cannot begin to explain how it came about that Gray and I became lovers. But once I had committed the sin, I felt unable to put an end to it. I was so sad and lonely. Lord Strathmore was unfaithful to me, you know. George Gray loved me, and I him.'

He held up a hand. 'Stop, Eleanor, please. Do not try to justify your actions. Have you learnt nothing? It was a sin, was it not?'

I waited for as long as I dared before I said, 'It was.'

'Then write it. Wait! I have a sudden thought.' Animated, he stood and came quickly across the room to seize my face and twist it up so that he could look into my averted eyes. 'Look at me, Eleanor.'

The zeal I saw in his face repelled me and I looked away on the instant. I knew which way his thoughts were heading.

'The bastard was conceived in ...?'

'November.'

He fixed me with those glittering eyes, a frank and challenging expression which made me blush and look away. I feared his next words. 'January to November. Eleanor, look at me. You are a fertile woman. A baby every year with Lord Strathmore. Are you telling me that you had relations with George Gray from January to November and only conceived once? Aha! I thought not!' His jubilation made me want to rise up and slap his face hard, but I forced myself to look ashamed.

To my horror, he knelt down at my side and took my hands in his. He spoke gently: 'Tell me, Mary Eleanor. How did you do it? How did you kill George Gray's baby?'

176

I raised a tear-stained face to him, my instinct hoping against all experience for some pity. 'Not a baby, Andrew. I cannot think of it as such. I did not bleed in May. I simply took a potion Eliza procured for me, and I bled. Not a baby: I cannot think of it as such or else I would run mad.'

'Ah, mad. That is the whole question, isn't it Eleanor? Are you mad? Are you mad enough to be put away from society, so that no more innocents will be harmed? For all were innocents. Despite what you say, Lord Strathmore was your husband, innocent of your base desires for another man. Baby John was innocent when you turned from him and could not love him. George Gray's baby died before it had a chance of life. All innocents.' He paused, the gleam of power in his hawk's eyes. 'And why kill that poor child if, as you say, you intended to marry Gray?'

'I did not intend to marry Gray. I intended to marry no-one.'

'And yet you told me, not a week into our marriage, that you had promised to marry Gray.'

'I had capitulated because I was pregnant again. You know as well as I the consequences for a baby born out of wedlock. I could not bear to take that black potion again.'

'Ah, but I think you did, Eleanor. I think you have taken that black potion many times. You must confess it.'

'I did not. I will not.'

'Oh dear. Then I see that you are quite mad.'

'How so?'

'You anger me. You do not tell the truth. I am your husband. You promise to obey me and yet you do not. You show some signs of sanity in submitting to my will, but then you lapse and the madness comes over you again. I fear you are destined for the lunatic asylum, Eleanor. So sad. George Gray's poor surviving baby will end up in the workhouse. A pity. She was so nearly saved.'

'No! I'll write it! I'll write anything you like if you promise me she will be safe!'

'You are in no position to bargain, Mary Eleanor Bowes. Oh how the mighty have fallen.' But he could not hide the gleam of satisfaction as he retired to his chair to begin his dictation. For dictation it was, all of it.

'Write "By medicines, I have reason to think I miscarried three times," ' he glanced at me to see whether I balked at this outright lie,

177

but I kept my eyes to the paper and wrote as he dictated. 'And attempted it a fourth; but thank God, failed in perpetrating that crime.'

What did it matter? He was clearly enjoying himself: this was no more than another exercise in control. As I wrote on, I reassured myself that no-one would ever see this tissue of lies. It even became an object of fascination to me, as his voice unspooled his fantasies: how did he know so much? Did he forget nothing that was ever said to him? How, when he showed so little concern for the welfare of his fellow man, for the reality of the lives of his creditors and victims, did he seem able to enter the life of another person and invent a monologue such as this? In another circumstance, I would have felt admiration for his skills.

He concocted a distortion of my friendship with my childhood friend James Graham and his sister: the innocent notes we had exchanged and codes we had invented became promises and messages of love and lust. Where I had simply secreted them in my little desk, tied up with ribbon, now I had burnt them and drunk up the ashes. The man was a fantasist. I even risked a little gentle humour, so clearly was he enjoying himself: 'My husband, you should write novels. I think Mr Richardson will be in fear of his reputation.' I waited in trepidation for his response, but he was clearly flattered and merely acknowledged the compliment with a nod.

'Now, to your lack of judgment.'

I confess to a wry smile which I tried to hide. Evidence of my greatest lapse of judgment was sitting in this very room.

'You have repeatedly shown that you have very poor judgment, Eleanor, and it is good that you are no longer to be left to your own devices. I shall protect you henceforth, now that you have acceded to me all control of your life. Let's see…'

I had to stop him. 'May I be excused?'

Instead of allowing me the dignity of a private visit to the water closet, I had to endure him standing at the door regaling me with a list of the people in whom I had placed my trust, all of whom, to a man, had proved themselves at best unreliable, at worst, a charlatan. He listed my female friends, harlots all. Male acquaintances were satyrs and pimps. My colleagues from the Royal Society, charlatans to a man. Eliza and Reverend Stephens, liars. I listened to all this with perfect equanimity, so outlandish were his fantasies and so far away were most of his subjects, but when he turned his attention to the staff of Gibside, my revulsion grew.

When I resumed my place at my desk, I was astonished to hear him say, 'I will leave you now and return at midday. By then, I expect to see an account of your imprudence as I have just outlined. The more detail you add, the greater the evidence of your commitment to this project.'

'But I ...' The face he turned to me was disapproving. He really had convinced himself he was a particularly high-minded priest supervising a confession, or a demanding professor disappointed in a student. I thought the better about what I had been about to say. 'I need to feed Mary.'

'Need? You have no needs, Lady Strathmore, beyond those I dictate.' And with that, he left the room and I heard the key turn in the lock. I heard a female voice in the passageway and knew it would be Mrs Holden bringing Mary for her feed. 'Lady Strathmore is indisposed, Mrs Holden, and asks not to be disturbed.' And then something else that I did not catch, but which caused Mrs Holden to giggle. They went away together.

Once he was gone, my strength suddenly drained from me, and I put my head down on the desk and lay for some time in a stupor from which I found it difficult to rouse myself. The tea was cold and I dared not call for any more. I dared not refuse to write an account of my lapses of judgement, for I deeply feared the consequences if he should return and find I had failed to do as he asked. I briefly entertained the thought of escaping though the window, letting myself down a rope of torn-up sheets to the icy ground and throwing myself on the mercy of the men whose voices I could hear echoing across the valley. A shepherd's voice amongst them, calling to his dog. Lambing had begun.

Under the snow, snowdrops would be stirring. I set to my task and soon found I could enter into it with bravado, losing myself in a reckless disregard for truth.

When I heard the chimes strike twelve, I stopped writing and put my head down on the desk, letting my aching hand hang down. I could not bear to look over what I had written.

The key turned in the lock as the last note faded, and he strode across the room to take the papers over to the window, where he set about perusing them intently.

'Hmm, yes, this is fine work. I'm sure your mother will be interested to read that you acknowledge your mistake in marrying Lord Strathmore against her advice. Headstrong, willful girl.' He shook his head sorrowfully. 'Ha! I like this part: "I was more than imprudent in encouraging and keeping company with people of such execrable and infamous principles: though, indeed, I did not think them such then; but that is no excuse for me, as I ought not to have trusted or allowed anybody to have frequented my house without a previous long acquaintance." ' I listened with incredulity: he had dictated that passage to me and I had actually felt a stirring of pity for him when I heard it now. It was a glimpse into a warped way of thinking, a lack of trust which I knew must be born of living in the midden of his own mind.

When he came to the part about Eliza and Reverend Stephens, I saw the satisfaction with which he read. It was as though his affair with her and her role in tricking me into marriage was some concoction for which I was to blame: ' "As to my madness in wishing Mrs Stephens to stay with me after I was married, I can only say that it was a diabolical infatuation, and that had I known her as I do now, I should have entreated you to turn her out of the house directly." Good, good.'

I rose and made to go once more into the water closet, but he restrained me with a hand upon my wrist without looking up from his reading. I stood unresisting until he had finished

'I think we need more detail, particularly on your affair with Gray. If you are to truly convince your reader of your repentance, you must acknowledge every sin.'

What could he mean? Surely he did not want me to enumerate every moment of a relationship which lasted almost a year?

'When constructing a narrative, a reality in which others can engage, it is important to include facts which cannot be denied.'

'To make the lies seem more real, you mean?'

He regarded me for long moments, but quite calmly. I saw that he felt we had reached an understanding. 'Quite. You are learning, Eleanor. We shall take our time over this, for we want to do it properly. You are tired now: I shall call for an egg for you. Then I think it best that I leave you to it, so that you can summon up all those little details from your memory. Make the story flow so that the reader knows the extent of your foolishness and depravity.'

'I have had no breakfast.'

'You are indisposed.'

'I am hungry.'

'Indeed. Hunger and discomfort are a necessary part of training. I have trained my dog. I have trained my horse. I shall train you.'

The outraged rebellion I felt, even in my weakened state, must be hidden, but I had to see a friendly face or else I could not stop myself from crying. 'Please could you ask for Martha to bring the tray? There is something I must ask her.'

'What is it?'

'It is no matter, merely to have a report on her daughter's baby, who is ill.'

'Martha has more time to tend to her family now.'

'How so?' although I already knew the answer. Only Martha's age had saved her for so long.

'You have a new maid with a much more comely face. Old Martha is ready for the knacker's yard, I fear.'

I could not help it. 'You have dismissed Martha?' I cannot think my tone was incredulous, only sad and defeated. Nevertheless, his face changed in an instant. Without speaking, he went slowly towards the dying fire and picked up the tongs, with which he grasped a glowing ember.

As he turned to come towards me, I fell to my knees. 'Please, no. I am sorry. The servants are yours to retain or dismiss as you see fit.' It made no difference. He lifted the hem of my nightgown with one hand and held the ember against my calf with the other. I bit my own hand and I tried unsuccessfully to stifle my cries.

Satisfied that he had made his point, he returned the ember to the fire with care, as though placing evidence.

'May I get some water?'

'Of course, my dear. I am not a cruel man. When you disappoint me or forget your training, you make me do things I do not enjoy. You get your water and I shall go and make arrangements for your egg. If you are a good girl, I might even bring it to you myself, solicitous husband that I am. The servants are most touched by my devotion to you in giving up my hunting to attend to your needs. You like your eggs lightly boiled, do you not? Perhaps some bread, but if you have too much to eat you will become sleepy, and we have work to do.'

That afternoon I wrote of George Gray and quite lost myself in the telling of it. Light-headed, and ignoring my hunger, I devoted myself to reliving those days when I had felt safe in the knowledge of his kindness and devotion. I remembered the way he took care of me through illness when I caught a terrible chill after getting drenched in Kensington Gardens. He had sat by my bedside for days, cooling my head with a flannel. Why had I taken that for granted?

I wrote honestly about my feelings, which I had openly expressed at the time. I had never been anything but truthful with George Gray: "I told Mr Gray that he had my friendship and esteem; that my heart had long been in the possession of Lord Strathmore...That I had been so unhappy in matrimony that I was determined never to engage myself indissolubly again." Oh for the time when I believed that things could be so simple.

In revisiting that time, when I had sensed freedom and had felt confident to lay down such conditions to a man, the hope came to me that one day I would have such liberty again. It felt such a tiny bulb of hope, but I thought again of the snowdrops and all that they endure and I knew that as long as I was alive, I would nurture that bulb.

When he read what I had written, he nodded approvingly, and then said, 'Now, I think we need some explanation of your admiration for me and the reasons which caused you to break George Gray's heart, despite the fact that you were carrying his baby. You conceived a great passion for me, you must admit, and the reader needs to know how that came about. You are clearly a faithless woman and you must own it.'

As the afternoon grew dark and the fire died, he turned his mind to the servants he had dismissed: 'I have strong suspicions about your faithfulness to me, Mary Eleanor. You were far too close to George Walker.'

'George Walker was my good and faithful servant. He has served my family all his life, and his father and grandfather before him. He was like a father to me after my own died.'

His eyes glittered but he did not get up. 'You deny having sexual relations with him?'

'Of course I do. Perhaps you have never experienced devotion yourself.'

For a moment I thought I had over-stepped the mark, and I saw him consider whether to respond, but his mind had turned to the next item on his list of my misdemeanours: 'Write about your deception with regard to the pre-nuptial deed. Do not be too specific, for you are a muddle-headed girl and your recollections cannot be trusted.'

My hand weak and stiff around the pen, I scratched the story thus: "I gave him, the day or two before my marriage, the deed drawn up on account of my intended marriage with Mr Gray, and bade him keep the deed till I called for it. I declare solemnly that I did not do this from any mistrust in your generosity or honour. How could I? I had a high opinion of both and had never seen or heard anything which induced me to think otherwise. Having taken such precautions on my children's account with a man who I knew I could trust, I ought not to be less cautious with one whom I could not be so strongly assured of: but I would not tell you of the paper lest it should look like mistrust."

At first, he did not like this honesty, but quickly persuaded himself it was perfect: 'You attempt to justify your actions. Let me cogitate a moment. Yes, this is realistic, I think. You would naturally do so. A reader would believe this. Capital.' Again, I wondered who this reader might be, and could think of no-one save his cronies. Perhaps he intended to entertain them with a reading. I was so tired that I could not give a jot.

Still he had not finished: 'Go on to explain how you came to revoke the deed. You decided of your own free will to destroy the parchment. ' I looked up involuntarily but luckily had the presence of mind to extinguish the light of challenge in my eyes. I had never revoked the pre-nuptial deed. At least, I had never knowingly put my signature to such a document.

He watched me, his eyes fiercely burning, and then I watched him gather himself to reiterate and his voice had taken on a steely edge: 'As I said, voluntarily. You learned to trust me. Write that.'

I wrote it as carefully as I could, suddenly aware that one day these 'confessions' could be brought before a court of law. The thought made me quail, for what judge would question their veracity when everyone knew that women were hysterical, lascivious beings incapable of moderating their behaviour?

This is how I explained away the apparent revocation of my pre-nuptial deed, though the reality could not have been more different: "Your fondness for my children, and the generosity I thought I discovered in you on all occasions relating to pecuniary matters; together with the apparent openness of your temper made me assure myself I had nothing to fear for my children and reproach my heart for ever having entertained a shadow of a doubt.'

When I had read it aloud to him, praying that this would be the end of it, he thought for a moment and then, to my complete dismay, continued. 'Now, let's think. George Walker is gone but is not to be trusted. We do not know his whereabouts. We need to establish his unreliability .'

A great dread of his true purpose in the creation of these confessions began to crystalise in my mind. At first I had believed it to be simply an exercise of power, but now I saw that he had a real purpose.

'Write about your madness in trusting this servant with a copy of the deed. Confess that you attempted to deceive me about its existence, that you wrote a note to him in French because you knew I despise anything but the King's English and would not understand it if it fell into my hands. You are a fool, Mary. See what a tangled web you have woven?'

"I ordered George to burn the paper and when we were at Gibside, I asked him if he had, and he declared he had. Not having time to tell him when I spoke with him, I passed him a note written in French in which I charged him never to reveal having had that deed, or of any other thing he knew relating to me." He listened and then said, 'This was madness.'

'Pardon?'

'Write it. Write the words "This was madness." '

I did as he asked.

He watched and then said, 'Write "I have now punctually, minutely and most entirely given you a full account of everything I ever did, said or thought that was wrong."'

I did as he asked, and then, laying down my pen, I looked at the papers where they lay. I knew what I had done, but what would have been the consequences if I had refused? I looked up at him, smiling in that cruel satisfied way he had. 'I have, by my own hand, furnished you with a perpetual fund for unkindness and even a good excuse for bad usage; but you are my husband and I must obey you.'

He took the papers and I watched, hardly daring to breathe as he read, and when he laid them down and walked over to the window, I decided to see whether he would find pity in his heart and make me a promise.

'Andrew? In return for what I have done today, may I ask something of you?' There was no answer, but I carried on, praying that he would agree to what I was about to ask. 'I beg your promise to burn these papers, that you will destroy them when I die, that I may not stand condemned and disgraced, by my own hand, to posterity.'

He turned back into the darkened room and it was as though I had not spoken: 'It's not enough. It needs more work. You are sounding altogether far too self-righteous, ending it like that, as though you trust your own judgment to know what's right and wrong. We have more to do.'

'No, surely you cannot mean that!' I sobbed. 'I am hungry and tired and I have not seen Mary. I cannot endure any more. I have done everything you said – please!'

He watched me, his expression unreadable in the darkness, but when he spoke there was a kindness in his voice that felt like balm. 'You're right. You are too tired to do it justice now. This is a great endeavour we are embarked upon. Together we shall save your soul.'

He regarded me in the half-light of the candle and his face softened. 'You have done well, Eleanor. We shall leave the next part until another day. After all,' and here he kissed me on the brow, 'we have all the time in the world.' He helped me to my feet and over to the bed. 'Lie down now, my sweet, and rest. I shall send your new maid to introduce herself. If you feel you can eat anything, send word with her and she shall bring you a little light supper. I shall not disturb you again tonight.' And he locked the door behind him.

The next morning, it began again. I saw no other person in the whole of that second day. He tended to the fire himself, and trays were left at the door with a discreet knock. My heart ached to see Mary, and once I thought I heard her crying in the distance, but a warning look from my captor had me subsiding back to my task.

'I want you to be sincere in everything you say. Write next what is in your heart at this moment.'

I thought a moment, and then I wrote: "To prove that I am sincere, I know not what method to take. I am already so loaded with misery that there is only one curse which is not mine already."

He read over my shoulder as I wrote, and patted my shoulder, murmuring, 'There there, things are not so bad as that. See this as a chance: a chance to look back over your whole life and expiate all the mistakes you have made, all the foolishness, all the gullibility, the self-centredness and indulgence, all the flirtation and teasing, all the times you exercised your feminine wiles. I want to hear it all.' He looked at me closely. 'You look very pretty today. Your eyes are sparkling.' In truth, I think my eyes were shining with tears.

Nothing he said surprised me any more. It was a long time since I had recognised the truth of John Locke's words: "An excellent man, like precious metal, is in every way invariable; a villain, like the beams of a balance, is always varying, upwards and downwards." This man was a villain to the core.

And now he said, 'You do love me, don't you? You do understand that I am doing all this for your own good, for the good of our marriage? I want to know you, Eleanor, in all senses of the word.'

His fingertips trailed across the tops of my breasts. 'You have such beautiful breasts. Will you think worse of me if I tell you that they were the first thing I noticed about you?'

I smiled despite myself. 'You were not unusual in that.'

I saw I had made a mistake, for his face hardened and his voice changed completely. 'You are my wife now. Your charms are for no eyes other than mine. You will dress modestly at all times. Is that clear?'

'Yes Andrew, it is clear.' I bowed my head to hide my fear.

'Your hair too. Such beautiful chestnut curls.' He took a lock and coiled it round his finger, whilst I reflected that rarely had my hair looked so neglected. It had not been washed for almost a week, and without Martha's 100 strokes a night, which we had both found so soothing, it was lank and greasy, but he seemed not to see. When he kissed me on the cheek, it sent a chill down my side. 'Such a beautiful woman, and all mine.' He kissed me again on the side of the mouth and then full on the lips.

It startled and repulsed me, but I must not risk angering him, so I kept still and hoped that his physical attentions would soon cease. In some distant part of myself I wondered at this, for rarely had I felt so dirty or unattractive, but then of course I realized that it reduced me to the level of the kinds of women he seemed to favour: desperate women brought low, low enough to have to make their way in the world with the only means at their disposal. As he undressed me and I passively let him go about his business, I reflected upon what this showed about him and wondered where this fear of women had been born.

Finally, when with a grunt he emptied himself into me and lay his full weight upon my body until I feared I should suffocate, I felt I had an understanding of him. I would remember this: that he had been aroused by my state of abject helplessness, and I would use it against him. I had another weapon in my armoury, or so I reassured myself, though when I look back now at the poor cowed creature that I had become, I pity her delusion.

At last, he rolled off me and fastened up his trousers. He never did like to show any vulnerability. He propped himself up on one elbow and looked down into my face: 'I shall get a child on you soon.'

'It does not always happen so easily.'

'With me it does. I think you will find yourself with child very soon. And then I shall have an heir, for it will be a boy of course.'

'How can you be sure?'

'They mostly are.' He really felt no need any longer to pretend. 'I shall be a good father to him, I think.'

'My father was a good father.'

Interested, he propped himself up on one elbow. 'Tell me about him.'

I never needed any encouragement to talk about my father, as if speaking of him could bring him to life in the air of the room. If only. And so I told him all, all the things of which my love and admiration were made, all his strengths and passions, all his intelligence and fairness, his compassion, his humour, his devotion to my education, his oft-expressed determination that, though a woman, I would have all the benefits and training, all the priorities and liberty of a man.

And when I had finished speaking, what do you think he did? He sat me back at the desk and made me write an account of my father which I did not recognise, in which all his devotion was turned to obsession, all his strength was turned to despotism, and all his compassion was turned to foolishness. What I wrote was a betrayal of my father and when I had finished, I looked at my hand as though it belonged to another, which of course it did.

Something in me, some sense of my own integrity, broke that day.

Chapter 19

By the time I had endured six years of marriage, even my father would have struggled to recognise me. I looked and behaved like the thin, disabled, much older sibling of the Mary Eleanor Bowes who once was.

Time and mistreatment had dulled my senses. Whether we were at Gibside, Streatlam or Gloucester Square, I hardly spoke to anyone other than Stoney. Those who might have felt concern for my well-being were assured by my husband that I was well-cared for in my mental incapacity, but that, as I often heard him say, 'Perhaps one day I shall have to bow to medical advice and commit Lady Strathmore to an asylum for her own safety, for she is a danger to herself. It is so sad. When I think...' and here he would wipe away a barely-discernible tear. I would look on, mute and cowed.

I saw my children only on occasional and all-too-brief visits, which were always closely supervised. The fear and dismay in their sweet little faces when they saw me: it breaks my heart to think of it even now. Only young John was steadfast when he approached me, his beautiful face so serene like his father's, but his eyes unreadable.

When my mother died, I received the blow like I received all the others, with passivity and helpless tears.

At Gibside, I stayed mostly indoors and hardly saw a familiar face, save for the estate manager, Thomas Colpitts, whom Stoney clearly liked and admired. It was a wonder to me how their relationship had survived the destruction of the ancient oaks. We had not been long married when news had come to me that the new master of Gibside was advertising timber for sale in the Newcastle papers. Colpitts had turned up in London unannounced, and there was such a row that I thought it must surely end in violence. At one point, I heard him shout, 'But no-one will buy it! You know that. You did the same at Coal Pike Hill and Hannah Newton's uncle posted bills warning people not to buy from you! It is remembered, Mr Stoney!' the last word almost spat out. There was silence then, and I felt sure one or other had been dealt a blow. They were both big men, but Colpitts certainly had the edge, and I felt a frisson of hope that Stoney would be bested in some way.

I strained hard to listen. Still silence. And then Stoney's voice, low and emollient, and then Colpitts, calmer now and lower, and then tea was sent for, and when he went way again, I saw Stoney pat him manfully on the back as he climbed into the carriage. Colpitts' face was not visible to me when he left to return to Gibside. I imagined the great oaks lying like a slain army and the thought of it pained me acutely.

When next they met, Colpitts had the look of a man who would not be intimidated. I saw Stoney greet him with civility and a certain wariness that I had not seen before. Perhaps the thought had occurred to him, as it often had to me, that Colpitts knew of men who would happily arrange for the new master of Gibside to fall down a disused mine-shaft.

It was a rarity indeed to hear him talk to a Gibside employee with respect, and I marveled when I later heard them laughing together. My father had been very proud of Colpitts, often boasting to other landowners of his integrity, his strength, his fairness and his diplomatic skills. He was one of those charismatic men, universally loved and respected by the tenants and estate workers whose living was in his hands. I found it hard to believe he could look at the wreckage of George Bowes' daughter and feel nothing.

In London, I was persona non grata in all circles. Stoney had been elected sheriff by then, and he had his clique of well-respected men: the Scott brothers, a lawyer called Gibson, the renowned surgeon and natural historian John Hunter, and of course the ever-present and ever-obsequious doctor, Jesse Foot. In their presence, he was charm itself, and whenever I was invited to join them for dinner, my husband acted the part of a solicitous carer to a helpless invalid.

Out in the wider world, his reputation was far from clean. Even I could discern that he had his enemies: there were often bangs on the front door and raised voices as the footmen dealt with yet another angry tavern-keeper or betting-shop owner. Sometimes, there were gentler knocks and I would hear soft voices, pleading and sobbing. Stoney never answered the door himself, and the footmen always turned those girls away, but sometimes I would see them going back to the tradesman's entrance where I assume they were given food. They were often carrying babies.

As for my old friends from the world of botany, I was infected not only by association with a known rake and debtor, but also because of what happened to poor James Paterson. Such a young man, so keen and industrious – I could not have found a better naturalist to explore the Cape on my behalf, but of course, as soon as Stoney took control of the finances, all payments to Paterson were stopped. Clearly excited by what he was finding and experiencing, he continued to send home his letters and seeds, undaunted by what must have appeared to be my indifference.

Eventually (I had this story from him some years later) he had become so indebted to his guides, bearers and hosts that he had to impose on some Dutch acquaintances to settle his debts and bring him to Europe. He wrote to me from the Netherlands, though of course I never saw the letter, to tell me all that he had found, still in hope that some misdirection in the mail had prevented him receiving the support he had been promised.

It was at dinner one night with Stoney's clique in 1780 that I had my first news of what had happened to Paterson.

We had just been served the fish course when John Hunter said, 'Now, Bowes, what about this money you owe me?'

Stoney flashed a look in my direction, a look that I could tell was meant to warn Hunter to go no further in my hearing.

'Yes, yes, we'll talk about it later. Over port. Has no-one ever told you, Hunter, that it's most impolite to speak of finance in a lady's presence?' He guffawed loudly at his own joke and took a deep drag on his cigar.

'Well,' said Hunter, and to my great surprise, he turned to me. 'Lady Strathmore has it within her power to settle your debt, Bowes.'

Stoney took his cigar from his mouth, speechless for once in his life. I knew he set great store on maintaining the respect of these men, and I was surprised to hear that he owed Hunter money.

I took advantage for Stoney's discomfiture and risked speaking directly to Hunter, though my voice creaked through lack of use.

'How so, Mr Hunter?'

'Why, Lady Strathmore, I think you know.' And he winked at me good-naturedly. 'The stand-out specimen brought back by your man Paterson. Now that is something I would give my eye-teeth to have in my museum!'

I was in a quandary, for Hunter clearly believed that I was fully acquainted with the results of Paterson's three years in Africa. I knew nothing about what had befallen him: soon after our marriage, Stoney had sold Stanley House along with all my glasshouses and carefully-nurtured plants and announced there would be no more talk of what he called "loathsome weeds." Given Hunter's interests, he was unlikely to be talking of a botanic specimen, and I yearned to know what it was. But if I angered Stoney, I would no doubt be solicitously escorted from the room and punished later. I chose the diplomatic option.

I smiled demurely. 'My husband must decide for himself, Mr Hunter.'

Stoney sat up straight in his chair: finely attuned as I was to his moods, I could detect relief where Hunter will have seen only pride and excitement. It was also clear to me that he had no idea what he was talking about when he said, 'I'll think about it. I may get a better offer.'

'If the body was preserved, perhaps, but there are few men with my skills. I can reassemble the skeleton and the skin, have it stuffed and mounted, and give it pride of place in my museum, though I may have to make a hole in the ceiling to accommodate it!' He turned back to me in his animation, 'I shall of course credit her Ladyship with its discovery. I can still scarcely believe that it exists! I imagine you share my excitement, Lady Strathmore. I cannot wait to examine those vertebrae, that astonishing attenuated neck! I must discover how it is articulated!'

A giraffe. Paterson must have brought back the remains of a giraffe. How exciting: it would be the first of its kind ever to reach these shores, and I could understand Hunter's enthusiasm. I never learned the nature of the debt, but Hunter did indeed obtain the specimen.

It was soon after the news about Paterson that I realized I was pregnant again, and Stoney was predictably smug. If I had any hopes that he would treat me with any more tenderness for the duration of my pregnancy, they were soon dashed, though he never risked any harm coming to the baby.

Little William was born at Gibside on 8th March 1782. I remember how dark the room was: the sky was heavy and yellow with threat of snow. He was a small baby, dark and solemn, as well he might be given the circumstances of his conception. Of course a male heir made Stoney jubilant, and he was already drunk when he first saw his son. He appeared in my room accompanied by a comely young woman with long red hair worn loose. It seemed from her confident demeanour and bold stare that she was already perfectly familiar to the midwife and definitely to her employer. Don't think any worse of me, but I did not even try to breastfeed him and put up no resistance when the two of them took him away.

I lay back on my pillows and watched the darkness gather outside. I used to love snow, the pristine beauty of a fresh fall, the hushed sounds, the crunch of footsteps. I lost myself in reminiscence and drifted off to sleep. When I awoke, I was alone and the fire had gone out, but the room was warm and after I struggled from bed to use the chamber-pot, I felt quite safe back in my mother's bed. I thought of my baby, of course I did, but with a bleak absence of feeling that took me back to the birth of Maria.

The next day, it was still snowing, great heavy flakes that blurred the landscape and built up in drifts against the buildings. Snow such as I had never seen before. When little Mary was brought to see me – she would have been five at that time – her face glowed red with excitement and the tip of her nose was icy when I kissed it. I must get up now! Now! Come and see! I allowed myself to be dragged to the window, which she would insist on opening, so that great flat flakes floated into the room and we caught them on our tongues, laughing.

Happiness is a curious thing: it comes unexpectedly, sometimes lit against the darkness. That was one of those moments.

Then there is the kind of happiness that we only recognise when it is gone. We rebuke ourselves because we did not recognise it when we had it. Rightly or wrongly, that is how I think of my first marriage. I could have been much happier than I was: if only I'd known then what I know now.

The first time I experienced a prolonged period of real happiness as an adult, it was in that single year of freedom after John died. The fact that it was tinged by guilt made it all the sweeter, for that meant I knew it was real. On the 4th July that year, 1776, the

American Declaration of Independence enshrined in law the right to 'Life, Liberty and the pursuit of happiness' and I felt as though I had written those words. What I have learnt since is that you cannot pursue happiness. It comes to you when you are least expecting it.

That memory of little Mary and I laughing as we caught snowflakes on our tongues is a perfect little gem of joy that I can bring out to warm me whenever I like.

And just as a cataclysmic weather event will be forever associated in my mind with the birth of George in 1771, William's arrival in 1782 was swiftly followed by more disaster for the people of the Tyne. When the snow stopped, the rain started, and so much water fell from the skies in those few days of March that the river rose once more to a height which brought tumult and destruction: Ridley Hall Bridge and five arches of Hexham Bridge were swept away, and Haydon Bridge was rendered impassable. When the torrent reached Tynemouth, more than fifty colliery vessels had to cut their anchors and be swept out to sea at the mercy of the elements.

Happiness is a thing we cannot control, and so is the power of nature. It's surprising how often we need to be reminded about both.

Little Mary was a great comfort to me, and the fact that Stoney allowed our closeness rumbled in the back of my mind like distant thunder. I often found him watching me as I knelt with her in the garden tending to her little plot or when she sat on my knee to read a story. When she was finally taken from me, I found that I had known all along that the day would come.

One bright morning in late summer, I awoke early. The harvest was safely gathered in and there was a celebratory mood out on the farms: if Stoney was absent or in a good mood, I would ask whether I could take Mary for a walk. He would insist that we were accompanied, but no matter. It would be good to be out in the open on such a morning, and I lived for the occasional chance to speak to working people, however watchful they might be, for everyone lived in fear of drawing Stoney's ire. It was only a couple of years after the paper mill had been mysteriously burnt to the ground after a dispute between Stoney and the tenant: no-one wanted to risk anything.

194

I had not heard him come home and assumed he had spent the night in Newcastle. Whenever he was absent in this way I nurtured a secret hope that he would have met with some accident and I would never see him again.

I dressed quickly, in the simple muslin gown that I favoured when I felt the day to be my own. Mary's nanny slept in her nursery, although I had sometimes found her unaccountably absent. On those occasions, I found the courage to creep into Mary's little bed for a cuddle, and sometimes if I could be sure Stoney would not find us, I had carried her to mine. Such times were blissful and I cherish the memories of our closeness, the warmth of her little sleepy body and the smell of rosewater in her hair.

I went to her nursery and found it empty. My mind instantly filled with panic. No innocent explanation could account for this, none. Shaking, I went rapidly downstairs to the kitchens, hoping against hope that I would find her there, for everyone adored little Mary and the cook had asked Cuthbert Palliser to make a tiny table and chair especially for her visits to the kitchen.

The stone flags were cold on my feet as I sped along the pantry corridor, trying not to call her name. A kitchen-maid was coming towards me, and when she averted her eyes and scuttled past, I felt a cold tremor of fear. I came to rest in the doorway and my eyes went straight to Mary's little table, where a small bowl and a glass stood empty.

The kitchen staff stopped what they were doing and to a man, they stood still with their eyes on the floor. Since Stoney has sacked all my house-staff and filled the place with fearful men and pretty slatterns, I knew no-body save the cook, and she was not there. I could not keep my voice steady. 'Where is Mary?' The cook appeared in the doorway of the larder and I saw the pity in her eyes. Then she turned to look out of the window. At first I thought it was fear or denial, but then I heard across the still morning air the unmistakable sound of a carriage being driven at speed away from the house. The next thing I remember, I found myself running barefoot on the gravel calling her name.

In my weakened state, a great cavern seemed to have opened in my chest, a great schism in my being, I did not care whether I lived or died. I may have lost consciousness – in truth, I have no memory of events after that. All was blackness, in my heart, in my head, in my soul, as though I had drowned in a muddy silted lake and the cold of death was seeping into my whole being.

I remember raised voices. Someone was carrying me and I was conscious of heat and we were inside, perhaps the hallway. There were voices, male and female, and the man carrying me was angry: I felt his voice reverberating through my head and his heart thudded against my ear. For a moment of sublime hope, I was a child, back in my father's arms and I was safe. But then another man's voice was raised and other, colder hands were taking me. I lost consciousness and the next thing I remember was coming to awareness of life, not wanting it and trying to bring the darkness back.

Other hands touched my brow and sometimes trickled water into my mouth. I took nothing. I wanted nothing. I sought oblivion.

When consciousness became unavoidable, there was no light in the room save a candle almost burnt out. I was lying on my side, my legs curled up and my knees against my chest. My hair was sticking to my face and there was a distant awareness that my shift was damp with sweat. I groaned and curled still further into myself, not caring, rejecting all awareness of self. I wanted to be dead.

The next time I drifted into consciousness, I thought at first it was blackest night, but the blackness was a presence and I knew from the stale smell of whiskey that it was him. I kept my eyes closed and knew when he moved away from the bed because the light of the dying candle seeped though my eyelids.

My voice, when it came, was a ghost of a thing that drifted from me like smoke: 'Where is she?'

He did not answer, and I could barely summon the will to ask again. I felt as though I was cast adrift on a boat without oars, a boat with low sides. The waters of a cold lake lapped at me. A tall figure was standing on the shore, staring impassively out across the lake, and though his face was cast in darkness, I knew who it was. I could simply roll over and let the water close over my head. The thought was a tempting, even comforting one.

But then in my cold imaginings, I discerned another figure beside him on the shore, a small girl who glowed gold.

I sat up, shaking. I peeled tendrils of damp hair from my cheek and sent out the ghost to ask again, 'Where is she?'

There was no reply. I strained my ears for any sound but the silence was so profound and the blackness so complete that the thought came to me that I was really dead. I slid a leg out from under the blankets and found the floor. I stood and walked to the window like a newborn lamb, my eyes straining to find some grey in the midst of the blackness. And there it was, a pale disc of moon like a delicate leaf of honesty quivering in the lightest breath of air.

By the light of that moon, frail as baby's breath on frosty air, I saw the roof of the chapel. Beneath that chapel was an empty vault supported by a beautiful pillar like a fountain of sandstone where the ghost of another small girl waited for her father to come home.

When I look back now on that poor woman, tiny, emaciated and bereft, sobbing her grief to the cold stars, my heart breaks for her. She thought she was broken. She thought all was lost. But it wasn't, because into her life came an angel of salvation.

In the days after Mary's abduction, for that was what it was, I was delirious, delirious with grief, with fever, with hunger, with despair. In my weakened state, I had caught a chill. Everyone who came into the room was asked the same question: the scullery maid who came to tend the fire, the kitchen maid who brought me a thin gruel and a piece of dry bread, even, eventually, the doctor I had never seen before, whose breath stank of whiskey. To every one of them: 'Where is she?'

Someone, not him, told me. 'She is gone to school.'

It was some tiny comfort. As the fever abated, I forced myself to drink the gruel and eat the bread, all the while holding before me the image of that small glowing child. I shrank to a burning core. As my mind cleared, I thought about what made us live, what tiny spark is it that ensures that a bulb will sprout? How does a snowdrop stay alive?

There was a strange kind of release in having lost Mary: I had reached what I thought was the absolute nadir. I was less afraid, if you can understand that, for the thing I most feared had happened.

One day, without asking anybody, I got up from my bed, put on my old muslin dress, wrapped a shawl around my shoulders and walked straight out of the front door. I must have looked a terrible fright, and the servants I passed made no attempt to stop me. It was late September and the air was a fine warm drizzle with a tinge of wood-smoke. The gravel pressed into the soles of my leather slippers and my legs felt like dandelion stalks.

I walked through the Ice House woods to the shrubbery walk. A blackbird lobbed across my path and its chinking alarm call was echoed by another.

When I got to the Orangery, there was no sign of life, so I slipped in by the side entrance like a wraith. The air inside was dry and warm and my lungs drank it in like balm. The presence of plants soon worked its magic: the exquisite Tritonia Flava was in flower, and I lost myself in examining the miracle of it.

As I passed the garden room, I saw an open letter lying on my small writing-desk. When I lifted it, it left a dark square in the pale yellow layer of dust and pollen.

It was a letter from Paterson, dated two years previously, and it was addressed to me, care of Robert Thompson. In it, he wrote: 'Dr Solander has recorded it in Hortus Kewensis under gladiolus, but gladiolus has an oblong capsule with winged seed, and this plant has a roundish capsule with round wingless seed. I hardly dare to challenge Dr Solander myself, but perhaps you might raise the matter with him? I beg you to reply to me, for I have received no word from you and my bills have been returned unpaid. I am in sore need of financial support and am surviving on loans from a kindly acquaintance.'

It was a kind of epiphany for me. This sweet and dedicated young man, whom I had sent so far from home to inhospitable territory and then abandoned to the mercy of strangers. Just one more victim of this monster I had brought into innocent lives. I had allowed the devil into Eden and he must be expelled.

I left the Orangery a different woman.

We were due to travel back to London in October, and although I always dreaded leaving Gibside, I could look forward to seeing my daughters on one of the pre-arranged visits which were strictly supervised by Thomas Lyon, sometimes in person.

I was waiting in the morning room, supervised by a silent hulking fellow who stood in the doorway as if to prevent me bolting. The carriage was loaded and I could hear the groomsmen through the open window. Still Stoney had not appeared. Eventually, I heard his footsteps emerge from his study with two of his agents and then he brusquely announced to anyone within earshot that we would not be leaving as he had business to conduct. I jumped up from my chair, so anxious was I not to miss a chance to see my daughters. I had hope that little Mary had been sent to the same school as Anna, and would be brought with her. The hulking man in the doorway regarded me with alarm, quite clearly convinced that reports of my derangement were true.

I steadied my voice, 'Would you kindly ask my husband if I might have a word?'

Clearly under orders not to let me out of his sight, he leaned out of the doorway, and by some silent gesture, indicated to Stoney that I would like to speak to him.

I heard quiet words being spoken between the three of them, then the two election agents appeared outside and prepared to mount their horses.

When Stoney entered the room, he appeared distracted and irritable. I looked pointedly at my guard before I spoke, and with a sigh which he didn't trouble to conceal, Stoney indicated that he should leave the room. The door was left open: my husband was clearly too distracted to have any concern for privacy.

'What is it now?'

'I'm sorry to hear you are unable to come to London.'

He gave me a look of frank astonishment. 'You're not under some delusion that I'll allow you to go by yourself?'

'Surely it would be better for you if I were out of the way? The coachmen will look after me, and I'll take one of the house-maids as I have no ladies-maid of my own.'

'I've arranged for a new one to be employed in London.'

I greeted this news with a pretence of delight, although in truth I dreaded being attended by yet another of his slatterns. 'Thank-you, that is very kind of you.'

He seemed to relax a little and I watched as he sat down with a self-pitying sigh, evidently mollified by my gratitude, and without the faintest suspicion that it was entirely false.

'Bloody creditors pursuing me, bloody agents wanting money, bloody tenants whining about rents. Bloody Colpitts gone without a word. What a bloody life! I'd go to bloody London, but there's more of them there.'

Despite the clenching in my chest at the thought of our families begging this dissolute wastrel for a reduction in their rents, I kept up my show of sympathy.

'Is there anything I can do?'

'You?' he seemed to find the idea risible. 'Hardly!' Then I felt a chill as I saw his eyes centre on me. He cocked his head to one side, as was his habit when an idea was forming.

'Your daughters are being brought to Grosvenor Square on Saturday.'

I lowered my eyes, not wanting him to see how much I was desperate to be there. 'I believe so, yes.'

'How old are they now?'

I knew instantly which way his thoughts were heading. Answering his question felt like offering them to him, and my mouth dried up. I affected to cough and took a drink from the cold tea on the table. By an effort of will, I kept my voice from shaking. 'Maria is sixteen and Anna thirteen' and watched as an unmistakable gleam spread across his features.

Straightening up in the chair where he had slumped only moments ago, he spoke almost to himself. 'Ripening nicely, I'll wager.'

I swallowed with difficulty: the constriction in my throat threatening to choke me. The fear that I felt was visceral. I never thought I would be grateful that Thomas Lyon had taken my girls into his protection, but at that moment I wanted to rush to him and warn him to take them far, far away.

My boys were safe, I knew: John at school in Edinburgh, George and Thomas in Neasden. I missed them with a constant ache, but knowing that they were safely away from this monster was a great comfort to me. My girls were an entirely different matter, and thoughts of them always brought a chill wind of fear. In my heart, I had always known that the day would come when the basilisk eye would fall on them.

'Tell me about Maria.'

'Well, I know precious little. You know as much as I.' I hardly needed to add that I had not received a single unopened letter in the six years of our marriage.

'Your impression?'

I must not show my fears. I would make Maria sound completely out of his sphere of influence and surrounded by powerful people. 'She is grown into a fine young lady. She favours her father's side, being tall and dark, and she has his poise and confidence. She is clever and serious; she has left school and now lives with her aunt, Lady Anne Simpson.'

'Where?'

'In Harley Street.'

'Tell me about Lady Anne.'

'She is a strong, independent, good person, very proper, very clever and charming. Through her, Maria is embarked upon society. She has powerful friends already. The king's sons frequent Lady Anne's salons.'

'Suitors?'

'Not that I know of, but then, I would not be told.'

He shifted in his chair, settling more comfortably into contemplation. Eventually, he said conversationally and with what looked like an indulgent smile, 'Anna is a charming little imp, is she not? She looks and behaves far older than her years.'

There it was. He had seen her. He must have been to the school. Amongst all the turmoil in my heart, I prayed that this meant he would soon confirm that that was where he had sent my Mary - that she was with her sister.

I smiled, though the muscles of my face were rigid with tension. It felt like a grimace, but he noticed nothing, even when he glanced at me and said dismissively, 'You must have been very similar at her age. She is amply endowed already, and those chestnut curls…'

My heart shook, but I steadied my voice and answered, 'Yes, I think so. If she were to visit Gibside, there are people still here who would remember me at that age and would no doubt see it.'

'Yes, perhaps she should visit us here. Perhaps we should invite her to Gibside for the Christmas holidays. Introduce her around. There are several young men I can think of, and some not so young, who would be interested to meet our little heiress.'

I could not help it, the blush of anger rising up my neck, I protested in a tone much more mild than I felt, 'Oh she is far too young for that! And besides, it seems unlikely that Thomas Lyon will let her out of his sight.'

'We'll see about that.' Suddenly, he rose to his full height, his spirits clearly raised. 'Yes, Eleanor, you shall go to London this very day. I will follow tomorrow, and together we shall present a devoted mama and papa who would love nothing more than to have their daughters living with them.'

'And Mary?'

He was already leaving the room, but he tossed over his shoulder the words I had longed to hear, 'Mary will be perfectly happy where she is. Best not to disrupt her so soon.'

On the journey down to London, my bodyguard spoke barely a word, staring morosely out of the window and idly flicking the letter which Stoney had entrusted to him. The tiny scullery maid whom Stoney had chosen as my chaperone slept like a dormouse. I was glad of a chance to think without fear and without having to act.

When we arrived at Gloucester Square, the door was opened by yet another new footman. There was no bow, no formal greeting, and his only words were, 'Your new maid is upstairs awaiting your arrival.' Then he slouched away down the hall. I bit my lip. The time was not yet right to show that underneath this meek and broken exterior a new Eleanor was taking shape.

The little scullery-maid helped me with my outer cloak, her eyes darting around the hall in wonder. I spoke to her kindly, for she was scarcely older than my Anna. 'You will find a welcome in the kitchens, Molly. They will give you food and find you a bed in the attic, though you may have to share. Do whatever is asked of you with a smile, but if anything makes you uncomfortable, anything at all, of whatever nature, you come directly to me. Do you understand?'

Bless her, Molly bobbed me a curtsey. 'Yes ma'am. Can I ask – will we be here long, do you think?'

'I have no idea, Molly, but between you and me, I sincerely hope not.' I touched her cold cheek and wished I could bring her to my fire, feed her soup and talk of home. Little mite, I would take care of her too. 'My sitting-room is there and my bedroom is on the first floor, at the front. You will always find me if you want to speak to me. Go now, and remember what I said.'

When I opened the door to my room, I expected to find the usual beady-eyed slattern lying on my bed or rifling through my clothes. Creatures of the night, all of them, so hardened by whatever trials had brought them to this state that any thought of concern or pity for me could not be further from their minds.

Imagine my surprise when I opened the door of my bedroom to a soft breeze. The windows were open, and though the smoky London air lacked the sweet fertility of Gibside, it was refreshing. Standing by the window was a tall, neat person of my own age with a strong brow and determined jaw. She stood still for a moment, watching me, her expression unreadable. I made myself stay still and wait for her to acknowledge my presence.

Just when it seemed that neither of us would move, she inclined her head slightly and moved forward to offer me her hand. She was almost as tall as Stoney, and being offered a handshake by a woman, especially an employee, was unheard-of. As she looked down into my face, I felt myself scrutinized and balked before her frank gaze.

'Lady Strathmore, I am delighted to make your acquaintance. Mary Morgan.' She extended her hand and enclosed my own in a brief but firm grip, then briskly took my light cloak from my shoulders and went into the closet to hang it.

'Thank-you, Mrs Morgan,' for I had noticed a wedding ring.

She reappeared in the doorway. 'As you please, Lady Strathmore. Shall I send for tea? Something to eat?'

'Yes, please, and for yourself. Let us sit and get to know each other.'

Her face closed and I had the distinct impression she was wary of me. What had she been told? That I was an hysteric? A madwoman, barely tolerated to be in society? An invalid? A fantasist?'

Her demeanour and clear, direct gaze had made me hopeful that by some oversight, surely some mistake, I had been sent a maid who knew how to conduct herself. Who could be a friend, even an ally. I decided to yield to my instinct to trust: it was something I had not allowed myself to do for six long years. Perhaps I would find that I had been unwise in approaching her so soon: wherever she had come from, she would not expect a society lady to want to make her acquaintance, indeed she would perceive it as a breach of etiquette. Anxious not to confirm whatever version of me she had been given, I moved to reassure her. I did not want her to be frightened by my desperation, but with Stoney absent for at least twenty-four hours, here was a real chance to form a bond.

'Perhaps you are unused to such informality, Mrs Morgan.' I smiled with a warmth that I genuinely felt, intuitively. There must be some reason for her presence: if she was not one of his mistresses, which seemed very unlikely, perhaps she was a spy. I must know how she came to be here, so I went on: 'As you'll be aware, I am from the north, and we tend to have a warmer way with our staff than I have sometimes observed in London. If you would prefer not to take tea with me, perhaps you could tell me something of yourself. My husband is very busy and did not have time to appraise me of your background.'

She stood very still and regarded me with a curious expression, and then seemed to make her mind up about something and replied, to my great astonishment: 'Mr Bowes did not recruit me, Lady Strathmore. I have not had the pleasure of meeting him. I was interviewed by the wife of Reverend Reynett.'

My astonishment and excitement knew no bounds, and I could not hide it. 'Oh! You surprise me. Mr Bowes takes a great deal of interest in procuring our female staff.' I watched her and saw the gleam of understanding light in her eyes: I had chosen the verb deliberately and she knew it. I experienced one of those pleasurable moments when we know we are understood.

She gave a slow blink of understanding. 'I will send for some tea and cakes.'

'Two cups?'

She smiled and revealed for the first time a row of perfectly white teeth: it transformed her face in a way I loved from the first. In that moment, it felt as though I was admitted to her heart.

While she was gone, I looked around my apartment, noted the fresh flowers, the bags of lavender in the wardrobe, the freshly-ironed pillowcases and hugged myself for pleasure.

When she returned with the tray, I had changed my dress and arranged myself on the chaise. I could hardly expect her to sit beside me, but she might. I honestly felt as excited as a young girl making a new friend, and had to keep reminding myself to have caution. It had been so long since I had met anyone I knew I could trust, or about whom I had such a strong intuition.

204

Once she had poured the tea and offered me a biscuit, I waited until she was settled in the armchair. We exchanged a few pleasantries about the weather and the journey, and then I said, 'So, please tell me about yourself, Mrs Morgan.'

Instead of demurring and protesting that she hardly knew where to start, she gave me a brisk potted history of her life so far. 'I was born in Cheltenham thirty-three years ago, the only surviving child of a vicar. My mother died in childbirth and I was brought up by my paternal grandmother, educated at a day-school and had hopes of being a teacher myself. I married at twenty and devoted myself to my wifely duties and the needs of our parishioners. My husband died four years ago, and although I have a small private income, I found it necessary to go into service. I came to London so that I could attend the theatre and lectures, for I love to learn. I have been fortunate in my employers thus far and was able to provide excellent references.'

'I have no doubt, Mrs Morgan. And I, I think, am most fortunate that you have come to me.'

The look that she gave me was an appraising one: Mary Morgan knew her own mind. She would allow my familiarity, for she instinctively understood that I needed it, but she would take her time in judging whether to trust me. She would see which way the wind blew.

It didn't take long for her to find out.

Chapter 20

I knew as soon as I saw him that something was afoot, and my greatest fear was that it had something to do with my daughters, most likely Anna. She had alarmed me on a previous visit by acting like a tiny coquette, dissolving into gales of laughter at anything Stoney said. Whereas Maria was always cool with me and acted like a distant relative or an exceptionally reserved acquaintance, Anna was a dramatic child of extremes, always gripped by one emotion or another. Thanks to Stoney's treatment and Thomas Lyon's propaganda against me, both girls were understandably watchful, but in Anna, that watchfulness had grown into disdain.

It pained me to hear her call Stoney 'papa' and she knew it. I remember the moment she seized on it as a way to gall me. She was ten years old, mutinous and looking for a reason. Stoney had been unusually solicitous of her, buying her an overly-generous gift of a giant doll almost as high as herself. Seeing it for the first time, she had burst out, 'Oh thank-you Papa! She's beautiful! None of my friends at school has a doll half so tall or well dressed as her! I shall call her Sarah.'

My children had all called their father Papa, and I could not bear to hear the term used to refer to Stoney. To my knowledge, he had at least a dozen children, not one of whom was properly supported by him. I often saw young women with a babe in arms or a toddler turned away from our door and was in no doubt about the reason for their knock. I had chided her gently, 'Mr Bowes is not your papa, Anna. Perhaps you might like to call him Andrew?'

She turned her fierce gaze on me and I saw her lip curl. Then, with clear intent, she gathered her skirts and rushed over to climb on Stoney's knee. 'Silly mama! Of course you are my papa! Don't listen to her! Oh thank-you, thank-you!' and she covered his face with kisses. It made my skin crawl to see his complacent gaze over her head. When he next spoke to me in her hearing, he had dropped all pretence of excessive politeness, and the intuitive little moppet picked up on that, adopting a similarly dismissive tone herself.

On every visit since, she had made a point of greeting him first, using the same endearment, then turning to me with a formal curtsey. I had not the courage to correct her again or to try to disarm her by gathering her into my arms, in case she rejected me further.

That Saturday, it was no surprise to me to hear her voice from an upstairs room before I knew her to be in the house. I had been in the garden and as I stood up to go indoors, heard a gale of unmistakable laughter from an upstairs window. I came into the hallway and saw the chaplain and his wife preparing to leave.

'Reverend Reynett, Mrs Reynett, how are you both?'

The couple looked startled and inadvertently both glanced upstairs. Seeing the landing empty, the reverend bowed politely and his wife bobbed a curtsey.

'Are you here to see Mr Bowes?'

'We have just brought Anna from her school. She is upstairs.'

'Oh, only Anna? I thought perhaps Mary…' The honest souls both looked sorrowfully at me and Mrs Reynett patted my hand, whispering, 'She is quite well. I'm sure you will see her at Christmas.'

Acknowledging her words of comfort with a smile, I said, 'Well then, Anna. I was not aware she had arrived. I thought she and Maria might come together.'

They looked at each other, Mrs Reynett nodded, and the reverend spoke in a low voice. 'I think Lady Maria has left.'

'What? But I have not seen her! They were expected at 2pm. It is only midday!'

With a furtive look up the stairs, the reverend inclined his head to my ear. 'I think you had better ask Mr Bowes about his plans. I am not sure what he intends, but I fear Lady Maria and her chaperone … took flight.'

I had heard a door open behind me and turned to see that Mrs Morgan was standing in the doorway and had heard the exchange. 'It is true. There were raised voices in the hallway about half an hour ago. I was upstairs. I saw a tall dark young lady and an older woman hasten through the door and leave in a blue carriage.'

I could scarcely believe it. 'What could have occasioned such a precipitous departure? And before I had even seen my daughter! Oh, I could weep!' And to the evident alarm of the Reynetts, I burst into tears. Mrs Morgan's arms closed round my shoulders and she spoke over my head. 'Be not alarmed, I shall look after her. I shall look after them both.'

I think it was Mrs Reynett who squeezed my arm, and then they were gone and Mrs Morgan was helping me into the front parlour.

'Come come, compose yourself please Lady Strathmore. You will see your daughter again. Some misunderstanding, I am sure. Perhaps to do with the timing of the visit. You know how highly-strung these young girls can be. Here, I have a clean handkerchief. Dry your eyes.' Evidently alarmed by the depth of my feeling, she sat for a moment holding the handkerchief out to me, perhaps embarrassed at witnessing a gentlewoman in such emotional disarray. I simply could not stop crying.

Eventually, she came to sit beside me on the chaise and put her hand on my arm, whereupon I dissolved afresh. She lifted the hair at the side of my face and I heard her gasp. 'What is this? How did you get this bruise? It is quite purple, and you have blood beneath your ear. What has happened?'

I kept my face averted. 'I walked into the door of the closet this morning.'

She did not answer and I sensed that she had gone very still.

Quite spent, for it was the second time that day that I had cried, I made an effort to compose myself. I went to take the handkerchief from her hand and found that her fingers were rigid. She released them and I dried my eyes, still avoiding looking into her face. Summoning my dignity, I stood up and brushed down my skirts, which were lightly dusted with soil. Stoney hated to see me in the dress I wore for gardening, and I was anxious to change before I saw Anna.

Another gale of laughter rang through the house, and Mrs Morgan said, 'Anna is quite happy, it seems.'

I gave a rueful smile and looked at her face, which was still and without expression. 'I wonder, could I trouble you to see to Anna on my behalf, Mrs Morgan. I must make myself presentable.'

She rose to her feet. 'I will help you. I have laid out a gown and your bath was ready for twelve, as you requested.'

But suddenly alarmed, I clasped her hands. 'Please, Mrs Morgan. Please attend to Anna. She should not be...' She understood me instantly, blinked once to show that she had done so, and left the room, only to return within moments. 'I have sent Mrs Price to Anna. Come, let's get you upstairs.'

She was just fastening me into my gown when the door opened and Stoney strode into the room, his face flushed. He stilled, watching Mrs Morgan, his head on one side. I could not see, but if she had not bobbed him a curtsy, he would not like it, and somehow I knew she would be unable to hide her feelings. I held my breath.

'Leave us.'

'One moment. I have almost finished.'

Unused to being gainsaid, he was nonplussed. I saw him gather himself. He stood at his full height, watching Mrs Morgan. It was a relief when he said, 'I will speak to Lady Strathmore over lunch.'

Anna was sitting on the stairs playing with one of the cats, and when she looked up at me, her eyes were bright with excitement. 'Mama, we are going to France!'

I bent and kissed her forehead, 'How lovely, darling. With school? In the summer holidays?'

'No, now. You, me and Papa! It was a surprise for us! Just think! None of my friends has been out of England yet! I shall be the first! And before the school holidays, too, while they are all at their desks, I shall be strolling down the boulevards of Paris!'

'I hardly think so, darling. There must be some misunderstanding. Come along, we'll have lunch and talk about it.' I kept my voice steady, but in my heart I knew that this was what he had planned.

I should tell you that I had a particular reason for fearing for Anna. When I was exactly the same age, fourteen, I narrowly escaped being kidnapped and forced into marriage. The plan was hatched by an MP, whose name we never found out. Via a shadowy intermediary, he had attempted to bribe a member of our staff. I was to be lured to a particular part of the grounds, where I would be bundled into a carriage and whisked away. A marriage ceremony would be performed abroad and the family would be presented with a fait accomplis. Such is the importance of a girl's reputation that they would have been forced to accept. I have no doubt whatsoever that the MP would never have attempted such an audacious plan if my father had been alive, but it would have been frighteningly easy

210

to achieve. We were saved by the footman fortunately recovering his loyalty and morality: he told my mother and the plot was foiled.

It was a startling way of learning that in the eyes of some people, I was nothing more than a commodity: a passport to wealth. And now, of course, I feared for Anna.

When we entered the dining room, she was prattling away in French; like me, she was a precocious linguist, and Stoney was looking on, nodding and smiling and pretending he understood. Mrs Price was standing by the door, and when I entered, I gave her a nod which released her back to her duties.

I sat down beside Anna and joined in conversation with her in French. Stoney loathed people speaking in other languages, for of course he had none, and such was his need for control that he viewed even this conversation between a mother and daughter as a threat. I deliberately avoided his eye, and when Anna said again that we were going to France, I replied gently, 'Ma non, ma petite.'

Stoney's chin was up, ready for a fight. As the footman positioned my seat, I kept my eyes on Stoney's in a challenge which he recognised. Somehow, Mrs Morgan's presence in the room above my head gave me the first stirrings of courage.

'Anna seems to be under the impression that she is going to France. I have explained to her that that is quite impossible.'

'She is right.'

'But my dear - thank-you James - ...Anna must return to school on Monday.'

'We are going to France this afternoon.'

Entirely disarmed, I said, 'This afternoon?'

'Yes, Mama! Isn't it exciting?'

'We leave in just under an hour. You had both better eat your lunch.' It was only then that I saw that the table was already laid with sandwiches and tea. Anxious not to cause a scene in front of Anna, I took a sandwich and thought quickly.

'It is a great surprise to me, too, Anna, but men have little understanding of how much preparation we girls like to put into a trip. If we are to go to France, perhaps in the holidays, you and I must go shopping first, don't you think?'

'Your cases are being packed as we speak.'

'Has the school been informed?'

211

Silence.

'Do Anna's guardians know of her departure?'

'That is no concern of yours.'

'No concern of mine? How can you say such a thing?'

'Oh, Mama, relax, we don't care about stuffy old Uncle Thomas, do we Papa?'

'Really Eleanor, anyone would think you didn't want to have Anna live with us.'

I turned to Anna, 'Of course we do, darling. I would give anything. Anything in the world.' Here, I looked pointedly at Stoney and I didn't care what he saw in my eyes. 'But it is out of our control. Uncle Thomas only wants the best for you and your brothers and sisters. We shall go to France one day, I promise, but this is not the day. We must make proper arrangements first.'

He stood up and flung his napkin to the table. 'Oh well, Anna, your mother clearly does not have our adventurous spirit. We shall have to go without her.'

'No!'

'I thought not. Go and get ready.'

'Hurrah! We're going to Fra-ance! Nous allons a la belle France!' As Anna danced out of the room, I turned to Stoney and watched a slow smile spread across his face.

'Why are you doing this?'

'Why do you think, my love?'

'I cannot imagine. Anna is only fourteen.'

'Old enough.'

My flesh crept and my hatred for him crystalised into real resolve. He saw it in my eyes, for he flinched and looked away. 'Old enough for what?'

'Why Lady Strathmore, to procure a wealthy suitor. I have several candidates in mind.'

'You cannot do this. Mary is a Ward of Chancery.'

'Oh my dear, I think you'll find I can.'

We left the house in a hackney carriage, by which subterfuge he hoped to avoid detention. So eager was he to get away that he didn't even raise an objection when Mrs Morgan climbed in beside me, though I saw him register her presence and consider objecting. His man rode beside the driver.

212

The whole journey was planned to avoid detection: the night in Dover under an assumed name, the channel crossing, not on the packet steamer with other travellers, but huddled in an open boat wrapped in blankets. Anna was terribly sick, but the silver lining was that for the first time she wanted comfort, and snuggled into my side. As I wrapped her in my own blanket and held her across my lap, I kissed her hair and murmured, 'Mummy will keep you safe, my darling.'

During our overnight stay in Calais, Stoney went off into the town and did not come back until the small hours, so I had the delicious pleasure of sleeping with my daughter curled against my side, for she was exhausted and had eaten nothing.

By the time we arrived in Paris, she had recovered, and as the carriage rattled through the bustling streets of Faubourg Saint-Germain, she was raptly exclaiming upon the foreign smells. I was able to keep up a conversation in French only because Anna had scoffed good-naturedly at his request for us to speak in English. In her world, everybody spoke French. He was clearly anxious to keep her calm, so he did not object any further.

The suite of rooms at the Hotel de Luxembourg was luxurious; even Anna was impressed, exclaiming over all the enchanting furnishings and decorative flourishes. She was to share her room with Mrs Morgan, which she at first resented, not having met the lady before, but Mary charmed her by discussing French fashions in a surprisingly knowledgeable way, and as I closed the door, I heard her promising to dress Anna's hair in the French style for dinner that night.

Still in his outer coat, he was sitting at the escritoire writing a letter. I sat on the bed, tired but quietly determined that no harm should befall my daughter. His lack of French and the presence of Mary Morgan on the other side of the door gave me courage to challenge him. I waited until he had finished, and as he folded the sheet, addressed no doubt to one of his fortune-hunting acquaintances, I said, 'I do not understand how you hope to get away with this. Thomas will have been to court by now. You will be a wanted man. You have abducted a Ward of Chancery.'

'No, my dear. You have abducted a Ward of Chancery. I am merely your loving husband. I could not let you undertake this desperate attempt alone. You will write to the courts now, pleading for custody of your children and explaining how your desperation, nay madness in the face of their absence, has driven you to this.'

'I will not.'

'Oh Eleanor, I think you'll find that you will.'

He hurt me in ways that it pains me to recall, and many times he threatened to kill me but always relented. Both of us knew that if I died, he would get nothing. His only income was from my tenants, and once I was dead, it would pass to my son. Suffice it to say that my arms and body were a mass of bruises of varying degrees, but he always ensured that my writing hand was unharmed. He dictated letters, and I wrote them. I wrote letters to the courts, to Thomas Lyon, to Stoney's financial agent, William Davis, to his lawyer friends John Scott and John Lee, who as MPs were both in strong positions of influence. And in all of them, Stoney dictated words that purported to come from me, pleading to be able to keep my daughter.

He was buying time, of course. Various men, French as well as English, were brought to our rooms to take tea with me and Anna. I have no idea what kinds of bribes were offered, how the negotiations proceeded, but I have absolutely no doubt that he would be trying to play one off against the other. He was conducting an auction for my daughter, and I could do nothing about it.

Mrs Morgan never let Anna out of her sight, and did everything she could to cultivate Anna's friendship with the daughter of some Swiss guests who had rooms on the same floor. The Swiss girl's maid stayed with them whenever Mary had to tend to me, and I felt instinctively that she had confided in her.

During all this time, Mrs Morgan attended to me with complete devotion and total discretion. In Stoney's presence, she was unfailingly polite: we both dreaded him finding some reason to expel her from our lives. Neither of us spoke of the bruises and cuts, though her mouth compressed into a fine line whenever she saw a new one. After a particularly vicious beating, when even he was startled at the flow of blood from a cut on my scalp, he grew genuinely alarmed and called for her. She was waiting outside the door.

I was sitting on the bedside chair, holding a towel to my head and weeping hopelessly. I heard him say, 'Mrs Morgan, I think it is about time we consulted a doctor about Lady Strathmore's mental health. She is a danger to herself. See to her.' And with that, he put on his cloak and left the room.

It was the turning point. I had had more than I could take, and she had kept silent long enough. As she bathed and dressed my wound, her hands were shaking. At first I thought it was fear, but when I saw her face, I knew it was anger.

'Lady Strathmore, I must speak.'

I gave her no encouragement, merely lay passive, submitting to her care.

'Many times before now I have thought to stand up to him. I have seen and I have heard. If I show my hand, he will throw me out on the street and you will be at his mercy. That is not going to happen. We must box clever. I am going to ensure that you are never alone with him again. You will act as if semi-conscious, and I will say you are concussed and must not be left alone. I will sleep in your room from now on.'

She saw my eyes widen in alarm.

'I will bring Anna's bed into this room if I have to drag it myself. Fear not, she will not be left alone either. I know, for I have heard him say it, that he needs you alive if he is to keep control of your money. I know also that he has severe debts, even here in Paris. I have made a number of acquaintances who may be useful to us.' Here she looked at me with great meaning and waited until she was sure I had understood. 'If he speaks again of having you committed, I will accuse him of attempted murder. I am a witness. He may throw me out on the street, but be assured, Lady Strathmore, I will come back and I will not be alone.'

My tears redoubled, but this time they were tears of gratitude. I murmured my name, but my lips were so swollen and my throat so dry that she could not tell what it was that I said. She supported my head and I breathed in the scent of lavender. 'My name is Mary Eleanor.'

'Well, Mary Eleanor, my name is also Mary, and you and I are going to defeat this monster. We may have the bodies of weak and feeble women, ' she smiled and tapped her forehead. 'but we have the strength up here, where it matters. When we get back to England, and we will, be sure of it, we are going to get you away from this monster. And, by our lady whose name we carry, we will live to see him in prison.'

'I cannot believe…'

'You cannot? Believe, Mary Eleanor.' She spoke gently, cradling my head and careless of the blood seeping into her bodice. 'I know you do not share my faith in God, but perhaps one day I can teach you the consolations of belief. Tell me, what do you believe in? What is your ideal?'

'I believe in Liberty.'

'Then let us raise our glasses in a toast.' She refilled my water-glass and poured another for herself. 'To Liberty.'

Chapter 21

Mary Morgan's ruse worked, and for the remainder of our time in France, she presented me as a barely-conscious invalid and never left my side, guarding me with the steadfast devotion of a bulldog. It meant, of course, that she found it difficult to keep an eye on Anna, who had fallen entirely under Stoney's spell and was clearly being wooed. We often heard deliveries arrive, and on the rare occasions when she came to see me on Mary Morgan's insistence, she was always wearing a gown I had not seen before, or a new head-dress in the Parisian style. Our conviction grew that if he could not secure a suitor for her, he intended her for himself, which of course meant greater danger for me.

Out of her own pocket, Mary engaged a member of the hotel staff as a maid and instructed her to chaperone Anna at all times. She was a mature Frenchwoman who would be safe from Stoney's attentions and whom we quickly trusted enough to allow Anna to resume her accompanied walks. She was growing bored and restless, and we hoped she would begin to pressure Stoney herself for a return to London.

His moods were increasingly mercurial and unpredictable. I had spent so long watching him carefully for every nuance of mood or expression, trying to guage his actions and avoid provoking that terrifying temper, that his distance from me was at first a source of great fear. I expected him every moment to burst down the door and drag me from the bed by my hair. But as the days passed, the rumbles of his voice seemed increasingly far off, like thunder. I felt myself to be lying in the still centre of a storm, but I was never alone and I felt safer than I had for years.

Perhaps it was frustration on his part: a self-declared man of action, he was reduced to distant puppeteer while his cronies strove to do his bidding, instructed only by letters which took days to travel in each direction. Every day, the household waited to see what news the post would bring, and it seemed to me, quietly reading in my room, attended by my faithful friend, that the mood of every day depended entirely on what arrived in the post. If it was not a letter from his lawyer friends relating the slow progress of 'our' custody case, it was a missive from his financial manager containing news of some creditor or tenant, which invariably sent Stoney into paroxysms of anger from which even the hotel staff cowered. Only Anna seemed able to calm him: I would hear her soothing voice and then all would be quiet.

If ever he attempted access to my room, Mary was at the door before I was even aware of his footsteps. From the first day, she had wedged a chair under the handle so that we should not be surprised by him, and twice we had heard him try to gain entry in the night. Instead of sharing my fear, both times Mary murmured, 'He takes me for a fool.'

One morning, a few days after our siege commenced, we heard a knock shortly after the maid had taken away our breakfast tray.

Mary called out, 'Who is it?' and we were both surprised to hear his subdued voice. 'It is Mr Bowes. I wish to see my wife.'

'She is indisposed, Mr Bowes.'

'Open this door, Mrs Morgan.'

We looked at each other, my fearful eyes riveted to the calm blue of hers.

'I shall be with you in a moment.'

We both distinctly heard his harrumph, but its tone was subdued and so Mary took one of the pillows from beneath my head and helped me to lie down on the side which ached least. She raised the coverlet so that only my hair would be visible from the door. I watched astonished as she took a brass candlestick from the mantlepiece and held it behind her back.

I heard the door open and the silence which ensued. I hardly dared breathe. Mary told me later that he had taken a step as though to enter the room and she smiled as she told me of the surprise and bewilderment that crossed his features when she held her ground and blocked his way. This was what I most feared. I had never before seen a woman unmoved by Stoney and I had no idea how he would react. Throughout their exchange, I prayed to a God I do not believe in that she would not make an enemy of him, for then we were lost.

'I should like to see my wife, Mrs Morgan.'

'I am most concerned about her, Mr Bowes.'

'So am I. As you see.'

'I think perhaps you should send for a doctor.'

He leant towards her then, conspiratorially. 'Her mind?'

'No, Mr Bowes. Her body. I think a doctor, and perhaps a constable, should see her injuries.'

'She inflicted them herself, you know. She is quite mad.'

Silence.

'I take it the chair is to prevent her escaping?'

Silence.

Clearly alarmed by such an immovable object in the unaccustomed shape of a woman, he took to bluster, like a little boy lying when caught red-handed by a respected grandparent. 'I was only trying to prevent her harming herself!' Silence. 'She tried to jump from the window, you know! I had to wrestle her to the ground and pin her there by the weight of my body. She many have sustained bruises. She was possessed. The very devil was in her.'

I smile now to imagine how Mary Morgan's face must have looked to him, as unimpressed and impassive as a stone angel.

'And the blood, well that was her own fault. She struggled out from under me, from where I had her pinned.' The unlikeliness of such a scenario appeared not to cross his mind. 'And made for the window again. I went to catch her by the hair, streaming out behind her, but I caught her ear and her scalp, but such was her strength…and the blood. Well, you saw the blood.'

'Indeed. I did indeed see the blood. And the injuries from which she is now suffering.' Silence, and who knows what exchange of expressions, of understanding. Mary Morgan was walking a tightrope and he seemed entirely oblivious, being apparently transfixed by those calm expressionless eyes.

Finally, she spoke and I held my breath. Her voice was soothing and rhythmic, almost an incantation: 'I believe the courts have demanded that we return Anna to England, and back to her school. She has had an adventure, and received an education, albeit of an unconventional kind. We are law-abiding people, and the law has decreed we should return, so I imagine you are making preparations. Fear not, Lady Strathmore will survive the journey, if that is why you hesitate. I am experienced in the care of invalids. She is very docile. I think perhaps a brain injury. You will have no further trouble from Lady Strathmore, Mr Bowes. And you can rely on me.'

And then, unbelievably, the two words I had never heard Stoney say to any servant: 'Thank-you.'

And so we returned to England. Wrapped in blankets, I stayed quiet, my eyes mostly closed throughout the journey, Mary Morgan pressed reassuringly against my side. Opposite me sat Anna, restless and chatty, though I detected a nervousness in her and worried at the cause of it. 'I simply cannot wait to see all my friends! I have so much to tell and so many new clothes to show off! Are we going to school first? I shall be in time for dinner if we do.'

Stoney was in a strange mood: he barely spoke to any of us, but whenever I sneaked a glance at him from under my lashes, his lips were working and his eyes darting this way and that, as though he were talking through scenarios, rehearsing speeches, looking for a way out. Like a rat in a trap.

This time we took the packet boat and I was relieved to be amongst the public. I still ached and my left hip pained me greatly, so it was no pretence for me to act like an invalid. Whenever I lifted my head, I kept my eyes vacant and my mouth hanging open. I even allowed drool to escape my lips and noted with satisfaction the repulsion on his face when he saw. When I saw the white cliffs looming out of the mist, I felt an unspeakable relief that at last I was on my way home, my trusty, resourceful, staunch friend sitting resolutely by my side.

When she heard Stoney instruct the coach-driver to take us to the Royal Hotel, I saw her wait for Anna to object, but Anna had subsided into a sulky silence, and so Mary asked what we were all wondering.

'Mr Bowes, when do you intend to return to Grosvenor Square? You must be looking forward to seeing little William.'

There was something about Mary Morgan that made Stoney want to impress her: she had a way of treating people as though they were the best version of themselves. It was a curious thing to see him respond to her and I wondered whether she reminded him of someone. Or perhaps he was genuinely afraid that he had gone too far in abducting Anna and felt that he needed all the friends he could get. Perhaps he intended Mary Morgan for a character witness. The thought made me smile inwardly.

'Yes, I shall see little William tomorrow. I shall send word for Dorothy to bring him to the hotel.'

Hearing that name, I twitched involuntarily, and Mary turned so that her face was blocking Stoney's view of mine. In the rattling of the coach and the creaking of the leather, he will not have heard me say, 'Ask about Dorothy.'

She smiled her understanding and tenderly wiped some imagined drool from my mouth, then sat back in her seat and said to Stoney. 'Poor Lady Strathmore, she is subject to such spasms now. I think she does not know where she is or understand what I am saying. It is very sad.'

I kept my eyes expressionless and averted, but I could tell that Stoney was looking hard at me.

Mary, bless her, went on pleasantly: 'Dorothy? I don't think I've met a Dorothy.'

Even in my peripheral vision, the nature of his smile was unmistakable, but he answered as though indifferent to Dorothy's charms. 'Brought her down from Gibside to look after William. Tall, long wavy blonde hair. Considered quite a beauty up there. William was most struck with her, so I gave her a job.'

There was mischief in Mary's voice when she said, 'And what is the nature of Dorothy's job?'

Stoney seemed uncharacteristically stunned by the pert question. 'Why, nanny to William of course.' I had no doubt whatsoever that he had already seduced Dorothy. The Stephensons would never have allowed her to be taken from them willingly.

'No, we shall not disturb Grosvenor Square. We are only passing through London on our way north. There is no point in having the household prepare for our arrival only to depart the following morning.'

Anna pulled a face. 'North? I shall not be accompanying you north, shall I Papa?'

'No Anna, I think it is time you returned to school.'

She clapped her hands together and bounced in her seat. Such an age, thirteen, one minute a poised young lady, the next an excited child.

At the Royal Hotel, I was put to bed and then Anna and Mary went down to dinner. Stoney left immediately after he'd eaten and didn't return until breakfast-time. There was no further discussion about seeing William, so I assumed he had been to Grosvenor Square by night to avail himself of his new mistress and perhaps spare a moment for his son.

It was late September, and the smoky London morning air had a sweet, mellow tinge of dirty golden light. We dropped Anna at the gates of her school, an unceremonious arrival for her, but she was so excited that she barely cast us a backward glance as she paraded up the steps in her Parisian gown, followed by two footmen carrying an enormous trunk. Our chaise departed almost immediately, so fearful was he of being apprehended, and the coach carrying our luggage did not catch us up until we reached Grantham.

From there, instead of leaving for Gibside, as I had hoped, we went to Streatlam Castle by a roundabout route. I imagined his tactic was to evade capture until he had ascertained that the fuss had died down in the wake of the safe return of Anna. And so it proved to be, for we did not return to London until the beginning of November.

Once I was comfortably installed in my bedroom at Grosvenor Square, I asked Mary to bring William to me. 'I would like to meet Dorothy, too. I have heard much about her. She is a famed beauty at home. She's the daughter of one of our oldest and most respected farming families, the Stephensons. She is their pride and joy. I don't know whether she is married, and I would be interested to learn the circumstances of her coming to London.'

When Mary was gone, I reflected on my feelings about Dorothy: curiosity and a degree of jealousy would sum it up. It was only when Mary returned with the new maid called Ann that I grew concerned.

I kept still. Mary and I had agreed that we would keep up the pretence of my mental incapacity until we could ascertain whom, if anyone, we could trust.

They closed the door behind them and both approached the bed.

'William is fine, Lady Strathmore. He's just having his bath and will be brought to you directly. Now Ann, tell Lady Strathmore what you've just told me.'

Ann blinked, clearly shocked by my appearance and nervous of telling me whatever it was she had to say.

'Go on, Ann, tell Lady Strathmore - Where is Dorothy?'

The maid would not look me in the eyes. 'She has gone.'

For a moment, I believed that somehow she had got safely home. Maintaining the appearance of imbecility, I looked to Mary for guidance.

'We can trust Ann.' I never doubted her word, not for one moment, and so I said, 'Gone home? To Gibside?'

'No, mistress, Mr Bowes has delivered her into the care of...an acquaintance.'

'Of Dorothy's? I don't understand. Come Ann, tell me. Quickly. You are not in any trouble. I am simply concerned for Dorothy's welfare.'

'Oh mistress, he took her to a brothel. Mrs Sunderland, whose house it is, came here shouting and making a scene, wanting money. Dorothy is delivered of a baby girl.'

Something in me crystalised then. The idea of lovely Dorothy, defiled against her will, used and abused in this way, alone, far from home and now living in a brothel with a baby to care for. My heart hurt.

In that instant, she became for me a symbol of everything I wanted to save. If I died in the doing of it, I would get Dorothy and her baby home to Gibside.

Chapter 22

That winter, 10, Grosvenor Square was a house of secrets. I barely saw or heard Stoney, but servants who to him were invisible often overheard things which they reported to Mrs Morgan, who in turn passed news on to me. Since the safe return of Anna had had no repercussions, he had assumed that his story of a misguided act by his desperate and unstable wife had been believed. His apparent success in hoodwinking the courts had emboldened him to seek custody of all my children: the suit had been presented to the Court of Chancery on behalf of his ailing wife, whose grief at their continued absence was causing grave concerns for her health. Threats of suicide were mentioned.

The very opposite was true. Much as I missed them, I knew my children were safe and that Anna's abduction would ensure that none of them was ever put at risk again. When I heard that my eldest, John and Maria, were refusing to see me at all, I even secretly smiled at their willfulness. George and Thomas were brought to see me, and it almost broke my heart to stay silent and apparently asleep through their whispered visit. Through lowered eyelids, I watched them approach the bed, fine healthy boys of thirteen and eleven. I did not move or show that I sensed their presence, though it grieved me not to be able to reach out and touch them, and when they had gone, I wept as though my heart would break.

On the very rare occasions that Stoney came into the sickroom, I never spoke or stirred: by then, he clearly believed his wife to be an entirely submissive invalid. He needed me to remain alive in order to achieve his aim, but I was under no illusion that he would have any concern for my welfare if he succeeded in becoming their legal guardian. It surely could not come to pass, but judges can be bribed. For the sake of everyone I cared about, I had to stop him.

In the dark and quiet of my room, alone with my books, fed and warmed and cared for by the trusted females of the house, I grew stronger. As my physical health improved, more importantly so did my mental health. Boosted by the care and attention of the maids Ann and Susanna, nurtured by Mary Morgan, I began to believe that I could survive this man. And as the days shortened and the nights grew long, so I hugged myself, nurturing the core of life in me. Not for the first time, I felt myself a snowdrop, and like a snowdrop, it was in the coldest days of January that I found the strength at last to begin to raise my head.

Mary Morgan slept every night in a truckle bed by my side, and often we whispered through the night. I will never forget the sense of intimacy I felt in those days, a feeling I had not experienced before. In the darkness, with no-one watching or judging me, I found I was able to speak of things I had never shared with anyone. And in that sharing, I found strength. No man is an island, nor woman either.

The moon was full and our room bathed in a silvery light when first I spoke of escape.

'Mary, do you happen to know any lawyers?'

'No, I've thankfully had no need of them. You must have a lawyer you can trust?'

'If I could get to Newcastle, perhaps, but then William Scott and his brother are well-respected and powerful, and they are Stoney's friends.'

'He can have few legal friends in London, for he has too many creditors. I do not know how you would be able to get advice without revealing your hand. Wait though! I have a friend whose husband's brother is a lawyer. It is possible I could talk to him.'

'Could you trust him, do you think?'

'I'm not sure. I will find out what I can, without giving too much away. What would you have me ask him?'

'I need to know whether the law can offer me any protection at all.'

'You have told me yourself that a man's right to beat his wife has been enshrined in law.'

'Yes, but the rule of thumb is a hopeful sign I think. If a judge has imposed a restriction as to the degree of punishment that can be meted out, it at least recognises that there is a limit.'

She looked at me for long moments before she spoke, and then a slow smile spread across her features. 'You are feeling stronger, are you not?'

'I am, Mary, and I have you to thank for that.'

'Strong enough to leave your home?'

'This is not my home. It never was.'

'What would you hope to do?'

'Oh, what would I not hope to do? I would hope to escape from this man, and hide. If I knew the law would help me, I would make representation and I would expose this monster for what he is. I would see him sent him to jail. I would achieve a divorce from him. I would ensure my children were safe from him forever. I would gather up my little ones, I would go to Mrs Sutherland's brothel and find Dorothy and her baby, and I would take us all home to Gibside, where we belong. I would sell this house, and I would never return to London. Never.'

She was almost shy. 'And me?'

I clasped her hands, my eyes shining with tears. 'And you, Mary Morgan. If you would come with us, come with me, it would make me so happy. You and I... we are such friends as I have never known. You would live with me as my companion. We could be free.' The beautiful vision swam in front of my eyes, and neither of us spoke.

Suddenly, the reality of my situation came crashing in on me and I dropped her hands. 'But alas, I have no money and nowhere to go.'

She regarded me silently in that way I had come to love, and then she took my hands in hers and dipped her head to see my downturned face. 'But you are Mary Eleanor Bowes. You are your father's daughter. You were forged in the land of oak and iron.'

I raised my head, my eyes shining.

'And now I see the spark of that forge alight in your eyes. Stoke it, Mary Eleanor Bowes, for with that fire and with our hearts of oak, we shall achieve our liberty.'

I have always felt my strength at its greatest in February, perverse as that may seem. I don't know why that should be. It is a momentous month for me, whether because it is the month of my birth, and babies born in February must be tough to survive, or because I can smell the spring beneath the earth and the snow.

Like the coming of spring, preparations went on below the ground; in the kitchens of that great house in Grosvenor Square, in the minds of those maids with their impassive faces and obedient curtsies and their stout hearts; in the darkness of the nights, when we whispered and planned and waited.

At last, through a chance remark overheard as Stoney and his friends were served port, we learned that he planned to dine out two nights hence. It would be our chance.

For forty-eight long hours, it seemed to me that the air of the house thrummed with tension, though few words were exchanged. I barely slept, I was so excited and terrified. I had fears for my own endurance, for my muscles were wasted through lack of use and my legs shook when I paced the floor.

On the evening of Thursday 3rd February, I was dressed and ready when I watched from the bedroom window as the carriage pulled away through the slush of the streets. I turned to Mary, who stood with her back against the door. Without a word, she nodded, gave me one long look and then left the room. I heard her knock on the nursery door, heard William's nanny answer, then the door opened and an animated conversation ensued. At the first burst of laughter, I opened my door. Below in the hall, I could hear Susannah singing, our agreed signal that Robert the footman was there. She stopped singing and said something, then came the deep rumble of his voice. She spoke again on a sharper note, and then he, sounding most aggrieved, for we all knew he had a soft spot for her. Her voice cajoled and then her tinkling laugh diminished down the hall towards the breakfast room and he followed, as we had known he would. I took my chance and left the room, clad only in the kitchen-maid's uniform that Ann had given me.

As I hastened down the stairs, my bare feet slipping on the wood, my heart hammering in my chest, I reassured myself that so far, I was doing nothing wrong. I slipped along the hall staying close to the wall, and felt my way down the servants' staircase to the below-stairs passageway. The cloak and bonnet were hanging on the peg, and through the darkness of the subterranean tunnel, I could see the pale oval of Ann's face by the open doorway in the light of the moon.

We left the house in silence, slipping through the empty streets on winged feet, two servant girls hastening home to their lodging. The hackney driver barely gave us a glance, and when he deposited us on Chancery Lane, he did not stay to see which door we knocked on.

Mr Shuter was a grey-haired gent who was reading by the fire when we entered: he wore an embroidered cap and a velvet jacket and at first I thought he was quite the dandy. His warm handshake and apple-cheeked smile reassured me instantly: I know not what he expected of the infamous Lady Strathmore, but when he saw how small I was and thin, how frightened my eyes must have been, he wrapped a paternal arm around my shoulders and guided me to a seat by the fire.

We spoke very briefly at that first meeting, for I was anxious to get to our hiding-place quickly, before the alarm was raised.

'Lady Strathmore, I can only apologise for having added to the difficulty of this evening by requesting that we meet. I have seen enough. You will not remember this, but I have met you once before, at the funeral of your first husband, God rest his soul, and I am most perturbed by your changed appearance. We do not need to go into any details now, for it is paramount that we get you to a place of safety as quickly as possible. I shall be pleased to represent you if you do wish to go ahead with your petition.'

'I do, Mr Shuter.'

'Then I shall visit you on Saturday morning at 10am. I always take a constitutional on my way to my club. Mary has informed me of the whereabouts of your lodgings. I will see you then. I've asked my valet to stop a hackney carriage. You are not alone, are you?'

'No, I have Ann with me. Mrs Morgan and Susannah aim to meet us there.'

'Then we must move quickly, for the absence of all four of you is bound to be noticed. Let me help you to your carriage.'

'No need, Mr Shuter, but thank-you. I am stronger than I look.'

'Yes, I think you must be.' He smiled and patted my hand like a kindly grandfather. 'Until Saturday.'

Our hiding place was three small rooms down an alleyway at the back of a baker's shop in Holborn. When we arrived, breathless and nervous, there was food in the pantry and clean sheets on the four truckle-beds. Mary and Susanna arrived shortly after us, and we lit a fire and hugged ourselves in elation at the success of our plan.

On Saturday, Mr Shuter arrived at ten on the dot. Mary and I showed him into the kitchen and the three of us sat down at the table by the light of a beeswax candle. He produced a notepad and pen and began without any formalities: 'Tell me, Lady Strathmore, what do you hope to achieve by leaving this marriage?'

'Well, where do I begin? If I am honest, my most deep-seated fear is that if I stay, he will kill me or have me committed to a lunatic asylum. Although I will admit to you that there have been times when I wished myself dead, I am a mother, and the thought of my babies is what always saved me from complete despair.'

'So, let's start with his physical mistreatment of you. I have no wish to cause you pain in the remembrance of specific incidents, but if you could give me an indication of the kind of punishment Mr Bowes has meted out to you, I will have a better picture of your chances of persuading the courts that your very life is in danger.'

'He has done so many things... Seven years...' To my own surprise, I started to cry. It seemed that all the planning and the secrets and the tension of the last few weeks had depleted me more that I knew.

Mary reached out and held my hand. 'I can attest to things I have seen in the short time I have been with her ladyship. Beating, scratching...'

I lifted my chin and found my voice. 'Biting, pinching, burning, whipping, kicking, imprisoning, insulting, provoking, tormenting, mortifying, degrading, tyrannizing, cajoling, deceiving, lying, starving, forcing, compelling...'

'What kinds of things has he compelled you to do?'

'To write letters, to his lovers and creditors, to my own friends and my father's friends, always for his own ends. To write a document detailing my own depravities, entirely of his own invention...'

'Where is this document now?'

'He has it! He has it in his own possession, and I fear he will use it against me. No-one can know the depths of his calculations. He never stops planning and lying and hiding and using people for his own ends. His own sister...'

'Thank-you, Lady Strathmore, you have given me a good indication of the grounds on which we will charge him with reference to your personal mistreatment. May I respectfully bring you back to my original question – what do you hope to achieve by ending this marriage?'

'I want to protect my people from him as well as my children.'

230

'Physically?'

'In every way.'

'Tell me about your children, please. Just a brief outline of your priorities.'

'Mary is only seven years old. He has sent her away from me but I think I know where she is.'

'He is her father, Lady Strathmore. You may have great difficulty in gaining possession of his own children, even in such a case as this. There are precedents, you know...'

'I must have Mary. Of all my children, Mary has only me.' I looked at Mrs Morgan, and when she nodded encouragingly, I took a breath: 'Mr Bowes is not Mary's father.'

Mr Shuter straightened his back and his automatic disapproval visibly altered his demeanour.

I watched him, suddenly calm. I would not plead, I would not explain. I wanted justice, not moral condemnation.

'Mr Shuter, Mary's paternity is told to you in confidence, not because I am ashamed, but so that you understand my determination to save her from him. He has no care for Mary, the only reason she is important to him is that he knows she is my most precious child. No mother should say that, I know, but she is the one who needs me the most. I am trusting you, Mr Shuter. Only William is Mr Stoney's child, and if I tell you that his conception was, in effect, rape...'

'A man cannot be charged with rape against his wife.' All the certainties of the patriarchy shone from his eyes.

'Mr Shuter, I think we have quickly arrived at a point where we get to know each other and discover whether we will be able to work together.' I kept my eyes on his, steady and challenging, and I saw him mentally adjust his picture of me. 'Are you ready to hear what I have to say?'

I held my breath while I watched him weigh his knowledge of the law against his conscience. If he rejected me now, I was lost, but I must not let him see it.

Finally, almost imperceptibly, he nodded. I breathed out through my nostrils slowly and summoned my thoughts.

'It is not merely in the interests of self-preservation and self-interest that I am making this stand. Until this happened to me, I trusted men. I trusted everyone: it is how I was raised. We live and learn. What I now know is the extent of the harm a man can do to a woman in the privacy of their home, not just her body but her mind. And call himself her husband, having entered into a pact in the eyes of God and the eyes of the Law to protect her. And hold his head up in society and count himself a man. And have the respect of other men. I have lived all my life in the public eye, and yet this can happen to me. So what of all the other women who are not known, or wealthy, or well-educated? What of them? Must they endure anything their husband chooses to do to them, and have no recourse to law? This is not civilization, Mr Shuter, this is barbarism.'

I watched the surprise and understanding grow in his eyes, and crystalise into humility and respect.

'With your help, I will bring this man's actions to the attention of the law of this land, and in doing so, will cause the judiciary to consider what is happening in private all over England. We call ourselves a civilized country, we speak of liberty and congratulate ourselves on our sensibilities...'

He stood up. 'Lady Strathmore, you need go no further. I salute you, and I would be honoured to represent you. Furthermore, I know of others who, when they hear your testimony, will be persuaded. I have heard enough for now. On Monday, I will institute proceedings in all three legal departments.' Seeing my incomprehension, he went on: 'The highest criminal court in the land is the King's Bench, so our priority is to obtain their protection. We must do this quickly, so on Monday, I will make arrangements for you to present yourself there. I will also make representation to the Ecclesiastical Court for the divorce and to the Court of Chancery for the matters of finance.'

'Present myself? I am in fear of my life, Mr Shuter.'

'I know that, Lady Strathmore, and you will have to disguise yourself. Fear not, the King's Bench sits in one corner of Westminster Hall. I do not imagine you will ever have experienced Westminster Hall? No, I thought not. The proceedings are open to the public and somewhat boisterous. In the melee you will not be noticed if you assume common clothes. I think it likely that once he has heard your case, Lord Mansfield will bind Mr Stoney over to keep the peace, and that he will assign you a tipstaff for protection.'

'Lord Mansfield?' The memory came to me of a conversation with Mrs Montagu long ago: Lord Mansfield had invoked habeas corpus to free a slave. My heart lifted to think that he would hear my case.

'I am anxious to convey to you that Mr Stoney will use every means within his power to defeat and discredit me.'

'I understand that, Lady Strathmore.'

'Pardon me, Mr Shuter, but I doubt that you can imagine the extent of his guile. Still, I must be patient. He will reveal himself. But know that he will use my children. They must be kept safe. Is there any way you can have them protected in law?'

'Do you have any evidence that he has harmed them?'

I thought of Anna. 'No, I do not. I don't think he would harm them, although I have no doubt he would attempt to compromise the reputation of my daughters. I have never known him harm a child, except you count neglect.'

'Neglect?'

'Not my children, others he has …sired … by various women.'

'You know this for a fact?'

'Yes, Mr Shuter, I do.'

'Would any of those women be willing to testify against him?'

'I know of one for certain, if we can find her. Dorothy Stephenson, a young woman from Whickham, the village adjoining my Gibside estate. I know her parents, respectable and hardworking farmers. They entrusted Dorothy to my household and my husband raped her. More than once.'

'Where is she now?'

'He took her to a brothel to have her baby, but I've heard she's not there anymore. They don't know where he took her. He knows full well that I want Dorothy and her baby safe, and once he knows I have gone to the courts, he will want to silence her. I am most afraid for Dorothy.'

'We will make it a matter of urgency to approach Lord Mansfield and obtain a writ of habeas corpus.'

'What is that?'

'Stoney will be ordered to produce Dorothy before the court.'

'Please do that quickly.'

'You will need more than one testimony.'

'There are medical men I could call upon. Mr Stoney retains a doctor named Jesse Foot who I know has many enemies in the medical profession. I am friends with the surgeon John Hunter, and he once warned me against trusting Dr Foot. I will write to him. There are numerous midwives who attended the births. There are brothel-keepers who are owed money.'

'This is all very sordid.'

'These are other women whose lives Stoney has ruined.'

Looking up from his notes, Mr Shuter said, 'As you know, we are somewhat backward for a Protestant country in having no secular divorce law. Your best chance of obtaining a legal separation will be through the ecclesiastical courts. It is a long and tortuous procedure and you are far from being guaranteed success. We will present your case to the bishops of the London Consistory Court. Testimony as to Mr Stoney's immoral conduct will be important in achieving your ends. Unfortunately, they will require witnesses, so I urge you to make every effort to locate anyone who has ever worked for you who might be willing to sign a sworn testimony.'

Mary Morgan spoke: 'I know of at least one. Mr Stoney's footman, Robert Crundall, is very devoted to Lady Strathmore, and he has stayed with the household for that sole reason. He has been keeping a record.'

I looked at Mary and she at me: the smiles we exchanged were further reassurance, if any were needed, that we had justice on our side. We watched in silence as Mr Shuter made his notes.

Finally, he put down his pen. 'Lady Strathmore, you do know that proceedings of all the courts are freely reported in the press? You may not be aware that there is an enormous public appetite for salacious stories. You are prepared for this?'

'I am, Mr Shuter. I do fear it, but I have been through so much that I will not feel shame, only anger. And anger is a fuel.'

'Good, good. Just as long as you know what to expect. Now, we have yet to discuss financial matters. Do you have income from any source other than your husband?'

'No, sadly, I do not.'

'Then pardon me for asking, but how will you manage?'

'I do not know.'

'Mr Stoney controls all incomes and capital?'

'There is no capital. Creditors abound. He controls all income from my estates, yes.'

'You clearly had no legal advice before you married him. He was, I understand, an Irish adventurer.'

'Your tone rebukes me, Mr Shuter, and if I was feeling stronger, I would tell you all the reasons why that is unfair, but the truth is that I did take legal measures to protect my fortune from any future husband.'

'You signed a pre-nuptial agreement? Why that is marvelous news! Where is it now?'

'He destroyed it.'

'Surely you made copies? Lodged a copy with the lawyer who drew it up?'

'He … persuaded me to sign a document revoking it.'

'Persuaded?'

'It matters not how he achieved it, but he did.'

'If only there were a copy of the original deed. You are sure he destroyed them all?'

'I entrusted one to my former footman, a family retainer called George Walker. But Mr Stoney sacked him and I never saw him again.'

'Does Mr Stoney know that George Walker had a copy?'

'I think so.'

'Would George Walker testify on your behalf if he could be found?'

'I feel sure that he would.'

'Then we will find him.'

Mary Morgan spoke, and what she said could not have astonished me more. 'This George Walker, what does he look like?'

'He is over sixty, as tall as you and with a full head of white hair. Bright blue eyes.'

'I don't want to raise false hopes, but a week or so before we left, a person of that description came to the house.'

'In Grosvenor Square?'

'Yes. He knocked the kitchen door one night when Mr Stoney had just gone out. Robert was the one who spoke to him. We'll get a message to him somehow.'

The thought that George Walker was alive and well and somewhere close was totally unexpected, and I found myself crying quietly.

Mr Shuter waited until I had composed myself, and then he went on: 'Now to the immediate issue of your sustenance. At home, are there any items which you could claim are family heirlooms? Items that could be legitimately taken into safe-keeping? Strathmore silver, perhaps? It might be possible to borrow money using some such item as surety.'

'Not Strathmore silver – I had it all sent to Glamis, but there are many items at Grosvenor Square that have been in my family for at least two generations: jewellery, works of art, silverware...'

'Then when we have appointed an attorney, we will make a move to retrieve these items and have them taken into safe-keeping. If you could supply me with an itemized list, please, but be sure to include not one single item that Mr Stoney could claim he bought, for that would invalidate the whole inventory.'

He stood up. 'I must go now, but here is the address of my club on Curzon Street. Perhaps you could send the baker's boy with the list this afternoon. I will be there until 4pm.'

He stood up and bowed his head. 'I take my leave of you, Lady Strathmore, Mrs Morgan. Until Monday.'

When Mary returned from seeing him out, I said, 'Bring paper and ink. I have letters to write.'

Chapter 23

To my mind, Dorothy Stephenson was an emblem of all that Stoney had defiled, and the key to stopping him, if only we could find her. On the day that he had been ordered to bring her before the bench in Westminster Hall, Mary Morgan begged me not to attend. More than anything, we were afraid of him finding out where we were living. When it became clear to Mary that I would not be dissuaded, she would give me no help in dressing, and only when my arm prevented me from fastening the cloak at my shoulder did she speak.

'Well you're not going alone. I'm coming with you.'

'I think it best that you don't, Mary. I have a good chance of going unnoticed, but if you are with me, it doubles the likelihood.'

'Then you must go with a man. Wait here.' She opened the door and slipped out into the passageway, returning a few minutes later with a plump lad of about sixteen whose dark shirt bore the outline of an apron in flour. 'This is the best I could do. Harry, say hello to Martha.'

The boy blushed and mumbled a greeting.

'Martha needs you to accompany her to Westminster Hall. Just stay with her and do as she says.' Turning to me, she whispered, 'Do not come directly home, whatever you do. I will be waiting and watching from across the street in the pawnbroker's. Come into the shop so that I can watch and make sure you are not followed.'

She was right. With my diminutive stature, in my drab clothes, hair hidden under a maid's mob-cap, smudges of soot on my face, and a cloak to hide under, I felt more secure with this child-man at my side. He kept up an amiable monologue all the way to Westminster, only falling silent as we jostled our way through the great stone arch.

I led Harry to the right as soon as we entered the hall: if Stoney should appear, I doubted he would look behind him and I would have time to melt into the crowd. We stayed snug against a pillar, which I thought I could slip behind in an instant. He had been ordered to bring Dorothy to the morning session, and as time wore on, I began to worry. If she and her baby were still alive, I did not put it beyond him to defy the courts and already be on the way to France or Ireland.

Harry was fascinated by the whole proceeding and his mumbling monologue started up again. 'Why look at that fellow. I never saw such a red nose! That boy has a cap like mine. My mother has a basket the same as that one.' He was such an amiable, simple soul, and when I gave him his instructions, he listened with his mouth agape, for I think I was not so successful as I'd hoped in adopting a Cockney accent. When I'd finished, he merely said, 'You talk funny.'

In the course of the morning, hundreds of people passed through the hall, and I flinched and ducked my head every time a tall man appeared. I craned from my vantage point to see every face. By the time he finally made his entrance, the hall was clearing and I felt more exposed with every passing minute.

I felt that my body recognised him before my brain: something inside me flinched with recognition and fear deep in my guts. I knew that erect bearing, the set of his enormous head on that bull neck, the way he strolled in like a dissolute emperor. I had to stop myself from stepping back further into the shadow of the pillar, merely slowly turning my head so that if his eye fell on me, all he would see was the side of a hood behind a stout boy. My hand to my face, I said quietly, 'Look at the bench, Harry, look straight ahead and keep still.'

Stoney paused and his gaze swept the room: I felt it through the thin fabric of my hood and my bones trembled. By the time I had summoned the courage to look back, my gaze crept across the stone flags to where he had last been standing. He had moved forward by several yards, and was now more safely in front of me. If Dorothy was beside him, she was hidden by the great barrel of his chest.

I cast around me for a safer vantage point and saw that the midday sun was now streaming through a window further along my wall. If I stood underneath it, anyone turning in my direction would be dazzled. I took Harry's arm, and keeping him between myself and the room, I strolled as nonchalantly as possible to a position under the window.

238

Stoney was by now standing before the bench, though there were people in front of him and he was looking round, a disdainful expression on his face that I hoped he would forget to wipe off before Lord Mansfield's gaze fell on him.

'Andrew Robinson Stoney Bowes.'

'Here, my lord.'

'Step forward, Mr Bowes.'

There was silence while Lord Mansfield gazed at Stoney over the top of his pince-nez, his face impassive. I still could not see Dorothy.

'Dorothy Stephenson.'

I heard no response, and my heart dropped. Was he going to defy the court? Had he come here without her? Was she already dead?

Suddenly, there was a commotion in the great doorway and voices raised, 'There! There she is! Dorothy!' and I saw the weather-beaten face of Dorothy's father amongst the crowd. There was still no sign of Dorothy from my vantage point, but then I saw that Stoney's elbow was bent back: he was clearly restraining her.

Lord Mansfield had not spoken, and watched impassively as two tipstaffs moved through the crowd to apprehend the Stephensons. They emerged with William and Mary Stephenson, holding them not unkindly, and walked with them to the side of the bench nearest to me. I could have taken ten steps and been by their side, but I must not, I must not.

'Now, Dorothy, for I presume from these people's reaction that you are she?'

I heard no response but Stoney was looking down to his left and Lord Mansfield nodded, clearly satisfied.

'Kindly oblige the court by letting go of the young woman's arm, Mr Bowes.'

'She will fall, my lord.'

'Will you fall, Dorothy? No, I thought not, for you look a fine healthy girl. I repeat, let go of her arm, Mr Bowes. Thank-you. Now, step forward, Dorothy, and tell me where you have been these past few weeks.'

But Stoney stepped in front of her. 'I have here an affidavit signed by Dorothy Stephenson in which she swears that she has not been held against her will.'

'Have you indeed, Mr Bowes? You do surprise me. Then I will read it.' Stoney clearly expected Lord Mansfield to put out a hand for the paper, and when no movement came from the bench, the tableau appeared to have frozen. Finally, he stepped forward and reached up to place it in front of the judge. When Lord Mansfield carried on regarding Stoney with an impassive gaze, he finally stepped back and away from the bench. Clearly assuming the judge would start reading straight away, he slipped an arm around Dorothy's waist and started whispering into her ear.

'Mr Bowes.'

'Yes, my lord?'

'Kindly unhand Miss Stephenson.'

'But you will see from the affidavit I am taking care of her and her baby, simply because, for all her moral weakness, she is my employee.'

'I repeat. Unhand Miss Stephenson. Thank-you. Dorothy, kindly approach the bench.' At last, her parents and I had a clear view of Dorothy and as she moved away from Stoney, her back straightened and she walked forward with admirable poise until she stood before the judge. I could not see, but I could imagine the impact on him of her famous beauty, if indeed she still possessed it.

'We are glad to see you, Dorothy, but where, pray, is your baby?'

At this, her shoulders slumped a little. 'With a friend of Mr Bowes. In Kensington. I don't know where that is.'

Lord Mansfield lifted his eyes to Stoney's, and then looked back at Dorothy. 'Perhaps Mr Bowes was unaware that the writ of habeas corpus extends to your child. Now Dorothy, tell me about this document.'

'I do not know, sir.'

'But you have put your mark to it, have you not?'

'I have sir.'

'But you have not read it?'

'No sir, I cannot read.'

Lord Mansfield lowered his head towards Dorothy. 'Mr Bowes read it to you, did he? Before you signed it?'

'Yes sir.'

'Would it surprise you to learn that it says that Mr Bowes has never forced you to do anything against your will?' He watched her face as he said this, and although she did not reply with her mouth, she clearly did with those famous brown eyes.

'Mr Bowes, step forward.'

Sensing which way the wind blew, Stoney did not attempt any bluster. 'As you are no doubt aware, Mr Bowes, this young woman is a potential witness in a case that has been presented to this court, and you have clearly ... interfered with her. Tipstaffs.' The two court officers moved away from Dorothy's parents to stand before the bench. 'Kindly escort Dorothy and her parents to Kensington to retrieve the baby and return to court immediately. Mr Bowes, you will give them the address. You will remain here until such time as the child and her mother return. Stand to one side.'

I watched, joyful, as Dorothy's parents ran to her and wrapped her in their embrace whilst Stoney stood immobile, staring at Lord Mansfield as though his face had been slapped.

'Mr Bowes, if you are considering some kind of insolent riposte, I would strongly advise you against it. Stand to one side.'

Suddenly conscious that Stoney would soon be facing in the opposite direction, I tugged Harry's arm and scuttled from the room, my face averted. Bright sunshine lit the great doorway. I must think quickly. Dorothy and the baby were to return here, and I didn't imagine her parents would lose much time in leaving the capital and heading north. Pushing aside my thoughts of how much I longed to go with them, I hastily turned Harry to face me. 'Did you see the people who were sent to get a baby?'

'With the two tipstaffs, yes. I think I'd like to be a tipstaff when I grow up.'

'Harry, listen to me. Can you see those people? There, by the Hackney carriages. Listen carefully. Go to them. Go to the father. Do you know your letters, Harry?'

'Yes.'

'Say to him MEB wishes to speak with him. I will follow you and stand there, near that gate. Speak to no-one else, just the father.'

As I hastened to the church gate, I watched Harry approach the group milling around the carriages. I saw Mr Stephenson incline his head to listen to Harry, then speak quickly to one of the tipstaffs. It seemed to me that he had indicated that he wished to relieve himself in the churchyard, so I ducked inside the gateway and waited for him, my heart pounding, my skin alive with excitement. When his honest brown face appeared in the gateway, it was all I could do not to run into his arms. His astonishment was palpable: 'Miss Bowes? I cannot believe it is you.'

'It is so good to see you, and I am so happy that Dorothy is safe. Can you bear to leave her here in my care?'

'Leave her here? In London? Where he may find her again? No, forgive me Miss Bowes, Lady Strathmore, but I cannot. We must take her and the baby home to safety.'

'I am sorry to ask you to do this, John, but please. She can lodge with my lawyer. She will be safe there. Just while she is guided through her testimony. Dorothy has seen much and endured much. I … I need her help if I am to succeed in saving us all from this brute.'

'Saving us all or saving yourself?'

'All of us. If I succeed, I will not only be divorced but he will be imprisoned. Gibside will be free of him. Please. Have faith in me. I know I have sorely tested your loyalty, but…'

'Our loyalty to you has never been in any doubt, Miss Bowes. Only you brought that devil into our heart and let him damn near ruin us all.' I could see he was relenting. My face must have spoken of my desperation. In the end, he took a deep breath and spoke the words I so longed to hear: 'We will return to Gibside with our little baby granddaughter and we will leave our daughter in your care. God help you both.'

I grasped both his hands in mine and could only blink my thanks. He looked at me and his eyes softened: 'Poor bairn. What a time of it you've had. Come home with us.'

For all the world, I could have fainted at his feet and let him take me north, but I must see this through, once and for all. 'Mr Shuter. Lincoln's Inn Chambers.' And I was gone.

Dorothy provided a witness statement of such lengthy and incriminating detail that when Mr Shuter brought it to my hiding place, his ruddy face was beaming with an openness I had not seen so far. It was as though, by hearing it from the horse's mouth, knowing that neither I nor anyone else had had access to influence Dorothy's tale, and watching those expressive brown eyes, the indignation and anger that fuelled her testimony, the case was won. If only it had proved so simple.

'Such recall as you would not believe! She can name dates, she can remember what people were wearing. She has seen so much! And you, my dear,' and here he held my hands, 'you have endured so much. As has she. I have no fear of offending your sensibilities: she was raped. Repeatedly. Often violently. She has witnesses who can testify to being ordered from the room. People heard her cries, saw her injuries. This man is the devil incarnate. But we shall have him,' and here he shook his fist in my face, 'we shall have the bastard and we shall have him in prison, if it takes a year!'

'A year!'

'Yes, my dear, I hardly dared tell you how slowly the wheels of the law grind on. But have no fear, I have a grand surprise for you! Harry!'

The door opened, and Harry and his father carried in a huge hamper, laid it down on the floor and opened it with a flourish. It was filled to the brim with carrots, turnips, parsnips, cabbages and onions.

'What is this?'

'This is vegetables,' said sweet simple Harry, and we all laughed.

'Yes, thank-you Harry, I can see that. But where are they from?'

'Can ye not guess?' said a voice from the doorway, and there was Dorothy, her colour restored, her bright eyes shining. She spoke again, and her accent had gone so far north that all the southerners surrounding us looked on in wonder. 'Divvn't ye knaa them clarts, bonny lass? Them veggies are from yem.'

My eyes filled with tears and I knelt to smell the Gibside earth.

After that, the letters started, family after family sending their story, their words of support, their promises of loyalty. On one envelope, I recognised the handwriting of old Robert Thompson the gardener, and savoured for a moment the memory of his hand on so many carefully-folded paper packets of seed. I remembered the times when I had entrusted him with a precious scattering of tiny granules that had travelled half-way round the world. At first, he had heartily disapproved of such foreign imports, but once he had laid eyes on a Cape bloom, he was converted.

243

In his letter, though he tried hard at first to sound full of promise, it became clear that he was finding it hard: it seemed he was working alone, and I was wondering what had become of all the apprentices and garden lads and potboys. When I got to the end of the letter, I read that he had been sacked but refused to leave.

With the letter from the gardener came one from Francis Bennett the gamekeeper, who made no bones about telling me of the destruction being wrought by 'Mr Bowes and his cronies.' Seeing those words in the hand of such a loyal servant - for Francis had been Glamis footman to my first husband, and had been so smitten with Gibside, which he called 'This Eden' that he had begged me to let him stay on after Lord Strathmore's death - I resolved to instruct all my correspondents to refer to him as Mr Stoney, as if by that simple act I could divorce him, reduce his power and save all these good people from his actions. Francis went on to warn me not to reply as Stoney was intercepting all the mail that came onto the estate. He spoke of finding a hare caught in a trap in the woods, and how he had wished it had been something else.

'People are frightened, and it's every man for himself. I have tried to collect rents, but men stand on their thresholds in defiance for no-one trusts the next man. Are you a Bowes man or a Gibside man? is the cry. Bowes meaning him. I should call him Stoney, we all should, for he is no more a Bowes than my dog. Forgive me ma'am – I know that you will. For all their bluster and fear and defiance, I swear that everyone here is praying that you will get the better of this Stoney Bowes and rid us of him once and for all. Many's the time it has crossed my mind how many ways a man could come to harm in these woods, with their foxholes and mine-workings. There is rumours that Tommy Colpitts is hereabouts, perhaps you have heard from him already. I have hope that if he knocks on doors, rents will be handed over, for he is a Gibside man through to the bone. For all my length of service, I am still a Scot and a foreigner.'

Thomas Colpitts had indeed returned to Gibside, and in the year it took for the courts to gather evidence and depositions, to examine and cross-examine witnesses, he brought a semblance of normality to Gibside. With Stoney so much occupied in London in bribing witnesses and hiding at Streatlam to send forth false reports of his own death, Colpitts became my representative, an emblem of the old order and a promise that it would one day return.

The decision, when it came, was swift. Judge Wynne, sitting in the Consistory Court, found in my favour. Mary Eleanor Bowes, Countess of Strathmore, was granted a divorce 'from bed, board and mutual cohabitation' from Andrew Robinson Stoney Bowes, on the grounds of his cruelty and multiple cases of adultery.

Imagine, if you will, the relief I felt upon hearing those words. I barely had time to savour the joy of being believed, of being released from the marriage, before the judge's next words brought the final stage of the battle to the forefront of my mind. 'Mr Bowes, you will pay Lady Strathmore alimony of £300 per annum.'

The worst was yet to come.

Chapter 24

As soon as I was sure Stoney had left London after the separation ruling, I felt safe to come out of hiding. A small number of friends and acquaintances from my previous life had come forward with offers of help, although I was still clearly shunned by the majority. I suppose mud sticks: the disapproval and distaste of wider society could not have mattered less to me. If all went well, I would soon be able to leave London forever.

I had been offered temporary occupation of a friend's house in Bloomsbury, as she and her husband were in the habit of spending the summer on the south coast. I was cautiously excited, for it felt like a real victory to emerge into daylight, and a respectable address would increase my chances of seeing my children. Whenever I thought of little Mary, my heart hurt. George and Thomas were fourteen and thirteen now, and I had been notified that they were at Eton. John had just gone to Cambridge University. It had been so long since I'd seen him that I could barely imagine him in a cap and gown. In my mind's eye, I gave him his father's beautiful face.

I had hoped against hope that Stoney would go back to Ireland, his tail between his legs, but news soon came that he had gone to ground at Streatlam Castle while he planned his next move: he clearly felt safer there, now that he knew the extent of the spirit and devotion to me of the people of Gibside. Streatlam had not been properly occupied by our family since John had died. Thomas had lingered some time there, for he too was fond of the stud, but since I'd married Stoney the place had been run by a skeleton staff, none of whom I knew.

It was clear that he was now wary of returning to Gibside, though until the Court of Chancery settled the matter, he was still master there. Although I had not been aware of it at the time, the man who picked me up from the gravel when Mary was taken away had been Thomas Colpitts. There had been a terrible row and he and Stoney had almost come to blows: Colpitts had left Gibside that very day. Now that he had returned and the people had rallied behind him, Stoney knew he had a formidable enemy, and when one of his vicious dogs was killed, I imagine he suspected he might be next. By all reports, he now had a gang of thugs about him, recruited apparently in Darlington.

His lawyers were preparing an appeal, and I was bracing myself for what that might bring. Thomas Colpitts had gone into hiding and the mythology swirled around his absence from plain sight: he was Gibside's Robin Hood. Through a complicated system of subterfuge, he and I kept up a weekly correspondence, and it was not long before I had it confirmed that Stoney was there, and raging about the place with his henchmen, demanding rents and issuing threats to anyone who showed any loyalty to me.

The courts were soon to retire for the summer, so Stoney's appeal against the divorce ruling would not be heard in the ecclesiastical court until October. My suit to reinstate my prenuptial deed was due to be heard in Chancery at the same time. If I was to have any hope of retaining my properties, I had to find George Walker; the rumour was that Stoney had had him killed or locked away to prevent him being subpoenaed, and I hoped against hope that it wasn't true.

I knew that Stoney would do everything in his power to overturn the judgment of the ecclesiastical court, and naturally, his tactic would be to discredit my morality. Whereas until now his efforts had been directed at manipulating others, he would now devote his energies into presenting me as a moral degenerate. I had a profound fear of what this might bring, simply because of the attitudes to women which prevail in our time.

My father taught me to mistrust the church, and one of the reasons he gave was its representation of women as the source of sin and temptation. For his own mother, an indomitable widow, he had the very greatest respect. His devotion to his first wife gave her the status of an angel, and in his second wife, my mother, he found a competent and intelligent partner. I rarely heard him say a bad word about anyone, but he raged against anyone who mistreated a woman, and had only contempt for the popular press and their taste for scandal, which was invariably presented as originating in the wanton profligacy, ungoverned desires or wicked temptations of 'fallen' women.

In London, popular prints of degraded subjects are displayed openly in the newspapers and shop windows, and distributed and sold for entertainment. Pornography is everywhere. To my mind and that of any right-thinking individual, the creator, the reader and the buyer of such publications degrade themselves. The same newspapers profess admiration for the people who fight for freedom and equality in France and America, or demand an end to the slave trade: they see no conflict when they turn to the page where a woman is treated as guilty or degraded because she is an object of fear or desire.

On the day we left our hiding place in Holborn, I found myself unexpectedly sad. Such tiny rooms had felt like a trap to me when I had first come here, but the baker's family had sheltered us so kindly and with such generosity. As Ann and Susannah packed our few bags into the hackney carriage, I went into the shop to say goodbye and I felt genuinely sad. I grasped Mr Baker's floury hands, regardless. 'I will never forget you and your kindness. One day, when I can repay it in some way, I will come back.'

As our carriage emerged from the warren of narrow streets into the open spaces of Bloomsbury, I felt an unexpected shiver. The four of us were tightly-packed in the carriage, and Mary felt the tremor go through me.

'What's wrong?'

'It's strange, I feel more afraid here than I did in Holborn.'

Ann, always blunt, said, 'Why? Surely you are safer here, among your own kind.'

'My own kind, as you call them, have been far from kind to me. There was a warmth and security in that small alleyway in Holborn.'

'You're romanticizing!' Dismissively, Ann looked out of the window.

Mary Morgan spoke, 'No, I think I understand. You believe that you know where you are with working people.'

'Yes, I feel that I do. My father always did. He always said that respect had to be earned, not demanded, and he had far more respect for an honest, hard-working man than for a landed toff who didn't know which side to butter his bread.'

'And to be fair, many of the people we think of as 'your kind' are not of the same mind.'

'No indeed. I was always conscious that Lord Strathmore was an aristocrat and he saw my father as an upstart with dirty hands.'

'Ha, but they needed your money though, those Strathmores, didn't they?'

'Yes. They made no real secret of that. I think many of the landed gentry are the same. They have the great houses but often little in the way of income. And they lose a sense of what work is. They forget about the people whose labour supports their lifestyle. I have heard that there are great houses where the servants have to move about through narrow passageways between the walls, lest they offend the sensibilities of their employers!'

All expressed astonishment.

'It is true. They forget. John Locke said "All wealth is the product of labour" and my father taught me never to forget it. At Gibside, the iron and paper mills and mines and kitchens are all visible and part of the fabric of the place.'

'Can I ask you something?'

'Of course Susannah, anything.'

'If you win your case in October, will you get everything back? All of it? Stoney will be left with nothing?'

'Yes. That is what I'm hoping for.'

'And if you lose?'

'He keeps everything until my eldest son reaches his majority.'

'And how old is he now?'

'Seventeen.'

'So he only keeps it for four more years?'

'Unless he succeeds in preventing the divorce, in which case he keeps it for as long as he can keep me alive. Once I am dead, John comes into his inheritance.'

Robert Crundall had been silent until now, but then he spoke my deepest fear. 'Of course you know he will try to take you by force?'

The three women turned wide, frightened eyes from his face to mine.

'Yes. Yes, I do. It is what I am most afraid of.'

Susannah and Ann broke into questions, clearly alarmed at the thought of this fearful bogeyman, whom they had heard so much about, coming to take their mistress.

'When we arrive at the house, I will talk to the staff about security.'

'Thank-you Robert.'

He was as good as his word: the servants were fully apprised of the threat. No-one was to be allowed access who was not known to them, and even visitors they knew must not be allowed to come up from the basement kitchens. On Robert's advice, I wrote to the owners and asked permission to install extra security measures. I was fearful of their reply as I imagined they might balk at the idea of their house being the target of a madman, but to my great relief, an answer came by return. It simply said, 'Do all that you feel you must to keep yourself safe.'

A system of trips, bells and levers was already installed but under-used. Robert reinstated it, much to the annoyance of the scullery-maid whose job it was to light the fires. Extra bolts and bars were installed on the doors and windows, and one day Robert came home in a carriage with a large metal box which the driver helped him carry into the hall. It contained two large swords, a smaller rapier and four cudgels, one for each of the women. He showed us the most effective way of using it on a man, which caused much nervous hilarity and an inadvertent injury which left him crumpled in a heap moaning.

Charles Shuter was a frequent visitor and always paternal and affectionate. The lawyer who had represented me in court was a gentleman by the name of James Farrer. He and his wife and daughters became my firm friends. When he became aware of the extent of my physical fear, James introduced me to his brother Henry, a ship's captain recently returned from South Africa. James suggested that he accompany me as a bodyguard whenever I left the house, and I accepted with gratitude.

The anguished letters from estate workers came thick and fast: Stoney and his henchmen were laying waste to the woodlands, venting his fury on my heartlands. Not only had more ancient oaks been felled, but now the newer plantations from my father's time. I filed an injunction as quickly as I could, and when it succeeded, lost no time in having handbills and posters printed warning anyone tempted to buy the timber that its sale was illegal. I wrote again to Thomas Strathmore, pleading for support to protect the children's inheritance, but again received no reply.

Soon I started to hear from tenants and farmers who were being threatened with eviction for displaying support for me. Things quickly started to escalate and it became clear he was acting on his threats: widows and orphans were being cast out of farms they had rented for generations. I grew convinced that he was doing this to lure me away from London. When I refused to respond as he'd planned, his next step was typically mendacious: he falsely claimed that the injunction had been revoked and then swiftly followed this up with handbills proclaiming to all and sundry that the Countess of Strathmore was now reconciled with Mr Andrew Robinson Stoney Bowes.

I received a heart-breaking letter from the gardener Robert Thompson pleading for reassurance that this was not true, and by the same post another from the Stephensons, who were being singled out for particularly vicious intimidation on account of Dorothy's role in the divorce case. Mrs Stephenson begged me to come home, being in fear not only of eviction, but of her husband's imprisonment for debt.

With Stoney's London reputation in tatters, I had assumed the judiciary in the north-east would never trust him, but when I heard that he had successfully sued Thomas Colpitts for collecting rents in my name, I knew that his charm was still working on them, else they were corrupt and in his pocket.

It was Mr Shuter, bless him, who had to break the news that I had joined the ranks of the poor degraded women whose images are distributed to serve the baser human instincts. I had endured much by the hands of Stoney Bowes, but I can honestly say I had never felt such a peculiar sense of pollution as he perpetrated on me in the name of entertainment.

I could tell as soon as he entered the room that something had happened, for he fumbled with his hat and avoided my eyes. As is the way with parents everywhere, my thoughts went straight to my children: 'What is it, Mr Shuter? Tell me.'

'I cannot, Lady Strathmore.'

I knew then that it was something other, something about my public persona, for he always called me Mary Eleanor.

'Come now, we know each other well enough. I have no secrets from you, so kindly tell me what is causing your evident consternation.'

He looked at me then, but in a new way, as though he hardly knew me at all. 'I hardly know how to begin.'

I tried to lighten my tone to encourage him, but my heart had contracted with fear. 'Begin at the beginning.'

'On my walk to work, I pass a print shop on Grub Street.'

'There are many print shops on Grub Street.'

'Yes, and usually I avert my eyes. Such loathsome images pollute the soul, to my mind.'

'To my mind too,' but now an inkling of what was to come was beginning to creep up my spine. 'And why did this particular print shop draw your eye?'

'There was a crowd outside, over-excited as they often are when there is something in the window about a notable person.'

'And that notable person would be...?'

'This particular shop sells pornography.' He watched me as my eyes widened and understanding began to dawn.

'Tell me what you saw.' I saw his eyes glance towards the leather briefcase he still held.

'You have a copy in your bag?'

In answer, he merely hung his head.

'Show me.'

'I cannot for shame, Mary Eleanor. You do not need to see it. I only felt it my duty to make you aware. Mr Stoney has clearly begun a war of propaganda, designed to sway the church court and to weaken your resolve.'

'Nothing will weaken my resolve, Mr Shuter.'

He put down his briefcase with a resigned air, came over to me, patted my shoulder and sat down opposite me.

'The thing is, Mary Eleanor, I cannot think how we can counter this. If we engage with it, we validate it, and worse, we draw attention to it. If we ignore it, it seems like an admission of truth.'

'Thank-you. You have done your duty in bringing it to my attention. But if I am to know what I am up against, I must see it in all its glory.'

'It really isn't necessary for you to see it.'

'Nonsense. Of course she must see it.' Mary Morgan had been sitting in the window reading.

The roll of paper he drew from his briefcase was large, almost two feet in length, and when I saw this, my heart contracted again for it seemed that the larger it was, the more detailed it was bound to be. I knew that some of the cartoons in the pornographers' windows were very explicit, and I pitied the women who had sat for their portraits in such degraded circumstances. Very probably, many of them would be plied with drink or laudenam, but many will have been coerced. I didn't imagine that many would be paid.

He handed it to me rolled up and walked away to stare out of the window.

I unrolled it with trembling hands. It showed a bare-breasted woman lolling back in her chair, her ample skirts hitched up and plump legs spread wide, though mercifully her undergarments were in place. I scanned the writing quickly for my own name, but could see nothing until I noticed the words Grosvenor Square. I looked back at the drawing: the hairstyle and clothes marked her out as upper class, but nothing else seemed to link her to me apart from the amplitude of her breasts, perhaps. But as my gaze took in the other figures, my disquiet grew and I suddenly understood. A young boy was being held by a lascivious-looking maid, who was unfastening his breeches and holding him towards the figure in the chair.

I hardly know how to say what I felt, such was the storm of unaccustomed emotion this image provoked. Until Mary's voice came over my shoulder, I had not known which feeling would come out of my mouth first.

'I see I have a starring role. He has captured my expression very well, though I cannot say the same for the lady in the chair.'

Catching her light-hearted tone, I swallowed my tears of humiliation: 'It is skillfully done, I'll give him that.'

Lovely colours and fine drawing. A shame the artist...who is it?...Gillray... has chosen to waste his skills on such drivel.'

'I imagine he makes good money from such commissions.'

'What does it say at the bottom?'

' "Lady Termagent Flaybum going to give her stepson a taste of her dessert after dinner, a scene performed every day near Grosvenor Square." ' I lifted a puzzled gaze to Mr Shuter. 'Lady Termagent Flaybum?'

'A character from the pornographer's previous work on...' He stopped, clearly embarrassed.

'Flagellation?' He nodded. 'And you know that ... how?'

Wounded, he looked up at me, but when he saw that I was smiling, he relaxed. 'I asked someone in the crowd.'

'So the implication is that I am about to beat my son?'

'Yes, I assume so.'

'Not breastfeed him?'

'No, I imagine the state of undress is merely to …titillate the viewer. Whoever commissioned this caricature…'

'Come now, Mr Shuter, I think we all know who paid for it.'

'His clear intention is to portray you as a moral degenerate, a drunkard…'

'A drunkard? How so? Ah, I see now the wine bottles.'

'And an unnatural and cruel mother.'

'Ah.'

'You seem remarkably calm.'

'Well, I presume there is nothing I can do. There are as far as I know, no laws which this has contravened.'

'Quite so.'

'How many copies of this do you imagine there are?'

'Well, judging by the number of poorer copies being leered over outside the shop, very many. But the colour print is of excellent quality and expensively priced. And of course, with an artist of Gillary's burgeoning reputation, they will reach a wide audience of your peers.'

Something about the way he said 'they' alerted me. 'There's another one, isn't there, Mr Shuter?'

'Regretfully, there is indeed. I showed you that one first to prepare you for the other, which, to my mind, is infinitely more shocking.'

I gestured to him to bring it to me.

'This one, I have to tell you, was causing a great deal of raucous hilarity.' And when I opened the roll of paper, I could see why. In this one, recognisibly the same figure, although the breasts were grossly enlarged, was, and I blush to tell you this, portrayed suckling two cats. I took a sharp breath and involuntarily found that my hand rested on the tabby who slept beside me on the sofa at that very moment. I opened the roll out to its fullest extent, and saw the image of a boy crying as he regarded this sickening scene, as well he might. Beneath the caricature ran the words: 'I wish I was a cat – my mama would love me then. It was entitled 'The Injured Countess.'

In the background, a footman whom I took to be George Walker was suggestively indicating a bed.

'So to my catalogue of sins we may now add some kind of bestial perversion and …'

'Promiscuity. With a servant.'

'Yes, because as we all know, intimate relations with a servant are worse than intimate relations with a person of the same class.'

'Quite.' He regarded my stricken face for a few moments, for all pretence had fallen from me. 'So now we know.'

'Pardon?'

'Sorry, so now we know what his plan of attack is.'

'Yes, we do.' Something dreadful had occurred to me, and it clearly showed on my face, for Mr Shuter saw it in my eyes.

'What is it, Mary Eleanor?'

No. I must not bring my fears into the open. Not just yet. By confronting the possibility, they would become more real, and this particular fear had been shut away in a locked room in my mind for so long that it had grown bigger.

'Nothing. I was only thinking.' I stood up and brushed down my skirt. 'It looks like a lovely day out there. I think I will go for a walk. Shall we go together?' I turned back into the room to find both of them looking at me very intently. In the end, it was Mary who spoke. 'I think Mr Shuter needs to ask you something.'

I knew full well what it was, but I could not bring myself to open that door in my mind.

I turned to him, affecting innocence, though my heart was fluttering in panic. 'Yes, ask away.' But he could not meet my eyes.

'Eleanor, I think what Mr Shuter needs to know is whether your estranged husband has any evidence that he might use against you.'

I could not lie to Mary and she knew it.

'Yes, I think he does.'

'Of what nature is this evidence?'

The door in my mind burst open. 'Of a gross and revolting nature, of a completely fictional nature, of the nature of a document which he extracted from me by beatings and burnings, by threats and cajolings. He threatened me with the loss of Mary, he told me I would be incarcerated in a lunatic asylum if I did not do as he said! A document in which HIS nature, the nature of the very devil, is fully revealed! Degraded, perverted thoughts given free rein. The

256

vile creature entered my very soul and had me speak in tongues not my own. He had already penetrated my body and with this act of creation he penetrated my mind! Oh shall I never be free of him? By this document he has me, and he knows it. Condemned by my own hand. Oh, I am lost, I am lost!'

Chapter 25

As the date neared for the hearing, I became more and more convinced that I was in danger. Several times, the servants reported seeing suspicious men who appeared to be watching the house. Once, when Captain Farrar and I set off for a walk in Kensington Gardens, we became convinced that we were being followed by a certain hackney carriage with the blinds drawn down. In the mornings, I could almost dismiss yesterday's fears, but at night, we checked the bolts and chains repeatedly and compulsively. I was determined not to be intimidated by fear any more, and told myself over and over again that I had nothing to be ashamed of. In public, I endured pointing, laughter, bold stares and sidelong glances, but I always held my head high.

One day towards the end of October, I had just set out in my coach, accompanied by Mary and Robert. As we turned into Mews, we came to an abrupt halt and I waited breathlessly for the horses to resume their canter. Robert had risen to his feet and drawn his pistol the instant he heard the coachman's shout, and Mary Morgan had fearlessly looked out of the other window. I pressed myself into the corner and hardly remembered to breathe.

The driver appeared at Mary's window, his face grave.

'What is it?'

'We were being followed.'

'Why are we stopped?' for I feared any moment that the door would burst open and I would be dragged from the coach.

'Ann saw a chaise with its blinds shut and a hackney carriage waiting in the street. When we left, she saw them follow immediately behind. She sent James on horseback to overtake them and warn us.'

'What is happening now?'

'They have gone past and not stopped. We have cudgels and Robert has his pistol. Fear not, it is a busy street. It might be nothing, but better to do this in a busy street than wait until we are out in the countryside. Better safe than sorry.'

Mary grasped my hand firmly and waited. I could feel her pulse against mine, and both our hearts were beating ten to the dozen, though she kept her external composure with admirable self-control. Surrounded by the noises of the street, the creak of passing carriages, snorting horses, the voices of pedestrians close by, every male voice made me shrink inside.

Finally, the door opened and Robert climbed inside. Without speaking, he opened the blind and window, and leaned out.

'Tell me what's happening.'

'The vehicles did pull in behind us when we stopped. No-one got in or out. When I showed myself holding a pistol, the driver of the chaise spoke to whoever was inside, and the occupant clearly instructed him to move on, whereupon both vehicles passed us.'

'Could you see who was inside?'

I saw him exchange glances with Mary. 'There were three men in the hackney carriage. I think I recognised one of them as a lurker from outside the house.'

'And in the chaise?'

He did not meet my eyes, and nor did he answer.

'It was him, wasn't it?'

Finally, Mary Morgan confirmed what we all suspected. 'A chaise passed the house yesterday, just as I was paying the window-cleaner. Though I saw it only in profile, I would swear in court that the face I saw was that of Mr Stoney.'

'Turn for home. I will remain locked in the house under armed guard until the hearing.'

The following day, Mary brought a young constable into the sitting-room. His watery eyes seemed to trouble him, but he was a tall young man with broad shoulders, so when I heard that he had apprehended some suspicious-looking characters lurking at the back of the house during the night, I thanked him profusely. Somewhat shy, he stuttered an offer: 'If you would like to engage a bodyguard, Lady Strathmore, I would be honoured to offer you my protection.'

So Edward Lucas was engaged as a night watchman. Over the next few days, he appeared devoted to his duties and rapidly made himself indispensible to me. In fact, it was he who brought me news that appeared to be deliberately concocted to establish Stoney's whereabouts. The newspaper reported that he had been injured falling from his horse in County Durham. I knew it to be a lie.

After almost two weeks of voluntary incarceration, I decided to accept an invitation to lunch on Oxford Street. It was Friday 10th November 1786. Captain Farrer and Robert were both armed with pistols, and they sat opposite Mary and me, their faces turned to look out of the windows on both sides for the short journey.

When we arrived at the address, I looked out at the frontage of the ironmonger's shop, above which my friends lived, and had a vision of myself as the carefree sixteen-year-old I had been when I first came here. So much had happened in the intervening years, but now I had real hope that such freedom would one day be restored to me. My bodyguards dismounted first and flanked us as Mary and I crossed the pavement and entered the shop. I must admit, I had a fit of the giggles once we were inside, such was the seriousness of their faces. I was over-excited, I suppose.

Mr and Mrs Foster received us most graciously, and we had just sat down to lunch when we heard raised voices and a scuffle from below. Mary and I froze. When a shout came again, Mary stood, her eyes wide, and took my hand. Speaking rapidly to Mr Foster, she said, 'Quick! What's upstairs? Is there a lockable room in the attic?'

'Yes, go quickly.'

The narrow wooden staircase was clearly unused, for cobwebs brushed our faces and skirts. We found a door, but it was locked and so all we could do was wait in the dusty darkness until we heard words of reassurance from below.

After about fifteen minutes, one voice emerged from the hubbub three storeys down: it was Edward Lucas calling, 'Lady Strathmore, it is safe to descend.'

Mary went first. 'What was it, Edward?'

'A ruffian attempted to gain entry to the shop insisting that he had to speak to Lady Strathmore.'

'And where is he now?'

'I apprehended him and another constable has taken him away. But we were clearly followed so I am anxious to get us safely back to the house.'

Bidding a hasty and apologetic goodbye to Mr and Mrs Foster, Mary and I descended the staircase and hastened through the shop, followed by Edward Lucas.

Mary let go of my arm and went through the shop doorway before me. Briefly dazzled by the midday sun as I stepped from the shop's dark interior, the pavement seemed crowded with people and I was jostled by a person I took to be a passer-by. I took a step back, and was reassured to feel Edward grasp my arm and push me forward towards the coach. I glimpsed for a moment a frozen tableau of figures to either side and in front of me, one of whom was Captain Farrer. Edward was still pushing me forward with what seemed to be unnecessary force. I was just about to mount the steps into the coach when I went to turn to remonstrate with him for his rough handling when I found myself looking down the barrel of a blunderbuss. I instinctively turned towards Edward, and saw that he held me at arm's length. His face had entirely changed. The glasses were gone, and his thin-lipped smile had hardened into a tight line.

'Lady Strathmore, I have a warrant for your arrest. You must come with us quietly.'

'What? Arrest for what? Come with you where?'

In answer, he seized my arm and propelled me into the coach. Desperate, I saw Captain Farrer, his hands outspread as if to show me that he had been disarmed. Mary had disappeared. There was such a melee, all the men around me speaking at once, and not one voice was one I recognised.

Edward Lucas climbed in behind me and the coach pulled away before he had even slammed the door.

'What is the meaning of this, Edward?'

'As I said, Lady Strathmore, I have a warrant for your arrest.'

'On what grounds?'

'I am not at liberty to say.'

'Don't be pompous, Edward. I am not at liberty at all.' He granted me a tight smile. 'Tell me where you are taking me.'

'To appear before Lord Mansfield.'

I glanced out of the window. 'We are now on the Tottenham Court Road. We are heading away from Westminster.'

'You are to appear before him at his home in Highgate.'

'I do not believe you, Edward.'

'It is of no consequence.'

I spoke with far more confidence than I felt. Convincing Edward that he must let me go was my only hope. Fear of my true fate constricted my heart but I would not let it constrict my courage or my voice.

'Edward, if you do not take me straight home I will be forced to conclude that you are working for my husband. If this is true, I advise you to think again. Mr Stoney is going to jail. By aiding him you put yourself in danger.'

There was a flicker of uncertainty when he turned to me, but I saw him extinguish it and his eyes hardened.

'This is an abduction, Edward. You are breaking the law. You are a constable, or so you tell me. Was that a lie?'

But Edward spoke not another word.

When we turned into the yard of the Red Lion in Highgate. I made myself sit still until the coach came to a standstill, then I rose to my feet and leant towards the door.

Without a word, Lucas pushed me back into the seat and opened the door. There, standing in the middle of the yard with his hands on his hips and a triumphant grin on his loathsome face, was Stoney. All my restraint left me and I instinctively cowered away from him. It was a curious sensation. I had mentally rehearsed this scenario so often: I knew I must create a scene, get help, expose this for an abduction, but my body refused to obey.

I watched helpless as Edward dismounted from the coach, leaving the door open, and walked towards Stoney. They exchanged a few words, and I saw Stoney give him a banknote, whereupon he turned and smiled at me, said something to Stoney and then they both laughed. That was what galvanized me. Before I knew what I was doing, I was out of the coach and running towards the tavern entrance, shouting, 'Help! Help!'

Edward caught me by the upper arm just as I gained the doorway, and hoisting it high so that I feared my shoulder would be disjointed, he hustled me back towards the coach. I kept up my cries, 'Help! They are abducting me! I am the Countess of Strathmore! You must help me!'

I did not hear what Stoney said to the grooms and stable lads who had gathered to witness the commotion, but the faces of the older men broke into grins, though I caught sight of one young stable lad whose fearful and horrified expression must have matched my own.

Edward bundled me into the coach and I banged my elbow hard against the doorjamb. Sickened by the pain, I had nonetheless turned to carry on shouting my pleas but found the door blocked by

Stoney, who was climbing into the coach. The bulk of him blacked out the daylight.

He settled himself into the opposite seat, tapped the roof with the head of his cane and the coach described a circle in the yard and headed north at a gallop.

'And so, my love. Here we are. Together again at last.'

Mutinous, I hardly knew myself, such was my fear and revulsion. The familiar smell of him, of leather and cigar smoke, of port and something sweeter, more cloying.

'You look well.'

'Where are we going?'

I saw him switch tactics, quickly thinking of a lie to puncture my defiance. 'Oh my dear, I hardly know how to tell you. It's little Mary.'

I felt the colour drain from my face and my head swam. Swallowing hard but keeping as still as I could muster, I watched him carefully. 'Go on.'

'She was taken ill at school. I have had her moved to St Paul's Walden so that...' he glanced at me, perhaps calculating how far to go in this clear lie. 'So that she may...' he blinked rapidly, plainly meaning to imply that she was at death's door.

I maintained my angry stare, challenging him to continue. All the while, inside I quaked with fear for my daughter. When he didn't at first go on, I prompted him: 'So that she may...?'

'Be more comfortable. She is calling for her mother.'

'She called for her mother from the moment you sent her away from me.'

'It was for her own good. You were spoiling her.'

'So now you have moved my daughter to the house I inherited from my mother?'

I saw him consider reminding me about married women's property but decide to maintain this caring façade. 'Indeed. I thought it for the best.'

'I'm very touched by your concern. I have not seen my daughter for two years. I have not known where she was. You have denied all the pleas I have made through my lawyers to deliver her into my custody. And yet suddenly you decide that you should go to great lengths to deceive me, violently abduct me and take me to her? It beggars belief.'

264

He considered me in silence. I felt his eyes on me like jabbing fingers. 'You really do look very well.'

I did not respond. Instead, I made my mind focus on anger. Not fear. I would have no more fear.

'Eleanor, I want us to be together.'

'You want to be reunited with my fortune, you mean.'

At that moment, the driver's mate knocked on the partition and then slid it open. An unfamiliar voice, distinctly north-eastern, growled, 'We're just approaching the turnpike.'

'Who's that?'

'An acquaintance.'

'From Newcastle?'

'Darlington.'

'What became of my driver and footman?'

He had the audacity to laugh. 'Don't concern yourself.'

I was struggling to control my shaking, but told myself that if I could give the appearance of calm, he was more likely to trust me. And if he trusted me, I would have more opportunity to raise the alarm.

At the turnpike, I seized my opportunity. 'I need to relieve myself.'

After regarding me for a few moments, he stepped down from the coach and handed me down, for all the world like an attentive and polite husband. As I stood breathing deeply the cold air of a November afternoon, I kept my composure and surveyed the surroundings and then the chaise. Two ruffians looked down on me with barely-concealed contempt, and from the coach behind, three others descended, their faces concealed in mufflers.

'My wife wishes to avail herself of your facilities.'

The tollbooth-keeper nodded at a woman who had been standing in the doorway. Murmuring, 'This way, madam,' she showed me round the back of the building.

'As soon as we were out of sight, I grasped her hand and spoke urgently into her pinched face: 'You must help me and I will repay you. Fetch me pen and paper. Quickly. Do not tell.' Bless her, she nodded and disappeared, and as soon as I had stepped into the tiny room she had indicated, she was there, holding out a small piece of crumpled paper and the stump of a pencil. 'It's all I have.'

Hastily, in the dark room, I knelt on the earthen floor by the pale light that crept under the door, scribbled a note to Mary Morgan at James Farrer's address: 'My dear Morgan, 'I beg you and James will come immediately upon the receipt of this to Paul's Walden, and bring any other of our friends with you, and for heaven's sake don't lose a moment.'

Taking a coin from my purse, I pressed the note into her hand. 'I beg you, send this note with the first person you can trust who is headed south to London. Here, take this for them. There will be more reward for you if it succeeds in getting to its destination tonight. I am the Countess of Strathmore. Remember my name.' I clasped her hands. 'I depend upon you. I am in dire need. Will you help me?'

Her eyes were wide in the gloom when she answered, 'I will ma'am.'

There were noises outside, a hard and sudden knock on the door, and a rough voice shouted, 'Ye! What are ye about?'

She opened the door a crack and hissed, 'How dare you? Her ladyship is about her business. Wait outside and have a civil tongue in your head!'

In truth, I was so nervous that my water refused to flow at first, there crouched upon the ground, my skirts billowing around me. It was only when she smiled in the darkness, 'No luck? What it is to be a woman, eh? Oh for a peck of flesh to poke out of our breeches like the men do.' I laughed, despite myself, and the waters flowed. Oh blessed relief.

Back in the coach, Stoney's mood had darkened with the weather. 'What were you about all that time?'

'What do you think?'

Without any warning, he reached out and slapped me hard across the face and then leaned back, a satisfied look spreading across his features.

'It seems you have forgotten how to speak to your husband. I demand respect.'

'Respect? You don't know the meaning of the word. And very soon you will no longer be my husband.'

He slapped me again, and although I was knocked sideways by the blow, I soon sat up straight and stared into his eyes undaunted.

The miles rolled by under the carriage wheels.

When I recognised the lighted arches of the coaching inn at Stevenage, I knew we were not going to St Paul's Walden. I had travelled the Great North Road often enough to recognise the markers, and Biggleswade and Sandy passed by without any relief, either for the horses, who were being driven hard, or for me, in the airless tension of the chaise.

Finally, we turned into the George Inn at Buckden. I had stayed there before, and my heart quickened at the thought of recognition and rescue. As the carriage rocked across the cobbled yard and the grooms came forward to greet the horses, I scanned the faces for one that I recognised.

The innkeeper showed us into a private room, darkly wooded, where bread and meat and beer were set before us at a long table. I thought at first I would be left alone with Stoney, but soon the door opened, the four ruffians entered and I was cowed into silence.

Gesturing rudely at me with a piece of meat impaled on his knife, Stoney commanded me to eat.

'I cannot.'

'Suit yourself.'

I shrank back against the hard wooden bench and watched as more beer was brought. The innkeeper, a kindly man, cast me concerned glances where I sat pressed upon both sides by large men in dark greatcoats, but said nothing.

The sound of happy voices from the public bar set me trembling. Rescue could be so close but I was at a loss how to reach it.

The inn-keeper's daughter brought in more bread, and her face showed the confidence born of security. 'Is madam quite well? Is there anything I can do for you, my lady?'

One of the ruffians spoke up: 'Don't concern yourself, poppet. Come and sit here on my knee.'

In answer, she jutted her chin and looked at me directly. 'Madam? Can I get you anything? A pudding, perhaps?'

Emboldened by the beer, Stoney didn't bother to disguise his contempt. 'Leave her be, she's a fool who starves herself by choice.'

My eyes told a different story, and the girl repeated her question. 'Madam?'

'I said,' and now his voice contained steel, 'leave her be.'

The girl rested her eyes on him just a moment too long, secure in the knowledge that her father would support and protect her if any trouble ensued. How I envied her that protection and the courage it engendered. Without curtsying, she left the room and did not return.

I could eat nothing, though I knew that I should if I was to keep my strength up. If that girl spoke to her father, I might have a chance when we got up to leave. As luck would have it, she was standing in the passageway holding two mugs of beer, and I asked her in as confident a voice as I could muster, where the ladies' room was, although I knew full well.

'This way, ma'am.'

His henchmen had clearly decided there was no risk that I would attempt to escape, and they jostled past us, but Stoney remained where he was, and fixed me with a warning look. I was conscious of him watching, unmoving, as she opened the door at the end of the passageway. She went to step aside, but in a movement which I hoped was invisible to him, I gave her a gentle push indicating that she should step into the room before me. When I turned to close the door, his face was fixed on mine, illuminated from below in a devilish fashion.

The moment the door was shut, I whispered urgently into the girl's ear. 'I am Lady Strathmore and I am being abducted by my estranged husband. Send a messenger on horseback as fast as he can to Lord Mansfield in Highgate. Do you understand?'

Just as the words were out of my mouth, there was a bang on the door behind me and it crashed open. Taking in the scene in one glance, Stoney laid a heavy arm around my shoulders and kissed the top of my head. In the warm honeyed, Irish voice I had heard him use a thousand times on women, he thought to charm the maid: 'She'll have been talking her nonsense again, poor dear. It is all I can do to keep her from the asylum, but I cannot bear the thought of having her incarcerated. I am taking her north in the hope that the country air will benefit her mind.' He bent and kissed my brow and steered me out of the room, saying, 'Perhaps we can entice you to eat again, my love. A healthy body in a healthy mind, that's what we want for you, my darling. Thank-you for taking care of her, my dear. She'll be safe with me.'

268

Nothing could have been further from the truth, for the moment we were back in the coach, he punched me hard in the side of the head, knocking me to the floor, whereupon he pulled me by the hair into a kneeling position. Stunned and disorientated, I vomited over his shoes.

Cursing, he lifted my head and roared into my face. My eyes must have been rolling in their sockets, for I have a dizzying memory in which my vision was filled with his great gaping mouth and my senses were filled with the glistening of his spittle and the stench of his beery breath.

'At our next stop, Lady Muck, you will sign a paper. And if you refuse, I tell you now, I will shoot you in the head and have done with it!' Whereupon he let go of my hair and let me sink to the floor of the coach, where I remained in the stench of my own vomit until we reached the next stop.

When the coach finally ceased its rocking, he nudged my shoulder with his foot. Not wanting him to think I was dead, I groaned. He stepped over me and I heard him instruct one of his men to lock the door and ensure that I was unable to leave while the horses were changed. It was clear by now that we were not going to stop for the night.

At 7am on Saturday morning, when we arrived at a place I recognised as Newark, I was left in the coach alone with one of his hulking henchmen, who showed a surprising delicacy by sitting with his head out of the window because of the smell.

Where does the north begin, I wonder? In my mind, though I know that geographically it makes no sense, I feel I am in the north by Nottinghamshire. It's in the rolling hills, the trees leaning on the horizons, the smell of the air and the voices of the people.

When we reached Barnby Moor, I begged to be allowed out of the coach lest I vomit again, though in truth there was nothing at all in my stomach and cold anger was fuelling me.

'If you agree to sign the paper.'

'What paper?'

He withdrew it from his pocket with a flourish and proceeded to talk in his singsong, Irish soothing voice. 'It brings an end to the divorce proceedings. We respect each other, you and I. We can come to an accommodation. Come come, little one, you and I were happy once.' He cupped my bruised cheek in his hand, and spoke to me for all the world as though he had my best interests at heart. I thought at that moment, and not for the first time, that he was certifiably mad.

But I must disguise my defiance, for I must get out of the coach, and so I said, 'I need to read it in the light. And I need to use the chamberpot.'

'Of course, of course.' He helped me to my feet, the solicitous husband once more, and I did not have to feign my dizziness. I was seasick from the rocking of the carriage, and one side of my head and neck felt quite numb.

The tavern-keeper and an ostler were watching as I was helped down, and I saw the surprise on their faces as well as what I hoped was recognition.

'My wife needs help, she is unwell. She fell and hit her head on the cobbles when we stopped in Grantham and she has vomited. I fear she is concussed. Have you a maidservant who can take care of her?'

Did I imagine the suspicion on the face of the landlord? I hoped not. He disappeared into the passageway and emerged a few moments later with two dark-haired young women who seemed to be sisters. Without a word, they took my arms and helped me limp over the cobbles before Stoney could summon any credible reason to stop them.

I leaned against the wall whilst they washed my face and hands and ran a flannel through my hair, speaking soothingly all the while. 'Poor lady, this is an outrage. What can we do to help you?'

I swallowed painfully, for my throat was raw. 'Please send an urgent message to Lord Mansfield in London from Lady Strathmore. Tell him I fear my husband intends to get me to Ireland. If he succeeds, I am lost.'

'I promise you, we will do as you ask, but you are not fit to travel and I will tell him so. Then I will send for a doctor.'

I did not stop her, but I knew she would not succeed in convincing him, and indeed when she returned, he was right behind her. 'My dear, we must get you home. I have sent ahead and your doctor will be waiting for you at Gibside. Thank-you girls, you may go now.'

Like Mary Morgan, they seemed instinctively to recognise how to handle him. 'We will prepare a little light refreshment in the parlour. Her ladyship must be tempted to eat something. She is quite faint.'

And somehow, the hope given to me by those two clear-eyed girls gave me strength to eat. I was ravenous, and alone in a small alcove, guarded by one of the nameless thugs, I ate a whole chicken leg and drank two glasses of lovely refreshing water.

Feeling much better, I waited, and sure enough when Stoney reappeared he was carrying paper and pens. He set them down on the table next to a candle which was almost burnt out. Its cold wax was congealed in a sickly yellow halo around the stump, embedded with cigar ash.

He leant across the table and again his face was lit from beneath in a sickly sulphurous yellow. His stale breath caressed my face when he whispered, 'We were happy once. We can be again.'

I looked at him, frankly astonished. Now that I was used to being in his presence once again, I was curious to find he had lost his power to cow me. 'You are deluded. You may have been happy when you tricked me into marriage. Can you in all honesty look me in the face and tell me you care about my happiness? You are quite mad.'

Without a word, he folded up the sheets, stuffed them in his pockets and pulled me to my feet. Bending down, he hissed in my ear: 'By hook or by crook, I will have you Mary Eleanor Bowes. Make a sound on the way to the coach and I will break every bone in your hand. I promise you.'

How must we have seemed to the onlookers as we walked slowly across the yard, he supporting my arm while his other hand enclosed mine in a grip like a vice. All the while, he whispered vile threats into my hair in a singsong, soothing tone. 'You will be committed to a lunatic asylum once we reach Ireland. The doctors will be easily persuaded. Look at the state of you. I shall recommend a straitjacket and a gag, for everyone knows what a debauched stream of filth would issue from your mouth were you allowed to speak. Liar. Adulteress. Murderer of unborn children. Unnatural mother. Whore.'

Chapter 26

After that, I did everything in my power to draw attention to myself with what felt like a liberating absence of fear. I had gone beyond some point of thinking about self-preservation. I had gone beyond the point of thinking at all. Even the pain of my injuries existed only in the background. I would subside, quiet and docile for long stretches of open countryside, but whenever we passed through a town, anyone who heard a shout or a scream or caught a glimpse of hands wrestling with the leather blinds as the coach thundered past must have wondered what was going on inside.

When I judged that we were approaching Barnard Castle, for I knew the sounds of the voices, the gradients and the bends, I grew more confident and more vociferous. I knew by then that we were approaching Streatlam Castle, and when Stoney finally raised the blinds, I recognised its outline against the moonlit sky. Here at least I was known, and there might be some retainer who just needed an opportunity to show where their loyalties lay.

When we finally pulled up in front of the stone steps, the clouds had covered the moon. The night was black and cold and no servants were there to greet us: our arrival was clearly unexpected. As soon as the carriage door opened, I screamed as loudly as I could, 'Help me! Help me! I am Mary Eleanor Bowes! Stoney has brought me here me by force!'

I caught sight of the startled faces of the two young men who had driven us from the last staging-post, the driver and his mate having stayed behind at the inn. Stoney pulled me down from the carriage, his arm clamped about my shoulders and his hand across my mouth. 'Fear not, Her Ladyship is unwell. She is prone to these hysterical fits. The doctor is on his way. Off you go lads.'

As he manhandled me into the hallway, he hissed in my ear, 'I will indeed take you by force. You are still my wife and I will have you, raucous trollop that you are.'

When I replied, 'Ah yes, raucous trollops are to your taste, are they not?' his face clearly showed that he was still finding it astonishing that he could not subdue me. In answer, he opened the door to a cloak cupboard and flung me inside.

In the muffled silence and darkness, with my ear pressed against the oak door, I heard him speaking to someone. 'Wake the cook and get some food brought up.'

Whatever the answer he received, it did not please him for he shouted out, 'The devil she has! I don't care who you wake, get some food brought up and tell someone to light the fire in my bedchamber for it's as cold as the gates of hell in here.'

I slumped down in the folds of a damp-smelling cloak and wrapped it round me. It was airless in that cupboard, and quiet, and soon I started to doze and then slumped into a deep and dreamless sleep.

I was woken suddenly by the door opening and a candle thrust in my face. Hot wax splashed my cheek and a rough voice said, 'Get up.' For a moment, I had absolutely no awareness of where I was or what was happening.

In the dining room, platters of bread and meat were spread out at one end of the trestle table. He led me by the hand and as he slid out a chair for me, he said, 'I imagine you have banqueted here many times with the faces of your forefathers looking down on you.'

'It's you they look down on.'

'Don't be pert.'

'Pert? Don't you understand? I loathe you. I despise you. You have no right to sit here. By your behaviour, you have forfeited your right to enjoy anything of mine.'

'I shall enjoy you after I have eaten.'

'You shall not.'

He laughed, a great bark of a laugh with a piece of meat in his mouth which I hoped would choke him, and then took a swig of wine.

'I much prefer you like this.'

'I care not one jot what you think of me. You are a criminal and now you are a wanted man. It won't be long before Judge Mansfield's constables and tipstaffs catch up with you.'

'I doubt that very much. We will be in Ireland before they know where we have gone. And besides, if they did manage to catch up, they will find us reunited as man and wife.'

'They will not.'

274

'Oh, but you see, they will.'

He carried on eating his food with a ravenous lack of concern, and by my count he drank three big glasses of wine, slugging it down as though it was beer. He was always an unpredictable drunk, violent one night, sentimental the next, often lascivious, never docile. I had no hopes whatsoever that he would fall asleep. The man never slept more than three or four hours in one night in all the years that I knew him, at least not in my company.

He had just finished the bottle and upended it over his glass as if expecting more to materialize, when two of his ruffians entered the room.

'Take her ladyship up to my bedchamber and keep her there.'

I rose of my own accord, and though my bones hurt and my muscles were stiff with bruises, I mustered as much dignity as I could. When they approached me, no doubt to manhandle me, I said to Stoney: 'Tell them not to touch me.'

He grunted and smiled, a perverse pride evident in his face. 'As she wishes.' But when I turned my back as I left the table, he added, 'Unless of course you need to.'

Alone in the damp-smelling room, I sat by the paltry fire and took comfort from its warmth, reflecting as I did so that the pleasures of life are momentary. We only need acknowledge them and they are passed. This time I did not doze, however, for I knew that I faced my greatest test.

'So. Here we are.'

He placed a pistol on the table near to me, and watched me as if daring me to try to grab it.

'Get into bed.'

'I will not.'

'If you do not, I shall take you by force.'

'If you do, I will scream rape and I will have you prosecuted for rape.'

'You think that frightens me? A man cannot be convicted of raping his wife. You are mine to enjoy as I wish.'

'I think you'll find that Lord Mansfield is rather more enlightened than you give him credit for.'

'You will not be believed. Your reputation hangs in tatters.'

'You know, that's the strange thing. Despite your best endeavours, despite your loathsome publications, in fact sometimes because of them, I have gained many new friends of power and influence.'

'We will be reconciled. Witnesses will see us in bed together. Your case will collapse.'

I went on, conversationally: 'Rape, as you know, is a hanging offence. News of my abduction will be all over London, and you will by now be known for the outright criminal that you are.'

He reached out to stroke my cheek and it was all I could do not to recoil but I would not let him see anything other than a woman in complete possession of confidence born from a sense of rightness and support.

'Come on, Mary Eleanor, you know you like it. Let me pleasure you.'

'I would rather die.'

Startled, he lifted my chin and looked into my eyes. 'You mean that, don't you?'

Unwavering, I stared back at him. 'I mean it.'

'Right then!' In what seemed like one movement, he had snatched up the pistol and pushed me to my knees. Feeling the hard push of cold metal against my forehead, there came a curious sense of peace. If this was where it ended, so be it.

'Say your prayers!'

'Why? You want to save me from Hell for fear of meeting me there?'

He pushed the barrel harder against my temple, forcing my head to one side.

'Go on! Fire! If you are man enough!'

I don't know what happened then, for there was a bang and a flash close by my ear, but no impact until he dealt me such a blow with his fist that I remember no more.

I awoke to find myself still on the floor, and such was the stiffness and coldness of my body that the thought came to me that I had awoken in a coffin. Pressure seemed to confine me from all sides, I could barely breathe and the cold reached icy fingers inside me and grasped my heart, which fluttered like a captive bird. My eyes were open but I could not see, and I as I strained and pushed my eyes to perceive something, anything, without success, I knew I must be blind. But you are alive, I told myself. Breathe, breathe. And though it hurt to expand my chest, the air that came into my lungs was warm and musty and smelled of damp.

Every part of me ached with a dull pain that I welcomed, for nothing hurt sharply, and all of it meant I was alive. With difficulty, I rolled onto my side and lay for some moments inhaling the dusty damp of the carpet. I raised my hand to my head and felt the stickiness of congealed blood. I took my fingers to my mouth and licked them, the tang of iron in my own blood giving me back my sense of taste. Now if only I could see. I slid my elbow underneath my side and lifted my head, supporting it on my hand. This was better. There were gradations in the darkness, I was sure. A horizontal line in dark grey: could it be the hearth? As I lay there, trying to focus and discern a shape beyond it, perhaps of a grate or a pile of ashes, I heard a shout from outside, not immediately outside the house but further away. It was answered by another shout, not angry in tone, more of a greeting, an acknowledgement.

Inch by inch, moving slowly and painfully, I got to a sitting position, keeping my eyes firmly fixed on the dark shape of the hearth to orientate myself, for my brain rocked as though I was aboard a boat. Once I had achieved the sitting position, I took a moment to focus on the sounds from outside and found I could hear a crackling and a murmuring of many voices. I turned my head towards where I judged the windows would be and pushed my eyes to find them. A vertical slit of light, grey against the blackness again, but near its base, a faint orange glow. Fire? A fire in the distance? On the low hill opposite the house?

My eyes agreed with my brain, and then I could see that the curtains were open a crack and the vertical strip had shape, gradations of colour. They made sense. The paler grey at the top would be clouds or moonlight, and then darker grey, then black, then a patch of bright orange, then black. I must see. I pushed myself onto my knees then reached out into the darkness to find something to hold onto. My fingers brushed padded wood – the arm of a chair, perhaps the one I had been sitting on. I grasped it and manoeuvered myself to my feet. My head swam and I thought for a moment I would fall, but my other hand found the back of the chair and I waited until my senses settled.

When I was sure I would not fall, I left the security of the chair and slid a foot along the ground toward the window, my hands extended into the darkness. Then the other. Then again, this time my toe pushing gently against something, perhaps a shoe. When my fingers brushed the fabric of a curtain, I held on, and then I was at the window and I could see.

A ring of small fires. And as I watched, people moving behind and in front of them. Men, all men as far as I could see, some bearing staffs, some tapers. What manner of men they were I could not see, but something in me knew. They were working men, not soldiers. Men who knew each other. There was a camaraderie in the voices, and the rise and fall of them told me they were local.

At that moment, the door opened and someone came in bearing a candle. If I had been faster, if I'd heard them coming, I could have quickly closed the curtains and been hidden from sight, but I was clearly outlined against the window.

'We're leaving. Come. Now.' Not his voice. Rough and north-eastern. And before I knew it, I was lifted and thrown over a broad shoulder, winded. No other words were spoken as he hastened down the staircase with my chest banging on his shoulder at every step, my ribs, oh my ribs, and then down into the kitchens and along a passageway with stone floors and out onto cobbles then subdued voices, three men, one of them Stoney, and then a rag stuffed in my mouth and bound around my head, oh dirt and cloth and no breath, gasping, suffocating, a cloak was thrown over me and I could see no more and I struggled to breathe and not swallow the cloth jammed against the roof of my mouth, gagging and choking. I heard a door close, then the smell and snuffling of horses and then I was flung over a saddle, and then at a sharp word from Stoney, righted and sat upright behind someone, a man, though the hood still covered my face I could smell man and horse and leather and then we were moving slowly, the rocking of the saddle, not properly fastened, I must grip with my knees, for my hands were tangled in this heavy cloak and my legs were bare and cold, and oh the pain in my toes, icy. But alive. Alive.

Hands free now, one to hold on and one to release my face from this hood and this gag, but we start to gallop and I must hold on tight or I die, I die. Down the dale at the back of the house and up the slope and into the woods, thunder of hooves more muffled now, there's a path through the woods but we veer off it and then twigs whip our faces and then we burst out onto moorland and uphill and horses panting and icy wind stings my eyes and look! There is snow! The tops of Upper Teesdale in the distance are iced with snow and the moon lifts its gauzy veil and looks at the snow and I settle and I'm calm and I slide the cloth from my cheeks and then my mouth and I drop it and I don't care about anything any more as long as I can stay in this world.

Eight days. Eight days we spent on the moors, in one of the coldest winters our country has known in this century. Eight days on the high moorlands at the top of the very backbone of this land. When we took shelter, I was always confined, in a cupboard or a trunk. If I was lucky, I would be tossed a piece of bread, though often no-one thought to give me water. I drank from streams, a horse's water-trough, a leather bucket in a yard after breaking the ice to get to it, I even drank dirty water left out for a dog. When I could, I got a handful of pure snow and counted myself blessed. Eight days criss-crossing the moorland in snow and ice, and on horseback. And do you know, not once did I cry, though hunger and pain and loneliness and mistreatment brought me close many many times. I knew fear, deep in the core of me, but the fear was not of pain or deprivation or cruelty, the fear was of dying. In those eight days, when I existed so close to death, my determination to stay alive grew stronger.

There were moments of warmth, moments of human contact. We spent two nights, not consecutive, in a poor shepherd's cottage high on the moors and the shepherd's daughter arrived later on horseback. When she removed her cloak, I saw her thin arms and her pale skin and I saw her eyes go to Stoney and then I saw that she was pregnant. And I did not need to be told whose baby she carried, though she did say it in a brief and whispered conversation when she brought me some bread where I sat chained in the outhouse like a dog.

And later another woman, nursing by a fire, who bridled when she saw Stoney and told him to be gone, but then she saw me and relented. And that was his baby too.

And when we circled back and came again to the poor shepherd's cottage, he told Stoney in my hearing that men from

279

London had been looking for him and that we could not stay again. My heart flared when I heard this, and I did not care that we were cast out into the night again. They were coming. It could only be a matter of time. We were being seen and noticed and word would spread and people who knew this place far better than Stoney would follow us and find us and save me.

And what was he about, this madman who held my life in his hands? I think he hardly knew himself. One moment, we were heading for the west coast and the ferry to Ireland, another we needed a guide to Appleby, another we would head for the Roman Wall and beyond into Scotland, then we were going to Carlisle, and then we would head back towards Darlington, for 'they will never expect that' and then we must get back to Streatlam, for the miners would surely have dispersed by now.

He told some he was taking me over the moors to my daughter, who was having a baby. He told others he was a doctor and I his patient on the way to the asylum whence I had escaped. After I saw him reading a poster, his stories ceased, and I knew for certain the hunt was on. There was no more suave chat, no more elaborate pretence, and after that we left the roads and ploughed across moors and peat-bogs where there are no roads and no people.

And though the sleet blinded us and the horses stumbled, and it seemed this would never end, I saw such beauty in this wild world. The fells and the rocks and the precipices and escarpments were merely a grand and intimidating backdrop for the exquisite beauty of sunlight on snow, of moonlight on gorse, of an exquisite Alpine plant, tiny and indomitable as a lost gemstone.

I had watched the weak winter sun rise above the horizon eight times, and each time I hoped that this day would bring rescue. We had spent the night in an abandoned shepherd's cottage with only half a roof, the first time we had prevailed on no-one. If one of his cronies had not been able to make a fire, I doubt we would have survived. By then, one of them had become fascinated by my continued survival. 'Such a scrap of a thing,' he muttered as he gave me his greatcoat to sleep under, while he wrapped himself in a horse-blanket.

Mounted behind Stoney once more, we turned south and I guessed we were heading for Darlington, where he had a lawyer who he boasted was in his pocket. The horses were tired: unaccountably, the last inn we had tried would not let us swap them. We had left the third behind for it was lame, and now the four of us had only two weary and hungry mounts. The days were short, for we were nearly at the turning-point of the year, and so I judge it was soon after noon that we passed a sign saying Neasham.

On the near horizon of the field beyond the sign, a tall man sat astride a great Shire horse and watched us pass. Something about this figure drew my eye. Many had seen us on our travels, and most looked on with open curiosity, as well they might, but I felt instinctively that he had been watching and waiting. I made to adjust my skirts and stole a backward look, but he had vanished.

A few minutes later, I saw two farm-workers standing in a field on the opposite side of the road fifty yards away. They were both holding rakes and stopped talking as we approached. They gave us only a glance and then turned and walked diagonally across the field towards the farm buildings.

This Stoney noticed, and he looked over his shoulder at his accomplices, following behind us on the other horse. The one riding pillion raised his hand and then indicated we should turn off the road and cross the field to our left. Stoney nodded and I saw his hand go to the pistol in the pocket of his greatcoat. On his left side, the blunderbuss was strapped to the saddle and hidden in the folds of the coat.

A few yards in front, there was a gap in the dry-stone wall, and not far beyond that, a great hedge on a mound at right angles to the wall, a field boundary which ran all the way to the horizon with gaps every hundred yards or so. It struck me then that the hedge seemed thick for the time of year, used as I was to the bare skeletons of trees we had passed. There was a darkness in it, a density, and I thought I sensed movement.

The two men had reappeared in the field opposite, with two others. All were carrying rakes and they were walking quickly towards us. We reached the gap in the wall and turned into the ploughed field. Stoney had just raised his feet to kick the horse's flanks and send it into a gallop, but something made me raise my own feet and press them against the backs of his knees as hard as I could. It was enough to make him falter. Suddenly, two men on horseback and four on foot burst out of a gap in the hedge and the bridle was seized. Galvanized, I slid to the ground and ran towards the group and into the arms of a grizzled old man, who held me close and backed us away through the people, who I now saw were all holding implements.

His horse captive and submissive, Stoney was brandishing his pistol and threatening to shoot anyone who tried to seize him. The pillion rider on the other horse was trying to draw his sword, but a swift blow on the wrist from a rake made him drop it. Two men were wrestling with Stoney's blunderbuss, and when finally it came clear of its bindings, one pulled him by his greatcoat and the other gave him such a blow across the head with the barrel of his own gun that he fell to the ground and lay still.

It all happened so quickly, and I was in such a state that I feared that I was delirious. All my strength suddenly left me and my legs could no longer support me; I was only prevented from sinking to the ground by the old man, and then I felt a blanket come round me and strong arms lifting me and then I fainted quite away.

When I came round, I was warm. All of me was warm, not just my face and hands from huddling near a fire made of twigs, but all of me. I was lying on something soft, a bed, under blankets on clean linen and the air smelled of food and heat and people and my hands were being held and I opened my eyes and it was Gabriel.

Chapter 27

'For you, my brother, nay my more than brother,
My guardian angel, who doth interpose,
Bringing me wished-for and much-needed help,
Thou art indeed a friend.'

Those words I wrote long ago in my play, The Siege of Jerusalem. As I looked up into his weather-beaten face, so kind and concerned and so very very dear, I spoke those words. His expression creased into wreaths of smiles, and he squeezed my hands. Then he turned from me and I heard him say, 'Dorothy, she's awake.' And then there was Dorothy, and when she held out her hand to touch my cheek, I clasped it to me and kissed the palm, and then I saw the wedding ring. I looked up at them both, her arm across his shoulder, and I smiled, clasped their hands together and kissed them.

They stayed with me until Thomas Colpitts arrived, and with him Mary Morgan and Captain Farrer, and what a thing it was to be reunited with these three, there in that farmer's kitchen, packed in with the heroes of the hour and the kind and the curious and their children. It had all the warmth and the gaiety of a party, and indeed when beer and wine were produced, we judged it was time to take our leave for there was serious business to do and it would not do for the hapless heroine to be produced before the court sozzled and singing, now would it?

Much as I wished I could go and lick my wounds at Gibside, the courts awaited, my children waited, London society was aghast, the press had their pens poised, and the prison gates stood ready for Andrew Robinson Stoney.

On the journey down, I dozed in the rocking coach. We changed horses at Grantham but carried on through the night and the next day. I slept a good deal, lying across the lap of my dear Mary Morgan, and when I awoke, she told me all about the hue and cry that had led at last to my rescue.

The message from the innkeeper's daughter had indeed reached Lord Mansfield; until then, though the alarm had been raised by Mary and Captain Farrer, and rapidly spread by the London Evening Post, no-one knew the direction Stoney had taken me. Lord Mansfield having immediately issued a writ of habeas corpus, the channel ports were alerted and messengers sent to the port at Holyhead, in case he was heading for Ireland that way.

Once they knew that he had taken me north, a tipstaff was dispatched to follow the trail, and with him went Captain Farrer, glad to do something in view of his signal but understandable failure to prevent my abduction. They followed the trail of sightings up the Great North Road until they reached County Durham, whereupon they had it confirmed that I was being held in Streatlam Castle.

They arrived to find the whole place encircled by a ring of blazing coal-fires: miners and estate workers from far and wide assured them that the fugitives could not have escaped by night or day. Mary told me that Farrer had described the determination and grit of these men, who were undoubtedly losing money through missing their shifts, and burning coal they had hacked from the earth themselves. 'He told me, with wonder in his eyes, "She is truly loved."'

Thomas Colpitts had reached Streatlam at the same time, and they had blocked the entrances and broken down the doors, confident that we were still inside. A thorough search yielded no trace, and they were forced to conclude that Stoney had escaped and taken me with him.

The crowd, which by then numbered upwards of four hundred men, had dispersed to their several villages, and from there the word spread far and wide. Rewards were offered, instructions were issued to innkeepers and turnpikes to report sightings and attempt to delay the fugitives, though a warning was issued that no attempt should be made to apprehend them as Stoney and his accomplices were known to be armed and dangerous.

When I heard about the efforts of the miners, I cried for the first time, and when I heard that my son had set off on horseback from Cambridge to rescue me, I thought my heart would break for pride and joy.

Mary held me while I cried, and when the storm was over, we held each other. 'I will never be able to repay you for the strength of your devotion to me, Mary. Never. How can I show you my gratitude?'

She demurred at first, as I suppose I had known she would, but when I said again, 'Anything. Is there anything at all I can do?' She gave me an answer I hadn't expected.

'I do want to ask something of you, and when you hear what it is, I feel sure you will say no at first. But I want you to hear me out. And then I want you to think very carefully about what I have said. I don't want an answer from you until all this is over. Be assured, I will be by your side throughout the trial and everything that is to come. And after it is over, then I will ask you for your answer.'

'What is it, Mary? You intrigue me.'

She settled herself and I could see her composing her thoughts. I moved across to the opposite seat so that I could watch her face and weigh her words with all the attention they deserved. I never knew Mary Morgan to waste a word in all the years I knew her.

'You have endured much and it is not finished yet, although I think you will find on your return to London that there has been a sea-change in the world's opinion of you. Your courage and endurance are out in the open now, for all to see, and your suffering has made the world think. And not before time.

'You will achieve your divorce and you will see Stoney put in prison, I have no doubt. George Walker has been found safe now and he still has your original pre-nuptial deed. One of the counter-signatories to the supposed revocation of the deed is Dr John Hunter, and he swears he never signed anything of the sort. I think it extremely likely that you will be awarded all your properties and incomes, and it will be a landmark case, and you will be remembered for it.

'You will be reconciled with your children. Thomas Lyon has been prominent in promoting your rescue: he offered rewards for your safe return. I think he feels guilty that he did not act before, and so he should.

'Your son John is a grown man now, the 10th Earl of Strathmore, and a man of courage and loyalty, as is evidenced by his setting forth from Cambridge to come to your aid.'

Listening to her calm voice, with its well-chosen words setting forth my situation, all the chaos of the previous eight years seemed to settle into order. When she stopped speaking, I held the words before me, as if written in gold on the air, and I could have recited them back to her verbatim.

Unwilling to break the spell, we continued in silence for a mile or so, until I finally spoke, and my voice sounded to me like the voice of another woman. 'And you, Mary Morgan, what of you? What do you wish for your life? What can I give to you?'

She didn't answer immediately and when she spoke, it was clear she had a purpose in mind. 'You and I have known each other only in adversity. Speaking for myself, I have never met a woman whom I so liked and admired. I would not presume to assert that you feel the same, but I hope that you do.'

Her eyes looked directly into mine and I assented without having to move a muscle.

Satisfied, she continued: 'I would hope that we will have a good deal more time together, for I would like to know you better and to spend pleasurable times where we can please ourselves in what we do. I have a clear intimation of the things that make you happy and I share them all. If it pleases you, for I must not forget that you are my employer, I will be your companion.'

Thinking that she had at last revealed her hopes, I grasped her hands and said, 'Yes, Mary! That would make me so happy.'

'Good, good. And now to my point. I am going to suggest something that your instinct will refuse. I ask you only to consider it in the forthcoming weeks, and give me no answer yet.'

Seeing that I would make no objection, she continued thus: 'I know your heart belongs to Gibside.'

I felt that very heart contract at the word, for pain, for loss, for heartbreak, for guilt, for the sufferings and destruction that my mistake had brought about, for all that must be done to make amends.

As if she could read my mind, she said, 'Your love of the place is compromised now. I feel that if you decide to make a future there, you will never be at rest. It is not what it was, and neither are you.'

I smiled ruefully.

'Your health has suffered and there are bound to be lasting effects. You owe it to yourself and to your children to take care of yourself and make yourself available to them. Much as the people of Gibside love you, there are elements of discontent and resentment. People have suffered greatly as a consequence of your marriage and it will not be easily forgotten, though I am convinced it will be forgiven. You must consider what is best for your employees and dependents, tenants and workers, as well as what is best for yourself.'

She looked at me with kindness, for I was quietly sobbing. She told me later that she considered stopping there, thinking she had said enough, but I am glad that she continued, though it was painful at the time. In my mind, as always, if I could get to Gibside I would be safe and all would be as it once had been, but if I ever really believed that, she wanted me to see that I was deluding myself.

'What I am asking you to consider is that you should sign Gibside over to your son.'

I was conscious of her watching me closely as I struggled to digest this thought. As she had predicted, my impulse was no and I was perfectly certain it would remain no, though I said nothing.

She had seen it in my eyes, but it was what she was expecting so she continued undaunted.

'His youth and energy combined with your experience, with the support of Thomas Colpitts, as well as Thomas Lyon and yourself. It is the fresh start Gibside needs.'

If she had said 'deserves' I think I would have rebelled, but she put it so sweetly and so logically that I listened without prejudice.

'You will no doubt be thinking that the role of a dowager will not suit you, with all that implies. I am proposing an entirely different kind of life, in an entirely different place.

'Where?'

When I said that, I saw the gleam of excitement kindle in her eyes like the beginning of daybreak. 'I know of a place that I would like you to consider. Now is not the time to go into detail, but when you are ready to talk about it further, you must say so. For now, I only ask you to consider what I have said.'

And consider it I did. Throughout the weeks of my convalescence and the months of hearings, throughout the tearful reunions and visits from well-wishers, throughout the discussions and communications which connected me back to the people I loved and who cared about me, Mary's words stayed in my mind.

The thought of a fresh start seemed almost unthinkable at first, but with time I began to see the truth of her vision, and the more I saw of my son the more I began to believe that what she had said was true: he was what Gibside needed. And if that were true, I would be free.

And so here I sit, dear reader, at a desk by a window with a view of the sea. I knew as soon as I saw Stourfield House that I would buy it. Its situation has everything one could wish for in a retirement villa. It was built in the year of my engagement to John, the year I met an angel by the river one morning.

I have beside me a letter from Elizabeth Montagu, and in it she writes: 'the calm autumn of life has many advantages. Both have a peculiar serenity, a genial tranquility. We are less busy and less agitated, because the hopes of the spring and the vivid delights of the summer are over; but these tranquil seasons have their appropriate enjoyments, and a well-regulated mind sees everything beautiful that is in order of nature.'

I couldn't put it better myself.

Afterword

You can read a detailed account of what happened after Eleanor's rescue in Wedlock. She fought a long hard legal battle, but she did at last achieve everything she deserved: a divorce, restoration of all her property, and Stoney was imprisoned for the rest of his life.

The case was a great leap forward in divorce law and in society's perception of women's rights.

Eleanor had ten years of contented retirement at Stourfield House, just outside Bournemouth on the edge of the New Forest. It was a beautiful house, built in 1766 on a gentle hill just half a mile from the sea. She had balconies, lovely wooded grounds and views of the River Stour and Christchurch Harbour.

She was welcomed into the community and became a much-loved benefactor to the poorer members of the parish. Some thought her eccentric because of her pampered pooches, but she soon she became very popular with her neighbours, though she did not often entertain due to her desire for seclusion and her difficulty with hearing.

Mary Morgan lived with her until her untimely death in 1796 at the age of just forty-six. She was buried at Christchurch Priory, and Eleanor erected a memorial to her good and faithful friend: it commemorates her 'heroic qualities, cool, deliberate courage and matchless, persevering friendship.'

Her youngest daughter Mary lived with them, although Eleanor had another fight on her hands to allow that to happen, because Stoney kept Mary's whereabouts secret from her. Five years after they had been torn apart, Eleanor was finally reunited with her youngest daughter. Stoney's public revelation of Mary's illegitimacy may have been one of the reasons she never married, but then again she may have wanted to avoid wedlock. After her mother's death, she settled happily in Bath and was a devoted aunt to all her nephews and nieces, living to the ripe old age of seventy-eight.

Eleanor was reunited with all her children, and for the rest of her life was regularly visited by them all, although her eldest daughter Maria was never fully reconciled to her mother. Maria married at twenty-one to a wealthy army captain, Barrington Price. They lived in Gloucestershire, had two girls and they were, as far as we know, happy. Maria died at the age of thirty-eight, just six years after her mother.

In the same year, her brother George died aged thirty-five. He had only been married for eighteen months, and was living at St Paul's Walden. This now passed to his younger brother, Thomas.

Maria's widower, Barrington Price, married George's widow four years later.

Thomas was married three times and eventually inherited Gibside and the title Earl of Strathmore and Kinghorne from his eldest brother, John.

Anna, as we have seen, was a little madam, and at the age of seventeen she eloped to Gretna Green with an impoverished young man called Henry Jessup, who was eventually accepted into the family. They too had daughters, but Anna was widowed young and then moved to Bird Hill House on the Gibside Estate. She died aged sixty-two in 1832, and her remains lie in the vault with those of her grandfather and grandmother.

Mary Eleanor Bowes died at Stourton House on 28th April 1800 at the age of fifty-one. Having suffered ill-health for quite some time, largely thanks to the treatment she had received from Stoney, she had plenty of time to consider her last requests. She arranged to be buried in Westminster Abbey, in Poet's Corner amongst the giants of literature she had always admired. She also asked to be buried in the wedding-dress she had worn when she married John on her eighteenth birthday.

In the capable and dedicated hands of her son, Gibside was blooming again. As soon as he had become master, John set about repairing the damage that Stoney had wrought and bringing stability to the estate workers and miners who had suffered so much at his hands. One of his first acts was to re-plant the oak forests: the estate records show that in 1790, he ordered one thousand young oaks, sixteen thousand oak saplings and five thousand elms. He completed the Chapel, and his grandfather's remains were finally laid to rest at Gibside in 1812.

John always followed his heart. At twenty-one, just a year after taking over the estate, he fell in love with Sarah, the exceptionally beautiful but married daughter of Lord Delavel of Seaton Delavel Hall on the Northumberland coast. Sarah eventually left her husband, Lord Tyrconnel, to live with the young Lord Strathmore at Gibside. They never married but were, by all accounts, completely happy until Sarah developed tuberculosis, the same disease which had killed John's father. Sarah died in October 1800 at the age of thirty-seven, just six months after he had lost his mother.

Like his grandfather, John was grief-stricken at the loss of his beloved, and it was ten long years before he fell in love again. His second relationship also showed that he put emotion over convention, for this time the object of his affections was Mary Milner, the daughter of an estate worker at Streatlam Castle. (I feel his mother would have approved whole-heartedly.) Although they were not married, he immediately acknowledged paternity of the son she bore him in 1811: he was christened John Bowes.

When the earl's health began to fail in 1820, he arranged to marry Mary and thereby legitimize his son as his heir. He died the very next day. Mary, now known as the Dowager Countess of Strathmore, lived for another forty years. In 1860 she was laid to rest in the Gibside Chapel with her husband, the 10th earl.

Their son John inherited Gibside and Streatlam in accordance with the terms of his father's will. His claim to the title Earl of Strathmore was successfully challenged by his father's brother, Thomas, on the grounds of John's illegitimacy. So Eleanor's third son, Thomas, became the 11th Earl of Strathmore, and he is the great-great-grandfather of Elizabeth Bowes-Lyon, whose daughter became Elizabeth II.

John Bowes went on to establish the wonderful Bowes Museum at Barnard Castle, whose most famous piece is the mechanical silver swan which his grandmother first saw in London. Her botanical cabinet is in pride of place.

Who's Who

All characters really existed. Some, notably Eleanor's lawyer and head gardener, are a combination of two separate people for simplicity's sake.

At Gibside

George Bowes, Mary Eleanor's father
Mary Bowes (nee Gilbert) her mother, originally from St Paul's Walden, Hertfordshire
Eleanor Bowes (nee Verney) his first wife, who died just after they were married
George Walker, valet to George Bowes, later footman to Mary Eleanor
Charles Avison (1709-1770) eminent musician and composer, Mary Eleanor's music tutor.
Martha, Mary Eleanor's old nanny
Gabriel Thornton, an estate worker at Gibside and Streatlam
George & Mary Stephenson, tenant farmers on the estate
Dorothy, their daughter, seduced and impregnated by Stoney
Thomas Colpitts, Gibside agent
Robert Thompson, Head Gardener who succeeded Thomas Joplin
Frederick the footman
Effie the chambermaid

The Lyon family of Glamis Castle

John Lyon, 9th Earl of Strathmore & Kinghorne.
Thomas Lyon, his brother
Lady Anne Simpson, his sister
The Dowager Duchess, his mother

Mary Eleanor's children

Maria Bowes-Lyon, born in April 1768, when Mary Eleanor was 19.
John Bowes-Lyon, born in April 1769
Anna Bowes-Lyon, born in June 1770
George Bowes-Lyon, born in November 1771
Thomas Bowes-Lyon, born in May 1773
Mary Bowes, born in August 1777, Mary Eleanor's daughter by George Gray
William Bowes, born in March 1782, her only child by Stoney.

Local wealthy/aristocratic families

Hannah Newton (1748-1776) wealthy coal heiress of Coal Pike Hill – Stoney's first wife
Jane Bowes, Mary Eleanor's aunt
Sir William FitzThomas, friend of George Bowes
Sir Walter Blackett – Newcastle's much-loved mayor for many years
Sir Matthew White Ridley – Newcastle landowner, magistrate and mayor
Sir John Trevelyan of Wallington
Edward Montagu of Denton Hall
Elizabeth Montagu, his wife, a Bluestocking

In London

Mrs Parish, Mary Eleanor's new governess
Eliza Planta, her sister, governess to the children of George III, mistress of Stoney
Joseph Planta, their brother, a naturalist at the British Museum
Rev Henry Stephens, chaplain to the family in London, who marries Eliza Planta
George Gray, a friend of Mary Eleanor's who becomes her lover

Botanists

Sir Joseph Banks (1743-1820) naturalist on James Cook's expedition to Australia, later president of the Royal Society and adviser to George III in establishing Kew Gardens
Daniel Solander (1733-1782) Swedish naturalist who had accompanied Banks on the Endeavour.
William Paterson (1755-1810) Scottish horticulturalist and army officer recruited by Mary Eleanor for a botanic expedition to South Africa.
John Hunter (1728-1793) Scottish surgeon and zoologist who established the Hunterian Museum
William Curtis (1746-1799) Botanist and lecturer at Chelsea Physic Garden, later establishing his own Botanic Garden and Botanic Magazine

Literary and Society figures

Hannah More, poet and playwright a few years older than Mary Eleanor
Benjamin Stillingfleet, botanist and author of Flora Anglica, friend of the Bluestockings
David Garrick, foremost actor of his generation, latterly theatre manager
James Gillray, satirist, caricaturist, cartoonist and printmaker
Dr Johnson – writer and lexicographer
Joshua Reynolds - painter
Horace Walpole – writer and wit
Thomas Gray - poet
Lord Mountstuart, son of Lady Bute.
Georgiana, Duchess of Devonshire

Stoney and his cronies

Jesse Foot, dodgy doctor
General Armstrong & General Robinson, his great-uncles
William Scott, Newcastle lawyer and future Lord Stowell. His brother was...
John Scott, Newcastle lawyer who went on to become Chancellor and 1st earl of Eldon
Thomas the valet who leaves soon after Stoney marries Eleanor
Edward Lucas, the constable who was meant to protect Eleanor but was Stoney's man
Durham baddies

Mary Eleanor's servants and supporters

Mary Morgan (1747-1796) widow employed as ladies-maid by Reverend Reynett
Susanna Church & Ann Dixon – maids at Grosvenor Square
Robert Crundall, ex-footman to Stoney
Reverend (and Mrs) Reynett, chaplain to the family
Harry the baker's son
Charles Shuter, solicitor
James Farrer, barrister
Henry Farrer, his brother, a ship's captain who worked as a bodyguard/companion.
Lord Mansfield, eminent judge
Judge Buller, famous for his 'rule of thumb'

Chapter Notes

To set the events of Eleanor's life in context and to illuminate where fiction is intertwined with fact, these notes include extra information, clarification and random interesting facts.

Chapter 1

The early-morning encounter with Gabriel would have taken place in 1766, when Eleanor was seventeen and engaged to John Lyon, 9th Earl of Strathmore. Gabriel really existed, and his role in her rescue is documented, but this scene is invented.

George Bowes died in September 1760, a month before the death of George II.

David Garrick's Heart of Oak was premiered New Year's Eve at the Theatre Royal.

'Old Mr Avison' is Charles Avison, the composer.

Chapter 2

Mary was born in 1749 and building work on the column to Liberty began in the following year. The scenes she describes would have taken place 1753-8, when she was four to nine years old. At the same time, the stables and Banqueting House were being built by Daniel Garrett.

Mary Eleanor had measles and then was inoculated against smallpox.

In February 1753, a sudden thaw caused floods on the Tyne, damaging ships which were driven from their moorings on the Quay.

George's bay horse, Cato, won 100 guineas at the Town Moor Races.

In 1756, the Column and its scaffolding miraculously escaped the hurricane which did a lot of damage on the estate.

At this time, Elizabeth Montagu 'The queen of literary London' was a frequent visitor to the family manor house, East Denton Hall. She enjoyed a vigorous social life in Newcastle and ordered Northumbrian delicacies for her houses in London and Berkshire.

Elizabeth enjoyed her miners' singing, but considered their dialect 'dreadful to the auditor's nerves.' On visiting Gibside, she described the woods as 'oppressively dark and vast; you would expect to be entertained by the howling of wolves.'

Chapter 3

She describes her experience of London as a child, when she and her mother would have accompanied George Bowes while parliament was in session. After his death when Eleanor was eleven, her mother stayed in deep mourning for two years.

During that time, George III & Queen Isabella were crowned in 1761; two hundred militiamen were sent from Newcastle to deal with the Hexham Riot, over drafting for military service during the Seven Years War.

Records show that work was proceeding on the chapel and Joseph Palliser was palisading Eleanor's garden in Green Close.

When Eleanor was fourteen, a kidnap attempt was foiled at Gibside. Soon after that, she was taken to London and left her in the care of her governess and her aunt Jane at 10, Grosvenor Square while her mother went home to St Paul's Waldenbury, Hertfordshire.

Chapter 4

Between the ages of fourteen and sixteen (1763-5) she was pursued by many suitors before finally accepting the proposal of Lord Strathmore.

On Sunday 1st April 1764, a solar eclipse delayed church services. Horace Walpole, whose Strawberry Hill Gothic home has recently opened to visitors in London, published the Castle of Otranto, considered the first Gothic novel written in English. Mrs Montagu was a friend of Walpole.

Chapter 5

Eleanor describes seeing Lord Strathmore at the theatre in the summer she was fifteen: Wycherley's version of The Country Girl was playing at Drury Lane that summer: it seemed apposite! They became engaged in autumn 1765. The Chapel was being roofed that year.

Chapter 6

Mary Eleanor married John Lyon on her 18th birthday, 24th February 1767. Their engagement had been long and difficult due to legal negotiations over her father's stipulation that Eleanor's husband should take her name. She is on record as having realized before the wedding that they were ill-suited, but says she felt obliged to go ahead and was unwilling to admit that her mother had been right.

Chapter 7

This chapter is about the birth of her first five children. Maria Bowes-Lyon was born on 21st April 1768; John on 13th April 1769, the year that work ceased on the chapel.

In 1770, there were huge celebrations at Gibside for Eleanor's 21st. The house and estate were thrown open for ten days, with a whole roast ox and hogsheads of strong ale. The birthday girl was five months pregnant with Anna, who was born on 3rd June.

George Bowes-Lyon born on Sunday 17th November 1771, the same day as floods destroyed the Tyne Bridge. The mayor at that time was Sir Walter Blackett.

Thomas, the youngest of her Strathmore children, was born on 3rd May 1773.

Chapter 8

The Orangery was being built and fitted out in this period, and Eleanor oversaw alterations to the east wing of Gibside Hall, including a bakehouse and new dairy, stewards' room, dressing room, back kitchen with cellars and brewhouse beneath.

Her relationship with her brother-in-law Thomas was hostile: they had a public row in Edinburgh which was reported in the newspapers. When work on the chapel was halted, it must have galled Eleanor that Glamis Castle was having extensive renovations: 'New kitchens, a Billiard Room and new service courtyards beyond the East Wing were all added in 1773. Two years later, the West Wing was demolished and re-modeling of the grounds into open parklands in the style of Capability Brown began.' (Glamis website)

On 23rd November 1772, the corporation of Newcastle petitioned the House of Commons on the scarcity and dearness of all sorts of grain, occasioned chiefly by a general failure of the preceding harvest.

John Scott, the future Lord Eldon, eloped with Bessie Surtees from the first-floor window of her father's house on Sandhill.

In January 1774, the river Tyne was frozen over for about four miles below the bridge at Newcastle. On the 18th, two young men skated six miles along the river in fifteen minutes.

Robert Sand's library in the Bigg Market was frequented in the 1770s by Jean Paul Marat, who was working in the city as a doctor. The famous revolutionary published his first political book *The Chains of Slavery* (1774) in Newcastle and a copy of the first edition is kept in The Literary and Philosophical Society Library.

The society, which continues to thrive today, was founded in 1793 by the Reverend William Turner and others, over fifty years before the London Library. From the start, the Lit and Phil enjoyed international contacts and concerns: its members, including Thomas Bewick, debated such issues as American science and Scottish political economy. The Society received the country's first specimens of the wombat and the duck-billed platypus from John Hunter, Governor of New South Wales and honorary member of the Lit and Phil, who also appears in the novel.

The Newcastle assemblies begun in the house of Sir William Creagh in Westgate Street, continued in David Newton's elegant Assembly Rooms of 1774, which replaced those of 1736 in the Groat Market, and still stand in Fenkle Street.

In London, Lord Mansfield (the guardian of Belle in the recent film) invoked Habeas Corpus to free a slave.

The Silver Swan (now in the Bowes Museum) was exhibited at the Mechanical Museum of James Cox in Spring Gardens, Charing Cross.

Chapter 9

War broke out in America in 1775.

Earl Strathmore began to be very seriously ill with consumption, which we now call tuberculosis. On 9th January 1776, Thomas Paine's Common Sense was published – a discussion of liberty and abuse of power.

John died on 7th March and four days later Stoney's first wife, Hannah Newton, died in childbirth, freeing him to set off in pursuit of his next target.

The words of Lord Strathmore's letter are verbatim.

Chapter 10

Eleanor's few short months of freedom and independence coincided with the American Declaration of Independence (4th July 1776) 'Life, liberty and pursuit of happiness.'

Garrick left the stage that year, and the premiere of The Bankrupt by Samuel Foote played at the Haymarket, which seemed a good choice for Stoney's first appearance in London.

In December, the scandalized letters about Eleanor appeared in the Morning Post.

Chapter 11

Eleanor is writing at her desk in Stourfield House, looking back over her life. The scene she describes, when Stoney first appeared in London, would have taken place in the summer of 1776. Lord Strathmore had died on 7th March.

Chapter 12

1776 was the year of Eleanor's widowhood, and the information about her botanic activities and purchase of Stanley House in Chelsea is all true. The information about Stoney's strategems, including anonymous letters in the newspapers and forged letters from admirers, are revelations which are included in Jesse Foot's account. To read the primary source, follow the link on my website.

Chapter 13

13th January 1777 Stoney had a 'duel' with the paper's editor, Henry Bate and on 17th January he married Eleanor. The same date is on the pre-nuptial deed.

Chapters 14-18

The records of the court case have witnesses testifying that the abuse started immediately after the marriage. 1st May is the date on the revocation of the pre-nuptial deed, and it was apparently signed by Eleanor and witnessed by Gibson, Hunter & Scott, though the origin of those signatures was contested.

Stoney's first attempt to be elected MP for Newcastle ended in failure.

On 8th May School for Scandal opened, and soon after, Hannah More's Percy opened at Covent Garden.

Stoney sold Stanley House with all its exotic plants and conservatories.

The wife of a king who was locked away was Sophia Dorothea of the House of Hanover. Her husband, George I, had her locked away after she had an affair. She was the mother of George II but she spent the last thirty years of her life imprisoned.

It is believed that George Gray's daughter Mary was born in August, though the birth was registered as 14th November. George Walker was sacked

In 1777, 'No Entry' signs appeared at Gibside and the paper mill was destroyed by fire after dispute between Stoney and the tenant.

In 1780, he was elected sheriff, a success in part due to his having arranged for opposition supporters to be entertained aboard a ship on the Tyne which for some reason failed to return to Newcastle in time for the ballot.

Patterson arrived home from South Africa, having been rescued and brought back to Europe by Dutch traders. The giraffe was presented to Hunter.

Chapters 19 & 20

Eleanor's mother died on 20th January 1781.

Thomas Lyon had her five Strathmore children declared Wards of Chancery.

Eleanor conceived William in June 1781 and gave birth to him on 8th March 1782. 'A great fall of snow, on March 10, was next morning followed by a very heavy rain, with a strong fresh wind, which raised the river Tyne to an alarming height. Ridley Hall Bridge, and five arches of Hexham bridge, were thrown down; and Haydon bridge was rendered impassable. Upwards of fifty light colliers, lying under Tynemouth Castle, were obliged to cut away or slip their anchors, and drive to sea.'

Stoney sent little Mary away to school aged 6, in 1783. The scene where Eleanor faints and Thomas Colpitts picks her up is fictitious.

Mary Morgan was employed in London in 1784 and shortly afterwards, Stoney took Eleanor and Anna (14) to Paris.

Chapter 21 to the end

On Thursday 3rd February 1785, Eleanor escaped and went into hiding with Mary Morgan.

'Articles of Peace' were granted by Lord Mansfield, by which Stoney was bound over to keep the peace, like a restraining order. He turned his attentions to trying to flush her out by harassing Gibside tenants and persecuting Robert Thompson, evidenced by the latter's surviving letters which were delivered to her in secret, often along with baskets of food from Gibside.

The Gillray cartoons were published in May 1786 and Stoney kidnapped Eleanor on 10th November. Gabriel Thornton was one of her rescuers, but I have to confess that his marriage to Dorothy is pure fiction.

On 12th May 1787, the British politician and philanthropist William Wilberforce held a conversation with William Pitt and the future Prime Minister William Grenville as they sat under a large oak tree (this later came to be known as the Wilberforce Oak.) As a result of that conversation, on 22nd May 1787, the Society for the Abolition of the Slave Trade was founded in Britain.

On 30th May, Stoney and his accomplices were convicted and imprisoned by Judge Buller.

Thomas Jefferson said, 'The Tree of Liberty must be refreshed from time to time with the blood of patriots and tyrants.'

Matthew Ridley died in 1788. His monument by the noted sculptor John Bacon is the best in the cathedral.

A menagerie visited Newcastle. Thomas Bewick drew the 'Royal Namibian Lion' which figured in his immensely popular *General History of Quadrupeds*. Bewick, like Avison, rejected a career in London and was enviously referred to in verse by Wordsworth as: 'The poet who lives on the banks of the Tyne'.

Following the lapse of the Licensing Act in 1695, Newcastle became the most important printing centre in England after London, Oxford and Cambridge. In the 1770s, the town published more children's books than any other outside London. Few towns had more than one local newspaper: Newcastle usually boasted three, of which the Newcastle Courant, founded in 1711, was the first newspaper north of the Trent. Periodicals were rare outside London, Dublin and Edinburgh: Newcastle had ten during the 18th century. By 1790, the town could number twenty printers, twelve booksellers and stationers, thirteen bookbinders and three engravers, including the internationally celebrated Thomas Bewick. In addition, there were seven subscription libraries, as well as St. Nicholas parish library with its 5000 books. There were also three circulating libraries, including that of Joseph Barber in Amen Corner, which had over 5000 volumes, one of the largest collections outside the capital. There were 180 inns and coffee-houses where the new culture was disseminated.

On 19th June 1788, without any precedent in English law, Eleanor was awarded her estates.

On 2nd March 1789 the divorce was finalized. The US Bill of Rights was published the same year. July brought the storming of the Bastille, and in August *The Declaration of the Rights of Man and the Citizen.*

5th October was the Women's March on Versailles.

In 1790, Eleanor was reconciled with her children. She and Mary Morgan moved to Purbrook Park near Portsmouth with young Mary and William, who had spent a long time living with his father in prison.

Mary Wollstonecraft published A Vindication of the Rights of Woman in 1792.

In September of that year, the French Republic was declared and on 21st January 1793 Louis XVI was executed.

Eleanor moved in autumn 1795 to Stourfield House on the coast of Hampshire

William Wordsworth was in Newcastle in January 1795, visiting his sister Dorothy, then staying with the Misses Griffiths in Northumberland Place.

Mary Morgan died in 1796.

Mary Eleanor Bowes died on 28th April 1800, aged 51. She was buried in Poets' Corner, Westminster Abbey. It is rumoured that she was laid to rest in the wedding dress she wore for her marriage to Earl Strathmore on her eighteenth birthday.

Gibside Timeline

Gibside belonged to the Marley family of Marley Hill from 1200 on.

1538   Elizabeth de Marley married Roger Blakiston of Coxhoe. In the absence of any male heirs, the estate passed into Blakiston ownership.

1603-20 The main house was built by Sir William Blakiston (1562-1641) probably incorporating the older building.

1693   Again in the absence of a male heir, the marriage of Jane Blakiston took it into the ownership of Sir William Bowes (1657-1707) of Streatlam Castle.

1721   Their third son, George Bowes, inherited both estates on the death of his two elder brothers.

1726   He and the other 'Grand Allies' built Causey Arch to carry coal more quickly to the Tyne.

1729   Extensive plantations began at Gibside as part of Bowes' landscaping design plans.

1733   Bath house & new walled garden begun. Retaining walls built along the Derwent.

1735   Bowes bought Hollinside Estate & altered the approach to the house

1738   New Coach Way completed

1740   Octagon Pond begun after visit to Stowe

1742   Gothic Banqueting House was started at Gibside. Temple of Liberty being built at Stowe.

1743   George Bowes marries Mary Gilbert, from St Paul's Walden in Hertfordshire.

1745   He raises a cavalry regiment to defend Durham from the Jacobites. The Scots & French Catholics got as far south as Derby

1746   Grand Avenue built

1746   Strawberry Castle built in the Strawberry Gothic style (cf Walpole's house)

1748   Ice house built

1749   Mary Eleanor was born and the column to Liberty was started.

1759   Work on the Chapel began

1760	George Bowes died
1767	Mary Eleanor's marriage to John Lyon, 9th Earl of Strathmore and Kinghorne transferred Gibside and Streatlam into the ownership of the Lyon family of Glamis. George Bowes' will stipulated that his daughter's husband should take her name, so John Lyon became John Bowes. The surname Bowes-Lyon was adopted later by some of their children.
1772-3	The Orangery or Green House was built and improvements made to servants' quarters in the east wing, including a new bakery.
1790	Eleanor's son John, the 10th Earl of Strathmore, came of age and took over.
1800	Mary Eleanor died.
1805	The 3rd floor was converted into a battlemented parapet.
1820	John Bowes-Lyon died, having married Mary Milner of Staindrop on his deathbed. Their illegitimate son, John Milner Bowes, inherited the English estates. Henceforward known as the Dowager Countess of Strathmore, Mary Milner Bowes lived on at Gibside, later marrying William Hutt, who became Sir William Hutt, MP for Gateshead in Gladstone's government. The Scottish properties and title passed to Thomas, Eleanor's only surviving son.
1860	Mary Milner Bowes, Dowager Countess of Strathmore, died. From then onwards, Gibside was little used by the family, being let to various tenants.
1885	John Milner Bowes died without an heir, so the English estates of Gibside, Streatlam and St Paul's Walden reverted to the Earls of Strathmore.
1900	Elizabeth Bowes-Lyon, daughter of the 14th earl, was born. The mother of Queen Elizabeth II, she was very fond of Gibside and remembered coming for picnics when she stayed at Streatlam. She last visited the crypt in 1968.
1920	The drawing room chimneypiece, depicting Samson and Hercules supporting a huge mantle-shelf, was taken to Glamis with other items of value.
1930s	The great oaks and beeches, many of which were planted to replace those cut down by Stoney, were felled.

1950s	The roof and floors had become dangerous and were removed.
1965	The National Trust acquired the Chapel to protect it. The Queen Mother came to the hand-over ceremony.
1974	The executors of the 16th Earl donated a large part of the estate to the National Trust.
1994	The column was repaired
1997	The old 'home farm' at Cut Thorn was bought by the National Trust
1998	The riverside meadows of Warren Haugh and Lady Haugh were purchased.
2002	The house was consolidated
2004	The Orangery was made safe and the Stables purchased: renovations began.
2013	The walled garden was re-instated when the new car parks were built.

For more information, visit:
http://www.nationaltrust.org.uk/gibside/

Truth and Fiction

The whiff of scandal still swirls about the name of Mary Eleanor Bowes: even people who've only heard of her as an ancestor of the Queen often feel that they know there's something notorious about her.

For those interested in getting as close as we can to the 'facts' about Eleanor, the primary sources are available. (There are links to the online versions in the Bibliography on my website.) If we would rather the facts were selected and interpreted for us, there are the three biographies, as well as her entries in Wikipedia, The Dictionary of National Biography and other supposedly objective accounts.

The trouble is, we always have to remember that even in the primary evidence, the writer has an agenda. In the case of Mary Eleanor, her letters and particularly her Confessions cannot be taken as 'fact': the former because she will always have been affected by mood, circumstance, who she's writing to, what she wants them to think, what she's chosen to leave out; and the latter because they were written under duress and partially, if not wholly dictated by Stoney Bowes.

The recent BBC production of Wolf Hall drew attention to the differences between 'fact' and fiction, as this letter from the Guardian makes clear:

'Mark Rylance's depiction of Thomas Cromwell as a soulful, family-centred, introspective, silently suffering spectator is totally removed from the ferocious tiger who set up a proto-Nazi regime in England. He created a cult of leader worship, tortured the innocent young men round Anne Boleyn to get false accusations, leading to her death, set up a black propaganda campaign to undermine the monasteries, led a vile process against the religious who tried to cling to their ancient faith, subjected the simple Carthusians to an agonising death, destroyed the noblest Englishman (Thomas More) because he would not conform to Cromwell's Führerprinzip.

'He had absorbed the brutal cynicism of Machiavelli during his twelve years in Italy and applied this realpolitik in London. Miss Mantel is not the first bluestocking to fall for a nasty, cruel man of power: her portrait of Cromwell needs to be balanced against the facts of history.'

Emo Williams
Shere, Surrey
The Guardian, 23rd January 2015
http://www.theguardian.com/books/2015/jan/23/wolf-hall-good-bad-codpieces

In all of this lies the fascination of history and human stories.

Hilary Mantel said: 'My own method is to wrap the fiction around the documented record, to let imagination lead us by touch into the rooms where history can't shine a light.'

The Guardian Review. 17th January 2015

For more information about all aspects of this novel, including photographs and bibliographic links to primary sources, please visit my website at www.valscully.co.uk

Bibliography

Primary Texts

It is possible to find print editions of the five primary texts, but not easy; luckily, they've all been scanned, either by the Gutenburg Project or Google Books. You can read the first four online, and the fifth can be downloaded. All are available print-on-demand. To be taken to links where you can read them, please go to the Bibliography page on my website: http://www.valscully.co.uk

The Confessions of the Countess of Strathmore

The Lives of Andrew Stoney Bowes Esq and the Countess of Strathmore, written from Thirty-Three Years Professional Attendance, from Letters and other Well-Authenticated Documents by Doctor Jesse Foot.

The Remarkable and Curious Trial Between the Countess of Strathmore and Her Husband Andrew Robinson Stoney Bowes, including Mr Bowes' Allegations Against the Countess for a Criminal Intercourse with George Gray ... in Answer to Her Charges Against Him of Cruelty and Adultery.

A Full and Accurate Report of the Trial between Stephens, Trustee to E.Bowes, commonly called Countess of Strathmore, and Andrew Robinson Stoney Bowes, in the Court of Common Pleas on Monday 19th May 1788.

The Siege of Jerusalem by Mary Eleanor Bowes, the Countess of Strathmore (1769) Download or print on demand by Gale Ecco Print Editions.

Biographies of Mary Eleanor Bowes

The Unhappy Countess by Ralph Arnold. Constable & Co. Ltd. (1957)

The Trampled Wife: the scandalous life of Mary Eleanor Bowes by Derek Parker. Sutton Publishing. (2006)

Wedlock: How Georgian Britain's worst husband met his match by Wendy Moore. Weidenfeld & Nicholson. (2009)

Gibside

Gibside and the Bowes Family by Margaret Wills. The Society of Antiquaries of Newcastle Upon Tyne. (1995)

Gibside – National Trust Publications (1999)

Gibside Landscape Park – National Trust Publications (Revised 2013)

From Blakiston to Bowes: The Development of Gibside during the seventeenth and eighteenth centuries by Peter G. Firth of Gibside Volunteer Research Group (2012)

The Influence of Eighteenth Century Landscape Gardening on the Development of Gibside by Susan Adamson of Gibside Volunteer Research Group (2010)

Newcastle & Durham

The Picture of Newcastle upon Tyne: containing a guide to the town and neighbourhood, an account of the Roman Wall and a description of the coal mines. (1807) Facsimile reprint published by E&W Books (1969)

312

Tynesides's Finest: a miscellany by John Gundy. Tyne Bridge Publishing (2006)

Eighteenth-century Newcastle by P.M. Horsley. Oriel Press. (1971)

The Making of an Industrial Society: Whickham 1560-1765 by David Levine and Keith Wrightson. Clarendon Press. (1991)

Whickham Parish: its history, antiquities and industries by William Bourn (1893) Portcullis Press (1999)

Some Chapters in the History of Whickham, written and illustrated by members of the Whickham Local History Class. Edited by Helen G. Bowling, WEA tutor. (1961)

Annals of Coal Mining and the Coal Trade, Volume 1 by Robert Galloway. (1971)

Coals from Newcastle by Les Turnbull. Chapman Research Publishing. (2009)

History of the British Coal Industry, Volume 2, 1700-1830: Industrial Revolution by Michael W. Finn. Clarendon Press. (1984)

The Dark Side of the Dale: the grim, gruesome and grisly history of the Derwent Valley by Tony Kearney. Dark Dale Publications (2004)

The Old Halls and Manor Houses of Durham by Neville Whittaker. Published by Frank Graham (1975)

Lost Houses of County Durham by Peter Meadows & Edward Waterson. Published by Carter Jonas (1993)